THE BEAUTIFUL PEOPLE

BOOK ONE OF THE NEW MAFIA TRILOGY

E.J. FECHENDA

Cover design by: Jessica Ouellette

Acknowledgments

I seriously wouldn't have made it this far without the unfailing support of friends, parents and family, especially "my boys" - my husband Steve and son Matt who have to deal with my distracted state the most – thank you for your encouragement and love. To my "Lit Bitches" Shannon, Beth, and Liz, I couldn't have asked for better beta readers. To the fabulous ladies of my writers group, Marlee and Nicole, you were the first to read *The Beautiful People* (the first to read any of my writing) and through the years as our friendship has grown, our writing has too. Thanks to the awesome Maine writers community for continuing to inspire and thanks to all of my friends, near or far, for your support. Writing is very personal and my stories are like horcruxes because a little bit of my soul is in each one.

Prologue

It was only a job. At least that's all it was supposed to be. Despite student loans, the occasional loan from my brother, Grant, and income from waitressing at T.G.I Fridays, I struggled to make ends meet. Grant was the head of security at Crimson, one of Philadelphia's top nightclubs, and he helped to get me a job there as a cocktail waitress, but I had to agree to one of his "conditions" first.

"This is just temporary, until you graduate, okay?"

"Relax and believe me when I tell you I don't have aspirations to be a career cocktail waitress," I reassured him. We were grabbing a slice of pizza before heading into work together.

"Well, believe me when I tell you a number of people have gotten sucked into the glamour and money – the whole scene – and are still there."

"Are you talking about yourself? It was the glamour that lured you in, wasn't it?" I teased, but really was curious what it was about Crimson that caused Grant to drop out of college.

He didn't answer and gave me one of his "don't mess with me" stares. I laughed and stood, picking up my grease soaked paper plate for the garbage. "Grant, I'm just kidding. Come on, I don't want to be late on my first day."

Grant drained the rest of his soda and I followed him out to his car which was parked in front of the pizza joint. He drove a new Lexus sedan, silver and fully loaded. This alone was probably the reason he never left Crimson. Obviously he was doing alright for himself without a college degree.

My brother was quiet during the brief ride from South Street until we pulled into the employee parking lot in the rear by the loading docks. Crimson was a refurbished brick warehouse that sat hulking over the Delaware River in the old industrial section, near the decommissioned Navy Yard. Blue, an after hours club owned by the same development company, was located in a twin building directly next to Crimson. We parked and a neon sign cast an eerie bluish glow across the hood.

"I want to give you some advice for your first night," Grant said, turning to face me.

"Okay…"

"First of all, if anyone gets inappropriate with you or too handsy, let me or one of my guys know. We'll take care of it. Second, there are a lot of egos that work here, so there will be drama. You're better off not getting involved, which leads me to the last thing…don't get involved with any of the guys here. Dating a coworker is not a good idea."

"Company policy?"

"No, company policies are kind of loose. It's my policy…for you."

"Oh a Big Brother policy," I said and tried not to roll my eyes. "I get it Grant, all work and no play. You don't have to worry." He didn't because I had no interest in hooking up with anyone. I'd done enough of that in high school. I was here for the money until I graduated college in the spring.

Turns out agreeing to Grant's policy was easier said than done. While he warned me that I would be tempted by the whole scene, he didn't tell me just how seductive it would be. Turns out, Grant didn't tell me a lot of things.

Chapter 1

The club thumped and I watched the crowd pulsate with the beat while waiting for drink orders to be filled. Dominic, one of Crimson's bartenders, smiled and winked as he put two beers plus an assortment of shots on my tray, which I hoisted up onto my shoulder before proceeding to weave through the wall of people. My short skirt and tight top showed more skin than I felt comfortable with, but it was hard to curl inwards like I wanted to without spilling drinks all over the place. Even though this was my first night working at Crimson, it didn't take long to realize how many men considered the skimpy uniform an open invitation to grab at my body. I didn't see any of the other girls running for security every time someone pinched their ass, so I followed suit and ignored Grant's earlier request.

When the club cleared out, I joined some employees around Dominic's bar. He was busy stacking clean glasses, the steam from the dishwasher causing his black hair to curl. He smiled when I approached, a flash of even white teeth, and this made me squirm a little. The fact that he was able to trigger such a visceral reaction from me with one glance was bothersome. I reminded myself of Grant's "policy" before sitting down on a stool furthest away from Dominic. I should have been relieved to find his attention no longer focused on me, but on one of the shooter girls, and for obvious reasons. Her cosmetically enhanced boobs tested the confines of her top. She had sculpted curves and platinum blonde hair, a regular Barbie doll. Instead of relief though, annoyance and a hint of jealousy pulsed through me. I glanced down at my B cups and silently urged them to grow on command, but no such luck.

I noticed the rest of the employees around the bar maintained various stages of perfection. The women could be bikini models and not just because our uniforms were that skimpy. Their hair and makeup were still as immaculate at the end of the night as in the beginning. I, on the other hand, felt disheveled and droopy. The men were equally flawless in their black t-shirts which stretched across fierce physiques. Shaking off the moment of low esteem, I turned my attention back to counting out tips. Peroxide Barbie sat down to my right.

"Hi, I'm Brittany. We didn't get to meet earlier. Are you Natalie, Grant's sister?"

I nodded and Brittany retrieved a wad of cash from in between her breasts and said, "Tonight rocked!"

I pulled out a less impressive wad of tips, which I'd kept in my skirt pocket, not my cleavage.

"Yeah, I had a good night. I made more than I would have in a week at my old job."

"Where?"

"Fridays."

"Oh yeah, totally. This is the place to work. Everyone wants a job at Crimson and they're hard to come by."

"It's who you know, isn't it?" I looked over at the opposite end of the bar where my brother sat, drinking a beer. He was surrounded by a bunch of the other waitresses. If I wasn't his sister, I would probably find him attractive. He was tall, muscular and had an air of confidence about him. He walked with his broad shoulders straight, ready to carry the weight of the world. In some ways he did and even carried my burdens every once in a while. Grant gestured for me to come down so I gathered up my tips and said good night to Brittany.

"Everyone, here's my little sis, Natalie," Grant said to his groupies. They would be lining up, vying to be my best friend, just to get to him. They usually did, like my freshman year in high school when he was the big senior football star. Fake, shallow bitches, I thought to myself as I smiled and said hi.

"I assume you two met?" Grant asked when Dominic replaced his beer.

"Yes."

Dominic regarded me with deep green eyes and I had to keep myself from busting out in a goofy grin. I didn't date much and mainly focused on my studies, but I would have been blind not to notice that out of all the Crimson men I had seen, he was by far the hottest and like my brother, moved with this cocky assurance which appealed to me more than his biceps. I imagined what he might look like naked just before he asked me if I wanted a drink and I found myself incapable of answering. Grant nudged my arm and glanced sideways at me. I needed liquid courage in order to have a normal conversation with this guy. So I ordered something I hadn't had in a couple of years.

"I'll take a shot of Cuervo."

"Whoa, Grant you didn't tell me your sister was so hardcore... or beautiful," he winked again. "You've been holding out."

Grant responded with an uneasy laugh and eyed me with caution, worry that this was going to be one of *those* nights clearly etched on his face. I used to drink...a lot, and Grant had to cover my ass on a number of occasions in the past. Even though I'd behaved for close to three years, those memories will reside in the forefront of his memory until I'm eligible for Medicare.

Alcohol made my muscles tingle and relax after a few sips. After a couple of drinks, I gained the confidence my brother came by naturally. Just being near Dominic made me nervous so I needed all the help I could get. Dominic set the shot down on the bar in front of me. Quickly glancing at Grant, I slammed it back without a flinch; no salt or lime. It didn't take long for the warmth to start coursing through my veins, loosening my muscles. I ordered another one. Like a turtle creeping out of its shell, with each shot I became more gregarious. After my third Cuervo, I was ready to flirt the pants off of Dominic, literally.

Miranda, the club manager joined us at the bar. The way she orbited around my brother, I had a pretty good idea about their relationship. I found this discovery interesting because Grant hadn't mentioned that he was seeing anyone. "Grant, you have a phone call. You can take it in my office."

"Okay. Nat, hang out for a bit and I'll give you a lift home."

He and Miranda walked away, leaving me alone at the bar with Dominic. Brittany joined me and sat on the stool, adjusting her low cut shirt to reveal more cleavage. She smiled at Dominic, but he turned away and focused on wiping down liquor bottles. Interesting, I thought to myself and snuck a glance at his ass which, like everything else, was perfect.

"So Natalie, are you up for a smoke session?" Brittany interrupted. I turned towards her. She tucked her hair behind an ear, mimed holding a joint up to her mouth and inhaled.

"No, I'm good with the shots. I stopped smoking pot a long time ago."

She raised her eyebrow and gazed at me with intensity. So she wanted to test the new girl.

"I'm in," Dominic said, his eyes scanning me up and down. My insides did a somersault and at that moment I tossed the "Big Brother Policy" out the window – in less than twelve hours I might add - a new record. Brittany eyeballed Dominic in a completely different manner. Her bright blue eyes glittered, not with tears, but some other emotion.

Moments later we were sitting in Brittany's car. She introduced me to Allegra, one of the two chesty shooter girls. Allegra smiled and passed me a joint which I almost dropped the first time around because I was shaking so badly from the cold and from being out of practice. Weed was something else I hadn't had since high school. One night at my new job and the old vices were popping back up.

The January night was frigid and the car took a while to warm up. Allegra and Brittany sat up front while Dominic sat in the back with me. Feeling brave after the tequila and a few tokes, I inched closer to him and the temperature instantly got a lot warmer. We leaned towards each other, our shoulders touching. Brittany occasionally glanced in the rearview mirror and scowled, which made me uncomfortable, so when Dominic placed his hand on my thigh, I adjusted the position to where she couldn't see. I placed my hand on top of his and linked our fingers together. Then I held my breath as he moved in for a kiss.

A loud bang pierced the silence around us. I jumped and my head jerked up, almost colliding with Dominic's face. "What the hell was that?"

"Probably a car backfiring," Dominic whispered against my neck, trying to get my attention back. It almost worked. His very presence distracted me especially when I inhaled his spicy scent.

A second bang cracked, ricocheting off of the old, brick buildings which surrounded the parking lot. This time I recognized the sound.

I waited for the sirens. In any big city, gunfire was pretty common and Philadelphia was no exception. There were many times I heard gunshots in the distance, but this was different. These were really close. A few minutes passed and the atmosphere in the car grew tense. Headlights whipped around the corner and a gray sedan pulled up to the loading dock located at the rear of Blue. A man in a long trench coat got out and the back door to the club opened up. He spoke to someone who remained in the shadows and something was exchanged. When the guy moved to get back in the car, his coat moved to the side and the light caught his badge that was clipped to his belt. The officer got back in his car and left.

My jaw dropped. Did I really just witness this? I turned and noticed everyone in the car staring at me. "Did you guys see that? I think the cop just got paid off!" Allegra and Brittany shrugged their shoulders and directed a weird look towards Dominic, who squeezed my hand.

"It's nothing. Probably a gun from the gun check went off. No big deal."

"But there was more than one shot."

"Happens all the time, don't worry about it and just don't go telling everyone. We…" He stopped mid sentence.

"What?"

"Nothing. Forget you saw anything." Dominic breathed this against my neck, but this wasn't as distracting as a few minutes earlier, I couldn't take my eyes off of the darkened back door of the club.

Finally I blinked, but still didn't say anything. Focusing back on my co-workers, I caught Brittany smirking at me in the rearview mirror, almost daring me to panic. My instincts were screaming at me to get the hell out of the car and run, but I quickly silenced them. I considered how excited I was to work at Crimson, how all my college friends thought it was cool, and plus I needed the money. Dominic massaging my thigh, just under the hemline of my skirt, provided another reason to ignore my gut.

Chapter 2

Allegra lit another joint and passed it around, but the atmosphere had become subdued. Dominic, sensing my distance, backed off. The gunshots seemed to have sobered everybody up.

I'd just inhaled when my door was yanked open. I screamed and began to choke on the smoke, dropping the joint on the floor mat when Grant popped his head in.

"Why are you out here? I told you to wait for me."

"I wasn't going anywhere. What took you so long anyway?"

"Last minute work stuff…come on, I'll take you home," he said, moving aside so I could step out.

Dominic decided to leave too and started walking to his car, a black classic Mustang, and turned back to me. "See you tomorrow night?"

"Err, uh, yes," I answered, internally cursing the return of my awkwardness.

"Good."

My mouth, already dry from the weed, dried up completely and I smiled.

"Let's go, Natalie," Grant said, while glaring at Dominic.

Grant drove me back to my apartment and I wanted to talk to him about what I had witnessed, but he was absorbed in his own thoughts. He would glance at me every few minutes until I had to break the silence.

"What?" I snapped.

"Nothing."

"Why the hell do you keep looking at me like that?"

"Like what?"

I huffed and crossed my arms over my chest. My typical reaction when he was being annoying.

"I'm thinking I shouldn't have gotten you a job at Crimson."

"Are you firing me?" I paused. "Do you have the authority to fire me?" I asked in a quieter tone.

Grant didn't answer right away which did nothing to encourage me. He still had a nervous, far-away expression; his eyebrows furrowed together in concentration.

"What happened tonight – well, it happens a lot. Crimson may seem all shiny and exciting, but there is a dark side too."

"What are you talking about?"

"The gunshots, the cop –"

"Oh, you saw that too!" I didn't recall seeing Grant anywhere, but I felt relieved that he knew.

"Yeah and I wish you hadn't."

"Dominic said that Blue has a gun check and sometimes there's an accidental discharge. It's no big deal."

"He did?" Grant seemed surprised, but his brow soon creased together again. He stopped talking as he pulled his Lexus up in front of my apartment building. I didn't get out of the car.

"Will you stop being so overprotective? I'm a big girl and can handle myself. Besides if you're the 'Head of Security'," I emphasized this by making quotation marks with my fingers, "how much trouble can I get into?"

Grant sighed, rubbing his hands over his face before looking at me. His face was a male version of mine with the same wide set hazel eyes, sharp cheekbones and full lips. We even had the same dark chestnut brown hair. He wore his short and slicked back, which emphasized his square jaw. Mine fell past my shoulders in thick waves.

"I can't fire you Nat and I am overprotective for a reason." He raised an eyebrow when he said this.

I knew Grant was referring to an episode that happened during my senior year of high school. Someone slipped rufies in my drink at the local dive bar in our hometown of York. I remembered taking a few sips and seconds later my body began to freak out. The room started spinning and I lost control of my limbs. I barely made it to the bathroom, where I collapsed in one of the stalls. I didn't care about the dirty floor or the mystery puddle my knee was submerged in. Who worries about something like that when you think you're dying? Somehow I managed to call Grant on my cell.

I screamed something unintelligible into the phone, but he must have been able to understand. His prior experience with "Natalie in crisis" helped. I managed to tell him where I was and minutes later, he came barging into the ladies room. Thank God he was home on holiday break. Philly was a good three hours away from York and I don't know what I would have done.

He scooped me up off the floor and rushed me to the Emergency Room where they pumped my stomach, hooked me up to an IV and lectured me about my choices.

Grant stayed by my side at the hospital and he insisted on paying right away. He gave the stunned receptionist $1,500 in cash and asked for the bill for any balance to be sent directly to him. I didn't ask where he got the wad of bills he had in his pocket and he never said a word to our mom. This is when I began to learn we both had secrets to keep.

Grant didn't go back to Drexel after that winter break and began working full time at Crimson. He quickly moved up to Head of Security. When the time came for me to pick a college, I chose the closest art school to Grant. Even though I cleaned myself up after the rufies incident, he was handy to have around whenever I decided to have a damsel in distress moment.

If our mom knew about half of the shit I had gotten into, shit Grant had bailed me out of, I would be in a convent. We sat in silence and he tapped his finger against the steering wheel – an indication he was thinking.

Finally he said, "Alright, you're only working there through graduation, the summer at the latest. Just keep a low profile, okay?"

"I already agreed to that," I reminded him before climbing out of the car.

Just before I could shut the door Grant threw out another caveat. "Keep some distance between you and Dominic. He isn't a good guy to get involved with."

"Grant, you said yourself that there isn't a company policy in place about dating co-workers and I'm twenty-two years old. I'll date who I want," I said and slammed the door. He was not going to tell me who I could or couldn't see. Typical Grant, he was always trying to act like my father.

I marched up the stairs to the second floor, calming down after reaching the landing. By the time I stood in front of my apartment, I was laughing at myself about how I got all worked up over a guy. I was truly acting irrational over a drunk and brief encounter. Taking a deep breath and swallowing the laughter, so as not to disturb my roommate, I turned the key in the deadbolt and quietly pushed open the door. To my surprise the light in the living room was on, my roommate practically pounced on me.

"Oh my God, how was your first night? Was it awesome? Did you see anyone famous?" I took a step back and laughed. Chelsea had taken her contacts out and wore her broken glasses, the same pair she'd had since eighth grade and which hung crookedly across her face; magnifying an already manic expression.

Any remainders of the bad mood Grant had put me in quickly vaporized as I had a captive audience. I couldn't wait to tell Chelsea about the club, leaving the part out about the gunshots though, having already had enough lectures for the night.

"I am so jealous! What a freakin' cool job. You are so lucky!" Chelsea declared. I sat back on the futon and agreed with her. "So, you didn't see anyone famous?" Chelsea asked again.

"No, but there's some sort of NBA charity event next weekend."

Chelsea's glasses almost fell off her face when her blue eyes bugged out, "No freakin' way! Can I come?"

I laughed again and yawned, "Maybe."

"Cool." Chelsea smiled at me like I was a celebrity. Yeah, there was no way Grant could convince me to not work at Crimson.

Chapter 3

Crimson proved to be busier the next night and the guys grabby, again. At the end of my shift I made my way over to Dominic's bar.

"Hi Natalie," he said as I approached.

"Hi back." Out of the corner of my eye I spotted Grant observing our exchange. Dominic seemed really uncomfortable which made me self-conscious and this bothered me. Why was I all of sudden concerned about how a guy felt? Sure I was physically attracted to Dominic, but there was something else lurking there under the surface I couldn't place.

"Did you want a drink?" he asked as he wiped the counter in front of me with a white towel that reeked of bleach, making my eyes burn. The wet surface reflected the blue and red lights that hung over the bar.

"Sure, I'll have a vodka tonic." I enjoyed the view as he walked to the other end of the bar. Before he could catch me obviously checking him out, I turned my head. Grant stood off to the side frowning at me, most likely none too pleased I had ordered a drink.

"So, do you think we'll hang out in Britney's car again tonight?" I asked after the alcohol instilled some courage.

"I don't know," he answered and turned away. His distance bothered me again and I thought about it as I took another sip. I adhered to one self-imposed rule: don't get attached. This was established six years ago, during my junior year of high school, after my last experience with a relationship. Toby Donovan was captain of the soccer team and also a gifted artist. We were in the same AP art class the first semester and he sat across from me. We spent hours using each other as models for sculpture, painting, you name it. He was different from the other guys I knew and we hung out on weekends. After soccer season, we started getting together during the week, despite harassment from his friends because I wasn't in the right "circle". One thing led to the other and we became an official couple. I felt so comfortable with him that when he asked me to pose nude for him, I did. No question.

My mom raised me to not trust men. My father left us and she became a bitter, abandoned ex-wife. She had the tendency to be a cruel mother too. I spent my childhood trying to live up to her high expectations and failing miserably. Where Grant could do no wrong, I couldn't do anything right. Toby helped me think about myself differently. When we made love for the first time, my first time, I never felt more wanted, appreciated and beautiful. With him, my insecurities disappeared.

How quickly they returned though, when two months after I lost my virginity, I caught Toby hooking up with Marlene Perkins, co-captain of the cheerleading squad, at a party. The pain and humiliation manifested in my chest, making it hard to breathe. I couldn't even say anything to him and just ran away from the house party. That following Monday a drawing of me, where I had posed nude, was taped to the front of my locker. I wanted to crawl inside my locker and hide from the world. My mom had been right, men can't be trusted. If she was right about that, maybe she was right about everything else; like I wasn't smart or pretty. Toby's betrayal sent me into a downward spiral. During the day I remained super-disciplined at school. I didn't need my mother to approve of my art work. My instructors' praise and awards from competitions told me I was a promising artist. My personal life derailed. I started sneaking out to get drunk and hooking up with random men. Since Toby, I hadn't had a relationship last longer than 24 hours (if that even qualifies as a relationship).

Since I started college I'd been on a few dates, stopped sleeping around and avoided getting involved with anyone. All of my focus went towards my course work. Dominic, however, made me feel unfocused and disoriented. I didn't know how to handle the physical reaction he triggered in me. An attraction was there and it was difficult to suppress.

As I zoned out at the bar, it dawned on me; I was beginning to like Dominic in more ways than lust. Or maybe it was just lust and he was right in distancing himself. I chugged my drink and stood up.

"Well, good night," I said, hoping he couldn't hear the panic in my voice. I walked up to the employee lounge to get my things. Brittany was getting ready to leave too.

"Hey! A bunch of us are going over to Blue, want to come?"

"Yes!" I jumped at the opportunity, grateful for the distraction.

We passed Grant on the way out. "Be careful. Remember what I said about drama?" He tilted his head toward Brittany. "Call me if you need anything." I rolled my eyes, but knew he would be the first I'd call if things got out of hand.

A huge line of people stood outside Blue. Many swayed in place and probably should have been home sleeping the booze off and not waiting to get into another club. I recognized several customers from Crimson as we walked past. I followed Brittany's lead and we were ushered inside by a bouncer at the door.

Blue was packed and steaming hot; the air heavy with perspiration and the stench of stale beer. We left our coats at the coat check and filtered through the crowd to the bar. Once I had my drink, I spun around to people-watch and instead came face to chest with Dominic. Vodka and tonic splashed all over my shirt.

"Shit!" I gasped as an ice cube fell down the front and became lodged in my bra, instantly beginning to melt against my hot skin. I reached in and fished it out.

"I would have gotten that for you," he teased.

"So you're talking to me now?" The smile vanished from his face.

"Yeah, sorry about earlier, your bro didn't like us getting so friendly in the back of Brittany's car last night."

"That's Grant for you. It's really none of his business."

"I can't say I blame him. I'd probably do the same if my little sister started to get involved with someone like me."

"What's that supposed to mean?"

"Nothing, he's being a big brother. I get it." He leaned over to order a drink, sandwiching me between his body and the bar. His closeness made my stomach flip. I shook my head slightly in an attempt to focus. Don't do it, Nat. don't start liking this guy, I warned myself. The counter dug into the small of my back so I shifted, resulting in me being pressed closer to Dominic. He smiled down at me. "I owe you a drink, don't I?" His voice was soft and husky.

Minutes passed while we waited for the bartender to return with our drinks. Dominic kept me pinned, but I wasn't complaining. "So what's your story, Natalie?"

"I don't have a story, well, not an interesting one anyway. I go to the University of the Arts and will be graduating in May."

"What are you studying?"

"My major is sculpture and my minor is art history. Do you go to college?"

"I took a couple semesters, but school didn't appeal to me. Besides, I'm going into the family business anyway."

"Which is?"

The bartender arrived and I never got an answer to the question.

Dominic kept me pinned beneath him and he leaned down. "I wanted to do this last night," he whispered in my ear. I closed my eyes, anticipating his next move. Sure enough his lips found mine and he moved closer. I grabbed his bicep when he pulled me against him. This kiss was like nothing I had ever experienced. Not wet, not sloppy, it was…incredible. His lips were soft, warm and fit perfectly over mine. I stopped holding back and fell into the moment. The loud club ceased to exist. When we pulled apart I had to catch my breath. My insides were begging and pleading for more. I could very easily have taken Dominic back to my apartment, slept with him and then been done. I was about ready to propose this, but stopped myself as another realization hit me.

I didn't want just a one night fling.

We moved in at the same time for another kiss. Our lips barely touched when Brittany suddenly emerged from the crowd, pulling me away from Dominic and onto the dance floor.

"Brittany, I was kind of in the middle of something back there," I yelled over the music.

She ignored me, or pretended to be oblivious, but the glittering in her eyes made me suspect she knew exactly what she was doing. I glanced back towards the bar, but Dominic was gone.

Damn.

Chapter 4

Returning to class on Monday was a harsh reality check. The number of projects that were due was overwhelming and it didn't help that I couldn't get thoughts of Dominic out of my head. I was in a permanent state of distraction. Mornings were difficult in the first place, but I had to go back to my apartment three times in a row because I kept forgetting things. This seriously amused Chelsea who laughed harder and louder each time I came through the door.

When I did arrive at my first class, a creaky hinge alerted the professor to my late entrance and he glared at me. I crept to the back of the classroom. To make matters worse, the teacher called on me and caught me mid-fantasy. I was too busy thinking about the effect of Dominic's body pressed against mine that I stammered out the wrong answer. Usually I would have had the correct one. This earned me a disapproving frown from my professor before he moved on to another student.

"You were off your A-game today Miss Ross," he commented as I tried to hurry past after class.

"Yes, I'm sorry."

"Well, must be something good because you're always so focused." He had no idea how good; I thought to myself and suppressed a chuckle. "Since you're here - have you given any more consideration about pursuing your MFA? You mentioned you were interested in the Art Institute of Chicago."

"I haven't decided."

"Well, let me know. I would be more than happy to write you a letter of recommendation."

"Thanks, I will. I have the application, but haven't filled anything out yet."

"You shouldn't waste any time. You are one of my best students and I think they would accept you right away."

"Okay, I'll think about it more this week," I promised before I left the classroom. Great, now my mind was going to be really preoccupied. I needed to get my shit together. Once back at my apartment, I dropped my backpack on the floor by my desk and changed to go for a run.

As I settled into a steady pace, my head began to clear. It felt good to do something positive with my body after the long weekend of working and partying. Running gave me a sense of clarity and by the time I rounded the corner of my block, I had put thoughts of Dominic aside and focused on post-graduation plans.

I had been considering getting a Masters in Art Therapy or Art Education so I could teach and support my independent projects. The 400-level courses this semester were grueling and I hadn't had time to focus on those pursuits. Philadelphia was soon going to be part of my past as I set out to create a future for myself. Sure I did a lot of growing here, but the time had come to move away from the crutch Grant provided. I needed to figure out the type of person I wanted to be. Getting romantically involved with anyone now would be ridiculous. This was reason enough to put any and all thoughts of Dominic aside.

Chelsea was home and cooking dinner when I returned. "What did you forget this time?" she joked.

"God, I'm lucky I even made it to class. The run helped and I'll feel even better after a shower."

"Good idea," she said, wrinkling up her nose.

"Shut up!" I laughed and chucked the dish towel at her. She was still laughing when I stepped into the bathroom.

The shower worked wonders and helped me get the last of my hormones in check. I felt better about myself and in control of the situation. After slipping on pajamas, I checked the messages on my cell phone. There were three; one from Chelsea to see if I was home, the second from our friend Jillian to see if we were still on to watch our Wednesday night shows and the last was from Dominic. My pulse quickened the instant I heard his voice.

"Hey Nat, it's Dom. Sorry I had to leave Blue last night – my uncle needed me to take care of something. Call me some time or I'll see you at work."

I jumped up and down and did a little happy dance before I realized what I was doing. Get a grip girl, no emotional attachments, remember? My calm, cool and rational self quickly reminded me. It didn't help. I took a couple of deep breaths and dialed his number.

We spoke for over two hours and it only felt like a few minutes. Chelsea kept peeking in to my room and I had to wave her away. Turns out we had a lot in common. He was a huge music fan, we both liked alternative rock. He loved horror movies and we shared the same favorite movie – Silence of the Lambs. And like me, he considered himself a foodie.

"Speaking of food, I haven't eaten dinner yet and I am starving," I didn't want to end the call, but needed to eat.

"I won't keep you. I'm glad we had a chance to talk outside of work. Also, I'm sorry we couldn't hang out at Blue last night."

"That's okay. It's not like we were on a date or anything."

"Yeah, but it was turning out to be a very interesting night." I laughed in response, knowing he was referring to our kiss.

"That's a whole other conversation, Mister," I joked. "This girl's gotta eat!"

He laughed, "Alright, I'll talk to you later. Are you working Thursday?"

"Yup, Thursday through Sunday."

"Cool, see you then."

I hung up the phone and fell back against the pile of pillows on my unmade bed. Chelsea must have been waiting in the hall, eavesdropping, because she popped up in the doorway within nanoseconds. Before she even sat down next to me, questions were flying out of her mouth.

"Who was that?"

"Dom, the guy from work I told you about."

"Really?" she asked; her eyebrow arched high. "Wow, you had a two hour conversation with a guy. When are you getting married?"

"What?"

"Geez Nat, I'm just kidding. Two hours is like the longest commitment you've given a guy since Toby – ha ha?"

"Oh, I get it. Not funny. Besides, I've already decided I'm not getting involved with anyone because I'm leaving Philly after graduation."

"Wait a second. So you actually considered getting involved? Wow, Nat, that's progress." Chelsea sat back and looked at me. "I'm proud of you. I know Toby really fucked you up and maybe now you're beginning to realize you're not completely broken after all."

"I wouldn't go that far! Like I said, this isn't going anywhere."

"Uh huh," she said and she stared at me like a parent whose baby just spoke her first word.

I rolled off the bed and Chelsea followed me down the hall into our small kitchen. I dropped a bagel in the toaster then chopped an apple, smearing the slices with peanut butter.

"Did Jillian call you about watching our shows?" Chelsea asked. She knew me well enough to stop discussing Dominic.

"She left me a message, but I haven't called her back."

"Well, the girls and Danny are going to come over here tomorrow night to watch. Everybody's going to bring a snack and a drink."

"Sweet should be fun," I said and took a bite of my bagel.

"So you're thinking about grad school again?"

I nodded as I chewed.

"It's going to be weird not being roommates anymore. I'll really miss you Nat." Chelsea was leaving for Italy for the summer after landing an internship. This was the first time I really thought about how we were going to be so far apart. We had been inseparable since fourth grade.

"We still have a few months," I put down my bagel and pulled her into a hug. "And I'll miss you more than you know." My voice grew thick with unshed tears and she was quick to return the hug, as usual.

Chapter 5

I was running late for work. Every pair of pantyhose I pulled out of the dresser had a run. Finally, I found a new pair shoved in the back of a drawer and managed to put them on without ruining them. I stepped into black high heels and threw my winter coat over my work clothes, a tight black skirt and low cut top. The cab was waiting at the curb and I caught the driver checking out my legs as I approached. I made a mental note to buy a longer coat.

"Club Crimson, Columbus Ave. and Oregon, please," I instructed the driver.

The closer we got, the more nervous I became. I was excited to see Dominic and seriously annoyed with myself for feeling that way. As the cab pulled up in front of Crimson, I decided I wouldn't go out of my way to seek Dominic out. It was better not to pursue anything with him. At least Grant would be happy about this decision.

I didn't see Dominic when I walked past his bar on the way to the employee lounge. Brittany and Allegra were sitting on one of the black leather loveseats smoking.

"Hey Nat, ready for a busy night?" Brittany asked.

"Are Thursdays busy here?"

"Definitely, they're crazy. Allegra and I are planning on going to Blue again after work, if you want to come?"

"I don't know. I have school tomorrow."

Brittany shrugged, put out her cigarette and stood up. I was amazed her tiny frame could support such giant breasts and wondered if her plastic surgeon had any ethics at all. "See you on the floor," she said and left the lounge.

Brittany was right, Thursday nights were crazy. I was grateful though because it kept my mind off of Dominic, although it didn't keep my eyes from seeking him out. I purposefully avoided his bar, even if it meant a longer trip to fill my drink orders. The other bartenders weren't as captivating. At the end of the night, however tempted I was to wind down at Blue after work, I knew I needed to behave and be prepared for class. Grant dropped me off and seemed more at ease. I think he was pleased I was being responsible.

Adrenaline from the busy night still coursed through my veins and I wasn't ready to sleep when I got home, so I pulled out grad school applications for a couple of the schools I was interested in attending. The Art Institute of Chicago, Cal Arts and the Rhode Island School of Design rounded out the top three. I managed to fill out all the necessary forms and made a list of what I needed to include from the school such as a transcripts, recommendations and my digital portfolio. It felt good to make progress and I slept peacefully.

The next night I wasn't as successful at avoiding Dominic. After the club closed, all of the other employees gathered around Dominic's bar to count out. It would have been too obvious if I didn't join them so I walked over. Dominic saw me approach and smiled. "Hey you, it's about time you came over. I thought you were avoiding me or something."

"No, just busy. You were pretty busy tonight too."

"I would have made time for you," he admitted. I smiled in response. Damn, he was making it hard for me to resist him.

Grant walked up to us with Miranda at his side. "Miranda is having a little after work gathering at her place, Nat, care to join us?"

"Sure!" I was still pretty wound up from the night and not ready for sleep, plus since it was Friday night, I didn't have to worry about classes the next day.

"I'm in too," Dominic announced. Grant glared at Dominic, but didn't say anything.

Grant and Miranda walked ahead to her car. Dominic and I followed close behind until he slowed to a stop and I stopped with him.

"Did you forget something?"

"No, I wanted to talk to you while we're alone."

"Um, okay?"

"Were you avoiding me last night and tonight?

I looked into his eyes prepared to lie, but found it impossible. "Sort of," I laughed and stared down at the tops of my shoes. He waited for me to continue. "I don't want things to get weird or complicated and –"

Placing a finger under my chin, he raised my head, and silenced me with a kiss. The kiss was anything but weird and it certainly complicated things. My knees went weak and I fell against him. He held me up, pulling me closer. His lips on mine felt so natural and way too good for me to try to stop.

He pulled away and I caught my breath. "You were saying?" he prompted me.

"What was I saying?" I joked. He smiled and moved in for another one. I put my hands on his chest and pushed away. "Grant is probably watching and I'm really not in the mood to deal with him. Besides, I need some time to think about this, about us. Okay?"

He nodded. "That sounds reasonable, but you don't have to avoid me." I was beginning to think I wouldn't be able to avoid him, especially if he kept kissing me like that.

Chapter 6

Crimson was packed. The celebrity NBA event drew a crowd. A line of people, desperate to get in, wrapped around the building. They stood there patiently dressed like it was summer, oblivious to the sub-zero temperatures. Inside the club felt tropical, the air was thick, moist and uncomfortably warm. Bodies writhed together on the dance floor and couples were entwined on large plush sofas that lined the walls. Each of the three bars had crowds of people waiting to get drinks. I didn't have to wait. Dominic gave me priority when he filled my orders.

It only took me a week to get used to making my way through the throngs of people, but I was not getting used to being grabbed by strangers. If my brother had his way, he'd throw out every guy who touched me. Fortunately, he was busy and distracted in the VIP Section; otherwise I wouldn't make any tips.

Weaving my way through the crowd, I spotted Grant talking to a group sitting at a table in VIP. One of the men in the group was staring at me. He was older and his beady, black eyes were intense. His eyes combined with heavy jowls that hung off of his jaw reminded me of a bulldog. His unwavering gaze made me uncomfortable. I looked away, but couldn't help but peer back to see if he was still staring. This time the guy was talking to Grant and pointing at me. The fear on Grant's face when he saw me was terrifying. I'd rarely seen him afraid. He was always so sure of himself. Shocked, I turned away and refused to hazard another glance.

It was too busy the rest of the night and I had forgotten all about it until I was walking over to Dominic's bar to count out my tips. The creepy guy was sitting on one of the stools and talking to Dominic. I stopped short and contemplated turning around, but it was too late because Dominic spotted me and waved. The guy swiveled around on his stool to see who Dominic was waving at.

He watched me walk the rest of the way to the bar, making every step an extremely uncomfortable one. I had no choice but to go up to Dominic.

"Hi Nat. Did you have a good night?"

"I did. Thanks for helping me out with my drink orders," I answered, trying to ignore the penetrating gaze of Mr. Creepy.

"Natalie, this is my uncle. Marco Grabano." Dominic introduced me to Mr. Creepy. "Uncle Marco, this is Natalie Ross, Grant's sister."

Not wanting to, but not wanting to be rude, I held my hand out to shake his hand. "Nice to meet you Mr. Cr – Mr. Grabano," I said.

"You can call me Uncle Marco, doll," he said in a gravelly voice. Instead of shaking my hand, he bent over and kissed the top. "I've been anxious to meet Grant's sister. Apparently you got all the looks." He winked before his x-ray eyes scanned me again.

I turned my head, embarrassed, when I noticed Grant. He was sitting at the other end of the bar. His jaws clenched and nostrils flared when he saw Marco kiss my hand. Concerned Grant was going to do something 'big brotherish", I withdrew it and turned towards Dominic. "Sorry, I have to go talk to Grant." I nodded in Mr. Grabano's direction. I could feel his eyes on my ass as I turned and walked towards my brother.

"What is with you?" I hissed at Grant as I got closer to where he was sitting.

"I don't –I mean, I want…let's talk about this later. I thought I told you to stay away from Dominic."

I exhaled sharply. "Not up for discussion, Grant." There was a noticeable edge to my voice. "Now, staying away from his uncle?

That I can do," I whispered this part, not wanting 'Uncle Marco' to overhear, "He weirds me out."

I noticed Grant was clenching his jaw again. "He's the co-owner of Crimson, Nat. He's a very powerful man here in Philly."

"Great, so he's my boss? Shit, I was kind of rude to him just now."

Grant leaned in close to me. "I don't think you can be rude to him, Nat. The way he is looking at you right now, you could flip him off and he'd be just as enthralled."

"What?" I jerked my head up to see what he was talking about, but Grant prevented me.

"Don't. Jesus…" Grant paused. "You seem to have caught Mr. Grabano's eye. He wanted me to arrange a meeting. But, I told him you're my sister and not available."

"Ewww. But why would he want to meet me? I mean, all the other waitresses, they're gorgeous!"

"Natalie now is not the time to delve into your low self-esteem issues, just listen to me. Try to limit your interaction with Marco. I know he's our boss, technically, but he is used to getting his way and abusing his power. Catch my drift?"

"Oh." I gasped as the realization hit me. "Is he dangerous?"

"Very. And he isn't used to being denied anything he wants."

"And you think he wants me?"

"I know he does," Grant said. There was a shadow of sadness in his hazel eyes. "Nat, I really wish I hadn't gotten you a job here."

"Is Dominic really his nephew?" I asked, anxious to change the direction of the conversation.

"Yes and the apple didn't fall far from the tree."

I laughed finding that hard to believe. Dominic was nothing but a sweetheart. He didn't have a dark, brooding presence like his uncle.

"If you have such an issue with Dominic, why did you let me hang out with him at Miranda's again last night?"

"Because he's Miranda's cousin."

"Oh."

"Natalie, will you please take me seriously?"

I could see the concern on my brother's face and didn't want him to keep nagging me. "Yes Grant. I am taking this seriously," I reassured him.

He relaxed a bit after that and let me finish counting out my tips in peace. I was shocked to discover I had made over $400. There was a lot of money being spent at Crimson. Despite having a creepy boss man, this was a great place to work.

Dominic walked down to stand in front of me. "Hey Nat, do you have any plans for after work?"

I was just about to answer when Grant butted in. "I'm her ride. We're heading out in a few minutes."

After shooting death rays at Grant I looked apologetically at Dominic. He was just being nice and Grant was behaving like a giant ass.

"I can give her a ride Grant, if she wants to hang out?" He regarded me with his deep green eyes. Thank God I was sitting because my legs probably wouldn't have been able to support me. It was utterly bizarre how Dominic's mere presence affected me. Before Grant could speak for me again I answered, with exaggerated enthusiasm. "That would be great! I'm not ready to go home yet."

I turned towards Grant with a big smile and batted my eyelashes. He frowned at me and shook his head. "Yeah, sure you're taking me seriously," he muttered. I heard the defeat in his voice and knew I had won, because Grant would have to physically pick me up and carry me out of the club. I wasn't going to budge.

***

Dominic and I were flying down Broad Street, heading towards South Philly in his Mustang. The worn leather seats smelled like a mixture of smoke, gasoline and Dominic's cologne - definitely a man's car. It was just the two of us and I enjoyed being alone with him. I found that once I got over my shyness, he was easy to talk to. I had no idea where we were going. He said he was taking me to a special place not too many people knew about. We could have driven around 'til dawn, I didn't care, as long as I got to stay next to him.

He asked all sorts of questions about me. When we had spoken on the phone the other night, we didn't talk about our family. I told him Grant was three years older and my only sibling. Our parents divorced when I was five and our Dad moved to Texas. I hardly knew him. He was remarried and had another family. We stayed with our Mom in York and Grant was forced to be the man of the house.

"He's kind of overbearing, but I don't think he really has a choice," I revealed to Dominic.

Dominic nodded his head. "I can see that and I think it makes him good at his job. He's always watching out for everyone."

"Yeah, but it's not easy when you're his younger sister, trust me."

"Does he hold you back?"

"He tries to," I said with a laugh.

"Like he tried to keep you from going out with me tonight?"

"Yes."

"But he didn't stop you."

"I try not to let things stand in my way of something I really want." I closed my mouth with a snap, completely mortified I let that slip. I turned my head and stared out the window.

"Am I something you really want?" he teased. I ignored him, not ready for him to know.

Dominic told me a little bit about himself too. I finally got the answer to my questions about the family business he would take over someday.

"Ah, Uncle Marco," I said.

"Yeah, I'm learning all of the positions. They had me start out as bar back, now I'm bartending."

"What's next?"

"I think I'm going to be working under your brother."

"That should be interesting." I said, imagining just how thrilled Grant must be at the idea.

Dominic slowed down as he turned off of Broad onto a smaller side street. Most of the row homes were dark, their occupants asleep. A few were boarded up. He parked in front of one of the abandoned homes. I got out and followed him up steps which led to a condemned building.

"Dominic, where are we?" I asked, recalling how the serial killer, Gary Heidnik lived in a similar neighborhood. I mean, how well *did* I really know this guy?

"You'll see." He knocked three times on the door. It immediately opened from the inside and a very large man peered through the crack. Dominic said something in what sounded like Italian and the door widened to let him through. I gathered myself together and quickly followed him in.

The large man eyeballed me. "Does she need to be searched?" he asked Dominic.

The thought of this man searching me with his bear paw sized hands was very disconcerting and I was relieved when Dominic told him I was cool and worked at Crimson. The man relaxed even more when he heard I was Grant's sister.

Once inside, I was able to take in my new surroundings. The home wasn't condemned at all. A long hallway led to a back room, where a group of men were sitting around a table playing cards. The smoke from their cigars hung in a haze above their heads. To my left, a steep staircase led to a dark second level. A living room or parlor, which had been converted to a bar, was to my immediate right. Several people sat around the bar counter and the bartender waved when he saw Dominic.

I followed him into this room and saw the front windows were boarded up, but aside from that the room was well maintained. The lighting was soft and jazz was playing quietly in the background. I noticed how people paid attention to Dominic as he crossed the room. They regarded him with respect. I quickly caught up so I was walking next to him. I wanted these people to know who I was with.

Behind the bartender and above the bottles of liquor there were three framed pictures. One was of the Pope, one of Marlon Brando and the last one was – Frank Sinatra. Only Rocky Balboa was missing. I felt like I had just walked into a scene from Goodfellas or The Godfather. I never thought places like this existed. This was definitely a first for me and I was determined to memorize every detail because my friends were not going to believe this shit. Dominic ordered us glasses of red wine and we relocated to a private table tucked away in the back corner of the room.

He took my coat and hung it up on a hook behind our table. I sipped on my wine quickly, waiting for the magical blanket to soothe and relax me. Dominic peered over the rim of his glass at me and winked.

"What?" I asked.

"You seem very relaxed, that's all. Don't you find this place a little weird?"

I sipped some more wine before answering. "Well, it's better than a condemned building – I was having some serious concerns there for a moment!"

He laughed. "I never thought about how it must have appeared. You probably thought I was some serial killer or something."

"Something like that," I admitted and smiled at him. "Where are we exactly?"

"This is a little after hours place my family has owned for generations. It dates back to Prohibition – used to be a speakeasy. We call it 'The Speak'."

"Your family owns this too? What else do they own?"

"Blue and the other club Trance. Um, they own the restaurants, Butter, and Tiramisu, plus some various real estate developments around the city."

"Wow, like which ones?"

"Independence Place is one."

My eyes widened in shock. Independence Place was one of the tallest skyscrapers in the Philadelphia skyline. The Grabanos had to be loaded and powerful. I thought back to Grant's warnings earlier and wondered if he wasn't exaggerating. Dominic's disarming smile distracted me from this negative thought. When he placed his hand on my thigh, all thoughts of Grant were banished.

This was our first time really alone together. There were the brief flirtations at the bar when I needed my drink orders filled, the occasional close encounters and of course that phenomenal kiss at Blue. But here it was just us and I liked it – and I was really beginning to like Dominic. He was more than just a hot guy and my resolve about not getting involved with him was quickly eroding.

We talked for what seemed like only a few minutes, when the doorman started to usher people out. I was surprised when we stepped outside and the sun was beginning to rise. We had been there for close to three hours. Dominic held the car door open for me and I dropped into the seat; which was freezing and the cold went right through my skirt. Hearing my teeth chattering, Dominic took off his jacket and draped it over my legs.

"Thank you."

He surprised me by kissing me, silencing the chatter. He pulled away from me slowly and all I could do was stare at him stunned. The engine of the Mustang still had to warm up, so I slid over closer to Dominic. He pulled me up on his lap to where I was straddling him. We didn't do anything more than kiss, but when we finally separated the windows were fogged up. I was dizzy and had to rest my head against Dominic's shoulder.

"Wow," Dominic whispered into my hair.

"Yeah, wow," I sighed, burrowing in closer to his warmth.

"I better get you home before, well, you know." He winked and flashed his dimple, which made crawling off of his lap a true test of my willpower, but I managed to make my way back to the passenger seat. I was wobbly and it wasn't the most graceful of moves.

He held my hand as he drove to my apartment building. When he turned onto my block I spotted a familiar silver car.

"What the hell?"

"What is it?"

"Grant," I answered and pointed at a silver Lexus.

There weren't any parking spaces so Dominic had to let me out in the street. We kissed again before saying goodbye. I couldn't wait to get to work later that night and had given up any hope of resisting Dominic at this point. I shut the door to the Mustang and watched it drive down the street. I turned and glared at Grant as he got out of his car.

"Spying on me again?"

"I wanted to make sure you got home safe since you choose to keep dangerous company."

"Whatever!" I rolled my eyes and turned to go up the three marble steps which led to the front door of my building. Grant reached out and grabbed onto the sleeve of my jacket. I shook his hand off and turned around to confront him. Even in my heels I had to look up at him.

"Knock it off Grant and stop acting like my father! I can spend time with whomever I want."

Grant stood his ground and didn't even flinch at my tone. He was always better at arguing. Whenever I got angry I wanted to cry and right now I was choking back the tears. This was not the time to appear weak.

"Natalie, I normally don't care who you spend your time with. But I know Dominic and I don't want to see you getting involved with him or anyone else at Crimson," he said rationally. "I think he's playing you, plus he's the owner's nephew."

I hadn't thought about it from that perspective. But then I remembered Miranda. "Oh really? What about Miranda?" I threw back at him.

"That's different," he replied, but I knew I had a reaction when his stance loosened.

"Grant," I said softly. "I know you're head of security and all, but you don't have to be my personal bodyguard. If I am making a mistake, let me find out the hard way. Otherwise, I won't learn. But, I think you're wrong about Dominic." And boy did I hope he was wrong.

Grant's shoulders dropped and I knew he was ready to concede, "I wish there was a way I could make you understand. I've done things I'm not proud of to get to where I am. I just don't want you to pay for my mistakes. "

"Please, what are you talking about? You are such a Boy Scout!" I teased.

"Do Boy Scouts drive Lexus' and carry a gun?" Grant said as if trying to allude to something more sinister.

"I'm sure some do when they grow up."

"Alright. Well what about your first night working at Crimson - the gunshots, the discreet transaction with the cop? What do you think that was about?"

"A corrupt cop in Philadelphia? Now there's an anomaly!" I laughed. "Dominic told me how many businesses the Grabanos own. It doesn't surprise me if there are a few city officials on the payroll."

"That doesn't bother you?"

"No. Should it?" I couldn't believe it. My brother was seriously annoyed that this didn't bother me. It's not like I was born yesterday, I knew how the world operated. Did he really think he had sheltered me?

"Never mind!" he snapped. I was suddenly very tired. The high from spending the night with Dominic was gone. Arguing with my brother as the day was just beginning was not what I had in mind.

"Grant can we talk about this later? I really need to get some sleep and you do too. We both have to work tonight," I whined.

"Fine," he sighed. "Just please be careful, okay?"

"Yeah, sure…see you tonight." I turned around and went inside.

Chapter 7

Chelsea wasn't waiting up to ambush me, much to my relief, and I was able to collapse. I was so exhausted that I didn't bother taking off my uniform. I just fell across my double bed, with my feet hanging off the edge. Gravity took the high heels off for me. Hours later my cell phone woke me up out of a deep, dreamless sleep. It was my mom wanting to know how the new job was going. Recalling the angry exchange with Grant, I felt like I lied to her when I said everything was great.

I was too awake to go back asleep after her call. So, I rolled over onto my back and thought about Dominic – the way his thick, dark hair framed his face and accentuated his green eyes, the taste of his lips, the spicy smell of his skin and how perfectly our bodies fit together when I was on his lap. I knew I had it bad when I started counting down the hours until I saw him again. Three hours. That didn't give me much time to get ready and I still had assignments to work on, which were due in the morning.

The apartment was quiet as I made my way into the kitchen, grabbed a diet coke and poured myself a bowl of Captain Crunch. The caffeine and sugar had their desired effect and I cruised through my paper on the Impressionists. I had just enough time to shower and get dressed, which included getting in a fight with pantyhose, before catching a cab down to the club.

Miranda was at the desk by the front door chatting with the doorman when I arrived. She reminded me of a World War II pin-up with her glossy, wavy black hair, natural curves and her penchant for red lipstick. She wasn't all hairspray and silicone like most of the Crimson girls. She carried herself with professionalism and maturity. These traits plus the fact that she had brains, was probably why Grant liked her.

She was all business when I walked in. "Natalie. I've been waiting for you."

I gulped, wondering what I might have done. She smiled when she saw my deer in the headlights expression.

"Marco requested you to work in the VIP section tonight."

"Oh," I said, relieved. "What do I have to do?"

"Just keep the drinks coming, don't spill on anyone and try not to come off as too intelligent."

"So, act dumb, look pretty and keep them drunk?"

She laughed at this. "You got it! Oh, and watch out for Brittany tonight."

"Why's that?"

"She usually has VIP and she is pretty pissed you bumped her – and that you were requested."

Then it really registered about who had requested me. The image of Marco Grabano's beady eyes popped into my head. It was all I could do to control a shudder.

"Brittany may seem tiny, but she has a temper. You don't have a car do you?"

"No. Why?"

"Good. Brittany's been known to take her anger out on cars – flat tires, broken headlights, windshields, etc…"

I tried to picture the petite girl terrorizing someone's car and laughed.

"Seriously, Natalie, watch your back."

This was the second co-worker I've been warned about and I was seriously beginning to wonder just how many drugs my brother and Miranda were doing together, because these warnings were absurd.

"Okay," I said to appease her.

I went into the employee lounge to hang up my jacket and bag. Brittany was sitting on the sofa reading a magazine. She glared at me when I walked in. I smiled at her and went about my business. One of the shooter girls sitting next to Brittany was hunched over the coffee table doing lines of cocaine – her pre-shift routine. Joey D., one of Grant's bouncers, walked out of the shower area wearing only black jeans, his muscles rippled with his every move. He sat down on the sofa and did a line with the shooter girl. Not interested in that extracurricular activity, I quickly applied some lipstick and left.

My heels clacked on the dance floor when I crossed on my way to the VIP section. The club was cavernous without all of the people and with the lights on, glaringly bright. I was disappointed to see that Dominic wasn't working the bar in the VIP area. It was Sal, another dark haired bartender, not nearly as beautiful as Dominic. After helping Sal set-up, I roamed around hoping to find Dominic. I found him in a separate room enclosed in dark tinted glass that was reserved for private parties. He was arguing with my brother- big surprise. They didn't see me as I quietly entered the room and stood in the shadows.

"I can't believe you took her there," Grant hissed at Dominic.

"It was no big deal, nothing happened," Dominic defended himself.

"You're lucky. If anything had happened to her, I swear to fucking Christ-"

"Don't threaten me Grant!" Dominic was pointing his finger at Grant's chest. Both men were about the same height, well over six feet tall, but Grant was more muscular. Dominic didn't seem the least bit intimidated, "Nothing is going to happen to Natalie. I'll keep her safe."

"I'll hold you to that promise." Grant stormed off and out the rear exit of the room.

I stood in the shadows, not sure if I should make my presence known. I really wanted to run over to Dominic and throw my arms around him. He must like me if he had defended me to my own brother.

"Dominic?" I called out. He looked around, but couldn't see me. My black clothes were like camouflage so I stepped uncertainly out into the dim light. His face lit up with a big grin full of straight white teeth. He strode over, pulled me to him and placed his lips on mine.

"How long were you standing there?"

"Long enough," I answered. "I told you my brother was overprotective."

"Yeah, but I guess he has good reason to be. You're worth protecting." I stared up at him, amazed. He bent down and kissed me again before I could say anything else.

"Well, I have to go get my bar ready. Make sure you stop by frequently tonight."

"I can't tonight."

"Why not?"

"Your uncle requested me to work the VIP section."

Anger flashed across his face. "He did." It wasn't a question. He exhaled deeply and reached for my hand. "Do want to go out again after work?"

"Yes!" I must have said this with little too much enthusiasm because Dominic jumped a bit, and then he grinned.

We walked out holding hands just as Brittany was exiting the employee lounge. She stopped when she saw us then glanced down at our joined hands. I could feel hate and jealousy radiating off of her, giving me reason to take Miranda's warning seriously and making me grateful I didn't own a car.

The VIP section filled up quickly and I had to hustle to keep up with the demand. It was hard to maintain my composure when I waited on one celebrity after another. The whole section was like a Who's Who of famous Philadelphians, mainly athletes. Fortunately I was too busy to allow Marco to get to me. He managed to lean just a little too close when I was taking his drink orders and his hand came in contact with my ass one too many times, but at least he had stopped staring.

I tried to coordinate my stops when Grant visited at the table. Uncle Marco seemed to behave himself a little better in the presence of my brother. It was hard to act unintelligent and I found it easier to just keep my mouth shut. I may have been playing dim, but I was still observant. The fact that Uncle Marco and all of his friends were carrying guns did not escape me. I guess the owner and his friends didn't have to go through the metal detector and use the gun check like the other patrons.

Miranda stepped in to give me a much needed bathroom break and on my way back I stopped at Dominic's bar. He was mobbed as usual, but he managed to sneak a few seconds in to visit.

"How is it going up there?" he asked.

"Pretty good!"

"Is my uncle treating you okay?"

"Yeah," I lied. He didn't seem convinced, but didn't say anything. His bar was packed and I knew he needed to get back to work so I quickly left.

Soon after last call, the VIP area started to clear out. Only Marco and his crew lingered. They were smoking cigars and talking loudly. Marco waved me over to join them. Not really in a position to say no, I set my tray down and eased into the booth, careful to keep a substantial space between Marco and my legs. They were busy talking about the Sixers and other teams. Not a fan of sports I tuned them out to stare at Dominic.

"Natalie? Hello, Natalie?" Marco was trying to get my attention.

I quickly pulled my focus back to the table. "I'm sorry, did you ask me something?"

"Yeah. I was wondering if you would like to continue this party elsewhere." He looked at me expectantly. I couldn't believe this fifty-something man was asking me if I wanted to go out with him, and I think he wanted to include his friends.

"I, uh...well, I can't. I already have plans. Sorry." It was true, I'm glad I did have plans, because I would have had to lie to my boss – not a good habit to get into – and I feared I might get stuck accompanying him.

Marco seemed very disappointed, almost angry that he was being denied. His eyes turned an even darker black. A sneer started to form on his doughy face. "Well, maybe next time?"

"Um, sure?"

Thank God Grant showed up then. I went to leave, but Marco grabbed me by the wrist and anchored me to my seat. Grant saw and pursed his lips, but didn't say anything.

"Marco, Stump and his boys didn't pay their tab again," Grant said.

"That arrogant, cheap son of a bitch! I warned him if he pulled this shit again it was going to be the last time!" Marco slammed his other hand down on the table and his face turned bright red. He released my wrist, but I was too afraid to move. He studied Grant, his eyeballs seemed to twitch in their sockets and he was suddenly eerily calm when he said, "You know what to do." Grant tipped his head in acknowledgement.

When Grant turned to leave the table I jumped up to follow him. "Excuse me gentleman, I need to close out."

Marco smiled and reminded me not to have plans the next time.

"What was that all about?" Grant asked as we walked across the dance floor towards Dominic's bar.

"Mr. Grabano asked me to 'continue the party' later. I think it was his creepy way of asking me out." I whispered.

Grant stopped mid-stride. "What did you tell him?" I squirmed under his interrogative gaze.

"I told him I already had plans - because I do."

"What plans?" he asked suspiciously as if he knew I going to tell him something he didn't want to hear and he was bracing himself for it.

"Dominic and I are hanging out again after work." Grant rubbed his hands over his face and shook his head, but he didn't snap at me.

"You're not going to the after hours place again are you?"

"You mean The Speak? How did you know about that?" I narrowed my eyes at him.

"Word gets around fast. I have a lot of eyes."

"Ugh! You are so annoying!" I growled and stalked off to the bar. Dominic was just finishing up, so I went to the employee lounge to get my things. As I was taking my jacket off of the hanger I overheard Brittany in the bathroom area talking to someone.

"...and he was holding her hand. Can you believe it? He never held my hand. You know what's funny? I think she really likes him. He's such a player and she has no idea."

"Yeah and she's Grant's sister, now that takes some serious balls. Grant will kill him if he burns her," the other person commented.

I froze when I realized who they were talking about. So Dominic was a player. That explained his interest in me. It was too good to be true. My heart sunk into my stomach. Grant was right and he tried to warn me. I could feel the lump forming in my throat and I tried to swallow it down, but it wouldn't budge. My eyes started to tear up with bitter disappointment. I cleared my throat, put on my jacket and with my head held high, marched out of the lounge. My guard was back up.

Dominic was waiting right outside the doorway and I hesitated.

"What's wrong?" he asked.

"Nothing," I lied. I couldn't meet his eyes, his beautiful eyes.

"Okay… are you ready to go?"

"I, uh, I just remembered I have to work on a project for school. It's due tomorrow," I lied again and he saw right through me.

"Come on Nat. Something's bothering you. What's going on?"

Brittany and the shooter girl walked out of the employee lounge then and she smirked at me. She picked up on the tension between us and seemed pleased. Dominic saw the smirk and scowled at Brittany. She laughed and walked away.

"What did she say?"

I didn't want to talk about this, but didn't want to leave it unresolved either. So I put as much armor up around my heart as possible and answered him.

"I overheard her talking about us and she said you're a player. This whole thing between us is just a conquest for you isn't it?"

"No, not at all! Brittany is a psycho. We dated…briefly, but it didn't work out. She is a little obsessive." He seemed like he was being honest and I wanted to believe him. But, then I thought about Grant's warning and still wasn't convinced.

"Natalie," he continued, reaching for my hand, "I really like you and I swear this isn't just a thing. I enjoy hanging out with you." I looked at him skeptically, but his eyes were sincere. Knowing I might regret my decision later, I smiled and squeezed his hand.

"I'm sorry. I shouldn't judge based on hearsay. It's just, well; I'm not exactly like a Crimson girl."

"No you're not. You're very different – you're real." He bent down and kissed me. His lips were soft and tasted of mint from his gum. "Now, are you ready to go?"

"Where are we going?

"Are you hungry?"

At the mention of food my stomach growled. It dawned on me that the only thing I had to eat was the bowl of cereal. "I'm starving!"

He laughed at my enthusiasm as we walked to his car. "You told me you like Chinese food. Are you up for that?" At the mention of Chinese my stomach growled even louder, this time he heard it. "I'll take that as a yes." He chuckled as he held the door open for me.

We went to a small restaurant in Chinatown and the hostess recognized Dominic.

"You must like Chinese food too," I commented as she led us to a table.

"My parents took the family here all the time growing up. "

We were the only customers, but being that it was three in the morning, I wasn't surprised. As we waited for our order I sipped on some tea. I didn't need alcohol to talk to Dominic anymore, conversation came naturally between us.

"So, when will your uncle make you manager of Crimson?"

"I'm not sure. It's really up to Miranda, I guess."

"Why's that?"

"She's Uncle Marco's oldest so she gets preference."

"Wait, I knew you were cousins, but Marco is Miranda's dad?" I asked, shocked. There was no way Marco could have fathered someone so beautiful. I examined Dominic more closely and saw the family resemblance I never noticed before. He and Miranda had the same eyes and black hair. Miranda was fair skinned though, where Dominic had more of an olive complexion.

"You seem surprised."

"Yeah, I am. I just thought Grant would have mentioned it."

"Those two are good at keeping things private. I'm sure there's a lot about Grant you don't know about."

"You're probably right. He's always busy getting into my business so I'm usually too annoyed to get into his."

Once our entrees arrived, we were too preoccupied feeding each other with chopsticks to talk. Sometimes food slipped and would land on the table, or in my glass of water; which set us off laughing.

It was almost five in the morning when he pulled up in front of my apartment building. This time there was a parking space and my brother's Lexus was nowhere in sight. I didn't want the night to end, but I had class in four hours and had to get some sort of nap in. I scooted over to kiss Dominic goodnight and he cupped my face in his hands, pulling my lips to his. Reaching behind his head I grabbed onto his thick hair. This wasn't like a shy first kiss or like an 'I've had too much to drink kiss' either. This was deeper, passionate and hungry. The same connection was there too, I hadn't imagined it last night. Dominic moved his lips down my neck and kissed my collarbone and I moaned with pleasure. His arms wrapped around me and pulled me closer. I went willingly. My body was pressed to his and he moved my jacket aside to slip his hand up under my blouse. I gasped when his skin grazed against mine. His fingers were cold and sent shivers down by back. I lifted his head up from my neck and kissed him hard. We were both breathing heavy and I was getting to the point of no return. It took all my willpower to stop and pull back.

"Oh my God this is hard. I want you so badly Dominic, but I have class soon and I need to get some sleep."

Dominic groaned in frustration. I kissed him again, slower this time. "I'm sorry," I said, pulling away.

He twined his fingers through mine. "I understand. But next time, I don't know if I'll be able to stop." He lifted my hand up and kissed the top.

"Next time?" I teased and raised an eyebrow.

"What are you doing tonight? It's Monday so we don't have to work."

The promise of a normal date with Dominic was too good to pass up, even if I had a ton of projects due this week. "I'm not doing anything."

"You are now - I'll pick you up at 8." With this plan set, he kissed me one more time and then I trudged up the stairs to my apartment. I didn't even make it to my bedroom and passed out on the futon.

Chapter 8

Chelsea shook me awake. "Wake up Nat. You're going to be late."

I groaned and mumbled, "Go away". She continued to try to rouse me. "You're persistent," I growled at her, but I was awake – barely. My eyes burned and it felt like the undersides of my eyelids were made of sandpaper. I sat up and yawned and caught a whiff of my breath - Chinese food morning breath, nothing worse. I rushed to the bathroom and started brushing my teeth. Studying my reflection in the mirror, I surveyed the damage. Dark circles had formed under my eyes; which were bloodshot. Medusa had had better hair days than this - a ponytail would have to suffice since there wasn't time for a shower. I threw on a pair of jeans, a sweater and my sneakers. I readjusted the ponytail, dropped some Visine in my eyes, grabbed a diet coke out of the fridge and bolted to campus.

My 9:00 class was Art History and in a large lecture hall. I knew the risk of getting caught sleeping was minimal so, I was able to doze. Chelsea was in my next class and she kept nudging me awake when she heard my breathing get deep.

The rest of the day dragged by in a fog and by the time I got home at three, I was ready to fall into a coma. Chelsea was dying to hear more about Dominic, but took pity upon me when she saw how badly my ass was dragging. Thankfully she sent me straight to bed without any questions.

I was still exhausted when my alarm went off at 6:30 leaving an hour and a half to work a miracle. Dominic might run away screaming if he came to pick me up and I looked like an extra from The Walking Dead. I had no idea what he had in store for our date and was at a loss as to what to wear. Chelsea came to my rescue and started pulling clothes out of my closet. After having me try on five different outfits and trying my patience, we both decided on black, boot cut pants and a deep wine red v-neck cashmere sweater. The pants paired with high heeled black leather boots made my legs seem longer and the sweater hugged my curves in the right places. The neckline actually made my boobs appear bigger. I never realized how handy it was having a fashion design student as a roommate. Chelsea let me borrow her black leather jacket to complete the ensemble.

"Don't do anything I wouldn't do in this," she teased.

"I don't even want to know what you've already done in this."

Chelsea snorted out a laugh and then left me alone to finish getting ready. I blew dry my hair until it was straight and smooth. It hung in long, dark shiny plaits down to the middle of my back. I found some lipstick, the same shade as my sweater, and dabbed it on, but not too much as my lips were big enough. When I stepped out of the bathroom, Chelsea whistled at me.

"You're hot!" I smiled at the compliment. For the first time, probably since Toby, I felt sexy.

The intercom let out a loud buzz announcing Dominic's arrival. Chelsea, perched on the edge of the couch, waited in anticipation. I probably made Dominic sound like a model in my description of him. I opened the door as he was reaching the top of the stairs. He had a dozen red roses in his hand. He stopped when he saw me and his eyes lit up.

"Wow! Have I ever told you how gorgeous you are?" He appraised me up and down and I dropped my head in embarrassment. He looked fabulous himself with dark blue jeans, which hung just right on his hips, and a black shirt that was unbuttoned at the neck. He too had a black leather jacket on. He handed me the roses and kissed me. I stepped closer, deepening the kiss. Then Chelsea quietly giggled, reminding me of her presence. I broke away and spun around.

"Please come in and meet my best friend."

Chelsea sprung up from the couch and shook Dominic's hand. She was appraising him too, but I think she appreciated his sense of style more than anything.

"Nice to meet you, Chelsea."

"Me too. I've heard a lot about you." Chelsea smiled at me and winked. I shook my head and blushed. Nice, Chels, very subtle. Dominic and Chelsea chatted while I put the roses in a vase. I set them on the breakfast bar and wished I had a more suitable surface for the bouquet. We left my apartment and walked down the block to Dominic's Mustang. He held my hand and I appreciated the warmth.

"What do you have planned for us tonight?"

"I'm taking you to the best Italian restaurant in the city," he boasted.

"Spaghetti Warehouse?" I asked, completely deadpan, referring to the remodeled warehouse converted to a restaurant which served all-you-can-eat spaghetti. He had the most horrified expression on his face, like I suggested we commit a murder or something. I couldn't keep a straight face and busted up laughing. It took him a few seconds to recover, but he soon joined in.

We drove to South Philly again and he turned onto a small side street like any other street in Philadelphia with brick row homes lining each side. One had a little sign extended out by the front door. The street was dimly lit so I had to squint to read it: Franco's Ristorante. The restaurant was so non-descript I would have passed by thinking it was just another house until Dominic opened the car door. Scents of roasted garlic and other deliciousness assaulted my senses and my mouth started watering. I inhaled the aromas deeply and Dominic smiled at me.

"Wait until you taste it," he said as he locked the Mustang.

He held the door for me and I walked in through a small foyer. The aromas inside were so much stronger. A girl, a little bit younger than me, was waiting at the hostess stand. Her eyes lit up when she saw us. "Dominic!" she squealed and threw herself at him. Dominic gave the girl a big bear hug and actually lifted her off the ground. He set her down and laughed. She looked at me curiously.

"Natalie, this is my cousin Bianca. Bianca, this is Natalie."

"It's nice to meet you," I smiled and held out my hand. She shook it enthusiastically. The girl radiated enthusiasm. She spun around like a pixie and grabbed a couple menus.

"The usual table, D?" she asked as we followed her through a small dining area.

"That'd be great B," he answered. Cute, D & B, I thought to myself. We entered what probably would have been a living room at one time. There were several occupied tables and a couple of people glanced up as we walked by, but most were absorbed in their dinners. I couldn't blame them, the food appeared delectable. We proceeded through this room and Bianca led us through a set of double doors straight into the kitchen. Pots and pans clanged, food sizzled on the stove by which an older couple stood, arguing in Italian. The speech was so fast, I didn't recognize any words. The dining room was calm and the kitchen was chaos.

Ignoring the arguing couple, Bianca sat us at a small dinette table in the corner by the brick oven. After she got us situated she spun around and shouted, "Ma, Pa, will you shut it for two seconds! Look who's here." The silence was deafening. Who would have thought such a little thing had such a big voice? The woman dropped a spatula she had been wielding like a weapon into a big pot of red sauce and, wiping her hands on her stained apron, waltzed over to us. She was short and round and her full cheeks were bright pink from steam. She opened her arms up and Dominic walked into her hug.

"Dominic, it's so nice of you to stop in!" After their embrace she held him back at arm's length surveying him. She clucked and shook her head, "You're too skinny Dominic. Are you feeling well?" Dominic laughed and assured her he was just fine then he introduced me.

"Aunt Gloria, this is Natalie Ross, my, um…my girlfriend." I'm surprised my jaw didn't hit the floor. Girlfriend? I wasn't ready for that, but didn't correct him. Instead, I recovered quickly enough and went to shake Gloria's hand.

"Oh, please, honey!" She cried and pulled me into a suffocating hug. Afterwards I went through the same inspection as Dominic. I too was declared too skinny, something I would never hear my mom say, and a loaf of fresh baked Italian bread was brought over to the table. I was introduced to Uncle Franco after Gloria had finished fussing over us. He brought over a bottle of red wine and popped the cork, pouring us each a glass. Uncle Franco was tall and skinny, with dark, olive skin. His soft brown eyes were kind, just like Bianca's.

"Sorry you had to hear us arguing, Natalie," he apologized in a deep voice.

"It's alright."

Even though they were arguing, the atmosphere wasn't tense. I could sense the love between Gloria and Franco. After being raised by a single mom it was nice to bear witness to a relationship like that. I bit into a piece of the Italian bread and practically swooned. It was still warm from the brick oven and the crusty exterior melted away to a moist, soft center. I would have been satisfied with just the bread and wine all night, but didn't dare suggest that to Gloria.

Franco fried up some calamari and brought a heaping plate over. Dominic dipped a piece in the marinara and popped it into my mouth. I had to close my eyes and savor the moment. The golden batter was light and flaky and the marinara had a bit of spice to it. I'd never had calamari like that before. Having an Italian God feed it to me wasn't too bad either. Dominic seemed entertained by my enjoyment of the food. Then he handed me a menu to pick out the main course. I couldn't make up my mind.

"What do you recommend?" I asked Dominic.

"Everything," was his answer. I had to play eenie meenie minie moe to pick my entrée and landed on eggplant parmesan.

Gloria and Franco were distracted making our dinners so I seized the opportunity to grill Dominic. I found out that Gloria was his mother's sister and Franco was the third Franco to run the restaurant, Franco's grandfather being the first - he was an Italian immigrant right out off the boat from Sicily when he started serving meals out of his house. Bianca was their youngest out of five children.

"She's cute," I commented.

"Yeah, she's like a little sister to me. "

"I can tell. She just adores you. That's sweet."

"She's a good kid and the same age as my brother, Anthony." I leaned forward, interested in learning more about Dom's family. "As you can tell, Aunt Gloria and Uncle Franco like to feed us, so I'd stop by after school for snacks with my cousin Dante. All the kids still do." Dom paused and took another bit of calamari.

I took a sip of wine, followed by a deep breath before addressing the elephant in the room. "Listen Dom, I really like you, but girlfriend? I don't think I'm ready for that."

His eyes met mine. "You're not?"

"No. It's been awhile since I've been someone's girlfriend and that didn't end well. We need to take it slow."

He frowned slightly and processed what I said. "It's been awhile for me too. I'm not a relationship kind of guy," he admitted. "But, I feel differently about you. I'll take it slow with you, but as far as I'm concerned, you're my girlfriend." He said this with a sort of possessiveness.

At first I thought he was feeding me a line, but he didn't break eye contact and seemed sincere enough. "I think I can work with those terms." Smiling, I reached my hand across the table. He entwined his fingers with mine and caressed the side with his thumb. We were interrupted by the sound of Aunt Gloria clearing her throat. She had a steaming plate in each hand. We separated so she could set them down. I caught her wink at Dominic before she turned and smiled at me approvingly. I giggled, embarrassed.

From the first bite I was in love and would never be able to eat eggplant parmesan from anywhere else, ever again. I managed to eat half before surrendering. My pants were going to split at the seams if I ate another bite. I sat back and watched Dominic eat his lasagna. He too was engrossed in his food. After he finished his serving he started to eye up my leftovers. I handed him my plate, unable to look at it anymore and sipped my wine, enjoying watching him eat with such fervor. Between the wine, my full stomach and the warmth from the brick oven, my eyelids grew heavy and I really didn't think it was possible to eat another bite until Franco brought over the Tiramisu. I rallied and reached for a spoon, savoring the sweet creamy goodness that slid down my throat. I could get used to this, I thought to myself.

After the meal was done we got up to say goodbye. I hugged Gloria and Franco and thanked them profusely for the best meal of my life. They both beamed and said I was welcome anytime. We walked through the restaurant, which had already closed. Bianca was bopping around with her iPod clearing the tables. We waved goodbye and she waved back without interrupting her groove. Dominic grabbed my hand as we walked outside into the calm, chilly night. Before we got in the car I stood up on my toes and kissed him.

"Thank you for introducing me to some of your family…and their cooking!"

"You're very welcome. "

Eleven o'clock is past bedtime for most people, but the night was still young for me and Dom. He drove down to the Penn's Landing River Rink and parked in the empty parking lot. The ice skating rink was empty too, since it was after hours.

"What are we doing here?"

"Do you know how to ice skate?"

"Yeah, but it's closed."

"Wait a few minutes. You'll see."

Moments later a rusty Buick Century parked next to us. A middle-aged man wearing glasses stepped out and walked up to Dominic's window. When he confirmed that it was Dominic he asked us to follow him. He opened up the rental area and flicked on the lights. He helped us pick out the right size skates. Once we were set, Dominic led me out on the ice. It took me a few falls on my ass to get the hang of it. It had been years since I last ice skated. Pretty soon Dominic and I were skating around the rink like pros, well, semi-pros. He helped steady me when he felt my legs get wobbly and never let go of me once. We laughed and goofed off like teenagers. It felt good to move around after the big dinner. The cold air beat back the drowsiness brought on by a full stomach.

The view out on the riverfront was beautiful too. Philadelphia during the winter months was just plain ugly. The landscape becomes gray and barren. Litter blows around the streets like urban tumbleweed and the cold penetrates every corner. Homeless people sit on steam vents like birds perched in a nest and Broad Street becomes an enormous wind tunnel that tries to suck your breath away. But down here on the riverfront, with the Ben Franklin Bridge lit up in the background on one side and the skyline on the other, Philadelphia was charming.

We skated for about an hour then put the skates back and the guy locked up behind us. He had even made us each a cup of hot chocolate. I thanked him as we walked back to the parked cars. He nodded and waved before we separated.

"Dominic, do you like own the city or something? How did you pull that off?" I asked as soon as we were in the Mustang.

"My dad knows the manager and he owed him a favor."

"That must have been a big favor. What does your dad do?" I realized that I knew more about his cousins, aunts and uncles than his immediate family.

"He owns a construction company and is involved in the real estate investment business with Uncle Marco." An image of a dump truck with Grabano and Sons emblazoned on the sides flashed in my mind. I remembered Grant worked for that company one summer.

"Well, I'm impressed. You sure know how to plan a date."

"It's not over yet," he said with a smile and stretched across the front seat to kiss me. His lips and tongue tasted like hot chocolate. I welcomed the yummy goodness. When we separated I was left wanting more. He caressed my cheek and then started the car. He pulled out of the lot onto an almost deserted Columbus Blvd. He only drove a few blocks and then turned right into the Waterfront Square Condominiums. I stared in awe at the giant towers that loomed into the night sky. Dominic slowed the Mustang down in front of the lobby and a valet appeared out of nowhere.

"Good evening Mr. Grabano." the valet greeted Dominic and held the door open for him. Then he spotted me in the passenger seat. "Oh, I'm sorry Miss," he said and hustled around to my side.

Dominic walked next to me with his hand on the small of my back. The doorman opened the main door and we entered the expansive lobby. It was all I could do to keep my jaw from dropping. Once I had attended a wedding that was held at the Four Seasons and this place made the Four Seasons lobby seem ghetto. Crossing the marble floors, my heels echoed up in the high ceilings. Thankfully Dominic was steering me towards the elevators, because I would have probably stood there in the middle of the lobby, like an idiot, completely slack-jawed and dumbfounded.

The elevator shot up to the twelfth floor in seconds. Dominic reached for my hand and gently pulled me out into the hallway. Our footsteps were silenced by the plush gray carpet.

"You live here?"

"Yeah. My dad's company built this whole complex. They're investors too."

Dominic opened the door to his condo. Windows stretched the whole length and the view was breathtaking. The Camden waterfront twinkled in the distance and reflected on the river. The white oak floors gleamed only to be outshined by the granite countertops and stainless steel appliances. The layout was open and the kitchen and living room shared the vistas. Dominic walked into the living room and flipped a switch. The gas fireplace roared to life and flames danced off of the dark brown leather sectional, making the room glow.

"This is amazing! Bartending must be working out for you to be able to afford a place like this."

He laughed and came up behind me to take my coat. He draped it over one of the bar stools at the breakfast bar and circled his arms around me.

"No, not bartending; the family helps me out."

I leaned back against him, his arms circled my waist and his lips moved slowly down my neck, making me shiver. "Mmmm…that's nice." I turned around and placed my arms around his neck, meeting his lips with mine. He moaned and pulled my hips against him, pressing his arousal against them. I gasped and our kissing deepened. Eventually, he led me over to the living room and we stood by the fire, our kisses growing more urgent. I started unbuttoning his shirt, but impatience won out and I ripped it off, scattering loose buttons everywhere. I yanked my sweater over my head and tossed it on the floor.

We fell to the carpet in front of the fireplace. He lay over me on one side while slipping my pants off with one hand. He paused and his breath hitched when he noticed I wasn't wearing any underwear. Then it was my turn, I admired his six-pack, tracing the ridges of muscle before reaching for his zipper. His excitement was evident as I worked at his pants and the bulge they contained. We attacked each other. He played with me and made my body react in ways I never thought possible. I had been with a few guys in my life after Toby, but didn't have the best experiences with them. Dominic erased all of that. Not once did I feel self-conscious. He wanted me just as badly as I wanted him. My hips rose to meet him and we moved together on the carpet. I moaned as my back arched in a spasm which rippled across my entire body. I felt very warm, wet and suddenly giddy. Dominic moaned, his body shuddered and then he rolled onto his back, panting.

"Oh my God that was amazing," I whispered into his neck and snuggled close.

"Yes it was," Dom kissed my forehead and pulled me closer.

We dozed off and when I woke, Dominic was spooning me. We were both still naked and on the floor in front of the fire. I nuzzled up closer to him for warmth. He physically responded to my movements and we started touching each other; slower this time, drawing the pleasure out. We ended with me draped across Dom. I moved so my chin was resting on his chest and really looked at him. The green of his eyes were barely visible through slits as he stared back at me. Satisfaction had softened the hardness of his jaw line where stubble had sprouted up overnight and his dark hair was tousled. I traced the tattoo spanning Dom's collarbone, shoulder and upper arm on his left side. It was all black ink and bold, geometric lines framing the word "famiglia".

"Family?" I asked.

"Yeah, it's the most important thing in my life. Without family, well, I can't imagine."

I rested my head on his chest, listening to his steady heartbeat, and tried to imagine a big family. Dom tightened his arm and pulled me closer, our bodies flush against each other. We stayed like that until the room gradually grew lighter and I peered out the window at the rising sun. Carefully extricating myself off of Dominic and stepping over our pile of clothes, I went to stand in front of the window. My naked body reflected on the glass and I made a quick assessment noting my abs were firm and toned, my breasts perky and my hair fell around me in waves, dark against my fair skin. My lips were fuller from all of the kissing and my eyes were bright – wide awake. I watched Dominic's reflection walk up behind mine. His was close to a foot taller and had a swagger to his walk. His body was muscular and his olive skin was smooth, flawless except for the tattoo. He had pulled a blanket off of the couch and wrapped it around us as we watched the sun rise, basking in the golden glow.

As the sun rose higher into the sky, reality began to sink in. The day was putting an end to a perfect night. I had classes to attend and a roommate to check in with. With a heavy sigh I turned towards Dominic. He looked down at me with understanding.

"Come on, I'll get you home."

He went into his bedroom to get a new shirt and I followed him in to investigate as we hadn't made it that far. The spicy scent of his cologne was more concentrated here and I inhaled deeply. A king sized bed pressed up against the window and the Delaware River sparkled below through the slats of dark wood blinds. The master bathroom was like a spa retreat in itself. A giant Jacuzzi tub called my name and I stared at it longingly.

"Next time we'll try that out."

"Next time?"

"Oh there'll be a next time, although I don't want this to end."

"Me either," I admitted, running through my class schedule in my head and determining I couldn't miss any today.

The Mustang was waiting for us when we got down to the lobby; the interior already warm – high rent had its perks. My purse vibrated so I reached inside and pulled out my cell phone. The display read that I had three new messages. There were two text messages and a voice mail all from Chelsea. Ever since Chelsea had broken up with her boyfriend she had a little too much time on her hands and had started living vicariously through my life. The first text message came in at 1:00 am – *What time r u coming home?* The next text message came in at 3:00 am and I perceived the annoyed tone – *I'm going 2 bed.* The voicemail had just been left for me at 8:24 am – Nat, I'm really worried and hope you are ok. Please call me!

Dominic overheard and chuckled. "You better call her before she calls the National Guard."

"Yeah, seriously," I laughed as I dialed Chelsea's cell. She picked up after the first ring.

"Nat! Are you okay?"

"Yes, I am more than okay," I winked at Dominic and he smiled back. "I had my phone on vibrate and didn't even hear it. I'm sorry to have worried you."

"You should have called to let me know you weren't coming home." She sounded sullen. I pictured her sulking, her lower lip sticking out in a pout.

"You're right and I will try to remember next time. I was just a little...preoccupied." Dominic reached for my left hand and squeezed it.

"Oh. *Oh!*" Chelsea gasped picking up on what I was alluding to and I knew all would be forgiven if she wanted the details. "Are you on your way back?" she asked, no longer sulking by the sound of her voice.

"I'll be there in a few minutes." I hung up the phone and glanced over at Dominic. He was trying to keep a straight face.

"What?"

"Preoccupied? Is that what it's called nowadays?"

"I was trying to be discreet."

"What we did to each other last night was definitely not discreet!" He squeezed my hand and a warm flush washed over my body.

The trip to my apartment was too brief and it was hard to say goodbye. Dominic promised to call me to make arrangements for later that night. As I was getting ready to open the car door he pulled me towards him and into a kiss. His stubble bristled against my cheek, but I didn't mind because his lips were soft and gentle against mine. I could feel Chelsea's eyes burning into my back from the living room window so I slowly pulled away from Dominic and somehow managed to get out of the car.

Just as I had anticipated, Chelsea was waiting at the door. I had barely set foot into our apartment when the inquisition started.

"Oh my God, he is gorgeous! Where did you go, did you stay at his place…did you sleep with him?" She was firing off questions like an automatic machine gun and I could barely keep up. I held my hands up to silence her.

"Geez, Chels. Can you give me a second?" She looked at me impishly and backed off. I dashed to the bathroom to relieve myself and splashed cool water on my face. I should have been exhausted, but was running on pure euphoria and endorphins at the moment. I glanced in the mirror and saw my eyes were bright and wide with excitement. There were dark smudges underneath from my mascara. It wasn't heinous though and that surprised me. The smudges added a smoky, dramatic effect. Hmmm, not bad, I thought to myself.

Chelsea waited in the living room and was twitching like an excited puppy when I walked in. I knew she was holding back a deluge of questions. I plopped down on the futon next to her and prepared for the assault.

"So, you spent the night with him?"

"Yes."

"Where?"

"His condo. He lives in the most unbelievable place. It makes our apartment look like a hovel."

"He's rich, huh?"

"I guess so. His condo sure isn't cheap."

"And the sex how was it?" I was embarrassed by her directness and flushed when I recalled the intimacy between us.

"Incredible." That was the only word I could come up with to describe it and then I thought of another. "Mind blowing. Quite possibly - no definitely - the best sex I've ever had!"

"Wow," Chelsea remarked. She inspected my face after my statements. "Oh, Nat you really like this guy don't you?"

I nodded my head in admittance. I hadn't allowed myself to get emotionally invested with anyone. After seeing my mom's heart ripped out and destroyed, I swore that I would never put myself in a position where something like that could happen to me. Then, after Toby, I swore off emotional commitments completely. Somehow, with Dominic, I found that promise hard to uphold. Flings were easy. I didn't put my heart up for grabs and ended the liaisons before they amounted to anything close to a relationship. I didn't want just a fling with Dom, though.

Chelsea peered at me waiting for me to continue. "I do like him. He referred to me as his girlfriend when he introduced me to his aunt and uncle." Chelsea's mouth hung open.

"Wait, back the fuck up! You met family members and he called you his girlfriend?" she paused. "And you didn't run away screaming?"

"No, I actually liked being called his girlfriend, even though I told him it was too soon for that. His aunt and uncle are so nice." I filled her in on Franco's Ristorante, the extraordinary food and the ice skating at Riverfront Park.

"Whoa." She sat across from me and regarded me with her sky blue eyes. "Are you ready for this Nat?" Her question triggered a little bit of the fear. I had let my guard completely down last night and showed Dominic more of my true self than I've shown anyone in a while. It was easy to be myself around him.

"I...think so? I really like Dominic and want to see where this goes."

Chelsea had a worried look on her face. She was still raw from her break-up and I'm sure she thought I was crazy to open myself up for hurt. Little did she know that I already opened myself up. That left me feeling both exhilarated and terrified.

Instead Chelsea surprised me. "Well I never thought I'd see the day..." and she grinned. "It's about time you gave another relationship a try. Sometimes they don't work out, but you learn a lot about yourself in the process."

"Oh yeah? And what did you learn about yourself this last go around?"

Chelsea may be living vicariously through my life now, but there were times when I lived vicariously through her relationships.

"I learned that I need to stay true to myself." Chelsea lowered her eyes when she stated this as if hiding the pain they revealed.

"True," I recalled how Chelsea had been consumed in her recent relationship with Chad and how she lost touch with her friends, including me. All of her time was devoted to Chad's needs and she lost sight of her own. "That's very good advice."

We both stared off and were lost in our thoughts until Chelsea saw the clock on the cable box and yelled, "Holy Shit, we're late for class!" It was a mad scramble as I ran to change my clothes and grab my backpack, there wasn't enough time for me to worry that I smelled like sex. Chelsea and I ran up Pine St. to campus, avoiding the icy patches and frost heaves on the uneven brick sidewalks.

Chapter 9

The euphoria that kept exhaustion at bay wore off early in the afternoon. I struggled through the rest of my classes and slumped back to the apartment, picking up a turkey hoagie from Wawa along the way. Dominic hadn't called my cell yet, so I had no idea what he was planning for tonight. How could he top last night? I struggled to get through some assignments, but kept dozing off. I gave up and crawled into bed for a nap. My bladder woke me and I stumbled to the bathroom. Chelsea was in the living room watching TV. She looked up at me when I walked in.

"You seem rested."

"Ugh," I grunted and yawned. "What time is it?"

"It's almost eleven."

"Eleven!" I was awake now. I turned around and ran back into my room to fetch my cell phone. There was a voice mail, but it was from my mom. There were a couple text messages from friends, but nothing from Dominic. I sat down on the edge of the bed as disappointment and doubt squeezed my heart like a vice. Did he just want to sleep with me and that's it? Was I wrong in thinking he liked me too? I rolled over in a fetal position, replaying every moment, every word that we shared. Did I set myself up for rejection? I groaned as I closed my eyes and tried to clear the negativity that clouded my thoughts.

"What's wrong?" Chelsea asked as she stood in my bedroom doorway.

"He didn't call. He was supposed to and we were going to go out tonight." My voice was strained with tears ready to be spilled.

"He'll call," Chelsea reassured me and sat down next to me.

"I knew I wasn't ready for this. I have no idea what to do…am I acting crazy?"

"Not at all. You're acting like a normal girl who has fallen for a boy."

"I am? What if he never calls?"

"Nat, you need to relax. He will call. He would be a fool not to." She rubbed my back as she said this.

"I hope he does. You're right, I didn't want to admit it, but I really do like him."

Chelsea stayed by my side until sleep claimed me at some point and I woke as the sun peeked through my blinds. This morning I'd be watching the sunrise alone. I sighed and hugged a pillow to my chest. I grabbed my phone from the bedside table - still no messages from Dominic. I debated whether I should call him, but didn't want to appear desperate or hear his rejection. Since I was up early, I dressed for the early morning chill and went for a run. By the time I reached Rittenhouse Square I had broken into a sweat. The run helped to clear my head and the long, hot shower afterwards washed Dominic's scent off of me and quieted my nerves. I wouldn't let it get to me. If he called, he called and if he didn't, that was his loss. My guard was back up and I chastised myself for letting it down in the first place.

I flicked on the TV on my way into the kitchen to make a pot of coffee; only half listening to the news as I toasted a bagel. A news story caught my attention and I stopped what I was doing to listen. The newscaster was discussing a shooting that had occurred overnight in South Philly on Lombard Street. They said it looked like a mob hit, even though the Philly mob was supposedly no longer in existence. The victim had been identified as George "The

Stump" Fratelli. It was "The Stump" that had grabbed my attention. I remembered the other night at Crimson when Grant and Uncle Marco were discussing a guy named Stump who hadn't paid his bill. Could this be the same guy? If so, wasn't Grant supposed to take care of it? I laughed at myself and the idea that Grant was in the mafia. This was probably just a coincidence.

The rest of the news was boring and the weather forecast I could have done myself - more freezing cold temperatures with no end in sight. I scarfed down the bagel, poured coffee into a travel mug, and bundled up to face the cold.

The studio lab helped to distract me and I immersed myself in a sculpture project. I was used to working with clay and embraced the challenge of working with metal. Once I got a handle on the welding torch, the metal was just as malleable. I enjoyed getting lost in the project and felt like I had accomplished something as I walked back to my apartment. I had tonight to get caught up on my work, before I had to work at Crimson again. One good thing about not being with Dominic was that I could get my work done. At least I tried to convince myself of that.

I turned the corner onto my block and immediately stopped. Dominic's Mustang was parked directly in front of my building. My heart stopped too. I didn't know what to do. I was ready to write him off and was not expecting him to be waiting for me. I thought about turning and going back around the corner but saw the driver's side door open and Dominic getting out. He must have seen me. I narrowed my eyes and made sure my emotions were in check before marching up to meet him.

His face lit up when he saw me approach and my step faltered. He saw my hesitation and frowned, the green of his eyes grew darker.

"Dominic," I greeted him with an emotionless voice.

"Hi." He leaned down to kiss me and I took a step back. "What's wrong, Nat?"

I couldn't meet his eyes and was beginning to wonder if I was acting psychotic. Sure, he didn't call me last night, but here he was standing in front of me, wanting to kiss me.

"Oh...I, um." I struggled for words and debated whether to give him another chance. I cursed the effect his very presence was having on my resolve. "Can we talk, upstairs?"

"Sure." He followed me up to my apartment. Chelsea was in the kitchen making ramen and we waved as I led Dominic back to my room. I shut the door for some privacy and dropped my jacket and backpack on the floor. My bedroom wasn't nearly as luxurious as Dominic's. My bed wasn't made and the comforter hung off the side onto the floor. The desk under one of the windows had a pile of textbooks on it and the easel in the corner held a canvas with a painting in progress. One of my bras hung on the back of my desk chair and I quickly grabbed it and shoved it in the top drawer of the Ikea dresser. Dominic poked around my room as I attempted to control some of the chaos. He picked up a framed picture of Grant, me and my mom that sat on my desk. It was taken at Grant's high school graduation; when we were wide eyed and innocent. That was almost eight years ago and we were both a lot wiser now.

I could feel Dominic watching me as I flitted about the room nervously, pretending to straighten up in order to buy some more time because I didn't know how to begin.

"Nat, what's going on?" Dominic broke the silence and I was out of time. Still unable to look at him, I began to speak.

"This is probably going to sound ridiculous or psychotic or both..." I risked a glance at his face and his expression was passive. I continued. "Normally it doesn't bother me when a guy doesn't call after...you know. But the other night was so different and it really, like, almost hurt me when you didn't." I could feel the tears creeping up to the surface and choked them back. I was over by my easel organizing the paints when Dominic came over and took my hand in his. He reached for my face and turned it, I had to meet his eyes then. I didn't see ridicule or insincerity lingering there only compassion and understanding.

"I'm sorry. You're right I should have called, but I wasn't able to. Uncle Marco needed my help with some stuff and that took up most of the night. You can ask your brother. He was with me. I was going to call you, but it was late. I figured you'd be pretty tired after the night before," he smiled at the reference. "And you're right. The other night was different for me too."

"It was?"

"Yes. Amazing, actually."

"Grant was with you?"

"Yes. Do you want to ask him?" Dominic pulled his cell phone out of his pocket.

"No. Don't call him, I believe you...and you can call me anytime, I won't mind."

"Well, Uncle Marco doesn't like distractions and I didn't have a break. I am really sorry." He cupped my face in his hands and leaned in for a kiss. I hesitated slightly, but didn't pull back. Reaching up, I wrapped my arms around the back of Dominic's neck. He pulled me closer and placed his lips on mine. All was forgiven the moment we connected.

We separated and I rested my head on his chest, "I'm sorry too. I didn't really have a right to react that way since you aren't my boyfriend."

"I want to be," he whispered in my ear.

Dominic was here in my room and holding me, revealing that he wanted to be with me. I couldn't refuse him, because deep down, I wanted it too.

This whole relationship business was new to me. I had to learn to trust Dominic and I had to learn to trust myself in a relationship. Knowing this, I squeezed him tight and whispered back, "Okay."

I heard him sigh with contentment and he kissed the top of my head. "Did you eat dinner?" he asked.

"No, I'm just getting back from class."

"Want to go grab something to eat?"

I paused because I was supposed to go with Chelsea to watch our shows at Jillian's apartment. "Give me a sec," I told Dominic and left him in my room.

Chelsea sat cross legged on the futon with a steaming bowl of ramen in her hand.

"See, I told you he wouldn't dis' you," she said.

"You're always right. I don't know how I could have doubted you!" I plopped down on the futon next to her. "I hope you won't be mad at me, but Dominic asked me out tonight. Are you okay going to Jillian's by yourself?"

Chelsea slurped noodles into her mouth before answering. "I guess so," she sounded disappointed. "You're going to miss some good episodes."

"I know, but I can watch them online later. I really want to go out with Dom. You see, I just agreed to be his girlfriend."

Chelsea almost dropped her bowl. "Are you serious?" My cheeks hurt from the ear to ear grin that spread across my face. "Holy shit, Nat this is huge! Go; get going… everyone at Jillian's will understand, although I don't think they'll believe me!"

I laughed at her enthusiasm because it mirrored the excitement I was feeling. Hopping up off the futon, I half ran half skipped back to my room. Dominic was still checking out the various pictures and paintings that hung on the walls.

"Did you paint this?" he asked, pointing at a watercolor.

"I did."

"Wow. You're really talented."

I savored the compliment. "Thanks."

"The landscape…it looks familiar."

"That's the beach at LBI. I love the sand dunes and the sea grass."

He proceeded to walk around my room in silence, as if he was in a gallery or museum, admiring each painting, drawing and sculpture. My room was cluttered with projects. The two windowsills served as extra shelf space and overflowed with multiple ceramic pieces.

"Nat, you're work is amazing. I had no idea."

"I applied to several grad schools. My professors kept encouraging me."

"I can see why they would. The only thing my hands are good at is getting people to do what I want."

I tilted my head at the odd comment. "What do you mean by that?"

"Err, never mind, that didn't come out right. I meant that my hands are good at giving you what you want." I could tell he was trying to make light of what he had just said. I had heard him the first time, but wasn't quite sure what he meant by it. "So, do you want to go out for dinner?" he continued.

"Yes, do you have a place in mind?"

"Butter, ever been there?"

I shook my head no. "Five-star restaurants don't exactly fit in my college student budget."

"Right," Dominic glanced down at the jeans and sweatshirt I was wearing and raised his eyebrow. "You'll probably need to change."

"Oh, right!" I hadn't noticed that Dominic was dressed up. He had on pressed black pants on and a dark green long sleeve shirt. I went over to my closet and started sorting through my clothes. I pulled out a black mini cocktail dress that was simple enough to be dressy, but not too dressy. I turned to leave to get changed in the bathroom.

"Where are you going?"

"To get ready."

"You can get dressed in here, with me. It's not like I haven't seen you naked before." He sat back on the bed and made himself comfortable. I could feel the heat creep up my neck and flare on my cheeks. Yes, he had seen me naked before. A nervous laugh escaped my lips.

"No need to be shy." He got up off the bed and walked over to me. "I'm your boyfriend, remember?" His hands reached down to the bottom of my sweatshirt and he lifted it up. I raised my arms in surrender and he pulled the sweatshirt off.

***

It took us awhile to get out of my bedroom. Finally, we emerged and Chelsea whistled when she saw me all dressed up.

"Wow, where are you two going?"

"Dom's taking me to Butter for dinner."

Chelsea's eyes grew huge. "I hear that place is incredible."

"I'll let you know how it is."

"I promise to have her home at decent hour this time," Dominic said in a serious tone, like Chelsea was a parent and she laughed.

"Don't worry about me. You two have fun!" She was still giggling when we left the apartment.

Chapter 10

We pulled up in front of Butter and the valet was quick to help when he recognized the black Mustang. Dominic slipped him a twenty dollar bill then escorted me inside. A tan man about Dom's age greeted us as soon as we walked through the door. He wore a dark gray suit that had to have been tailored made for his broad shoulders.

"Dom!" He exclaimed, pulling my boyfriend into a hug.

"Dante, good to see you. This is Natalie. Nat, this is my cousin Dante."

"Nice to meet you." He shook my hand."Wow Dom, you sure know how to pick them," he commented as he watched me take off my coat and place it on his waiting arm. Nice. What did he mean by that?

"I have a table reserved for you guys over here." We followed him through the dining area. I felt out of place in this restaurant that oozed opulence. The color scheme consisted of rich creams and ivories with a very pale yellow as an accent like, well, butter. These colors contrasted against the dark mahogany furniture. Candles flickered everywhere with flames reflecting off of crystal chandeliers. So this is what five star dining was all about, I thought to myself, and tried to remember which fork to use and when. Several of the diners watched as we walked by. This only added to my insecurity.

Dante sat us at a table towards the back of the restaurant in a more secluded area. Dominic acted the perfect gentleman and held the chair out. As I adjusted myself I noticed someone was checking me out. I followed Dante's gaze as he took in the low neckline of my dress. Dominic noticed too and glared at his cousin who smiled apologetically and quickly left us alone.

"God, this place is amazing," I said to Dominic, trying to keep my voice down.

"Wait until you try the food. My Uncle Al, Dante's dad, recruited the chefs from all over the country."

"I'm noticing a trend here. Your family seems pretty serious about food," I teased.

"You haven't seen anything yet. Wait until you attend a gathering that involves the entire family. It's like a cook-off and can get pretty competitive." I liked how he said this, like I was already going to be included.

"It sounds like you have a huge family."

"Huge. There is always something going on. Someone getting married, having a kid or dying."

"I have no idea what that's like. It's always been Grant, my mom and I."

"No cousins or grandparents?"

"Nope…well, not close. My mom was an only child and her parents died when I was young - actually not too long after my Dad left us."

"That must have been pretty tough for your mom?"

I nodded. "She didn't handle things well." I didn't elaborate about how depression swallowed her whole. Or how Grant had to step in and make sure I got to school with breakfast in my stomach. I didn't tell him how my mom would berate me when I got home and accuse me of being selfish and lost in my head just like my father. She might as well have accused me of being the devil.

"You and Grant are close though."

"I guess so. I think he feels obligated to look out for me or it's just become a habit for him. He's always been there. The flip side is that he can interfere."

"Well, at least you have some family around. I don't know what I would do without mine."

"Probably starve," I joked. The trip down memory lane was bringing me down and I didn't want to ruin our date.

Dante made sure the service was impeccable and it matched the food. We ate in silence, enjoying every last bite. The portions here were reasonable and not falling over the sides of the plates like at Franco's. After I finished eating I sat back with my glass of wine and watched Dominic. I really couldn't believe that I had agreed to be his girlfriend. When I started thinking about it, panic began to creep up from the pit of my stomach. I took a sip of wine, hoping to wash the fear back down.

The waiter came around and cleared our plates. "Dante wanted me to tell you that the meal is on the house," he said.

"Tell him thank you and this is for you." Dominic handed the waiter a one hundred dollar bill.

"Thank you sir, enjoy the rest of your night," he said before he left the table.

"Oh, I plan on it," Dom said and winked at me. I knew what he was implying.

After dinner Dominic took me back to his place and I texted Chelsea that I wasn't coming home. This time we made it past the living room and christened his bedroom. We stayed up exploring each other and fell asleep as the morning sky began to lighten.

I woke with a start and glanced over Dominic's shoulder at the alarm clock on his bedside table.

"Shit!" I exclaimed and jumped out of bed. Thursday morning had already come and gone.

"What?" Dominic murmured, still half asleep.

"I'm late for class!" I ran around the room and picked my clothes up that were strewn all over the floor.

"Come back to bed. You can miss today," Dom beckoned as he patted the bed.

"I can't. Midterms are coming up and I have so much to do!"

"What's one day? You can catch up."

Seeing him lying there naked made me weigh my options. I was already late for my third class and by the time I made it back to my apartment and got changed, my fourth and final class would be over. I sighed and let the clothes drop back onto the floor before climbing back into bed. Dominic pulled me up close against him and lightly kissed my neck and shoulders. Any stress about school dissipated with his touch.

Dominic's cell phone pierced the silence and woke us from our slumber. He groaned and buried his head underneath one of the down pillows.

"Aren't you going to answer that?"

"No, they can leave a message," he said, his voice muffled. "I'm not getting out of bed."

The phone stopped ringing, but seconds later started pealing again. I knew it wasn't possible, but it seemed more insistent this time. It was my turn to groan as I rolled away from Dominic so he could get up.

"Hello?" he answered. "Hey Uncle Marco, what's up?"

He walked out of the bedroom to take the call. I stayed in bed with my eyes closed, half listening to the one sided conversation.

"I can be there. It'll take a few minutes though; I have to take Natalie home."

I frowned at the thought of having to leave.

"Yeah, she spent the night," he paused. "That's none of your business!" he snapped, sounding annoyed. "No. She doesn't know."

What didn't I know?

"Tell Grant that everything is under control. I'll be there as soon as I can." I heard him click his phone shut and imagined that if it were a real phone, he would have slammed it down on the receiver.

I heard him walk back into the room, but I kept my eyes shut, I didn't want him to think I was listening.

"Natalie," he whispered and kissed my forehead.

"Hmmm?" I opened my eyes.

"I have to go. You can stay here or I can take you home?"

"Who was that?" I asked as I pushed the covers aside.

"Uncle Marco. He needs me to take care of some stuff."

"Oh. I'll go back to my apartment."

"Nat, you might want to prepare for a shit storm – Grant was with Uncle Marco and he heard me say you were here. He wasn't too happy about it."

"Shit. Well, he was bound to find out sooner or later. I'll deal with him."

"Sorry."

"You have nothing to apologize for. Grant is the one being an ass."

Dominic dropped me off at my apartment and we had a quick kiss goodbye. He promised to call when he was done and then he was gone. I watched him drive down the street and wondered what he was up to and what he meant when he said: "she doesn't know."

Chapter 11

Miranda was waiting for me at the front door again. A line had already started to form, even though Crimson didn't open for another hour, the line was just going to get longer.

"Hi Miranda!" I had been in a perpetual good mood since Dominic and I had come to terms, even if I was exhausted from all the late nights. It had been a week since we declared ourselves to each other and every moment spent with Dominic was incredible.

"Hi Nat. You're working VIP again tonight."

"Okay, same drill?" She nodded and then looked at me funny.

"What?" My tone was defensive.

"So you and Dominic? Is this like an official thing?"

"Yes," I answered hesitantly, uncomfortable about discussing my personal life with my boss, who was also my brother's girlfriend and not to mention my boyfriend's cousin.

"Grant doesn't like it." This was an understatement. I thought Grant was going to have an aneurism when he found out about us. This was four days ago and he hadn't spoken to me since.

"He'll get over it," I grumbled.

"Do you know what you're getting yourself into?"

"Why does everyone keep asking me that?"

"I'm talking to you as a manager. Ordinarily I don't care who my employees are dating, except when they're dating each other."

"Oh." I wanted to respond by saying she was being a little hypocritical, but decided it would be best not to push it. "I get it," I said instead and turned to go.

"One more thing…" I glanced over my shoulder at her and marveled at how similar her eyes were to Dominic's. "Grant told me that my dad has expressed an interest in you." My mouth went dry. "I told him that you were with Dominic, maybe he'll back off now."

"Oh…thanks! I hope so." I liked the tips I earned in the VIP section, but didn't like the looming presence of Uncle Marco. Miranda smiled at my reaction. Then I left to get set up. I passed Grant on the way to the employee lounge and he avoided me – again.

Brittany was in the lounge and I ignored her. She still hadn't gotten over that Dominic was my boyfriend and that I had replaced her in the VIP section. Her pouting was almost audible as I checked my hair in the mirror. It wasn't big and poufy like the other Crimson girls, but shiny and soft. Dominic said he liked it because his hand didn't get stuck in it when he ran his fingers through my hair. Like last night, when I lay underneath him and ran my hands down the length of his broad back to his firm…a toilet flushed behind me and snapped me out of my reverie. Having lost a few minutes to daydreaming I rushed over to the VIP section to get ready. Grant was leaning against the bar talking to the bartender when I walked up.

"Hi Grant," I said softly.

"Natalie," he greeted me through pursed lips. This was progress – at least he acknowledged my presence. I didn't want to push my luck and went about my business.

This was the busiest night I had worked at Crimson and that surprised me because it was a Sunday. Didn't people have to work in the morning? I ran around ragged trying to keep up with everyone's drink orders. Uncle Marco left me alone just as I had hoped. Not having this anxiety helped me focus and get my job done. The night flew by and soon the club had cleared out except for Uncle Marco and his boys. Marco asked me to sit with them again and this time I didn't mind.

"So, you and Dominic?"

"Yes."

"Huh. Is he treatin' you good doll?"

"Absolutely."

"Good. Let me know if my nephew misbehaves and I'll smack some sense into him." He gesticulated a lot when he spoke and he emphasized the word smack by slamming his hand down on the table. I couldn't help but flinch.

"I'll keep that in mind."

Grant walked up to the table and Marco shifted his attention away from me.

"Grant!" Marco shook my brother's hand. "Good job getting Stump to settle up on his bill. He wasn't any trouble?"

"Not at all and I don't think he will be any trouble in the future," Grant answered.

"Excellent! Now I have some more business to discuss with you. Natalie, you can leave." Grant visibly relaxed, his shoulders not as tense, once I had been dismissed.

Dominic saw me descending the stairs from VIP and waved me over to his bar. "Hey babe," he said and leaned across the bar and we kissed. "How was your night?"

"Good. Miranda told Marco that you and I are together and he left me alone tonight."

Dominic tightened his jaw. "Was Uncle Marco bothering you?"

I clamped my hand over my mouth and my eyes got wide. "Oops." I said through my hand and then lowered it. "I'm sorry I didn't tell you, but I didn't want you to get upset. Grant told Miranda and she handled it."

Dominic's face grew dark with anger. "How was he bothering you?"

"I don't want to say, you'll probably just get more upset. And he's your uncle"

"What about our agreement to be up front with each other?" Damn. He had to play that card.

"Okay," I caved. "I'll tell you later; let's finish work first."

This seemed to appease Dominic, but I knew he wouldn't drop it. One of the things we had in common was our persistence. I left him to finish cleaning up his bar and brought my tips to Miranda, she took fifty percent for the bartender and handed back the rest. I quickly counted the wad and was amazed at my take - $530. I had already paid my bills for the month, so all this was spending money and it instantly started to burn a hole in my pocket.

I bounced back to Dominic's bar and he handed me a gin and tonic, my preferred drink of late. I sucked it dry in seconds and asked for another. He eyed me curiously. "I'm celebrating," I explained. "I made some good bank tonight."

"We'll have to celebrate later." He gave me a suggestive look which caused me to squirm on the bar stool and gnaw on my straw. I hung out until he finished wiping down his bar. He walked with me to the employee lounge where I grabbed my bag.

"What would you like to do, besides discuss my uncle?" he asked.

"We could go back to your place?" I pressed up against him, stood on my tiptoes and nibbled his ear lobe. "We don't have to talk about your uncle tonight," I whispered, brushing my hand against his crotch.

"I do like your suggestion!" He held the exit door open for me and was almost out behind me when Grant yelled his name. We turned to see him jogging across the dance floor towards us. I prepared myself for a confrontation.

"Marco needs us to take care of something tonight."

"Can't it wait? Nat and I have plans."

"It has to be tonight. Marco said so." Hearing footsteps approaching, I glanced towards the VIP section and saw Marco heading in our direction.

"Dom, what the fuck are you and Grant standing around bullshitting for? You have a fucking job to do!" Marco bellowed.

"Yes, Uncle Marco," Dominic lowered his head in a submissive manner. This surprised me as he was usually so assertive.

"What do you guys have to do? It's almost three in the morning."

"Nothing you need to worry your pretty little head about, doll," Marco answered. "Come on, I'll take you home." He grabbed my arm. I tensed up and saw Grant and Dominic stiffen too.

"You don't have to go out of your way, I can take a cab." I tried to maneuver out of his grip.

"It's not a bother." He snapped his fingers at Grant and Dominic with his free hand. "Get the fuck outta here!" They both jumped and hurried out the door. He turned his attention to me. "So Grant's sister is dating my nephew? Very interesting...how does Grant feel about this?"

"He's not too pleased," I admitted as Marco steered me out of the club and locked the door behind him. He still had my arm in his iron grip.

"Yes, Grant is very protective of you. He's done a lot for me so he can take care of his family. I respect that." He led me to his black Cadillac and opened the passenger door for me. He finally released my arm and I slid into the seat and shivered. Not because of the cold, but because I was going to be stuck in a car with this man who, quite honestly, scared the shit out of me.

Marco got in and started the car, the engine purred to life. I could smell scotch emanating off of him and remembered how many drinks he had been served. This didn't help my comfort level at all.

"Where do you live?"

"9th and Pine."

He navigated the Cadillac out onto Columbus Boulevard. He seemed to have control of the car and didn't drive like he was drunk so I gradually eased off the 'oh shit" handle that I had in a death grip.

"Do you like working at Crimson?" he broke the silence after a few blocks.

"Yeah, it's great!"

"Best place in town," he bragged. Marco blew through a red light without even tapping on the brakes. I resumed my grip on the handle. A cop was parked on the street and saw Marco go through the light. I waited for the lights and siren, but nothing happened; the cop let Marco keep on driving. Thankfully the fifteen minute drive ended without incident and Marco pulled to a stop in front of my apartment.

"Thanks for the ride," I said. As I turned to get out of the car, Marco grabbed my left wrist and twisted me back to face him.

"What?" I asked.

"Don't I at least get a kiss?" His beady eyes gleamed and his licked his lips before they formed a malicious grin, his lips glistening with spittle. He started to yank on my arm as if trying to drag me across the seat and closer to him. I resisted and felt my wrist pop. "Just kidding," he said and suddenly released my arm. "Have a good night."

"Um, goodnight," I said and struggled to open the door with my shaking hand. Finally it opened and I practically tumbled out onto the sidewalk. I ran to my apartment building. As soon as I was inside with the front door secure behind me, my entire body started to tremble. It took a few minutes, and a few deep breaths, to get myself under control. Dominic's uncle had some serious issues and I never wanted to be alone with him again.

I waited until I had calmed down to go upstairs. Fortunately Chelsea was asleep because my face probably would have indicated that something was wrong. With the apartment door locked and my bedroom door closed, I finally began to relax. Lying in bed alone was not what I had in mind for tonight. What could Marco possibly need Dominic and Grant do? I thought about this as my eyelids grew heavy and sleep claimed me.

My cell phone woke me up. Disoriented, I felt around in the dark for it.

"Hello?" I mumbled.

"Hey, it's Dom."

"Hi," I sat up. "What time is it?"

"It's a little after five. I just wanted to call and make sure you're alright?"

"I'm fine. I was sleeping."

"Sorry to wake you. I just wanted to make sure my uncle behaved himself."

"For the most part," I yawned and could hear Dominic breathe a sigh of relief. "No offense, but your uncle's a little off."

"Yeah, I know. I'm just glad you're okay. He can be unpredictable." Unpredictable, that was a good way to describe him. Other words like menacing, disturbed and crazy would describe him well too.

"What did you guys have to do anyway?"

"Just stuff."

"Oh." I yawned again and tried to focus on the conversation.

"I'll let you get back to sleep; I just wanted to check on you."

"No, don't go, I'm awake now." My phone beeped then and I quickly looked at the display. "Ugh, I need to take this call, it's Grant."

"He's probably checking in on you too. I'll call you later. Sweet dreams."

"Goodnight," I whispered before I clicked over to receive Grant's call.

"Nat, how are you?"

"I'm fine. Dom just called too."

"I really shouldn't have gotten you a job at Crimson." Grant's comment woke me right up.

"Grant, shut up, I'm fine. Marco was a little creepy, but I handled it." I said, downplaying the incident. If Grant knew how tight Marco held onto my wrist, I probably would have to get another job.

"What did you guys have to do anyway?"

"Marco needed us to do something for him. I can't talk about it." Big surprise, Grant was being tightlipped. What did he and Dom do that they couldn't talk about?

"What's the big secret? I won't tell anyone."

"Natalie, it's confidential. I can't tell you," Grant snapped. "I'm glad you're alright. I need to go get some sleep." With that he hung up the phone.

Chapter 12

The alarm went off and I swatted at the snooze button for the millionth time. The momentary interruption wasn't enough to rouse me and I rolled back over with the comforter pulled up around my ears. When I finally did wake it was almost noon. I missed my morning classes again.

"Damn it!" I yelled at myself as I jumped out of bed, threw on clothes and bolted out the door. I didn't stop running until I reached the door of my classroom where I skidded to a halt, taking a few deep breaths before opening the door. The professor eyeballed me and frowned. I hung my head and found an empty seat. After class the he flagged me down.

"Miss Ross, do you have a minute?"

I braced myself for what was certainly going to be a serious talk.

"Is everything okay?"

"Yes. Everything's fine. Why?"

"Well, you missed class last week, you were late today. It's not like you. Plus, your work hasn't its usual quality. You seem to be slipping a bit."

"I know. I am sorry about that. I started a new job, at Crimson? Anyway, it's been difficult adjusting to the hours and I worked late last night."

"Don't slip too far. Remember you're a student first." It wasn't harsh, but an admonishment nonetheless. I promised to improve and hurried off to the next class.

Chelsea had saved a seat for me and I plopped down.

"I didn't know if you were going to make it," she remarked.

"Yeah, little bit of a late start today." It was Friday and my ass was dragging.

"I tried to wake you."

"You did? I don't remember that."

"Who were you talking to so early this morning? Did Dom spend the night?"

"No, but he called and so did Grant. They both had to do something last night for the owner of Crimson. They won't tell me what though."

"You're aware of your priorities, right?" Chelsea asked, sounding more like one of my teachers.

"Of course I am!"

The professor shot us a look so we both quieted down and focused on the lecture.

On the way home I stopped at Wawa for a soda. While waiting in line to check out, a headline on the front page of The Philadelphia Inquirer caught my attention:

LATE NIGHT MURDERS REMINISCENT OF SCARFO DAYS

Curious, I grabbed the paper and continued reading.

> Early this morning, two men were murdered in cold blood. The homicide took place near the Italian Market only hours before shoppers would begin to crowd the sidewalks. This is the second incident in recent weeks that emulates the mafia hits from the days when Nicky Scarfo's mob ruled South Philly's streets.

The Philadelphia Mob has long been rumored to be extinct. Are these murders indicative of a comeback? Police aren't revealing much about the investigation, including the victims' names. Detective Calvin Flynn, the lead detective on the case, did cite similarities between these murders and that of George "The Stump" Fratelli, who was killed two weeks ago.

"Details can't be released this early in the investigation. We are looking into a possible connection between this pair of homicides and that of George Fratelli, but nothing has been confirmed. As soon as we know more a statement will be released to the media," Flynn said.

Even though the Philly Mob has been believed to be all but extinct, these recent homicides and the pending investigations will determine whether this belief is still valid.

The article was brief, but contained all the information my imagination needed. Had Fratelli not been mentioned I would have thought the story interesting, but that's it. I thought back to the morning when I heard the news report about "The Stump's" murder. I had immediately thought of Grant, but laughed the notion off. Did the work that Grant and Dominic had to do for Marco last night have anything to do with these new murders or was it just coincidence?

"Ma'am, are you going to pay for that too?" The cashier asked. I hadn't been paying attention and was holding up the line.

"No, just the soda." I put the newspaper back and chastised myself for being ridiculous and knew that Grant and Dominic had something legitimate to do last night. They certainly weren't out murdering people.

Chelsea was sitting on the futon sketching on her large pad. She looked up when I walked in and waved then went back to drawing. I dropped my bag on the floor and went to sit next to her. She was focused on her work and I leaned over for a peek. She had sketched out a willowy figure that was clothed in an elegant evening gown.

"That's beautiful," I commented.

"It's for my final project; I have to design a whole line. I'm going for evening wear."

"You'll rock it!"

"Thanks! Are you working tonight?"

"Yeah, Dom's picking me up at like quarter of eight."

"He'll probably take you somewhere fabulous after work. You better watch out you're going to get spoiled!" She teased.

I laughed and stood up. Chelsea wasn't the only one who needed to do some homework. I picked up my bag and headed to my room. The desk was a total mess so I opted for the bed instead. The 400-level Art History course I was taking needed some serious attention. I had a paper due on Monday and that only left three days. I flipped open my laptop and started typing based on the outline and notes I had already pulled together. After working for over an hour straight, I welcomed the distraction when my cell rang, even though it was my mom calling.

"Hi Mom."

"Natalie. How are you?"

"Good…busy, but really well."

"Is that why you haven't returned my calls?" Guilt washed over me. I had been avoiding my mom. I didn't know how to tell her I was seeing someone.

"Yeah, sorry about that."

"Grant says you have a boyfriend – is this true?"

There it was, the very reason I didn't want to tell her. On the surface it was all accusation with an undertone of betrayal. *Thanks Grant, thanks a lot.*

"Yes, that's true. His name is Dominic, we work together."

"Has he cheated on you yet?"

A knot began to form in my stomach and I sniffed back tears. *Why did she have to say such cruel things to me?*

"No and he won't. He adores me."

"I thought your father adored me, all the way up until he walked out on us."

"Mom will you just stop it! Believe it or not normal, healthy relationships do exist."

"I thought you learned from Toby."

"Did Grant tell you he has a girlfriend?" Silence.

Disgusted, I hung up the phone without saying goodbye and dropped it like it was radioactive. I wasn't in the mood for her head games, not that I ever was. Angry tears rolled down my cheeks and I brushed them aside. My focus was gone so I packed up my laptop and got ready for work.

Grant smirked when he saw me. "Did Mom call you?"

"Yes she did, asshole. She can't wait to meet your girlfriend." Walking away I could hear him cursing under his breath. This put a smile on my face.

"Hi beautiful!" Dominic called to me. I made my way over to his bar and he met me halfway. "I missed you." He kissed my ear and then my lips. I practically disappeared in his embrace. He stepped back and reached into his pocket.

"I got you something to make up for last night." He pulled out a small present, wrapped in silver paper and handed it to me.

"What did you get?"

"Open it and find out." His green eyes sparkled.

I ripped the wrapping paper off before he even finished. I opened the white box and gasped. Inside a diamond solitaire stud sparkled.

"Dominic! You shouldn't have!"

"It's a navel ring."

"Is it a real diamond?"

"Of course it is - nothing but the best for my girl."

"Thank you." I fell against him, wrapping my arms around his waist. His lips grazed the top of my head.

I squeezed him once more before I reached for his hand and pulled him with me into a dark alcove.

"What are you doing?"

I lifted up my shirt to reveal the silver stud in my bellybutton. "Do you want to put it on?"

Dominic's Adam's apple bobbed when he swallowed hard. Licking his lips, he knelt down in front of me. His fingers brushed against my stomach, tickling me and causing me to giggle.

"Hold still." Dominic said, grabbing my hips.

Biting my lower lip, I kept the laughter in check while he finished. Suddenly, I felt his hands move up underneath my skirt. Cupping my ass, he pulled me towards him covering my belly with soft kisses. Groaning, he released me and stood up.

"You have no idea what you do to me, woman. That was the sexiest thing ever."

"Looks good," I said while studying my new naval ring.

"Looks better than good. I'm going to cover you in diamonds."

"Dom, no, I'm not worth it." His eyes grew dark when I said this, resembling Marco's glare. Shocked, I took a step back.

"Yes you are. Every diamond in the world doesn't add up to your worth." His eyes softened and he pulled me into his chest. Tears welled up as I wanted to believe him. Breathing in his spicy fragrance helped calm the swell of emotion, allowing me to savor the moment.

"Ew. Get a room!" I jerked my head up and glared at Brittany. Her normally pretty face was twisted into a sneer.

"Fuck off Brit," Dominic spat. She shot him an evil look before stalking off towards the employee lounge.

"What is her problem?"

"She's used to getting what she wants. God help the world if she doesn't. You know what? Keep your stuff in Miranda's office. You don't have to use the lounge anymore."

"Dom, I can handle Brittany. She'll just have to learn how to deal. I'm not afraid of her." I wasn't the tallest of girls and still towered over Brittany. What was the tiny blonde going to do anyway?

"Just watch your back."

"Yes, dear." I gave him a quick kiss and left to get ready for work.

Brittany sneered at me when I entered the lounge. The heavy, dark liner around her startling blue eyes made her appear meaner. Ignoring her, I went to an open locker to hang up my jacket and bag.

"Slut."

"What did you say?" I asked, whipping around to face her.

"You heard me. I called you a slut."

"You're just jealous." I slammed the locker door shut.

"It's so obvious what you're doing. Throwing yourself at the owner's nephew," she spat.

"Brittany, you're being fucking ridiculous. Dominic doesn't want you. Get over it!"

"He's just using you."

I closed my eyes, willing her to go away. Rubbing my belly I felt the navel ring and smiled.

"Let me ask you something Brittany," I said in the sweetest voice I could muster. "Did Dominic ever give you diamonds or did he just fuck you in the back seat like a cheap whore?"

I thought I saw her blanch before she charged at me, squealing like a banshee. "You bitch!"

"Careful, Brittany, you're true colors are showing...and so are your roots." She wasn't a natural blond and her part was dark in contrast.

Joey D. stepped into the lounge as Brittany was barreling towards me. His eyes widened and he ran after her. Just before Brittany could take a swipe at me, he yanked her back. She struggled against him, kicking and screaming. Poor Joey looked like he was wrestling an alligator.

Everyone heard the commotion and came pouring into the lounge. Dominic ran in and stood beside me. His arm wrapped protectively around my waist, setting Brittany off even more.

"What makes her so special Dominic?" Brittany yelled. Her face almost matched the shade of her red lipstick.

"Brittany, you need to stop." Dominic turned us to leave, but the doorway was blocked. Grant and Miranda had arrived. They rushed over to me.

"Oh, I get it you're all one big happy fucking family!" Brittany's rage hadn't ebbed and Joey was still struggling to contain her. "She's not one of us. I don't even know why that bitch works here!"

Those words stung as if Brittany had physically slapped me. She was right, I wasn't a Crimson girl and I hadn't really felt like I'd fit in since my first day.

"Shut up!" Grant bellowed. "Joey, get her out of here."

"Go home Brittany. You're not working tonight," Miranda said. The crowd parted, letting Joey and his angry cargo through.

"What the hell happened?" Grant asked.

"Brittany's a tad jealous," Dominic answered.

"That's an understatement. She came completely unhinged. Is that why you carry a gun, Grant?" I asked with a shaky voice. Brittany's outburst had rattled me more than I thought.

"Very funny." Grant stared at me for a few moments, then turned and left.

"He's still pissed, huh?" I asked Miranda.

"Yup. Are you okay?"

I nodded. Dominic rubbed the small of my back and kissed the top of my head. We left the lounge together and walked with Miranda to her office. Dominic turned towards me.

"I'm sorry about Brittany."

"Don't apologize for her. Besides, I instigated some of it." I told Dominic what I said and he grinned.

"Man, I wish I could have seen the look on her face when you said that!"

"Yeah, it was pretty good." I stared down at the floor, my false bravado quickly fading.

"What?"

"She's right though, you know? I'm not one of you."

"And I love that about you." He leaned down and kissed me. "Ignore anything Brittany says. She's just a mean, spiteful bitch."

"Dom, don't mean to break up the love fest, but you need to go set up your bar," Miranda said.

"Yes, boss." He saluted, a playful smirk twitching across his face, and left.

I decided to take advantage of the time alone with Miranda. "Why is Brittany so intense?" I had seen many cat fights in my day, but never involved in one. Brittany's temper was fierce and quick to flare. Now I knew why Miranda warned me about her.

"Her life's been kind of fucked up."

"Well, mine hasn't been a fairy tale either and you don't see me acting like that."

"Brittany's father died when she was ten years old and her younger brother is in jail."

"Oh, that is bad."

"Yeah, she has a lot of anger." Understatement of the year, I thought to myself. "Her dad was a friend of my dad's so he got her a job here to help out after her brother got sent to prison. She helps to support her mom."

"I had no idea."

"And she's had a crush on Dom since puberty so that is why she has you in her sights," Miranda explained.

I had been unwittingly encroaching on Brittany's territory. From working in the VIP section to dating her childhood crush, I was taking things away from her. After losing so much in her life already, I could understand why she would try to hold onto everything else so tightly.

We reached Miranda's office and I stopped while she unlocked the door.

"She needs some time to cool off and I'll talk to her. She needs to know this behavior at work isn't acceptable."

"Well thanks for giving me some background on Brittany."

Miranda turned before entering her office. "Everybody has a history and everybody has secrets," she said and shut the door, leaving me to stand there and contemplate her cryptic statement.

The night passed by without any more drama. Marco and his boys didn't make an appearance either and that made for a low key evening. It was a relief to walk into the employee lounge and not worry about confronting Brittany. I passed Joey D. on my way out and noticed he had fresh scratch marks all over his forearms.

"Are those from Brittany?"

"Yeah, she's one crazy bitch. I'm glad I came in when I did, she can be nasty."

"I'm glad you did too! Thanks for intervening."

"No prob. Take it easy."

I was still shaking my head in disbelief when I walked up to Dom's bar. He smiled and went back to cleaning. He seemed distracted and not as cheerful.

"Rough night?"

"Huh? Not really."

"You okay?"

"Yeah. I'll be done in a minute. I was thinking we should go out afterwards."

"We can just go back to your place."

"No. I wanna go out." He placed a drink in front of me. His abruptness made me feel uneasy and my gut twisted into knots.

Chapter 13

The ride was quiet. Dom's dark eyebrows creased together forming a pensive expression. There was something on his mind. That much I could tell. My repeated attempts to find out didn't yield anything, sending my imagination into overdrive. Dominic navigated his Mustang down the dimly lit street. By the time he parked in front of the now familiar condemned building, I was convinced he was going to break up with me. Once inside The Speak, he placed his hand on the small of my back and guided me to the same small table we always sat at. Dominic went up to the bar and ordered drinks. He came back with a bottle of Dom Perignon and two champagne flutes. His face was brighter and the smile he flashed reached his eyes.

"What the hell?"

"We're celebrating." He said as he popped the cork and poured the bubbly. He held up his flute to toast. "To us!" He clinked his glass against mine and we sipped. After a couple of glasses I was feeling the buzz. We were both laughing uncontrollably at anything. I rested my head on his shoulder to catch my breath. All of a sudden a commotion broke out in the back room. I heard a bunch of men yelling and the doorman, Sam, took off down the hall. Gunshots exploded and I hit the floor. Dominic hunched over me protectively. Our champagne bottle was on the floor having been knocked over when I bumped against the table. Several other patrons were crouched down in similar positions. Dominic made sure I was okay and then leapt up.

"Where are you going?" I hissed.

"To see what happened."

"Are you crazy? You're going to get shot!"

"Relax Nat. Everything's fine." He spun around and left the room.

I stood up slowly on shaky legs to follow him. Acrid gun smoke clouded the air, tickling my throat. I peeked around the doorway and down the hall. My eyes saw the blood first. A pool crept outwards from a man lying motionless on the floor. The man was lying on his back. The force of the bullet had knocked him backwards in his chair when it entered his head. What was left of his skull was the source of the pool of blood. I couldn't turn away. The slow creep hypnotized me. I could identify bits of bone, stark white islands in a red sea. Chunks of brain matter settled in the pool like gelatinous mounds. The dead man's right arm was flung up over his head, damming the flow, which had already started to coagulate and collect in the grooves of the wooden floorboards. A gun lay a few inches from his open hand.

I wasn't aware of the sets of eyes staring at me. The sound of my brother's voice broke my trance, "What is she doing here?" There was an accusatory tone to his voice.

My head snapped up at the sound of Grant's voice. I looked away from the body and focused on the back room. Grant was standing on the other side of the table flanked by Dominic and Sam. All three were looking at me. Sam's expression was of wariness, Dominic's of concern and Grant's was all anger. I then took on the rest of the scene. Two other men were lying face down on the table in smaller pools of blood. My eyes moved to Grant again, he was the only one holding a gun.

The vodka tonics and the champagne burned up the back of my throat. I bent over and vomited onto the floor of the hallway. Dizzy, I reached one hand out against the wall for support. I wiped my mouth with the back of my other hand and stared at a spot on the floor that wasn't covered in vomit, blood or brains. My heart pounding in my ears, I tried to slow my breathing. I needed to sit but was unable to move at first. Slowly, I slid down the wall and hugged my knees to my chest. I closed my eyes and willed myself to get a grip. The heavy metallic smell of blood that hung in the air wasn't helping to clear my head, but I was eventually able to calm down and became vaguely aware of people talking in the bar area behind me. No one else had gotten up to investigate.

"Hey Uncle Al," Dominic called down the hall, "Can you help Natalie for me?" Dominic was trapped on the other side of the body and the lake of blood. A tall, wiry man with salt and pepper hair and a goatee appeared at my side and helped me up. He wrapped his arm around my back in a fatherly gesture and helped me across to the bar. My legs were still shaking and I welcomed the bar stool. The bartender set a glass of ice water in front of me and I gingerly took a sip, grateful to wash down some of the bile residue. Uncle Al sat down next to me.

"How ya doin'?" he asked.

"I…I don't know how to answer that." I honestly didn't. I was scared, sick, horrified at the gruesome scene I had just witnessed and in shock that my brother was responsible for the carnage. I was even more unnerved that everyone else was so calm. It was like nothing had ever happened. "I need something stronger than water."

The bartender set a glass of cognac in front of me. I took a healthy swig and braced myself for it to come back up. Fortunately, it soothed my stomach instead and the warmth spread out through my muscles, acting as an anesthetic for my nerves.

"There. Do you feel better?" Uncle Al patted my hand. He must have seen me relax. I turned to look at him and saw the same green eyes as Dominic and Miranda, only lined with crow's feet. His skin had an olive complexion, like Dominic's.

"I do. Thank you."

"You just sit here. That mess will be cleaned up in no time." My hands started shaking again and I quickly took another sip. "I'm Dominic's Uncle, Al Grabano." He shook my trembling hand.

"I'm Natalie Ross." It seemed to be an odd time for introductions. He was looking at my profile and I could feel him evaluating my behavior. Now that the initial shock had worn off and the booze had started to kick in I thought I was ready to process the situation, a little bit at a time. "What happened?" I asked, hesitantly.

"I think we better wait for Grant and Dominic to answer your questions." We sat in silence. The smell of bleach wafted into the room and soon filled it up completely. Scrubbing sounds drifted down the hall and a door slammed a couple of times. The other men in the room carried on their conversations over drinks, oblivious to the activities around them. After the second glass of cognac my stomach burned a little and my eyelids grew heavy. I rested my head against my hand and dozed off.

Chapter 14

Men were arguing and I recognized the voices as I became more coherent. Grant and Dominic were shouting at each other.

"What the fuck were you thinking bringing her here tonight?"

"She needed to know."

"No she didn't and even if she did, for her to find out this way? Brilliant fucking plan!"

"Well it's done. I don't like keeping secrets from her. She deserves to know who I am."

"What about my secret, Dom? There you go, always thinking about yourself."

"Fuck you, Grant. Would you have ever told her? "

"I don't know - probably not. What's up with you anyway? Why Natalie? You'll probably be bored with her in a month, like everyone else you've fucked around with."

"She means a lot to me," Dominic admitted.

"She'd better, because if you hurt her, I'll kill you myself."

"Now, now Grant, don't go making threats against my nephew."

Recognizing the gravelly voice of Marco, I tensed up. This statement silenced Grant and the charged atmosphere dissipated.

"I'll deal with Dominic later, but right now we have a situation. Your sister, as pretty as she may be, has become a fucking liability."

I fully woke then and opened my eyes. I was curled up on a leather couch and my head was on Dominic's coat. At first I thought everything had been a bad dream until I smelled the bleach. It cut right through the leather and cologne of Dominic's jacket. Feeling more alert, I sat up straight and looked around.

We weren't alone. Uncle Al, Sam the doorman, Dominic's father, Rico, and Miranda were all in the dimly lit room along with Uncle Marco, Grant and Dom. Some were standing, some were sitting, and all were observing me. When Grant noticed I was awake, he moved closer to Miranda. Dominic sat down next to me and his lap replaced the jacket. He gently stroked my hair.

"Natalie, we need to talk." It was Grant who broke the silence. Miranda touched his arm. He reached over and rested his hand on top of hers and stood up straighter. It was like they drew strength from each other's presence. "What you saw tonight cannot leave this room." He glanced over at Uncle Marco, who sat in silence across from the sofa Dominic and I were on. Marco gestured for Grant to continue. "Our lives depend upon it." I was taken aback at this statement and at the serious expression on Grant's face.

"Grant, did you kill those men?" He confirmed by nodding his head. I shrunk back against the sofa. Dominic put his arm around me. I shrugged it off and hissed at him. "You knew about this."

I looked to Miranda for help. She had her arms crossed in front of her and was eyeing me warily. "What is this? Are you guys like the mafia or something?"

Marco shot a warning look at Grant. I gasped as realization sunk in. George "The Stump", that guy that was on the news, the mob hit. "Oh my God, this isn't the first time you've killed someone is it?"

Grant flinched slightly at my words before answering carefully, "No, it isn't."

I stared at my brother as if seeing him for the first time. He had a hard time meeting my eyes. I didn't know what to say and Grant didn't seem to either. The room filled with an awkward silence.

Miranda left Grant's side to sit next to me on the sofa. "Natalie, I know this all must be…overwhelming," she looked at me, her eyes burning with intensity. "We need to know that we can trust you to keep quiet."

I repeated Grant's words in my head. *Our lives depend on it.* Dominic reached for one of my hands. They had balled up into fists on my lap and he was struggling to wrestle my fingers free. "Nat, please," he begged. "I can't lose you."

"It would be a shame to lose Grant too. He'll be hard to replace," Marco threatened. I was running out of time. Of course I was going to keep my mouth shut. That was the smart thing to do when faced with an ultimatum like this. Keep quiet or die? Hmmm let me think… it was a no brainer, but what scared me was what I was agreeing to do. I knew three men were dead, murdered in cold blood by my own brother. I didn't know the reasons why, I didn't know if they were bad people who deserved it, but by agreeing to stay quiet their blood would forever be on my hands…and their death scenes would be forever engrained in my memory.

"You can trust me," my voice quivered and I looked directly at Marco. "You have my word. I won't turn against my brother, he's family." Dominic squeezed my hand. Miranda breathed a sigh of relief and got up to stand next to Grant.

"I told you it would work out," she whispered in his ear.

Uncle Marco stood up, commanding the room's attention. "I'm glad to hear that. Just remember if you tell anyone – anyone, both you and your brother are dead," Uncle Marco warned, his black eyes void of all emotion.

"I understand."

"Well, now that that's all cleared up, welcome to the family, doll! You're going to get to know all of us a lot better." With a flip of an invisible switch Uncle Marco was jovial. He crossed over to me and yanked me up off the couch. He kissed each cheek before giving me a big hug that lifted me off of my feet. He set me down, grabbing a quick handful of ass and I had to steady myself. Dominic stood up and wrapped his arm around my waist.

"I'll talk to you later about this," Marco said to Dominic, then turned around and left the room with Uncle Al and Dom's dad close behind.

"Nat, I am so sorry," Grant said. His shoulders were tense, like he was carrying the weight of the world.

"How long have you been killing people Grant? Is this a hobby of yours?"

"Not a hobby, a job."

"Now that I'm involved, I want to know everything." I looked around the room at Miranda, Grant and finally Dominic. "Everything."

Dominic nodded, he understood. We had agreed to be honest with each other. I swore to protect his family in order to protect mine, he owed me the truth.

"Let's go back to my place. We'll eat some breakfast and talk," Dominic offered. Grant and Miranda agreed. We stepped out of the room into a small hallway. To the right was a set of stairs that led down a flight. I realized that we had been in the same house the whole time. Just one floor above where the three men had been shot.

The sun had come up while we were cloistered inside and it felt like we were in slow motion as the rush hour traffic buzzed around the Mustang. A million questions raced through my mind. None of these were answered until we were inside Dominic's condo. We gathered around the granite breakfast bar drinking coffee.

"Grant when did you get involved in this shit?"

He set his mug down and paused before answering. "Five years ago. You were a senior in high school."

"How?"

"Remember that construction job I had over the summer? That was Grabano and Sons."

"Oh...but that was construction. When did you start blowing people's heads off?"

Grant inhaled deeply before beginning. "These guys showed up on a job site and Dom's dad was pissed they were there. It was one of those brutal, muggy July days and tempers were pretty hot. Things started to escalate and one of these guys pulled a gun on Dom's dad. I didn't even hesitate and ran up behind the guy and tackled him. The gun skittered across the ground out of reach. Well then his buddy jumps on me and instinct took over. I threw him off, grabbed the gun and turned to see the guy charging at me. I shot him in the chest, point blank, and he crumpled to the ground at my feet." Grant paused to see how I was handling the story.

Despite the fact that he was describing a murder, I was actually fascinated. My boring, serious, take-the-fun-out-of-everything big brother had a side to him I never knew existed. Grant continued, "Dom's dad was impressed with how I handled myself. He also liked that I protected him. So, he introduced me to Uncle Marco.

Turns out killing people doesn't really bother me. Plus, the money is really good."

"Whoa and I thought I was the one keeping secrets from Mom."

Grant's mouth twitched. "Yeah, if she only knew," then he got serious again. "Mom can never know."

"I know, I know. Geez, calm down."

Miranda laughed at our exchange. "Grant, I think she gets it." I regarded Miranda and her poise. She was so petite yet had such a big presence. I could tell she was used to being in charge.

"Where do you fit into all of this Miranda?" I asked, diverting attention away from Grant.

"Well, Marco is my father and he is considered the Boss of the Philly Mob."

"You're serious – the mob? For real, like the Godfather?"

"Yes. Dominic and I are part of the next generation. Dominic's dad, my Uncle Rico, is the underboss. I'm the oldest and have been learning to run the legitimate businesses as is Dominic. Right now we're focused on Crimson." At least Dominic hadn't been lying when he told me he was learning the family business. I just never would have guessed that the family business was the mob. "Apparently, because I'm a woman, I can't be a ranking member, so Dominic's next in line. But, we'll see…if a woman can run for president, than I can run the mafia. "

"Yeah right, like Uncle Marco would let that happen!" Dominic chuckled. "I can hear him now 'over my dead body…'."

"That can be arranged," Miranda said and nudged Grant with her elbow. They all burst out laughing and I stared at them horrified.

Dominic saw my expression and calmed down enough to explain themselves. "It's mafia humor. Get it?"

"Ha, ha...hilarious," I said and rubbed my temples, as if massaging the information overload. Dominic leaned over and kissed my forehead. "So why did you kill those guys tonight? What did they do wrong?" My morbid curiosity needed to know.

"A couple of reasons. They owed Marco money and they were telling secrets to the Nucci family," Grant revealed.

"Who's the Nucci family?"

"A rival family," Miranda answered. "They want to control the Philly mob. Technically "The Commission", which is made up of leaders from the Five Families in NYC, decides who runs the show here, but you have to prove that you're capable. Our family has been doing a good job, and Uncle Marco has improved relations between the Philly mob and New York, but a rival family can take us out. It's happened before."

"It has?"

"About twenty years ago, there was a real war with people getting killed left and right. Scarfo was convicted when his own capo and soldiers ratted on him in a classic example of a total power struggle. The Philly Mob used to have a spot on The Commission, but it was revoked during this time and lasted for close to ten years."

"The Feds really started cracking down and practically wiped out the mafia...or at least they have the media believing that," Dominic chimed in. "After the last boss got sent to prison, the Grabano brothers stepped up and helped settle things down. It's been somewhat peaceful since. We've repaired a lot of the damage with the New York families, but it hasn't been easy."

I sat in stunned silence processing the brief history. "What's a capo?"

"A capo is ranked underneath the underboss, sometimes there are more than one." Dominic laid out the hierarchy for me so I could understand. First there is the boss, who was Marco, and then the underboss, who was Dominic's dad Rico, Uncle Al, was a capo being that he was the youngest of the brothers and Dominic and Grant were considered soldiers.

"So you don't have to be blood-related to be a soldier?"

"No. If you do good work and play by the rules, you can get promoted fairly quickly. Loyalty goes a long way. That's how I got here," Grant answered.

I shook my head, still in disbelief over all that had happened. There was a lot to absorb, but it explained a lot of things; the expensive cars, the beautiful homes and Dominic's ability to have the ice skating rink opened up after hours for a date. Not to mention the endless stream of cash and the respect Dominic received when we were out. Not just respect, but fear. The same reaction Grant received, although I never really paid much attention until now.

"Do you guys like own the city or something?" I asked.

"Almost. We have a lot of pull and can get things done," Dominic answered. I shuddered knowing I had just witnessed one of the ways they get things done.

"Where did you guys put those men that Grant..." I couldn't bring myself to say killed.

"My dad had a crew come and get the bodies. They're probably already buried underneath several tons of freshly poured concrete at a job site in Wayne." I stared at Dominic speechless. There really wasn't anything to say. Those men would probably be on the missing persons list for eternity. Only the Grabano family, Grant, and now me, knew what happened.

Grant and Miranda left after breakfast, but not after my brother made me swear up and down that I was going to be okay.

"Grant, what choice do I have but to be okay with this? I just need some time to process everything."

"I'm sorry," he said before he shut the door.

Dominic came up to stand behind me and he rested his head on top of mine. "It really isn't so bad, Nat. You'll get used to it. And there are definite advantages."

"Why didn't you tell me – I mean this is really who you are?"

"I wanted to tell you right after we spent our first night together, but Grant begged me not to. It's been killing me, not being able to say anything. Having you there to see it firsthand seemed the best way to tell you. That way you would believe me."

Remembering the vacant stares of the dead made me shudder again. Dominic leaned in, brushing my hair to the side and kissing my neck.

"Maybe it wasn't the best way for you to find out, but I'm glad you know," he said softly in my ear.

"Have you killed people too?"

"Yeah. It goes with the territory."

I turned around to face him. "How many have you killed?"

"I don't know, five or six," he said with a shrug.

"Five or six? How can you be so nonchalant about that?"

"It's easier not to think about it, I guess."

"Do you know many people Grant has killed?"

"Dunno…a lot more than me though."

I couldn't look him in the eyes and focused on the floor. "I'd like to go home now."

"What? Why? Don't you want to talk some more?"

"No. I need to be alone. Please take me home."

Dominic backed off and called downstairs to have his car brought around. My head ached with exhaustion and I half dozed on the drive home. Dominic pulled up in front of the building and I leaned over to peck his cheek.

"Hey," he held my hand, preventing me from getting out of the car. Dramatically different from when Marco did it. "Are *we* alright?"

I really hadn't considered how our relationship played out in the scheme of things. How many more secrets did he have? "I just need some time. Give me a few days…I'll call you."

Before releasing my hand, he stared at me for a few seconds, as if searching my face for an answer I didn't know yet. "Okay, but don't take too long. And remember, don't tell anyone – not even Chelsea."

I nodded and got out of the car.

Thank God Chelsea was already at school and the apartment was empty. I really should have been at class too, but knew that was an impossible feat. Instead I took full advantage of having some alone time by immediately falling asleep.

A huge, hulking shadow of a man ran after me with a gun trained on my back. No matter how fast I tried to sprint, my legs moved in slow motion, like I was running through knee deep mud. A loud bang erupted from behind. I screamed and fell forward.

"Nat, Nat wake up!" Chelsea was shaking me and I woke up, still screaming. "Jesus, you scared the shit out of me!"

"I'm sorry," I murmured, my heart was pounding and my mouth was dry. "I was having a bad dream."

"I noticed. What was it about?"

"I was being chased. What time is it?" I asked, changing the subject.

"It's sometime after four. You missed classes again today."

"I know, but school just wasn't happening."

"This isn't like you Nat. Sleeping all day and missing classes. Do you have to spend every night with Dominic?

"I don't spend every night…last night was different. What business is it of yours anyway?" I rolled over so my back was to Chelsea. "I don't want to talk about it."

"Fine – whatever, Little Miss Mood Swing, I'm just being a friend." The mattress shifted and a few seconds later I heard my door shut. It was nice to be alone again.

I forced myself to go to classes the next day, even though it was a complete waste. I couldn't focus on any of the lectures and my creativity was flat in the studio. At least I would get credit for showing up.

Grant called as I was walking back to the apartment, but I let it go to voicemail. I still wasn't ready to talk to him or Dominic. Conflicted would best describe the way I felt. I was pissed that

Grant and Dominic hadn't been honest with me. I was pissed at Grant for getting involved with the Grabanos. Dominic didn't really have a choice, but Grant did. I was also relieved because it explained Dominic's weird hours and Grant's hesitation for me dating Dom. I was also scared. Yes, I dabbled with drugs and had been promiscuous, but that was about as far as I planned to take the immoral behavior. Two nights ago my life's path was seriously altered and I didn't know what the future held. Murder and violence were sure to be part of it and that idea was terrifying.

Dominic wanted to know how the truth about who he really was affected our relationship. How could I answer that? I liked Dominic, but that was before I knew he killed people and was part of the largest crime family in Philadelphia. Now I didn't know how I felt about him. Why didn't I just have a fling with him and leave it at that? No, I had to go ahead and start a relationship. If I did end things with Dominic, did that place me and Grant in danger?

These thoughts weighed heavily on my mind as I entered the apartment.   Chelsea   waved   from   the   futon.
"In a better mood?"

"Not really."

"Look in your room. I think there's something in there that will cheer you up."

I walked down the hall to my room and instantly spotted what Chelsea was talking about - it would be hard to miss. The most extravagant bouquet of red roses I had ever seen was on my desk. The scent filled up the small room and I inhaled deeply. I crossed my room in seconds and picked up the card.

I'm sorry about the other night. I couldn't go another day without you knowing the truth. - D

The roses were just a nice gesture, something I would ordinarily be thrilled to receive, but their very presence reminded me of the situation at hand.

"Somebody really likes you," Chelsea chirped from behind and I jumped.

"Jesus, you scared me!"

"I take it those are from Dominic?"

"Yes."

"Did you guys have a fight or something? That would explain your mood."

"No we didn't have a fight, but we did have a something. I can't talk about it, it's complicated."

Chelsea was the one person in my life, aside from Grant, who I went to during times of crisis. Now when I needed her the most, I wasn't able to talk to her. No matter how frustrating it was, I refused to put her life in danger by telling her what happened.

"I'm going for a run. I'll talk to you later." I turned my back to Chelsea and she got the hint. The door shut quietly behind her as she retreated.

***

I ran mindlessly through the city until my lungs begged for mercy and my leg muscles screamed. Even then I didn't stop. Finally, when exhaustion threatened to send me tumbling to the sidewalk I slowed to a walk. The run had helped to get my head on straight. Dominic would be pleased with my answer. It wasn't going to be easy, but I would continue dating him and act like nothing had changed. Marco was capable of being dangerous, this was obvious and I would do everything in my power to keep that danger away from Grant. I already liked Dominic and working at Crimson was lucrative. How bad could it be, really?

Chapter 15

The apartment was quiet except for muffled music coming from behind Chelsea's bedroom door. Feeling guilty for being so nasty towards her, I walked down the hall and knocked.

"Come in."

I entered her room and took in the extreme organization, which bordered on obsessive compulsive, such the opposite of my clutter. Chelsea was lying on her bed flipping through a fashion magazine.

"Hey Chels, I want to apologize for earlier."

"Feeling better?"

"Yeah, the run helped. I had a lot on my mind. Sorry."

"It's cool, we all have our moments. I'm glad you're in a better mood. I'm always around if you need to talk."

"I know."

I left Chelsea to her magazine and hit the shower. The run had thoroughly exhausted every muscle in my body, but my mind was still going at a hundred miles an hour. After getting dressed I checked my phone. Grant had called three more times while I was out. He could wait.

A bottle of vodka in the freezer had my name on it. I pulled that out along with a bottle of orange juice from the fridge. "Chelsea Reed, it's cocktail hour!" I hollered from the kitchen. Seconds later her stereo shut off and she opened her door a crack, peeking her head through. "Come hither." I beckoned, holding up a drink. She skipped down the hallway and grabbed the glass from my hand. I followed her to the futon with the bottles as back up.

Soon my mind had mellowed and we sat back with a box of hard pretzels between us. Chelsea flipped through the channels. The constant changing was perfect for our short attention span. We hadn't hung out like this since Dominic and I had started dating and I had forgotten how much fun it was to just chill.

A loud banging on the front door sent me leaping towards the ceiling, knocking a glass over in the process.

"Shit!" I yelled and ran to grab a roll of paper towels.

"I wonder who that is," Chelsea commented as she went to answer the door. "It's just Grant," she called. I turned to see Grant pushing past her. He took up the entrance to the kitchen.

"Is your phone broken?" he demanded.

"No, I -"

He cut me off. "Did you get my messages?"

"I saw that you called, but -"

He interrupted again. "Would it fucking kill you to answer the phone when I call? I've been trying to reach you. "

"Grant, relax! I can't deal with you like this." He was bringing me down and the mellow atmosphere was now charged with his intensity. He moved aside to let me pass and followed me.

Grant surveyed the living room spotting the glass on its side and the half empty vodka bottle on the coffee table.

"Is this why you couldn't answer the phone? You're too busy getting drunk?"

"Maybe you need a drink because you, like, totally need to chill," Chelsea remarked. She knelt down to blot the area rug where orange juice had started to seep in. Grant stepped into the hallway and pulled me with him.

"Marco wanted me to check on you. He was worried that you might take off. When I couldn't reach you…" he whispered in my ear.

"Oh!" My eyes widened with understanding. "He doesn't trust me, does he?"

"No. But don't worry, he hardly trusts anyone."

"Hey, what are you two whispering about over there?" Chelsea interrupted. We turned to look at her and she was holding a drink out like a peace offering. "Come here Grant, it's been a while since you and I got drunk together," she teased.

Grant laughed, visibly more relaxed. "I will, I just need to make a phone call," He gave me a significant look and slipped into my bedroom. I followed him. He called Marco and reassured him that I had not skipped town.

While he spoke I checked my phone and saw that there were thirteen missed calls. All were from Grant, except for one, and none were from Dominic.

"I wonder why Dominic isn't trying to get a hold of me." I asked when Grant hung up.

"He said that you told him you needed a couple days and was giving you some space. Sure pissed Marco off; he kept trying to get Dominic to call you too. Pretty impressive, Dominic must like you more than I thought." Grant grew quiet and stared at me.

"Is Marco still worried about me?" I asked.

"Yeah, but you stick with me…and Dominic," he said with reluctance. "That should help."

"Okay, I'll take your word on that," I mustered up a smile. We filed out of my room and joined Chelsea around the coffee table.

Chapter 16

After I got home from class the next day I called Dominic. He had been patient waiting for me. My stomach threatened to spill its contents as I waited for him to answer.

"Nat?"

"Hey, it's me."

"Hey you, it's good to hear your voice."

"It's good to hear yours too. Thank you for the roses."

"You're welcome. So, how're you doing?

"Better. I think I've gotten over the initial shock. Thank you for giving me some time to think."

"And?"

"I think we're going to be okay. But I want to know you, the real you. No more secrets." My voice cracked at the end. I really hoped that there weren't any more skeletons in the closet. "I'd rather know than be blindsided again."

"I understand. So we're good?" I could hear the excitement in his voice. "I want to see you, can I come over?"

"Yes to both."

"I'll be right over."

The second I hung up the phone I collapsed on the bed in a state of nerves. *It's just Dominic* - I kept repeating in my head as I rushed around to get ready. I did a quick clean up of my bedroom, brushed my teeth and ran a wide toothed comb through my hair. This didn't help quell the apprehension.

There was a light knock on my door before it opened. Dominic stood in the doorway.

"Chelsea let me in."

It wasn't until I saw him that I realized how much I had missed him. I jumped off the bed and ran to him, practically throwing myself at him, and he caught me. He smelled as good as I had remembered, and felt as good. He kissed the top of my head and squeezed me close.

"You have no idea how much I missed you. It's weird, I don't recall ever missing anyone so much," Dominic said in his husky voice.

"Same here," I said into his chest then grabbed his hand and led him over to the bed.

We sat down together. Dominic reached into his leather jacket and pulled out a small box.

"This is for you."

I took the box out of his hands and untied the ribbon. Inside, a diamond tennis bracelet sparkled against the black velvet lining.

"Oh my God!" My mouth hung open in surprise.

"Happy Valentine's Day!" He retrieved the bracelet and held it out to me. "May I?"

Even though I was dumbfounded, I managed to hold my hand up. He clasped the bracelet onto my wrist. I didn't know what to say. It had completely escaped me that it was Valentine's Day and I didn't know if I could accept such a generous gift. I opened my mouth to protest and he silenced the words.

"I told you I was going to cover you in diamonds. This should match your navel ring." He whispered in my ear and then kissed me. His tongue was probing and his caresses grew more urgent. He lay me down on the bed and started to unbutton my shirt all while still kissing me. The longing stirred deep and I responded. This was just Dominic. Had he killed people with the very same hands that were cupping my breasts? Yes, but I wasn't going to think about that. Instead I just focused on how good his hands felt as they explored my body – inside and out.

Afterwards we lay in bed facing each other, our foreheads lightly touching, staring into each other's eyes.

"What are you thinking?" Dom asked.

"I'm conflicted. You've killed people. I should be terrified of you, but I'm not." Dominic kissed my nose. "Also, I feel bad. I totally forgot about Valentine's Day and didn't get you anything." I lifted my arm up and watched the light glint off my new diamonds.

"Shhh," he brushed his hand across my cheek. "You stayed with me – that's a gift in itself."

Chapter 17

Dominic parked in the shadows alongside Crimson next to Grant and Miranda's cars. I gathered my bag and went to open the door.

"Wait. Before we go in, I should tell you something."

My hand broke out in a cold sweat around the door handle. What other bombshell was he getting ready to drop?

"I know, I'll keep quiet."

"No, that's not it. You don't have to keep a low profile here. Everyone's cool."

Dominic filled me in that all of the bouncers at Crimson were soldiers and Grant was like a mini boss among them. All of the employees were connected in one way or another to the Philadelphia Cosa Nostra.

"Everyone?"

"Yeah."

"I was the only one that didn't know? How come I was able to work here then?"

"Grant. My Uncle Marco treats him like a son and let him get away with it."

"Do you think that's why Grant didn't want us together?"

"I think that is part of the reason. I did have a reputation with the ladies though. That's probably what bothered him the most."

"I don't want to know!" I held up my hand to silence him. "That's in the past."

"I thought you wanted to know everything. No secrets remember?" He teased and got out of the car.

I walked into Crimson with a whole new perspective that night. Now I understood why all the employees had nice cars and could afford expensive drug habits. Dominic held my hand as we entered the club. Grant and Miranda crossed the empty dance floor to meet us.

"Did you tell them?" Dom asked Grant.

"Yes, they all know that Natalie knows. It was hard for everyone not to talk about it, so they're glad, well except for Brittany."

Dominic shrugged. "She'll get over it."

"Yeah when she finds another man to obsess over," Miranda added.

True to form, Brittany had a sneer on her face when she saw me enter the employee lounge. Everyone else seemed friendly enough. Allegra and Joey were getting ready to snort some coke when Allegra surprised me.

"Natalie, did you want to do a line?" She had never offered me any before.

"I'm good. Thanks though."

"Sure!" Her glassy eyes glittered when she smiled at me before hunching over the table, holding one nostril closed with her finger. Brittany scowled at Allegra. She probably felt betrayed by her coke buddy's invitation. I had never really felt like a Crimson girl, but I was definitely one now.

After the club cleared out and the tips were counted, Dominic and Grant left to attend to some business. At first I was tempted to ask what they were up to, but vivid flashes of the murder scene flashed in my head and that snuffed out my curiosity. Miranda came out of her office and saw me standing by the exit.

"I take it the boys are gone?"

"Yes, they just left. I was just getting ready to go out and hail a cab."

"Wanna hang out? I'll drop you off at home."

We walked out together. Even though the days were losing their winter bite and the crocus were peeking up out of the ground, the mid-February nights were still chilly. A brisk wind kicked up off the river and we hurried to Miranda's Mercedes. The vacant, dark parking lot also contributed to our haste.

Miranda didn't hesitate starting the car and cranking the heat to max. I blew on my fingertips which had been exposed to the elements. Soon the car was warm, even the seats were heated and especially toasty. If I had to live out of a car, it would be this one, I thought to myself as I relaxed into the leather.

I heard the flick of a lighter and looked to my left. Miranda was lighting up a joint. She took a deep drag and held it. Slowly she exhaled and handed the joint to me. The halo of smoke around her head had a dramatic effect, reminiscent of film noir.

"Now that you've had a couple days since...well, you know, are you doing alright?" Miranda asked.

"At first I didn't think so. Seeing those men dead..." I shuddered. "Then finding out about Grant and Dom and everything else, I was pretty freaked." I took another hit off of the joint. "I've had time to think about it and I think I'll be okay. I'm still surprised about Grant though. He is a little too good at keeping secrets. For instance, how long have you been going out?"

"About six months. We flirted a lot and my dad thought the world of him. It took Grant forever to ask me out and even longer for us to become an official couple."

"That seems to be a family trait," I laughed and took another hit.

Miranda put the car in drive. "Let's get something to eat."

"Sheesh, you Grabanos and your food!"

Miranda drove to the Spring Garden Lounge, a favorite late night haunt in the city. I could tell from the steamed up windows that the place was packed. A large group filed out as we walked through the door. I surveyed the restaurant. It was set up like an old diner from the fifties, what used to be the counter where you could order milkshakes and root beer floats was now occupied by well dressed drunks. The hostess recognized Miranda and waved us over. We followed her to an unoccupied table in a far corner.

"I'm impressed. It's always hard to get seated right away here," I remarked.

"The employees come into Crimson a lot and we put them on the guest list, so it's a fair trade."

We both ordered the sweet potato fries and chocolate shakes. Our conversation was limited as the noise level was off the charts. After devouring the whole basket of fries, I couldn't hold back a yawn.

"It's late. I'll take you home."

Miranda led the way to the exit. Several cat calls and whistles followed us out the door. We ignored them. Within a few minutes we were pulling up in front of my apartment building. Miranda turned to me before I got out of the car.

"Listen, I know it's not easy being a woman in the mob. If you ever need to talk, I'm here. You're Grant's sister and I'll look out for you."

"Thanks, I'll keep that in mind."

"It was cool hanging out with you."

"Same! Thanks for the ride."

Miranda waved and flashed a brilliant smile as she navigated away from the curb. Even Miranda was warming up to me. Maybe things were going to work out after all.

Chapter 18

Dominic really tried to help me adjust. He took things very slow with me and didn't push me into the lifestyle. My initial reaction towards him when I found out the truth was caution. Starting a real relationship was a huge step for me. Factoring in that he came from a long line of criminals *and* was a Mob boss in training needed some serious consideration. I appreciated the fact that he understood and gave me time.

Dom pulled up in front of my apartment building and parallel parked effortlessly. It was an unusually balmy night for early April and he had the convertible top down. I had been holding my hair up with my hands to keep it from whipping my face and it tumbled around my shoulders, down my back. Dominic brushed a few stray hairs off my cheek and kissed me, moving his lips down my jaw and neckline. I shivered in response and felt the now familiar pull in my stomach.

"Are you sure you can't spend the night?"

"As much as I want to, I can't. I have a big review tomorrow." It was true, in a little over a month I would be graduating from the University of the Arts, as long as I pulled my grades up.

"Are you sure?" He asked as he tweaked one of my nipples through my thin shirt. I groaned in response. He was going to make this difficult.

"I'm positive." I whispered in his ear before I nibbled on his lobe. It was a little salty; he must have worked up a sweat bartending that night. Now it was his turn to groan. I pulled away at that point and flashed a devilish grin. "Hold onto that thought until tomorrow night," I said as I opened up the car door and got out.

"You're killing me woman!"

"No, but I could have that arranged," I joked back with some mafia humor. He burst out laughing and turned the key in the ignition. The Mustang roared to life. He looked so fine in his car. The black paint as shiny as his black hair and the tan leather interior complimented his skin.

It was hard to see him pull away from the curb and I watched him drive down the street until he was out of sight. Feeling edgy from the pent up hormones I knew sleep wouldn't come easy tonight. I looked up at my apartment and saw the living room light was on. Chelsea's silhouette was in the window. I sighed and braced for another argument.

Our neighbors probably thought we're lesbians because we argue like an old married couple and we'd been arguing a lot lately. The hardest part about being keeping Grant and Dom's life a secret was not being able to tell anyone, especially Chelsea. She was the most persistent in trying to get me to tell her what was going on. She blamed Dominic for my sudden emotional distance and the drop in my grades. Little did she know shielding her from the truth was the best form of protection.

I opened the door to our apartment with trepidation. Chelsea stood in the living room with her arms crossed in front of her, glowering. I didn't even attempt to fake enthusiasm at seeing her.

"You're up late."

"I could say the same about you," she snipped.

"I'm home aren't I?"

"It's a miracle you're spending one night away from your Italian Stallion!"

"You don't have to wait up for me like some nervous den mother," I retaliated.

"I wanted to make sure you got home for your review in the morning," she admitted shifting to a less defensive position.

"That's why I'm here."

"Good, because your priorities have been out of whack since you decided to take on a boyfriend." She sounded resentful. "Remember my advice – don't let it consume you?"

I glared at her. She always took on this high and mighty tone, like she was some kind of relationship guru. I think she was just jealous. Dominic and I had a connection, despite both coming from very dysfunctional families, our relationship was tight. "Are you really going to start this again?"

"I'll keep bringing it up until you actually listen. By the way you got a letter from the Art Institute of Chicago."

I walked to the stack of mail sitting on the counter. The letter sat on top of the pile. Inhaling deeply, I tore the envelope open, silently praying it contained a rejection letter. It didn't. I was accepted and that's when I realized I wasn't going to be able to go. I crumbled the paper up and threw it into the kitchen sink.

"You didn't get in?"

"No. I was accepted."

"That's awesome Nat!" Chelsea grew quiet, watching me. "Why aren't you excited?"

"Because I've changed my plans and I'm going to stay here." I struggled to form the words.

"Because of *him*?"

"That's part of the reason."

"Jesus Nat! Are you going to throw your dreams away for a guy? Come on, where's your independence? Chicago was it for you and you're just not going to go? Don't do this because of Dominic."

This was the last straw. Every time I came home I was under attack. I would have loved to tell Chelsea the truth about Dominic and the gruesome crime I had witnessed – the crime that ate away at me 24/7, but I couldn't. She didn't accept any excuse I came up with, it always came back to being Dominic's fault.

"You know what Chelsea; I don't have to take this." My words might as well have physically slapped her because she flinched back. I pulled a wad of hundred dollar bills out of my purse and peeled off fifteen of them. Her eyes got huge when she saw how much cash I was carrying. "Here's rent, plus extra for utilities for the rest of the lease. I'm moving out early." I dropped the bills on the coffee table and marched to my room, slamming the door behind me. Yeah we'd probably get another call from the landlord in the morning. The second the door shut I let the tears fall.

I called Dominic on his cell and he could barely understand me I was sobbing so hard. I managed to choke out "Come and get me." I could hear tires squealing in the background and horns blaring.

"I'm on my way," he said and hung up the phone. I pulled my suitcase out from under the bed and started throwing clothes in. I already had toiletries at Dom's. Next, I packed up my laptop, paints, portfolio and all the books I would need for the week. My cell phone rang as I was zipping up the bag. Dominic was out front already and the timing couldn't have been more perfect.

I walked out into the empty living room and could see the light on underneath Chelsea's door. The cash was still on the coffee table. Moving as silently as possible, I grabbed my purse and left.

Chapter 19

Dominic held me as I cried. His gray shirt grew darker with tearstains the more I wept. He didn't say anything and just let me be. We sat on his sofa in the living room. The only light filtering in came from the hallway where Dominic had dropped my bags.

My breathing started to calm down, no longer hitching in ragged breaths. I sat up and wiped my eyes.

"What happened?"

I sniffed back snot and felt tears well up in my puffy eyes again. "Chelsea and I had a huge fight because I received an acceptance letter to this art school in Chicago. I was going to get my masters there. When I told her I decided not to go she flipped out."

"And you can't go because of me?"

"Well, kinda." I looked down at my hands resting on my lap.

Dominic was silent. I glanced over and he had his head in his hands. "Dom, what's wrong?"

"I wish I could take it back and never have let you see Grant in action. It was wrong of me. You deserve so much more! Your brother was right. It was a selfish move on my part."

"Dom, baby, please don't beat yourself up. What's done is done. I firmly believe everything happens for a reason."

"I'm sorry Nat."

"I know you are." I kissed his cheek and he smiled at me.

"So, I take it you're moving in?"

"Um, I guess so. Is that okay?"

"Are you kidding?" He moved suddenly and was leaning over me, his arms resting on the back of the sofa by my head. "I would love to have you move in with me." Lowering himself down, his lips met mine and just like that I had a new place to live.

Dominic jumped up and held his hand out for me. "Come on, let's get you unpacked."

I took his hand and let him pull me up off of the couch. He picked up my suitcases and I followed him to the bedroom. Unzipping one of the bags, his eyes lit up. Reaching in, he pulled out a lacy bra and raised his eyebrows. "I get to unpack this one!" He said with a suggestive grin.

He looked so wicked I couldn't help but chuckle.

"What is this?" He yanked out my favorite bathrobe. It was originally red, but had faded to a pinkish hue. I'd had it since high school and even though it was ratty looking, refused to part with it. "Sexy!"

I snorted that time. "Yeah right!" Snatching it out of his hands I hung it up on the brass hook behind the bathroom door.

Dominic's cell phone rang, interrupting our banter.

"Hello?" He looked at me before stepping out of the room. I heard him tell someone to come up.

"Who was that?"

"Dante, he needs to drop something off."

"Oh." I went back to unpacking.

Minutes later I heard Dante and Dominic talking. I went out to say hi and stopped when I saw what was on the dining room table.

"Is that cocaine?" I asked, referring to three large white bricks that were wrapped in plastic.

"Hey Natalie, I didn't know you were here," Dante said, shooting a sideways glance at Dom.

"Natalie lives here now. She's just moving in."

"Really? Huh."

"Is that cocaine?" I asked again.

"Heroin," Dominic answered. Dante groaned and shook his head. "Be cool Dante. She won't tell anyone, will you Nat?"

"Uh, no…no I won't." I couldn't take my eyes off of the drugs. There was enough there to put us away for a very long time.

"Well, if you trust her…"

"I do." Dom emphasized this by coming over to stand next to me and wrapping his arm around my waist. "I'll bring the stuff to Crimson for delivery. We should be able to turn a nice profit on this batch."

"Cool, I'll leave you to it." He picked up an empty backpack and slung it over his shoulder.

After Dante left, Dominic placed the blocks of heroin into his black gym bag that was on the floor by the front door.

"Dom, I know you're involved with distributing drugs, but not on this scale."

"Nat, I'm sorry I didn't tell you sooner, and I was going to tell you."

"Oh really?" I stalked back to the bedroom and started stuffing my stuff back in my bags.

"What are you doing?"

"It was bad enough learning that you were in the mafia, but then to find out you're dealing dope too? I'm leaving before some other secret sneaks up and bites me in the ass."

"Are you going to go back to your apartment?"

"No."

"Where are you going to go then?"

"I can go to Grant's place."

"He's just as involved in this shit as I am, so what's the difference between living there versus here? Well, I know what the difference would be." He came up behind me, pulling my body to his. He moved my hair aside and started kissing my neck. I flinched and tried to move away. He held me tight, his lips persistent on my skin. My nerve endings began to respond despite my attempts at suppressing them.

"If, I'm going to stay here, and that's a big if, you need to fess up." I knew as I was saying these words, I was going to give in. "What else are you involved in?"

"Do you really want to know?"

I elbowed him in the ribs.

"Alright, fine…besides the drugs, there are several illegal gambling houses in the city, some in South Jersey."

"I knew about the gambling houses. What about the firearms trafficking, I overheard Joey D. saying something about guns and I'm pretty sure he wasn't talking about his biceps?"

Dom laughed and ran his hands through his hair. "Yeah, I'm not too involved in it, only every once in a while when an extra man is needed. You know the gun check at work and at Blue?"

"Yes."

"Most of those guns were our merchandise at some point."

"Jesus."

"I didn't tell you that because I hardly do it anymore." He kissed my neck again. "Am I forgiven?"

"Maybe." I turned around in his arms to face him. "I'm too tired to argue anymore and need to be ready for my review in a few hours. "

Dominic held my gaze for a few seconds before releasing me. "I promise not to get you too involved. If I know when a delivery is being made, I'll let you know so you don't have to be here for it."

"Thank you, but I'm trying to be open minded about this whole thing. This is going to be what it's like for me living with you, I might as well get used to it…just don't ask me to deal for you."

"I never would have considered that." He pulled me to him again. "You really are being amazing about everything. I don't deserve you."

We went to bed a few minutes later, but I couldn't sleep. Worries about my review ordinarily would have plagued me, but instead it was concern over my new living situation. Was Dominic honest with me about what all he was involved in?

Chapter 20

If I didn't hurry I was going to be late for my review. I broke out into a jog and darted between traffic. Rushing through the front doors of the hall, I almost took Chelsea out. She stepped back and avoided eye contact. I didn't have time to stop and talk to her. The slamming door echoed after me as I ran down the corridor.

The review went better than I thought, much to my relief. Maybe I would graduate after all...at least I would have that accomplishment to my name. There were several items at my old apartment I had left behind in my haste. Knowing Chelsea would be on campus for at least another hour, I took advantage.

Opening the front door, I was surprised to find Chelsea in the kitchen. She turned and looked at me and then turned away without any acknowledgement.

"I'm just here to pick up some stuff," I said to her back. She shrugged her shoulders in response.

I hurried to my room and shoved the rest of my things into two large shopping bags. Chelsea was sitting on the futon when I walked out.

"Well, that's it. I'm going to post my furniture for sale on campus. If you know of anyone who needs –"

"You're not going to apologize?"

"Me apologize?"

"We've been friends forever Natalie and you can just pick up and move on... you couldn't even talk to me on campus today."

"I was running late. Besides, there's nothing to talk about. I've made my decision and have moved in with Dominic."

"Good, happy for you. See you around." Chelsea shut me out and tuned back to the television.

Choking on a fresh round of tears, I hurried down the stairs and out to the street. It hurt, like a part of me was amputated, but it was impossible to make Chelsea understand when I was unable to tell her the truth, so I let her think the worst. I was willing to sacrifice our friendship if it meant keeping her safe.

Chapter 21

When I got back to the condo, Grant was there. He and Dom were sitting at the breakfast bar and stopped whatever they were talking about when I walked in. One look at my tearstained face had Dom running over. He pulled me into a crushing hug and I wrapped my arms around him, breathing in his scent that had become so comforting to me.

"What's wrong, baby?" He whispered in my ear, dusting kisses along the top of my head.

"Chelsea...it hurts," I said before burying my face in his chest again.

"I know, baby. I'm so sorry." His hold loosened and I stepped back to look up at him. Reaching up, he brushed an errant tear off my cheek and gave me a sad smile. He grabbed my hand and we walked over to Grant.

"I know it's hard, Nat," he said. "Now you understand why I stopped hanging out with my friends from high school."

"Oh." I paused to consider this information. "I wondered what happened."

"Yeah, it gets easier over time." He finished his beer and stood up, pulling me into a hug. "I'm here for you, sis."

"I know." This made me realize that somewhere along the way I started to lean on Dom for help and called him instead of Grant. I returned his hug with a little more fierceness.

**

By some miracle I was able to graduate college. A feat my brother wasn't able to accomplish since his job got in the way. My mom couldn't have been more proud. Grant had always been the responsible one and perfection in her eyes. When he dropped out of college to work at Crimson full time, his halo became tarnished. Now I was finally living up to my mom's high expectations.

We had a huge graduation bash at Crimson, the private room was ours for the night and Uncle Marco spared no expense, giving Miranda free rein.

"My goodness Natalie, this is something else!" My mom gushed as she took in the raw bar and top shelf liquor that was being served.

"Miranda really outdid herself." I left her chatting with one of our neighbors from York. Dom was leaning against the bar talking to his parents. He stood up and smiled at me as I approached. He held his hand out and I quickly placed mine is his.

"Having fun?" he asked.

"Yes, this is amazing!"

"Your mom having fun too?"

"I think so. I don't know if she quite knows what to make of it all. She probably feels bad she didn't throw the party for me. I know she can't afford anything lavish like this."

"Your family is our family, Nat. Throwing you this party is the least we could do," Rico, Dominic's dad, said before giving me a hug.

Dominic's mom stood to the side watching me in silence.

"Well, if she thinks that this is lavish, wait 'til she gets a load of this," he said, pulling a small black box out from his pocket. My heart stopped beating. I really hoped this wasn't his way of proposing. I was nowhere near ready for that level of commitment.

I took the box with shaking hands and popped the lid open. A solitaire diamond pendant sparkled at me. "Oh my God, Dominic - it's gorgeous!" I flung myself at him and practically knocked him over. "Thank you...oh my God!" I stared down at the giant, glittering diamond. He laughed at my enthusiastic response.

Several of my girlfriends hurried over to see what the excitement was about. They probably had the same idea I had when they saw the jewelry box in my hand.

"Wow!" Sara, a friend from high school gushed.

"Beautiful!" Jillian, my friend from college agreed.

They all waited for Dominic to fasten it around my neck. I had to hold my hair up so he could clasp it securely. I had never owned a lot of jewelry, until Dominic started spoiling me, and it was slightly daunting wearing such a valuable piece – it had to be at least two carats.

I looked up from the gem and glanced around the room for my mom. When I found her, she had a disapproving look on her face. I had expected as much. Happy moments involving couples irritated her. I just thought that when it came to her own daughter, she might make an exception. I refused to let her issues ruin my night. I looked around at my friends from high school and from college that had showed up to celebrate. Chelsea's absence was noticeable. I missed her, but we had never been able reconcile.

Grant walked out with our mom and I after the party had ended. He handed a valet ticket to one of the drivers. I thought this was odd because he didn't use the valet to park his car. A bright red BMW convertible came to a stop in front of us. The valet hopped out and tossed the keys. It took me a few seconds to realize they were sailing through the air at me. I caught them and gave him a puzzled look. My mom looked just as confused.

"Congratulations Nat," Grant said with a big grin.

"Wait, what? Are you serious?" I wrapped my arms around Grant and squeezed him tight. He laughed at my reaction.

"Do you like it?" he asked.

"Do I like it? Is the Pope Catholic?"

"Grant, how could you afford this?" our mom interjected. She looked at the shiny convertible in awe. I glanced nervously at Grant waiting for him to answer.

"I've been saving up. Nat deserves it."

"I didn't say she didn't, but Grant this is so much."

"Mom, I only have one sister. This is a big occasion."

Mom eyed us both suspiciously. She looked at the two carat diamond sparkling against my throat and the diamonds sparkling on my wrist, then at the car. She inspected Grant's Armani suit and the Tag Hauer watch on his wrist. She raised her eyebrow like she was trying to piece something together. Instead she shook her head and pulled us into a family hug. She had had some wine and was a little tipsy. I was hammered.

"Uh, Grant? I don't think any of us are in any condition to drive." I slurred and looked sideways at my pretty car. It would suck to crash it on the first night.

"I got it covered. Joey will drop it off at the condo. The valet will handle it from there." I smiled at my brother. He always took care of things. Dominic walked out of the club with his parents and Miranda. He whistled when he saw the car.

"We might have to take this to Atlantic City next time." He bent down and kissed my cheek. "Are you happy?"

"Definitely! This was all so…unexpected."

"You deserve it. Well, enjoy the rest of your night. I'll see you later." He kissed me goodbye before he and Miranda walked to the employee parking lot. My mom didn't like the fact that I had moved in with Dominic and he was making himself scarce while she was in town.

My mom and I sat out on the balcony at Dom's condo, well our condo, and watched the traffic on the bridge. She was quiet and contemplative.

"Nat, honey?"

"Yeah Mom?"

"What are your plans now that you've graduated?" I was prepared for the question. It was inevitable that she would ask.

"Marco, the owner of Crimson, offered me some commission work painting murals at the club, in addition to waitressing."

She turned in the deck chair to look at me, her brown eyes were unreadable. "That doesn't have anything to do with your degree. What about working with special needs kids, didn't you want to use sculpture as a way for them to express themselves?"

"Yeah, but…"

"But what?"

"I like working at Crimson. I never thought I'd say it, but it's cool spending time with Grant."

"Uh huh, I'm sure it's Grant you like spending your time with." Oh God, here we go, Relationship 101, I thought to myself and managed to not roll my eyes or groan. "Of course with a place like this and a gift like that," she pointed at my necklace, "who wouldn't be swayed?"

"Is that what you think? I'm not for sale, Mom. God!" My eyes stung with tears as I glared at her.

"I didn't mean it like that! I'm sorry." She reached over and grabbed my hand. "I was commenting on my life. Your father was so smooth and seemed to have endless funds for extravagance." She looked at me and I could see the pain that still haunted her eyes. My father had left her high and dry, drained the bank accounts, trashed her credit and left all of us behind in a house that was in foreclosure. To say she had trust issues with men was an understatement. "I just want you to be careful. And don't settle. And put yourself first. It may sound selfish, but you need to come first."

I rolled my eyes. "Are you done with the lecture Mom?"

"Yes," she smiled tentatively and patted the back of my hand before withdrawing hers. I yawned and stood up. She stood with me and we walked inside the condo together. We hugged goodnight and she went into the guest room and I into the master bedroom. I was tired, but knew sleep wouldn't come so I drew a hot bubble bath in the big tub. I moved stealthily through the condo to snag a bottle of red wine and a glass out of the kitchen.

I shut the bedroom door behind me and then the bathroom door. With the candles lit and a full glass of wine in hand, I was ready to enjoy my bath. Soon I relaxed enough and began to doze off in the tub. Sleep might come after all tonight. I dried off and crawled into the king sized bed, which seemed enormous and empty without Dominic. I was asleep before my head hit the pillow.

The dream started out nice. I was swimming in the ocean, the sun high above and reflecting bright white off of the sand. I floated weightless in the water and bobbed with the gentle lapping waves. Dominic and Grant were on the shore waving at me. I waved back and dove under the surface. When I came up for air the atmosphere had changed. Dark, stormy clouds boiled in the sky and the sea had become choppy. Alarmed, I looked for Dom and Grant on the beach. They were gone. Something bumped into my back and moved away then collided with me again. I spun around and screamed. A body floating facedown in the sea moved with the surf. Panic set in and I started to swim toward the shoreline. When I turned, a different body, also facedown blocked my path. Then I noticed the water was blood red and corpses floated on the top of the ocean, in every direction as far as I could see. I opened my mouth to scream again and nothing happened, the air around me was void of sound, muted.

I woke in a cold sweat and with a pounding heart. I reflexively reached for Dom, but he was gone. Disoriented, I briefly panicked, still caught between my nightmare and reality. Finally, the surroundings of our bedroom became familiar and I remembered where Dominic was. My head ached and I had cottonmouth, the beginning of a hangover setting in. I rolled over and stared at the closed bedroom door wanting the comfort of my mom. On her good days she would make the nightmares disappear so I could fall back asleep. This time I couldn't tell her the source of my terrors. The boogeyman wasn't in my closet and there wasn't a monster under the bed, the horrors in my dreams were real.

Chapter 22

With college out of the way I had more time on my hands than I knew what to do with. My days fell into a pattern of sleeping, usually restlessly, until noon and driving to Fairmount Park for a run. I would grab a bagel, pretzel or hoagie for lunch and then meander around the Art Museum. Something about the calm interior and hushed reverence visitors had for the exhibits were soothing.

After spending a few hours in the museum I would zip home in my fabulous new car. Dominic was usually waiting for me and we would go to dinner before work. It didn't matter which restaurant he took me too, everyone knew him and we always got the best treatment. There were definite perks to dating a Mafioso. Our favorite restaurant, and one we had to visit at least every other week, was Franco's. Aunt Gloria would fuss over us like nobody's business. Bianca would grill me about college as she was going to Temple University in the fall.

Up until late June I had been waitressing in the VIP section until one night Miranda interrupted me while I was setting up.

"I need your help." She pleaded.

"Sure, what's up?"

"Joey and Grant got called away on 'business' I need someone to work the gun check."

"Oh." I was suddenly nervous. I had never touched a gun before. "Okay."

"Brittany will work VIP tonight. She'll be beside herself with joy."

There was something disconcerting about taking firearms from drunken people. Even more disconcerting was handing the weapons back to them when they could barely speak, let alone stand. I handled the guns like they were made of extremely fragile glass. It would be just my luck that I accidentally shot someone or myself. Up at the front desk I was able to observe who didn't have to check a gun. Quite a number of people were allowed to go around the metal detectors and I suspected that they were all packing.

At the end of the night Miranda handed me $400 and asked if I would be able to work the gun check one night a week. I agreed as it really wasn't as intimidating as I had imagined it to be. After work we all met up in Miranda's car to smoke up. Ever since I moved in with Dom, Miranda and I had gotten really close. Any animosity Grant had previously felt toward Dominic slowly dissipated too. Now that I was aware of the mafia ways, Grant had given up on attempts to keep me from Dominic – there didn't seem to be a reason to anymore. Other people used to join in Miranda's after work decompression sessions, but lately it had become exclusive to just us four.

We were parked in the side lot of Crimson that provided a view of the Ben Franklin Bridge. I leaned back against the door and rested my legs on Dominic's lap. He caressed my thighs as we passed a joint between us. We were mellow and relaxed listening to the radio. Grant's cell rang and broke the silence.

"Hello?" I could hear the agitation of the person on the other end, but we couldn't make out what he was saying. Grant turned his head and caught Dominic's eye.

"Yeah, he's with me. We'll be right there." Grant snapped his phone shut.

"Dom and I have to go. Something went down at Butter." Grant leaned over and kissed Miranda.

"Careful," she whispered as he pulled away. "Always," he promised. I lifted my legs off of Dominic's lap and moved closer to him. We kissed and hugged each other goodbye. It was hard to let him go. The boys shut their doors at the same time and ran across the parking lot to Grant's Lexus.

"I wonder what's going on," I said to Miranda.

"I don't know, but I'm sure we'll find out soon enough." She picked up her phone and dialed her father. He picked up after the first ring. "Dad, what happened at Butter?" Her eyes got wide and then narrowed "Really?" She gave me significant look in the rear view mirror. "Yeah, he and Dom left like a minute ago. Okay, lemme know. Bye."

"Wow," she said as she put the phone back in her purse.

"What?" I asked, curious.

"One of the Nucci boys just tried to take out Uncle Al."

"What!" I gasped. "Is he okay?"

"Yes, the bullet only grazed his hair, thank God. This move is ballsy. We've only taken Nucci Soldiers, but to go after a rival Capo…" she paused. "They're planning to retaliate. All of the boys are having a meeting." Miranda looked dejected at that statement. She was not and never would be considered one of the boys. I flashed back to the murder scene I witnessed months ago; another bloodbath was in the making. My stomach rolled with unease. Miranda must have seen the distress on my face.

"Don't worry Nat. Everything's fine." She seemed so confident.

"How can you be so sure?"

"Because the Grabanos aren't going anywhere," she replied, which wasn't really a good explanation.

When I got back to the condo I anxiously paced the length of the living room waiting for Dominic to get home. The pacing didn't help so I sat on the leather sectional to wait. Exhaustion caught up to me and I passed out. I didn't hear Dominic come home but woke when I felt him sink into the sofa next to me. Relief washed over me; he was intact. I crawled onto his lap and covered him with kisses.

"I'm glad you're home. I missed you." I didn't admit how I was worried sick that he was a target for the Nuccis. Sensing my concern he laid me down on the sofa, trapping me beneath his body. Lowering his head he kissed my lips; I opened to him and his tongue slid in. What started out as agonizingly slow grew in urgency. Wrapping my arms around his neck, I drew him closer, matching his intensity. My legs fell open and I cradled his body with mine, feeling all of the hard and soft parts. I surrendered completely and with each caress, each stroke, he made me forget my worries. Spent and sated, we fell asleep wrapped around each other. There, in the comfort of his arms, I slept; a peaceful, dreamless sleep.

Chapter 23

Most nightclubs were slow in the summer since at least half of the city migrated to the Jersey shore on the weekends. Crimson wasn't affected by that trend and continued to thrive. One hot and steamy Saturday night in July, I was working the gun check, desperate for the front doors to stay closed long enough for the air conditioning to cool the entryway. Sweat dripped down the back of my neck under the heavy blanket of my hair.

Joey B. was working the door when I noticed him stiffen. A large group of men walked up to the door. Joey radioed Grant and moments later he appeared and went to greet the party.

"Welcome gentleman." He held out his arm in a welcoming gesture and let the group pass without going through the metal detectors. To the naked eye Grant seemed perfectly normal, but I grew up with him and knew him better than anyone. He was stressed. The film of sweat above his upper lip was the first sign, the next was the way he rapidly licked his lips. Something was up and the tension seemed to infect all of the employees. The strained atmosphere increased when a half hour later Uncle Marco, Uncle Al, Dominic's dad, Rico, and about ten soldiers filed through the front door.

The second Miranda came up to the front desk I jumped at the chance to find out what was going on.

"Did you see that big group come in?" she asked. I nodded. "Those are some of the Nucci boys. A few capos and soldiers," she explained. That would explain the tension.

"Why did Grant let them in, and with their guns?" I hissed.

"It's all a ridiculous façade if you ask me," Miranda confessed. "It's like some macho thing. We show that we are completely unaffected and unafraid of their presence. Meanwhile, we're all on edge because people are drinking and armed. Anything can happen." I nodded again, my mouth was dry. "I don't think anything will happen here tonight though," she continued.

"Why do you think that?" I asked.

"The Mayor and District Attorney are sitting in VIP. It would be foolish to try anything with them around."

"That's good," I said and breathed a sigh of relief. The relief didn't last long. Shortly before last call Joey B.'s cell phone rang. Almost instantly he took off in a run down the walkway to the club, leaving the front door unattended. Gina, who ran the cash register, and I were the only ones up front.

"What was that all about?" Gina asked me.

"I have no idea." A small group of regulars walked in and they looked around surprised to see the door bouncer-less. "Something going on?" one of the men asked.

"Bathroom break," I lied. The man shrugged his shoulders and continued on. Minutes passed and Joey B. still didn't return.

"The door usually isn't left unattended like this," Gina remarked.

"Well, it's not busy so it isn't that big of a deal, is it?"

"I know the boss likes to have some muscle up here…it deters thieves. The register gets pretty full."

"Oh…" I hadn't thought of that. The front desk area was cut-off from the rest of the club. There was a door to Miranda's office, but that was it aside from the long walkway, which led into the main part of the club. The entire entryway was glass and we were as visible as if we were sitting in a fishbowl. Someone could easily walk in, rob us and walk back out into the night. If anyone ever did attempt this, they would have to be crazy to hold up a place owned by the mafia. "I pity the person who robs this place."

"Yeah, I know, right?" Gina laughed. "Marco would not be happy."

We passed the time chatting, stopping occasionally so I could return guns to their owners. We heard the DJ announce that the club was closing in ten minutes and we braced ourselves to handle the exiting crowd. Fortunately Joey B. returned and helped funnel people through. Several men hit on me and Gina; the more persistent ones were physically ushered out. Joey B. got noticeably more irritated when Gina got hit on. I wondered if something was happening between those two. They wouldn't be the first co-workers to date each other.

Miranda walked up with the Mayor, the District Attorney and their wives. She was laying on the Grabano charm as she personally escorted them out. Finally, the last customer left and Joey B. secured the doors. His hulking size almost blocked the entrance. Gina closed out the register and I grabbed the gun check cash box. Gina and I went through the side door to Miranda's office. She wasn't there so we walked through and out the other door that lead directly to the club, right by Dominic's bar. I looked up eager to see his handsome face and was disappointed to find him absent. Then I noticed that several employees had gathered around Allegra. She was sobbing uncontrollably and Brittany had her arm around her in an attempt to console her.

"Uh oh," Gina muttered under her breath and left my side to go see Allegra. I glanced up at VIP and immediately wished I hadn't. The Nucci boys and the Grabano boys were arguing intensely. Marco and Rico were in the front yelling at the two front leaders of the Nucci group. Grant and Dominic stood behind them, ready to draw their weapons. I knew Dominic had used a gun before, but I'd never seen him with one and so eager to use it.

Forcing myself to look away, I hurried over to the bar to find out what was going on. Miranda saw me approaching and stepped away from the cluster to talk. Her face was pinched and anxious.

"What is going on?" I asked her.

She pulled me to the side and answered in a hushed voice, "Allegra's father was killed tonight."

"Oh my God! Poor Allegra! Was this a hit?" I asked although I had a feeling I already knew the answer. Allegra's father was an accountant who assisted with certain business transactions and was good friends with Dominic's dad. It made sense that Brittany would be the one to help Allegra since her father had been killed under similar circumstances.

"We think so, although the Nuccis are denying it. That is what all the shouting is about." She tilted her head in the direction of VIP. My heart was stuck in my throat. The situation up there seemed to be unraveling and I feared someone else was going to get killed tonight. Summoning up courage I didn't know I possessed, I proceeded to march towards VIP. Miranda caught up to me on the dance floor and grabbed my arm.

"What are you doing?" she hissed.

"I'm putting an end to this."

"Are you fucking crazy?" I didn't answer her; afraid my courage would falter, and continued to march forward. "Oh for the love of Christ, I'm not letting you do this alone, both Grant and Dom will have my head," Miranda said as she caught up to me. Grant eyed us warily as we approached. He grew more alarmed when we walked up the steps and moved behind the Grabano group. Dominic mouthed "What are you doing?" to me, I ignored him. Miranda followed my lead as we moved to the center, standing between both groups. Each side quieted instantly at the unexpected interruption.

"Gentleman," I addressed the two groups. "Before you all get trigger happy can I say something?"

The front man on the Nucci side looked amused. "By all means, Miss?"

"Ross."

"Miss Ross, you have our full attention." His lips twitched as he tried to suppress a laugh. I would probably find the situation amusing too if I was in his shoes. What would possess two young women, unarmed and outnumbered, to stand in the middle of an imminent showdown?

I could tell that the Nucci side became less defensive in their stance. I couldn't say the same for the Grabano side, especially for Dominic and Grant. They both looked poised to fight and were watching the other side for any movement. I was shaking badly and really wasn't sure what to say next.

"Thank you," I began. "I just wanted to point out a couple of things." I paused to look at everyone. "First, I understand that family means a lot around here. You are all here because of family, right?" A few murmurs of agreement could be heard from both sides. "Take away the differences between your families for a moment; the fact is that there is a girl down there," I pointed at Allegra, "who just lost her father. Now, I don't know who was responsible, but I think enough blood has been spilled tonight." I stopped and let that statement sink in. "Secondly, the mayor and district attorney just left. They can identify everyone here tonight…probably not a good time to start shooting up the place." I heard more rumblings of agreement and could feel the atmosphere change. It wasn't as charged with hostility anymore. Even Dominic and Grant seemed to relax.

"Natalie, you are absolutely correct," Marco stated. "This isn't the time or place." The underlying message was clear; there would be another time, another place. A score still needed to be settled.

"I agree Marco. The lady has a point. Let's go." The front leader of the Nuccis lowered his guard and motioned for his boys to follow.

Grant escorted the group out. When they were out of eyesight Dominic hurried to my side. I could tell he was upset. "What was that all about? You could have gotten yourself killed!"

"I think that was bold and just what we needed." Uncle Marco remarked as he came to join Dominic, Miranda and I. "The situation was going to get out of hand and we needed a cool head. Good move Natalie," he praised. Uncle Al and Rico nodded in agreement, they came to stand behind Marco.

"Um, thank you? It wasn't my idea though."

"It wasn't?"

"No, it was all Miranda. She thought it would be better if I did the speaking. They might not have listened to her since she's a Grabano." Marco turned to appraise his daughter. He looked at her with a little more deference. I snuck a wink at the bewildered looking Miranda.

"Well, Miranda, I'm impressed! Very clever." He put his arm around her shoulders and kissed the top of her head.

"I learned from the best," she reciprocated the compliment and smiled up at her father.

Grant returned and was about ready to light into me when he saw the glow on Miranda's face and that Dominic was more relaxed.

"What did I miss?"

"That you're dating probably the most brilliant woman in the world." Marco answered and he filled Grant in on the recent disclosure.

"That was a risky move and I'm glad we had the outcome that we did," Grant remarked. He still didn't look pleased with our actions. We probably hadn't heard the last of it, but Grant wouldn't say anything in front of the hierarchy.

"I know. But you all are willing to listen to reason every now again, I assumed the Nucci boys were capable of it too," Miranda responded, joking lightly, willing to play along that it was her idea from the start.

"I may have underestimated you Miranda. Keep on surprising me okay, kid?" Marco complimented his daughter again before leaving with Al and Rico to go see Allegra. One thing I knew for sure was that Allegra would be taken care of. When one of their own is slain, 'the family' is always there for emotional and financial support and can be counted on to avenge the murder.

I was happy to give Miranda the credit. She was constantly struggling to find her place in the misogynistic hierarchy and didn't want to be discounted because she was a woman. Tonight may have given her a chance at more.

Chapter 24

Smog shrouded the skyline in a never ending haze that went from yellow to a poisonous orange as temperatures soared. Humidity oppressed air and sleepless nights led to irritable masses. As if in synch with the weather, the feud between the Grabanos and the Nuccis escalated. Violence gripped the city as the Grabano family defended their territory. Allegra's father's murder set off a bloody crime spree that kept the media busy. They reported on car bombings and drive-by gangland shootings erupting all over the city. Grant and Dominic were busy attending top secret strategy sessions during the day and working at night.

With the spare time on my hands and spare cash in my pocket, I rented a small space at a local artist's co-op in Manayunk. It was nice to get back to my creative roots and I hadn't realized how much my new life had consumed my old one. Getting away from the drama of the mob to carve a little niche for myself was just what I needed.

The atmosphere at the co-op was laid back and had a hippy vibe. A bong sat in the corner and everyone contributed to the pot of weed that sat on the table. Days would be spent opening up my creativity. Some days I would paint, others were spent on the pottery wheel or sculpting freehand. It was a release and enabled me to block out the murders that were taking place all over the city.

At the end of the day I would leave relaxed and mentally prepared to face the drama again. One night I arrived home and was surprised to find Dominic already there. His face lit up when I walked through the door. His smile and brilliant eyes still made my heart melt.

"Hi baby," he said softly into my ear as he wrapped his arms around me.

"I'm glad you're home," I said against his chest, inhaling the spice of his cologne. We stood there embracing each other, enjoying the moment. I shifted my head and smelled something other than cologne. My mouth started to water.

"Mmmm. What's that smell?"

"I made dinner."

"You can cook?" I looked at him amazed. "All this time we've been eating out and you can cook?" I followed my nose to the living room where Dominic had set up a candlelit dinner on the coffee table.

"Yummy, steak and asparagus - some of my favorites!"

"I know," Dominic chuckled at my enthusiasm. "I also made garlic mashed potatoes."

"Sounds delicious. I'm impressed."

"I got a special recipe from the head chef at Butter," he revealed.

I sat down cross legged on the floor. Dominic filled our wine glasses with merlot and sat down next to me. The food was superb.

"This is so nice, thanks." I reached for Dominic's hand and he met me halfway.

"I know this summer hasn't been easy for you and I haven't been around a lot." He lifted my hand to his mouth and kissed it.

"I've missed you," I admitted, "Although I am enjoying the studio."

"I can tell. You look so serene when you come home. It erases the worry from your face." He brushed his hand across my forehead and I closed my eyes, enjoying the caress. "Are you doing okay, Nat? Things have been getting crazy and this is still new to you and all…"

"You're right. It hasn't been easy. I've never been a violent person and now I am surrounded by violence. Plus, not a day goes by that I don't worry about you and Grant."

"You don't have to worry about us. We can handle it," he attempted to reassure me.

"You guys are both in the middle of everything though. You must be considered a big target to the Nuccis." Emotion caused my voice to crack and I choked back tears. Dominic moved over so he was sitting behind me, he wrapped his arms and legs around me.

"Shhh, baby, it's okay," he whispered in a soothing voice. "Grant and I are being careful."

"I'm sure Allegra's dad told her the same thing."

"We are being careful. Do you trust me?"

"Of course," I didn't hesitate answering because I did trust him.

"I'll be careful for you, I promise." I had to take his word even though the promise would be hard to keep, especially if a target had been placed on his back. I kissed the top of his arm.

"Okay, I'll try not to worry too much," I promised in return.

"I think your promise to me will be harder to keep," he joked. I playfully nudged my elbow into his ribs. Dominic kissed the top of my head and extricated himself out from behind me.

"Where are you going?"

"To get dessert," he said over his shoulder, walking into the kitchen. He quickly returned with a dessert plate in each hand. When he set the plates down I saw that each had a cannoli.

"Yum! Are these from Termini Bros.?" I asked, referring to the Italian bakery that had been around for decades. As far as I was concerned, they had the best cannoli in the city.

"Yup," he answered with a grin.

"I'm sure glad I exercise every day because I would be a total cow right about now. You Grabanos know how to feed a girl!"

"Not to mention the Manganellis," Dominic reminded me of his Aunt Gloria and Uncle Franco.

"Especially the Manganellis – especially Aunt Gloria," I agreed.

"It's nice to be with a girl who appreciates food and isn't afraid to eat in front of me. So many girls I dated were always on a diet or would only eat salad." His nose scrunched up at this thought.

"Let me guess, Brittany."

"Yeah, she was one. How'd you guess?"

"She is always complaining about how fat she is in the employee lounge and claims that cocaine is the best diet drug ever."

Dom nodded his head in silent agreement because he knew exactly what I was talking about. We got off topic when he fed me a piece of his cannoli. Some of the creamy filling remained on his finger so I sucked it off, licking the very tip before drawing his finger back in my mouth. He moaned in response.

"God, I'm glad we don't have to work tonight."

"You don't have to meet with the boys tonight either?" I asked, crawling onto his lap.

"Nope." He smiled at me. "I thought we'd hang out and spend some time together." I liked the sound of that – some actual couple time. Placing my hands on his cheeks, I lowered my mouth to his. Traces of sweet cream were on his lower lip and I drew it into my mouth, nibbling, sucking, causing Dom to groan and grab onto my hips. He was already hard and I felt my insides melt. Rocking forward to press closer, I gasped when he thrust to meet me.

Dessert was forgotten.

We went to bed early, leaving a trail of clothes in our wake. I lay on my back and Dom lifted a leg, slowly kissing from my ankle to my inner I thigh. He'd pause and watch me squirm with anticipation before continuing. Lust pooled in my center and spilled out to meet Dom's eager tongue. He licked and sucked, testing my limits. Balling the sheets in my fists, my hips rose to meet his mouth and I cried out as his tongue dove in deep. My body arched on its own as my muscles separated from bone and I collapsed back against the mattress, panting and weak, but wanting more. He rose over me and took my mouth. I wrapped my legs around his hips, pressing my breasts against his chest. Our naked bodies molded around each other and despite the air conditioning, we were working up a sweat.

Dom abandoned my mouth and lowered his lips to my breasts, sucking on a nipple, grazing his teeth across the tip. I moaned and thrust against his erection, which was heavy against my thigh. "Dom, please," I begged, scratching his back, trying to find any means possible to release the pressure building within. He moved onto the other nipple, sucking hard, making me gasp and writhe even more beneath him.

He chuckled, a low throaty sound, almost like a growl before thrusting into me. Surprised and relieved at his sudden entrance, I cried out and opened my legs wider, wanting all of him. He hovered over me, chest glistening with sweat, as he pulled almost all the way out before slamming into me again. My body went nuclear and burst around him, but I didn't slow down and met him thrust for thrust. He watched me with a gaze almost equally as penetrating and that turned me on even more. Shuddering, I came again and swore my bones had completely melted away, but Dom wasn't done. In one fluid motion, he flipped me onto my hands and knees and slid in from behind. I moaned and pushed back against him, loving the pressure. He filled me completely and with each thrust, hit some spot deep inside that made me quiver. The pressure built again and I felt Dom slow down, getting deeper right before he exploded and I came with him.

I fell asleep with Dom curled up behind me, his arm draped across my side, keeping me tucked up next to him. Then the dreams came. I was standing in the hallway of The Speak. The pool of blood was creeping closer to me and I was frozen in place. The bits of skull and the globs of brain moved with the blood. I watched in horror as it approached, but that wasn't what had me frozen in place. The source of the blood, the person lying dead on the floor was...Dominic.

I woke up screaming, my body soaked in a cold sweat. Dominic jerked awake when I screamed. His arm hugged me closer.

"Nat! Shhh, it's okay, I'm right here. You had a bad dream."

My heart pounded and I took big heaving gasps of air in an attempt to calm down. I rolled over so I could see Dominic and make sure he was real. I started sobbing and pressed my face into his bare chest. He hugged me closer and smoothed my hair. "Shhh baby, it's okay," he kept murmuring until my sobs dissipated. He kept me pressed close to him until my body stopped shaking. I could feel him looking down at me and I looked up at him, my eyes puffy and sore from the tears.

"Are you alright? What was your dream about?"

I couldn't tell him what I really dreamt, so I told him that it was the scene from The Speak with the three men that Grant had shot. Technically, that was the source of my bad dreams.

"Oh baby," he cried as he pulled me closer to him. "I'm so sorry you had to see that." He kissed my forehead. I laid there pressed close to Dominic grateful that the dream was just a dream. I couldn't bear to lose him. I had fallen hard for this man, harder than I thought possible. He felt right to me and despite the chaos going on around us; he was the calm inside the storm. Never before had I felt comfortable enough with a man to allow myself to be completely exposed and vulnerable and not care. I knew in my heart that Dominic would never hurt or betray me. I sighed as I let the calm that Dominic emanated envelope me. "Love you, Nat," he whispered and kissed my forehead. My heart froze for just a second, froze with fear, surprise and…recognition.

"I love you too, Dom," I lifted my face to look up at him and he kissed me. Yes, I loved him. I had promised my silence to the mob so that Grant and I could live. I never thought that I could find happiness here too.

Chapter 25

July was speeding by. Dominic and Grant continued to be busy, the mob war showing no signs of ending. I hopped into my car one morning with the top down. A cool front had moved in that dropped the humidity. The beastly mugginess had disappeared overnight and I could actually drive with the convertible down without the risk of heat stroke. I pulled out onto Columbus Blvd. and continued up to Spring Garden on my way to Fairmount Park, looking forward to running without choking on humidity and smog. I turned left onto Spring Garden and noticed a blue sedan behind me turned too. I continued up Spring Garden and crossed over to Fairmount. The sedan turned with me. I zipped up Fairmount and found a parking spot near the path that looped through the park. A glance in the rearview mirror showed the same sedan pulling into a spot a few cars down.

Not sure if I was being paranoid or if it was just coincidence, I paid extra attention to my surroundings as I ran through the park. Nothing seemed out of the ordinary, but I felt uneasy when I walked back to my car and spied the sedan still parked in the same spot. A man in a suit was sitting inside reading a newspaper. When I reached my car, I stretched and glanced casually back at the sedan, the guy still hadn't budged. This wasn't unusual though; a lot of people take lunch breaks and just sit in their cars.

I hopped into my car and took off back towards Center City. As I went around City Hall to continue south on Broad St., a blue sedan appeared in my side view mirror. Startled, I looked again and confirmed it was the same car and driver. This left me slightly unnerved. Determined to shake the guy, if in fact I was being followed, I made a quick right onto Walnut St., just as the light was turning red. I parallel parked a block away from Rittenhouse Square and waited. My car isn't very inconspicuous so if I was being followed, they would be quick to spot it. Sure enough, a few minutes later, the same non-descript blue sedan appeared in my side view mirror as it drove up the street. The car pulled into a loading zone a few cars down and sat with the engine idling.

I called Grant on his cell phone, wondering if his overprotectiveness had returned with a vengeance.

"Nat, what's up?"

"Are you having me followed?"

"What! No. Why?" He asked, sounding surprised.

I filled him in on the sedan that had been following me all morning. After I gave him the description of the car he identified who it was.

"The Feds. They've been tailing us for a few weeks; they might have been tailing you long before today. This is to be expected."

"So, they just follow you around? For how long?" I was feeling violated.

"Until they can make an arrest."

"An arrest?"

"Relax, Nat. It happens every time the body count starts to rise. They suspect it's mob related and they need to make it known that they are watching."

"But why me? I'm not involved in any criminal activity."

"I don't like talking about this on the phone; it's not secure. Where are you?"

"I was trying to lose my tail," I admitted. "My life is beginning to sound more like a bad TV movie." Grant chuckled when he heard this. "I'm right by Rittenhouse Square."

"Can you come over to my place?"

"Sure, I'll be there in a few minutes." I put my car into gear and pulled back onto Walnut Street. Seconds later the sedan pulled out and fell in line two cars behind me. Grant lived at the Lofts 640 off of Broad St. and it was only a matter of driving a few blocks. Grant opened the door to his studio as I was still knocking.

"Were you followed over here?"

"Yeah, they aren't really good at being inconspicuous are they?"

"They want you to know they're watching…to shake you up a bit."

"Well, it's working," I stated. Grant gave me a concerned look. "I don't like the idea of being watched…it creeps me out."

"You don't have anything to worry about. It's the Grabanos they want." That revelation triggered something territorial in me.

"You mean Dom?" I clarified.

"Not so much, but definitely Uncle Marco, Rico and Al. They'll try to pick off the lower ranks until they get to them."

"Pick off?"

"Yeah, have them turn and testify against the family. The feds will build their case until it is solid. It happened with Scarfo. Many of his presumably most loyal soldiers and capos turned against him."

"Why? That's awful."

"They were pinned. It was either them or Scarfo going to prison. They chose to save themselves. It was their way out."

"Oh…and I'm Dominic's girlfriend so I'm of interest to them?"

"Not only are you Dom's girlfriend, but my sister *and* you work at Crimson. You're probably considered Mafioso by now."

His words shocked me. Sure most of my acquaintances were affiliated with the mob, but I never considered myself one of them. But, to the outside world, I must look like it.

"Nat, are you alright?" Grant gave me the concerned look again.

"I think so. I just never thought that I would be…you know."

Grant sighed and put his hand on my shoulder. "I know. I should never have gotten you involved." I thought of Dominic and the love I felt for him. He made the sacrifice worth it.

"I can handle it. I'll be fine," I paused. "So now that I'm considered Mafioso do I get a gun too? Do I get to whack somebody?" I joked. Grant scowled at my bad humor.

"Seriously, if any of the boys try to get you more involved, come talk to me. I won't let you get any more involved than you already are."

"God, I was just joking! Do you really think that I could kill someone?" Grant must have envisioned me toting a gun because his face broke out in a smile and he laughed. His hazel eyes sparkled and the smile broke away the tension that had taken up residence on his face.

"I'm starving. What do you have to eat?" I helped myself to his kitchen. The refrigerator contained a pizza box with one dried up slice, a carton of rancid milk, a dessicated orange and something fuzzy in a microwave dish. A quick search of the cabinets revealed a can of tuna fish and a box of stale croutons. The sleek ultramodern apartment with all of the modern conveniences lacked one simple thing – food.

"Seriously Grant, how does Miranda let you live like this? It's sad…no it's beyond sad, it's pathetic. Do I need to call mom?" I threatened jokingly.

Grant gave me a sheepish look. "I don't stay here that much. I'm usually at Miranda's. Actually, since you brought it up, my lease is up soon and Miranda and I are going to move in together."

"Really? The commitment-phobe is moving in with a girl?" I teased. Grant and I were both known for being non-committal.

"I figured if you can handle it without a violent allergic reaction, then I can definitely handle it," he joked back.

"Ouch!" I laughed. My stomach growled angrily not liking to be ignored. "Damn. Dominic has me used to regular five course meals. I really need to eat - you hungry?"

Grant smiled and said, "I could eat."

"Wanna drive my car?" I dangled the keys out in front of him. He snatched them up eagerly. His lead foot was probably already twitching.

***

A week had passed since Grant and I had lunch and the VIP section was busy, busier than usual for a Thursday. I ran around at warp speed to keep the drinks flowing. Being busy caused the night to fly by and it was over before I knew it. I plopped down on a bar stool exhausted.

"You look wiped," Dominic commented.

"I am." I replied, stifling a yawn.

"Were we up too late last night?" he smiled mischievously. I blushed and smiled innocently at him while batting my eyelashes. "I have no idea what you're talking about." We both chuckled at our private moment. I saw Brittany in my peripheral vision pretending to gag – dramatically. I ignored her.

"You need to go home and get some sleep." Dominic urged. "My dad and I have some stuff to deal with after work." They were probably plotting the next hit on a Nucci boy. I didn't need to know the details. Since I had learned that the FBI had an interest in watching me, I figured the less I knew the better. I may be considered guilty by association and that was as guilty as I wanted to be.

"I won't disagree with you there." I stifled another yawn. I leaned over the bar to kiss Dominic goodbye. He gently massaged the back of my neck as we kissed. "Love you." I whispered.

"Love you too." He kissed the tip of my nose. This time I didn't see Brittany pretending to gag, but I heard her. I looked over at her and smiled gloatingly. She stopped and glared at me.

Joey B escorted me to my car. It didn't take me long to notice the non-descript sedan sitting in the shadows of an abandoned warehouse next door to Crimson. I fought the urge to wave to them, but Joey B. looked at me and shook his head as if reading my mind. "Don't encourage them Nat," he warned in his gruff voice.

"I won't Joey," I promised.

"You going straight home?" he asked protectively as he held the door open for me and shut it once I was in the driver's seat. Grant's bouncers had the same annoying need to watch over me.

"Yes, I'm exhausted." He nodded in approval and tapped on the hood as I pulled out of the parking spot.

I passed by the sedan and, as per usual, it turned to follow me home. What wasn't usual was when the car followed me up the driveway. The valet opened my door and I stepped out of the car overwhelmed by uncertainty. Were they going to approach me? The driver's side door of the sedan opened up and answered my question. I inhaled sharply and braced myself as the agent approached. His partner stayed in the car.

"Miss Ross, can I have a word?" *Shit, he knows my name.* I nodded and tried to swallow, but my mouth was too dry. I followed him to stand over by his car, away from the lobby entrance.

"You probably already know that we're monitoring the activity of the Grabano family," the agent began. I nodded again.

"We're also investigating the suspicious disappearance of Carmine Bruno, Vincent DeMateo and Joe Benucci."

"Who?" I asked, confused.

"They were part of your boss' circle until a few months ago. They all disappeared the same night."

"I don't know who they are."

"We thought that since you work at Crimson and who you're associated with, that you may have heard the names mentioned?" The agent suggested.

"Sorry, I haven't. Agent?"

"Oh, right. I'm Agent Phillips." He held his hand out. I shook it, briefly.

"Is that all you wanted to talk to me about Agent Phillips?" I asked and stifled yawn. I was so tired I wasn't even nervous any more.

"Uh, yes. That's it for now. Thank you for your time Miss Ross."

"Goodnight." I dismissed myself and walked to the lobby. The doorman held the door open for me and eyed me curiously. I schlepped across the lobby willing my feet to carry me to the elevator.

As soon as I was inside the condo, I started undressing not caring that my clothes were being left on the living room, hallway and bedroom floors. I scrubbed the make-up off of my face, brushed my teeth and crawled into bed.

Sometime after dawn Dominic curled up beside me. He kissed my shoulder and I grunted to acknowledge his presence, too tired to do anything else. Dominic chuckled as he drifted off to sleep.

The brightness of the room woke me up. The blinds were up and the sun was pouring in through the picture window. Dominic's arm was draped across his eyes in an attempt to block the light. I got up to shut the blinds and looked across to the Camden waterfront, even the murky Delaware River managed to sparkle. With the room much darker, I crawled back into bed to get some more sleep. Dominic pulled me up next to him.

"Thanks for getting the blinds," he muttered in a sleepy voice.

"No problem, it was so bright."

"How was the rest of your night?" he asked.

"Fine, I pretty much went straight to bed, except for the FBI wanted to talk to me." I could feel Dominic tense up behind me.

"What did they want?" His voice was more awake now.

"They were asking me about these three guys, Bruno, Benucci and someone else...I can't remember." Dominic tensed up even more when I mentioned the names. "I had never heard of them before."

"And you told them that?"

"Yeah, I didn't have any information. Even if I did I wouldn't say anything. Uncle Marco would have my head, remember?" Dominic still hadn't relaxed. "You know those names, the guys the FBI are looking for, don't you?" He didn't answer right away.

"You know them too."

"I do?"

"Yeah. Those are the guys that Grant killed last spring at The Speak." Now it was my turn to tense up. I rolled over to look at him, neither one of us was going to go back to sleep anytime soon.

"Are you serious?" The bodies on the floor had been nameless until now. Now that I knew their identities it made the crime so much more real. An involuntary shudder shook my body. "I didn't want to know that."

Dominic hugged me close and kissed my forehead. "You're handling all this amazingly well," he whispered. I guess he was right. Aside from the occasional nightmares, FBI surveillance and first - hand knowledge of a triple murder, life was great. I was in love and made good money, which enabled me to pursue my creative side. If I kept my nose out of the mafia's business I could get used to this life. I had no other choice. I thought back to Marco's threat and how menacing the expression on his face was when he gave me the ultimatum. Another shudder shook my body and Dominic held me tight, his naked body, tan from the summer sun, contrasted against my fair skin. I could feel the familiar warmth stirring deep in my core and I pressed even closer. Yeah, I could definitely get used to this life.

Chapter 26

Miranda was barking out orders like a drill sergeant when Dominic and I arrived a few minutes late for work. We had spent the entire day in bed and it was difficult to tear ourselves away. She glared at us and continued her rant. Employees were bustling around Crimson obeying her every command.

"What's going on?" I asked her. Miranda could run a tight ship, but I'd never seen her on a tear like this. She gave me an exasperated look. "Didn't Dom tell you?"

"Tell me what?" Now it was Dominic's turn to get the look.

"The five families are coming here tonight!" she hissed.

"The New York five families?" My eyes grew wide. "Why?"

"There's going to be a meeting. The Commission doesn't like what the Nucci family has been doing and wants to set them straight."

"The meeting is here?"

Miranda gave me another look. "No, they're going to meet at the fucking Holiday Inn. Of course they're meeting here."

"You're in VIP tonight Nat, I don't want Brittany in there interfering. Go set up," she ordered.

"Dom, Dad wants you up there tonight behind the bar as an extra set of ears."

"I'm on it."

We walked to Miranda's office and Dom unlocked the door. I set my purse on the desk chair. Since Dominic and I had gotten serious, I didn't have to use the employee lounge. We walked over to the VIP section where Grant was going over the security detail with some of the boys.

"This is closed tonight for the private party. If they aren't with any of the families, they don't get access." Wow, it must be a big deal if they were closing down VIP.

"Babe, who all is going to be here?" I asked Dom.

"Dad, Uncle Marco and Uncle Al, the top members of the five families, they make up The Commission and top members of the Nucci family."

"The Nucci family and the Grabano family under one roof again? This can't be good, especially after the big shooting in the Italian Market last week." I responded, feeling a little panicky. The Grabanos were out for blood after that shooting that took out two of our soldiers.

"Don't worry, they won't do anything while the five families are here," he reassured me. I was feeling on edge and hoped Dominic was right.

Crimson started to fill up, except for the VIP section. Several people tried to gain entry, but were blocked by Anthony, one of the largest bouncers on staff. I heard he tried out for the Eagles offensive line. With his bulk, that was easy to believe.

It was close to midnight when I saw Grant parting the crowds to make way for a group of men who were following close behind. I recognized the Grabanos and a couple of the Nucci boys so it was easy to pick out the New York contingency. They carried themselves with an air of superiority. All wore expensive, well tailored suits. The men ranged in age from early forties to late seventies, one of whom looked more dead than alive.

They all filed into VIP and I went to work collecting drink orders. At first everyone stood around chatting amicably. After a few drinks everyone sat down and the meeting began. I hung back in the corner and only went to the table when I was gestured to. Dominic barely paid attention to the drinks he was mixing as he was focusing on the conversation at the table. It was rather genius, actually, because the music was so loud that they didn't have to worry about being overheard outside of the section. There were a few moments when the conversation heated up and hands slammed down on the table. Overall everyone seemed to behave themselves and treated the New York families like they were gods.

One of the Nucci boys waved me over to the table. I stood next to him prepared to take his drink order. His cheeks were rosy and his eyes glassy from the alcohol. Too bad I wasn't allowed to cut this group off, because they needed it. "Hey, you're that girl," he slurred.

"Excuse me?"

"Yeah, you're the ballsy little lady that broke up the fight a month or so ago."

A couple members of the five families were suddenly listening. Marco was quick to jump in and capitalize on the attention.

"Natalie and my daughter, Miranda, waltzed in between my boys and Rocco's boys. It was right here in fact. Nat got us to cool off before we did anything stupid. It was Miranda's idea, but Nat pulled it off," Marco gloated.

One of the men in the New York group kept staring at me and it made me anxious. He sat away from the others, on the end of the booth, as if uncomfortable with close contact. His gray hair was slicked back and his skin, even the whites of his eyes, was yellowish, probably from the chain smoking. I had observed that the entire night he always had a lit cigarette in his right hand. The man leaned over and whispered in Marco's ear. Marco's expression changed from slightly arrogant to vacant. This made me uneasy. He looked at me and his eyes were cold.

"Natalie, Mr. Genovese would like for you to sit with him." I could tell from his tone that this wasn't a request. I looked around uncertainly. Marco's face grew darker the longer I hesitated. Fearing the consequences if I disobeyed, I sat down next to Mr. Genovese and clung to the very edge of the booth, trying to keep our bodies from touching. He reached up and tucked my hair behind my ear, his hand lingering on my chin. The burnt tobacco smell from his fingertips stung my nose and made me want to gag. Who was this man and what gave him the right to touch me? I attempted to inch further away. Mr. Genovese grabbed my wrist and yanked me closer to him. I resisted and he yanked harder.

"Ow! Let go of me!" I yelled and looked to Dominic for help. He was raging and I thought he was going to bust a vein, but he didn't come to my aid.

"Natalie, Mr. Genovese is interested in your company this evening. Behave." Yet another order.

"She is a feisty one isn't she?" Mr. Genovese wheezed approvingly. His hand moved up my thigh and under my skirt. I flinched. Dom's dad, Rico, and Uncle Al wouldn't meet my eyes. I saw Rico's jaw clench. Still, no one would stand up to Mr. Genovese. Miranda breezed up the VIP stairs and froze when she saw me sitting in the booth. Fear registered on her face, only briefly and then, composing herself, walked to her father.

"Miranda, glad you're here. Natalie won't be working the rest of the night. Send Brittany up here to replace her." I wasn't working the rest of the night? Was I going to be stuck here next to this awful man?

"Right away, Dad." Miranda radioed down to the main floor.

Grant escorted Brittany up and she happily bounced into action. Her pupils were dilated, leaving no doubt she was high as a kite. I could see the fury in Grant's eyes, but it wasn't for me. Mr. Genovese seemed amused at the anger being directed towards him. He reached up and caressed my cheek. I cringed, repelled by his clammy, smoky skin. I thought Grant was going to bust a vein too, but he stayed frozen in place. What was wrong with him? Of all people, Grant was the one I could count on to kick some ass and get me out of this situation. Instead he stood by, letting this nasty old man rub his smelly hands all over me.

Brittany entertained the group with her hyper antics and her incredible, overly enhanced boobs captivated the attention of most of the men at the booth, all except Mr. Genovese. He was insistent on exploring my body. I clenched my thighs together in a death grip, blocking his probes. Just when I thought it couldn't get worse, he leaned in close and sniffed my hair, inhaling deeply. Brittany kept throwing sympathetic glances my way. Every time I tried to move, Mr. Genovese pulled me back. He would laugh as if he liked my resistance.

When I realized that I wasn't going to be allowed to leave Mr. Genovese's side, I waved for Brittany. She didn't bounce over, instead she approached with trepidation.

"I want a Stoli and Tonic…and keep them coming." I was going to get so drunk that I didn't remember tonight. I needed to be numb. After I placed the order I glanced over at Dominic again. The rage was still there but he also looked sad.

"I'm sorry," he mouthed and hung his head as if defeated, the fight had deserted him.

With each drink I became more removed from the situation. The voices and faces blurred around me. By the time I was on my sixth round, I couldn't feel my legs, which was perfect because then I couldn't feel Mr. Genovese touching them.

I vaguely remember getting up as the group prepared to leave. I started to walk away, but was pulled back.

"You're coming with me." Mr. Genovese commanded. Narrowing my eyes, I tried to concentrate what he was saying. It sounded like he was speaking underwater. The room spun and I teetered to the left, unsteady on my black leather heels. Mr. Genovese had a vice like grip on my upper arm and prevented my fall. For a man with small stature, he was deceptively strong. We walked by the bar and I reached my free arm out towards Dominic. His eyes were a dark, mossy green and full of desperation. He started to come around to the front of the bar towards me.

"Do not interfere," Marco warned him. Dom stopped and I was yanked along with the rest of the group and taken out the rear exit. Right before I left Crimson I looked up and saw Grant being held back by Anthony "The Giant" and Miranda stood in front with her hand pressed against Grant's chest. Anthony seemed to have a hard time holding my brother back. Grant looked like he was ready to kill.

A black Cadillac sat idling in the lot behind Crimson. A driver opened the door and Mr. Genovese forced me in the back seat. The group dispersed to other cars in the lot. Like a funeral procession, the dark sedans moved in a line down Columbus Blvd. At some point along the way I passed out. Mr. Genovese shook me awake and roughly pulled me out of the car. We were in front of The Speak. I hadn't been here since that fateful night. Visions of bodies lying in pools of blood filled my head. I closed my eyes and was instantly dizzy. Mr. Genovese grabbed my arm again and started leading me to the front door.

I balked and stood my ground. "I am not going in there."

Without warning or hesitation, Mr. Genovese backhanded me. My head snapped and I rocked backwards on my feet, grabbing onto the railing for support. Stunned, I rubbed my stinging cheek and glared at the older man. Adrenaline was coursing through my veins and I felt more alert, more sober. Reflexively, I slapped him back. He grinned, a crazy, unsettling grin.

"I do like the feisty ones," he commented as he looked me over. I was suddenly self-conscious of my revealing outfit. The unspoken rule at Crimson was that the sexier you dressed, the more tips you received. Dominic understood and enjoyed watching me pour my body into tight outfits. Tonight I had chosen a ridiculously short black skirt with a black leather corset top. The corset enhanced my average breasts, which helped me to compete with the cosmetically enhanced ones of my co-workers. Black pantyhose and high black heels completed the ensemble and made my legs look endless. I considered my legs my best feature, the running I did helped to keep them sculpted and muscular. Now, I wished I had chosen a nun's habit to wear instead.

Marco, Rico and Al walked up the sidewalk and stood behind me. The rest of the men from New York arrived seconds later and I was surprised to see Brittany with them. None of the Nuccis had joined the party.

"Stop being difficult Natalie," Marco demanded. "Get inside." The menacing expression on his face made my skin cold. Defeated, I followed Marco up the stairs and into the house.

We moved past Sam, the doorman, and into the bar area. The bartender was extra attentive when he saw who had entered the room. He hustled around accommodating the men from New York, especially Mr. Genovese. I had surmised that Mr. Genovese was the boss of NYC. Why else would everyone dance around at his beck and call? Mr. All Powerful kept a firm grip on my wrist, forcing me to stay by his side. My buzz was wearing off and the numbness subsiding. I ordered more drinks, determined to block as much of this night from my memory. Brittany pulled out a vial of cocaine and sorted out lines on the bar counter. She was surprised when I took the rolled up twenty dollar bill out of her hand and snorted a line up each nostril. I tilted my head back, pure bitterness sliding down the back of my throat. The effects were felt almost instantly. My heart sped up and my pulse was audible. A sip of the vodka tonic washed the rest of the bitterness down. The numbness was almost complete.

After the cocaine was brought out, the party really started to get out of hand. Everyone was wasted. Brittany started to do a strip tease and I had to look away. The sexual tension of eight men in one room and only two women was tangible. Despite all of the alcohol and the coke, my nerves were on edge.

Mr. Genovese – Luigi to his friends – started to get a little too friendly. I tried to shrug him off and he got more aggressive. I stepped away and broke free of his grasp.

"I need to use the bathroom," I grumbled. The bathroom was off of the hallway. When I turned into the hall I half expected the bodies to be there with blood oozing from broken skulls, but no evidence of the crime was visible. I was too caught up in my memory that I didn't notice Uncle Marco following me out of the bar. Grabbing me from behind, he spun me around, pinning me against the wall with his hand on my throat. I gasped for air and struggled against his grip.

"You will do whatever Luigi wants and you will stop being difficult. I own you and I own your brother, remember? You will do as I say." It felt like my eyes were going to burst from the pressure and little black spots danced in front of me.

He released me and I collapsed in a heap on the floor, sucking in big gulps of air. "I und-er-sta-nd," I managed to choke out.

Satisfied, Marco left me on the floor. Down by the front door Sam stared off into the corner, pretending to be oblivious. Crawling into the bathroom, I struggled to regain my composure. I looked into the mirror to assess the damage. My eyes were wide with shock, and dark next to my pale skin. An impression of Marco's hand remained a red phantom on my neck. I combed my fingers through my hair, splashed cold water onto my face and focused on getting my breathing under control. I really wanted to hide in the bathroom and wait the nightmare out, but I wasn't easily forgotten as Marco was soon pounding on the door.

I started to open the door slowly, but Marco forced it open. "Mr. Genovese is waiting for you upstairs, the first door on the left."

So this is how it was going to be; pimped out like some cheap whore? I was backed into a corner without any options. Unwillingly, I made my way up the stairs. The door on the right was slightly ajar, it revealed the sofa I had woken up on months ago, Brittany was pinned down, naked and was being brutally raped by one of the men from New York, and two others waited in line. Her screams were silenced by the gun forced in her mouth, but her eyes pleaded for help. I looked away consumed by the fear that I was about ready to face the same fate.

I bolted down the stairs, missing the last two as I leaped for the door. One of my high heels snapped from the impact of the landing. Sam blocked the doorway and pushed me back. Marco appeared in the entryway of the bar. "I thought we had an understanding," he glowered.

Sam escorted me, shaking and on the brink of hysteria, back up the stairs. Ignoring my begging and pleading, he forced me forward to the first door on the left. In one fluid movement he opened the door, pushed me inside the room and slammed the door shut. Mr. Genovese sat on a bed, the only piece of furniture in the room. He was wearing boxer shorts and a wife beater. His suit was folded in a neat little pile on the windowsill. The white fabric of the wife beater made his skin look jaundiced.

"Ah, Miss Ross, glad you finally made it." He sat on the edge of an old, bare mattress decorated with a pattern that was popular twenty years earlier. It might as well have been a throne the way he sat there with authority, his back straight and shoulders squared. He didn't say anything to me, just patted the empty space next to him, inviting me to sit. I stayed rooted to the floor and didn't budge. He smiled at my defiance. Then he stood up and walked over to me so he was right in my face. I held my breath and turned my head away so I wouldn't have to inhale his noxious odor. Grabbing my chin, he dug his fingers in and forced me to look at him. I glared back. He smiled, briefly, before he kissed me. He pried my lips apart and invaded with his tongue. He might as well have shoved an ashtray in my mouth. I started to gag, bile rising in my throat. I placed my hands on his chest and tried to push him away. His arousal grew the more I struggled and he made sure to press against me as I protested. I lifted my knee up and hit him square in the balls. Instead of dropping into a fetal position, which is what I expected, he backhanded me again and I felt my lip split open. The pain was sudden and surprising, but I would take that over his nasty mouth on mine.

He shoved me against the door, my skull cracking hard on the wood. Dazed I shook my head, trying clear my vision. Mr. Genovese used his body weight to subdue me and attempted to rip my skirt off. His shoulder leaned in towards me so I bit, sinking my teeth into the flesh as deep and as hard as I could. He howled in what I thought was pain, but when he looked at me I saw a tobacco stained grin and anticipation in his eyes.

"Feisty and a biter – even better," he declared. I was horrified. All my self defense efforts were working against me. He was getting more aroused the more I fought back. Catching me off guard, he grabbed me, spun me around and threw me onto the bed. My one hundred fifteen pounds didn't offer much resistance. He ripped off my skirt, shredded my pantyhose and went for my underwear. I kicked and thrashed, trying to inflict as many blows to his head as possible. He laughed as if enjoying the challenge.

My thrashing got weaker as exhaustion set in and my head throbbed with every movement. Finally I stayed still. All the fight in me was spent. I prepared for the violation. Mr. Genovese licked his lips with anticipation as he traced his fingers up my legs to the waistband of my underwear. His hand slid underneath the corset and he twisted my left nipple, painfully. He paused as if waiting for a reaction. I stared vacantly at the blank wall, my vision blurry from tears. I felt the mattress shift as he moved off of me.

He glared at me frustrated, the tent he'd pitched in his boxers was deflating. He turned away from me, put on his clothes and silently left the room.

I don't know how long I laid there. I heard faint voices downstairs, the front door slamming and then silence. The room lightened to gray as the sun began its ascent in the sky. People would be getting up to go to church, to the grocery store, or maybe take a day trip to the shore. I just stayed there, beaten and bruised, afraid to move.

The stillness of the house was disrupted by a soft whimpering. My ears perked up and focused on the location of the sound. Someone else in the house was also crying and in pain. Then I remembered Brittany. She had been through worse than me. I forced myself into a sitting position and when the dizziness subsided, slowly stood up. My broken shoes were useless so I kicked them off before I walked across the room to retrieve my skirt. When I opened the bedroom door, Brittany's cries were much louder and filled the small landing. I crept across to her room. She was completely naked and curled up in a ball on the floor. Blood stained the back of her thighs. She twitched when she heard me approach. Both of her eyes were bruised and swollen shut, it was obvious she couldn't see who was in the room with her. Her whimpering grew louder.

"It's okay, Brit, it's me, Natalie." At the sound of my voice, she broke down into deep heaving sobs. I knelt down beside her and pulled her partly up, so she could lean against me. The force of her sobs wracked my body too. I rocked her gently, like a baby and her sobs slowed down. The damage to her body was far worse than mine. In addition to her swollen eyes, her nose was crooked and bloody and her lips were puffy, most likely from the gun being forced in her mouth. Bruises were beginning to darken and covered the front and back of her torso. I looked around the room for her clothes and couldn't find them. I remembered her strip tease downstairs and figured that's where they were.

"I'm going to go get your clothes. Can you stand?"

"I...I think so," she answered in a hoarse voice. I helped her to her feet, steadying her as she trembled on uncertain legs. Blood was smeared down the inside and front of her thighs too. I grimaced at her condition and was grateful she wasn't able to see herself. I helped her over to the sofa. As I straightened up, the front door downstairs slammed. We both stiffened, fear raised the hairs on the back of my neck.

"Nat, are you here?" a familiar voice echoed through the house. Dominic. I almost cried in relief.

"Up here!" I managed to yell out. Footsteps thundered up the stairs. Dominic appeared in the doorway, Grant's head barely visible behind him.

"Oh my God!" Dominic stopped in his tracks when he saw us. Brittany was cowering behind me.

Grant forced him through the door and followed Dominic into the room. Miranda was right behind them. Her eyes grew wide with horror when she saw us; color fled from her face before she bent over and threw up. Grant rubbed her back and sat her down in one of the club chairs. He and Dominic rushed to my side.

"I'm fine," I lied. I wasn't, but compared to Brittany I was perfect. "We need to get Brittany to a hospital." Grant grabbed his cell phone and spoke quietly into it. He snapped it shut. "A doctor is waiting for us. He's able to see both of you now." He inhaled sharply when he saw the full extent of Brittany's injuries.

"I was just going to get her clothes. I think they're by the bar downstairs."

Miranda had recovered from her initial reaction and she ran down the stairs. She returned in seconds and helped me dress Brittany.

We slowly made our way down the stairs. Dominic helped me get Brittany into the back seat of the Mustang. Brittany was clinging to me and refused to let go so I slid in next to her. We followed Grant's Lexus as he weaved through the South Philly neighborhoods; block after block of row homes passed in a blur. A few minutes later he stopped outside of a small clinic. A wiry, middle aged man paced out in front. He jumped when he saw us pull up front and he hurried over to talk to Grant. He gestured for us to follow him inside. Dominic helped me out of the car and I turned around to help Brittany. She winced in pain with every movement. I suspected she had some bruised or broken ribs.

The cool, sterile atmosphere of the small clinic was refreshing. The doctor started to take Brittany back to the examination room and she threw a fit, demanding I go with her. Grant went to follow us and I stopped him.

"I don't think Brittany's ready for more male company."

"Oh, right," Grant responded awkwardly, taking a step backwards.

"Miranda, can you come with us?" She didn't hesitate and joined us; taking Brittany's other hand in hers.

Dr. Russo helped Brittany up on to the examination table. She hissed with every movement. But the doctor was quick, thorough and gentle. He filled a basin with warm soapy water and asked Miranda to wipe away some of the blood with a sponge.

"Brit, I'm going to help clean the blood off your legs, okay?" she reassured Brittany before getting close to her private areas. The doctor reset Brittany's broken nose and she yelped in pain, squeezing my hand hard. He laid her back on the table and set an ice pack over her nose and eyes to help reduce the swelling. Overall, she had three broken ribs, multiple contusions, a broken nose and possible ocular nerve damage, once the swelling was reduced he would be able to better assess. Brittany had some rectal and vaginal tearing, but that would heal over time. He stared down at the battered and bruised blonde beauty and shook his head. "Who would and who could do this? What kind of monster..." he wondered out loud.

"Monsters," I corrected him. I saw him shake in reaction to the plural.

"Physically, she'll heal, but mentally...she is going to need help." I nodded in understanding. We were both going to have to sort this out.

It was my turn for the physical exam and except for a split lip, some scratches, bruises and a minor concussion, I was in good shape. I was lucky the doctor said. I wouldn't exactly describe it as luck.

Dr. Russo injected Brittany with a sedative which took almost immediate effect. "She needs some peace right now," he explained. I on the other hand needed to stay awake because of the concussion.

Miranda went to get Grant and he lifted Brittany up, carrying her out of the exam room. Dominic stood when he saw us walking down the hall.

"I want Brittany to come back with us," I explained to him. "She can stay in the guest room. I don't think she should be alone right now."

"I understand," Dominic agreed. Grant carried Brittany out and set her on the backseat of the Mustang. Dominic held the door open for me and I gingerly sat down on the passenger seat. My whole body ached. We drove in silence to our condo.

The doorman opened up my door and did a double take when he saw the condition I was in. He grew even more alarmed when Dominic lifted an unconscious and disfigured Brittany from the backseat. Speechless, he held the door open to the lobby. I could feel the eyes of the concierge follow us as we strode across the marble floor.

I folded down the comforter on the guest bed and Dominic set Brittany down. I pulled the comforter up to her chin. Her bruised face stood out against the white sheets.

Dominic put his arm around me as we stared down at Brittany. I couldn't help but flinch at the contact. He withdrew his arm.

"I'm sorry," I whispered. "I can't help it." Tears welled up in my eyes. "It's just that the past few hours I've been trying to keep that pig from touching me!" I cried out. My skin still crawled at the memory of the assault. Dominic reached out and pulled me towards him. I shoved away from him. "Why didn't you do anything?" I yelled. "That monster – why did you let him take me?" I slammed my fists into his chest. "Why? Why? Why?" I couldn't yell anymore, the tears were choking me, my fury dissipated as quickly as it sparked. Dominic crushed me against his chest and let me cry. And cry I did - bawled until the tears wouldn't spill anymore. The crying jag made my head pound even more and I slumped against the sturdiness of my boyfriend. He scooped me up effortlessly and brought me to our bedroom. He set me down on the bed and then turned and walked into the bathroom. I heard water running and Dominic moving around the room. He came back out with a glass of water and some Advil.

"You have to be hurting," he said as he handed me the pills. I nodded. It felt like I had been through a tornado. I couldn't even imagine the agony Brittany was going to be in when she woke up.

"Your bath's ready." Dominic took the glass from my hand and left me alone in the room. When I walked into the bathroom my eyes started to water again. Dominic had made me a bubble bath, lit candles and laid out a change of clean clothes. I took off my skirt, struggled with the corset top and my underwear. They all got tossed into the garbage. I caught a glimpse of my reflection and gasped. Blood was dried and crusted in the corner of my swollen mouth; scratches covered my legs and stood out bright pink against my fair skin. Marco's handprint was still visible on my throat. That would explain why it hurt to swallow. Feeling faint, I forced myself to look away. The bath beckoned to me and I sunk in. The hot water relaxed my aching muscles. First I scrubbed every inch of my skin, trying to erase the feel of Mr. Genovese's hands. If I could have scrubbed my nasal passages to get his smell out my head, I would have. Drained, I sunk in deeper so the bubbles covered my chin.

I stayed submerged until the water started to cool and slowly stepped out. The combination of the Advil and the bath had eased a lot of the pain. Exhausted, I stumbled back into the bedroom and curled up in bed with the covers pulled over my head. Just as I was drifting off, Dominic yanked the covers off and I screamed.

"Oh Jesus, I'm sorry!" Dominic apologized as he tried to calm me down. "Dr. Russo said I needed to keep you awake." He picked up a mug of coffee from the night stand and handed it to me. I sat up wearily and took the mug. He sat down cautiously on the bed next to me, but careful to keep a safe distance. We sipped our coffee in silence.

"Dom?"

"Yeah baby?"

"I want to know. How come you and Grant didn't do anything, back at Crimson?" I asked, more rational this time around.

He winced and stared out the window unable to meet my eyes. "We couldn't..." his jaw clenched slightly. "Even Marco is terrified of them." I had a hard time believing Marco was terrified of anything. "It's always been that way. They come down here and do whatever. Had I bashed Genovese's head in tonight like I wanted to...we would all be dead right now."

I took another sip of coffee before I continued with my questions. "Why didn't Uncle Marco do anything?"

"Because Uncle Marco is the most like them, it's like he understands them." I recalled how quickly Marco could switch emotions and detach himself from the situation. The handprint on my throat burned and I reached up to gently massage the skin. Dominic followed my movement and stared at the handprint. "Jesus, Nat. What did that guy do to you?"

I smiled weakly at him. "Your uncle did this."

"What?" he yelled and threw his mug against the wall. It exploded upon impact and pieces flew in every direction. I jerked away from his reaction. Coffee sprayed onto the beige carpet and dripped down the white wall.

"He forced me to join Mr. Geno – that guy." I couldn't bear to say his name, "upstairs."

Dominic seemed to vibrate with rage. He clenched and unclenched his fists as he paced the room. The nostrils of his straight nose flared and his chiseled jaw was clenched tight.

"Dominic, your uncle is not a nice guy – you just said he's more like those guys from the five families."

"I know Nat, but I can't believe he went that far." He walked over to the window and rested his forehead against the glass. "You're practically family." His back was to me and I could see his breathing beginning to slow. When he had calmed down he came back to the bed and sat next to me.

"Natalie?" he looked at me. "Did you and that guy…um, you know?"

"No." I could hear Dominic let out a sigh of relief. "He came really close…" I started to cry again. My hands were shaking so badly I had to quickly set the mug down.

"How did you know where to find me?"

"My dad called me once he was by himself. He did not like what went down at all. I had no idea how bad it was. I mean, my God, look at what they did to Brittany…" It went unsaid, but we were both thinking how it very easily could have been me. Dom's cell phone started to ring in the kitchen. He got up to go answer it. I was suddenly very tired and didn't want to talk anymore. I lay down on my side and closed my eyes. I had just dozed off when Dom shook me awake. I cringed away from his touch and he dropped his hands to his side. "Sorry baby, you need to stay awake." I moaned and rolled over so my back was facing him. "Grant and Miranda are on their way over. Are you hungry? They're bringing bagels."

"I'm not hungry."

"I can't let you sleep, if you stay in bed that's all you'll want to do." He urged me to get out of bed and I complied. He was just trying to look after me.

"I don't want to talk about last night anymore."

"Okay, whatever you want." I don't think he wanted to hear the details either. I crawled out of bed and followed him out into the living room. I curled up on the end of the sectional. Dominic went into the kitchen to make more coffee. I zoned out on the sound of the coffee brewing and Dominic moving around in the kitchen. Normal sounds. Normal was good right about now.

There was a light knock on the door and Dominic let Grant and Miranda in. They had both changed out of their work clothes. Miranda wore yoga pants and a t-shirt, her sleek black hair was pulled up in a twist. Grant wore jeans and a button down shirt that was rolled up at the sleeves, exposing his muscular forearms. Dominic still wore his work clothes. He had been too busy fussing about me to change. Had he been wearing a light shirt, bloodstains from Brittany would probably be visible.

I was too tired to move from the couch, so they all joined me after they had made their bagels. Ordinarily I wouldn't pass up fresh bagels, but my appetite was nonexistent. It didn't go unnoticed.

"You're not hungry?" Grant asked, sounding surprised.

"No. I'm not." I answered defensively. "Would you be?"

"Probably not," Grant muttered. They ate in silence, which I embraced. I wasn't in the mood to talk.

Miranda set her bagel down and looked at me. "Natalie, I am so sorry. What my father allowed to happen...it's, it's unforgiveable!"

I shrugged my shoulders. "It's not your fault."

"I should have seen it coming – had you work the gun check and not VIP, this could have been prevented." Miranda's face scrunched up and she started to cry. Grant reached his arm behind her and rubbed her back.

"It happened and we can't change that. Let's just move on!" I snapped. Exasperated I stood up. "I don't want to talk about it anymore." I stomped off to the bedroom and slammed the door. The room was cool and dark, the bed inviting. Despite Dr. Russo's warnings I was going to sleep. My body and especially my mind needed a break.

I could hear Dominic, Grant and Miranda talking about me, but I tuned them out and slipped into a deep, dreamless sleep. When I woke up the sun was beginning to set. Dominic was getting ready for work.

"You're going in?"

"Yeah, Miranda needs as many hands on deck," Dominic answered before he pulled a black t-shirt over his head. It clung perfectly to his muscular torso. "How are you feeling?"

"I'm…I don't know just yet." I gave him a weak smile. "Is Brittany still here?"

"Yes, she got up for a few minutes and then fell back to sleep. She looks like hell."

"I bet she feels worse." I shivered at the image of her with the gun shoved in her mouth.

Dom walked over and sat on the edge of the bed. He placed his hand on top of mine. The expression on his face when he looked at me was a combination of concern and sorrow. "Are you going to be alright tonight?"

"I'll be okay. I'll probably just sleep. Are you going out after work?"

"No. I'll come right home," he promised.

"You'll lock the door behind you?"

"Absolutely. Your cell is on the nightstand. Call me if you need anything, okay?"

I nodded and struggled to keep my eyelids open. Sleep was ready to claim me again. I felt Dominic's lips brush against my forehead. "Love you Nat," he whispered.

"Love you too," I mumbled as I drifted off.

A noise woke me up. The condo was quiet and dark, too dark to see anything in the room with the exception of the alarm clock, which cast a red glow on the surface of the bedside table. I heard the sound again and froze, afraid to breathe. Someone was in the room with me. My heart pounded in my chest as I strained my eyes in the darkness. I focused on the noise, a faint clicking, it was familiar.

Curious, I flipped on the lamp. Brittany was standing next to the bed visibly shaking, her teeth were chattering together at a rapid rate – like a woodpecker against a tree. Alarmed, I inched back in the bed and lifted the down comforter. "Brittany, come lay down next to me."

\She silently complied and climbed in. Her shivering made the bed shake. I curled up behind her to help warm her up. She flinched and tensed up at my touch, but as my body heat warmed her she relaxed. Eventually her shivering stopped and she fell asleep. I was wide awake.

Dominic came home and was surprised to see us in bed together. Probably, under different circumstances, this would be a fantasy of his. "You guys okay?" he asked.

"Yeah, Brittany was freezing. She's warm now though," I whispered.

"She's probably still in shock. Dr. Russo said that's one of the signs."

He went into the bathroom to brush his teeth and change. He walked out wearing cotton pajama bottoms and a t-shirt. I wasn't used to seeing him wear clothes to bed, but since we had company, it was only appropriate. There was plenty of room for all of us on the king bed. Brittany was more petite than I was and didn't take up much space. Dominic curled up behind me and I suppressed the flinch. I knew he wasn't going to harm me. He slung his arm over me protectively.

Brittany woke us up with a start, screaming and thrashing in her sleep. Her hands clawed at the air in front of her.

"Brittany, wake up! Wake Up!" I lightly shook her. Her eyelids flung open, as far as the swelling allowed, and her crystal blue eyes stared at me, not recognizing me at first. "You're safe. It's me, Natalie." Relief and recognition flashed across her face and she calmed down.

"Oh Natalie, it was awful..." she trailed off and broke down into sobs. Dominic sat up in bed watching us, not sure what to do.

"Shhh, Brit. I know." I spoke to her in a soothing voice. Two days ago, if someone had said I'd be consoling Brittany in the same bed I shared with Dominic, I would have told them they were fucking crazy. But, here we were. Brittany choked back her sobs and tried to get her breathing under control. When she looked up and saw Dominic she jumped and started shaking again. Her eyes filled with fear.

"Brit, it's Dom. He won't hurt you. You're safe here," I reassured her. Her shaking slowed and her eyes became more relaxed.

Brittany's face was mottled with bruises and her eyes, although still swollen, were more black and blue than anything else. Her shoulder length platinum blonde hair stuck out in all directions and she still wore her uniform; the skirt was torn at the seams on one side. Bruises and scratches ran up her legs, like they did on mine.

"Dom, can you run Brittany a bath, like you did for me?" He didn't hesitate at my request and scooted out of bed. I rolled slowly out after him, my body still sore, and went to the dresser to pull out a change of clothes for Brittany. Even though I was petite, my clothes would still be large on her, but at least they'd be clean.

I went into the bathroom and saw that Dominic had put a spare robe out for Brittany. I went to the linen closet and set out a new toothbrush, a comb and a new stick of deodorant. I used the toilet, brushed my teeth and used mouthwash. My mouth still tasted like that chain smoker, like the smoke was stuck to my taste buds. Even though I had slept for close to twenty-four hours my eyes had dark circles underneath. My lips were still puffy and the split was an angry red against healthy pink, at least the handprint around my neck had faded.

I looked up in the mirror and saw Dominic in the background watching me. The expression on his face was startling. He looked murderous.

"What? What did I do?" I asked his reflection.

"You didn't do anything."

"Why do you look like you want to kill me then?"

"Not you. Mr. Genovese. I want to kill him. He needs to pay for what he did to you!" His eyes flashed. "I should have stopped him at the club." God, how I wished he had. "And those assholes who did that to Brittany…they need to be punished too. You just don't treat people like that!" I could feel the anger emanating off of him in waves. I stepped away from the vanity, shut off the faucet to the bathtub and walked over to Dominic. I grabbed his hand and led him out of the bathroom. Brittany had rolled over to face the bathroom door. She stared vacantly in our direction with lifeless eyes. The spark and energy that usually lit up Brittany's ice blue eyes had been extinguished. Brittany and I had had our differences, but no one should have to go through what she had just endured. I agreed with Dom, they all needed to be punished.

"Let's talk about this in a few minutes. I'm going to help Brittany." Dominic nodded; his jaw still clenched with anger, and left the bedroom.

Brittany needed to lean against me as I helped her into the bathtub. She looked up at me gratefully with watery eyes after she got settled into the hot, sudsy water.

"Thanks, Nat. This feels good."

"I know. It did wonders for me. Do you need anything else?"

"Did we go to a doctor?" she asked and looked confused.

"We did. He gave you a sedative and knocked you out. I think it was a horse tranquilizer because you were out cold," I joked weakly.

"Are there any more?"

"Any more what - sedatives?" she nodded and hissed in discomfort when she shifted in the tub.

"No, but he gave us a few pain pills. Do you need one?"

"God, yes!" she exclaimed. "I feel like I've been split in two." I flinched at this description. The way those men had their way with her, they came pretty close to doing that.

"Okay, I'll go get them." I hurried out of the room to ask Dominic where the pills were. He was on his cell phone talking to someone and shut up the second he saw me. I asked him where the pills were and he pointed to the kitchen counter. I grabbed the bottle and a glass of water then hurried back to the bathroom. I heard Dominic continue speaking again as soon as I left the room.

After making sure Brittany was all set I went to see Dominic. He was off the phone and staring out the window. He must have heard my movements and turned to look at me. He still looked angry, but seemed to have calmed down considerably.

"Who were you talking to?" I asked.

"Grant. He wanted to know how you're doing."

"What did you tell him?"

"That you seem to be handling everything pretty well…on the outside."

"But not on the inside." It was more of a statement than a question.

"How are you doing, Nat?" he asked softly.

"Do you really want to know?"

"Of course, I love you and want to know what I can do, what I need to do." He walked over, pulling me gently against his body. My head rested on his chest and I inhaled the familiar smell; a little woodsy from his cologne and spice from his deodorant.

"You need to talk about it. You shouldn't keep it bottled up inside," he prodded. I thought about what I was going to say first before responding.

"I still feel his hands on me and taste him in my mouth. It's awful and won't go away! And I still feel your uncle's hand around my throat. It's hard to breathe. I don't know whether to cry or to puke! All I really want to do is sleep; hoping maybe I'll wake up and it would have just been a bad dream." Dominic hugged me tighter the more I revealed. "Despite all that I consider myself lucky…it could have been so much worse." Despite my efforts to stay strong I started to sob again, soaking the front of Dominic's t-shirt. He didn't seem to notice.

"I will kill him," Dominic announced. The finality in his voice caused me to look up at him.

"Dom, as much as I want him to suffer an excruciating death, it's suicide! What would happen to you if you attempted to kill him? You'd be dead. I can't deal with that."

"He can't, they can't be allowed to get away with what they did to you and to Brit." As much as I wanted to agree with him and have him avenge me, it would be stupid to allow it. Dominic would be dead before he left New York City.

"Didn't you tell me that Mr. Genovese is the most powerful out of the five families?" I asked him.

"Yeah," he answered unwillingly.

"Do you really think that you can get away with it?"

"Yes, Grant and I were talking-"

"What!" I cut him off. "Not Grant too! You guys are crazy. Just stop thinking about it, it's not an option." I pushed myself out of his embrace and glared up at him.

"But, Nat —"

"No. I don't want to hear anymore. I don't want to know." I crossed my arms over my chest and turned away.

Dom moved up behind me and rested his chin on my shoulder. His stubble tickled against my skin. "You're right. I won't talk about it anymore," he whispered in my ear.

"Thank you." He gave in way too easily. I had a feeling that this wasn't going to be the end of his crazy scheme.

Chapter 27

The week passed quickly, despite becoming a recluse in the condo. Brittany stayed with me and we passed the time up at the rooftop pool or sitting on the deck. We would get up around noon and mix margaritas or green apple martinis and the lounging would begin. An hour into our day we would be relatively numb. Our bruises were fading to yellow and Brittany's vision was no longer impaired, but our psyches had yet to heal. Dom would leave us alone and was busy on some side project that the Grabanos were working on. I had no desire to know any particulars about the project.

Brittany and I had gone from foes to friends. Our shared experience forced the friendship upon us. When Dom left us alone, we talked about that night. Brittany didn't know I witnessed part of her attack. She recalled hearing a struggle from across the hall, like a body being slammed against the wall. I explained that was me getting thrown into a door.

Saturday afternoon, a week after the horrific night, Brittany and I sat on the deck, with our martinis in hand. We both sat in silence, deep in our own thoughts. Out of the corner of my eye I saw Brittany's hand tremble. She lifted her glass to her lips and drained it empty.

"I need another drink," she declared and stood up. "You?" she asked me. I drained my glass and followed her into the kitchen. We had already polished off the bottle of green apple martini mix, so we moved onto straight vodka. Dominic came home from the gym to get ready for work and found us close to passing out on the sectional. Brittany's glass was knocked over on the coffee table, an ice cube slowly melting into a pool on the finished wood.

He gave me a disappointed look and walked into the bedroom. I probably should have followed, but I was incapable of getting up off the sofa.

"Was that Dom?" Brittany slurred.

"Uh huh."

"Do you think he has any coke?"

"Probably not," I answered. Dominic was like me and preferred smoking a joint over snorting lines.

"God, I could really go for something stronger," she slurred, almost unintelligible.

My eyes were drifting closed when Dom came out into the living room. He had changed into his work clothes and the smell of his body wash trailed out behind him.

"Dom, when you come home, can you bring some coke?" Brittany asked in a pleading voice.

Eyeing her warily, he said, "I'll see what I can do." His answer was noncommittal. "You two are a sight." he stated and looked at me.

I couldn't meet his eyes. We must have seemed pretty pathetic to him; hiding away all week and drinking like it was our job.

"Did you eat anything today?" he asked.

"No, I haven't been hungry." Dom lowered his head in frustration. I hadn't eaten more than a handful of crackers all week. My usual ravenous appetite still hadn't returned. Even though it had only been a few days I could tell that I lost weight. My face looked gaunt and my clothes fit looser. I couldn't explain to Dom that my mouth still tasted like ashtray and only the alcohol was palatable. He would just get pissed off and start talking crazy again.

Brittany suddenly stood up and took off in a dash towards the bathroom. Seconds later we could hear her hurling in the toilet.

"Nice," Dom remarked before he turned his attention back to me. "Will you try to eat something? Please? I'm really worried about you." His concern was visible.

"I'll try," I promised.

He bent over and kissed my forehead. "I'll be home later than usual. Call me if you need anything."

"Ok." I slouched back against the sofa. "Dom?" He looked back at me. "Love you."

He smiled at me, "I love you too." As he walked away I noticed his gun was tucked in the back of his pants. Before I could say anything I passed out.

Chapter 28

A phone was ringing in the background. As I surfaced to consciousness the ringing grew louder and more insistent. I opened my eyes and was blinded by the sunlight. I moaned and rolled over towards the sound. My head was pounding and I was so thirsty. The phone stopped and I embraced the silence. Almost as soon as it had stopped, it started again. The ringing was coming from the bathroom. I dragged myself out of bed to grab my cell phone off of the vanity.

"Hello?" My voice was scratchy.

"Nat, it's Miranda. Is Dom there?" I detected distress in her tone. I walked back out into the bedroom to get Dom and saw that the bed was empty. His side of the bed looked like it hadn't been slept in at all last night.

"Hold on, let me check." After a survey of the condo, I found Brittany passed out on the floor of the second bathroom, but Dom wasn't anywhere to be found. "No. He's not here."

"Shit. Have you heard from him or Grant?" The hysteria in her voice was increasing.

"No. Why? What's going on Miranda?" I demanded. She was freaking me out.

"Grant's car is still outside Crimson and he didn't come home last night."

"It doesn't look like Dom did either. Were they going somewhere after work?"

"They didn't work last night."

"But, Dominic was going to work, that's the last time I saw him." Then I remembered the gun in his pants. That wasn't part of his uniform.

"What did they do last night? Do you know?" Miranda was silent on the other end. "Miranda, are you still there?"

"Yes. You're not going to like this," she paused. "They went to New York City last night." My heart stopped.

"Oh no," I whispered. My legs gave out and I collapsed on the floor. I pictured Dominic and Grant lying in pools of blood. Their eyes open, vacant and beginning to cloud over. "Why didn't you stop them?"

"They wouldn't listen to me and were hell bent on evening the score."

"And they're not answering their cell phones are they?" I asked.

"No. I've tried repeatedly."

"Who else was in on it?"

"Just them. They didn't want to involve anyone else."

"So, your dad doesn't know or Dom's dad?"

"I don't think so; they would have prevented something like this. A hit on Mr. Genovese is very serious."

"What were they thinking?"

"I'm going to make some more calls. Will you call me if you hear from them?"

"Of course, you do the same." I hung up the phone and stayed on the floor. I called Dom's cell and it went straight to voicemail. "Please call me as soon as you get this." Next I tried Grant and got his voicemail. I left the same message. My nerves were shot and I was thirsty. I heaved myself up off the floor and marched into the kitchen. The bottle of vodka was still on the counter. I poured myself a glass and took some big gulps. It didn't take long for the warmth to settle in and relax my nerves. The pounding in my head began to ease off. I poured another glass and went to go check on Brittany.

She was curled around the toilet, her head propped up on a towel.

"Brit, wake up." I nudged her leg with my bare foot. She groaned and mumbled something. "Brit, come on." I urged, nudging her again. She shook her leg, mumbling incoherently, but still didn't wake up. She looked cold lying on the tile floor in shorts and a tank top. The air conditioning vent was directly overhead and blasting arctic air down on her. I grabbed the other towel off of the rack and draped it over her.

Hours passed. Brittany slept and my phone never rang. Even though I had consumed two glasses of vodka, it hadn't eased any of the edginess. I rolled a joint and smoked it. This helped a little. My eyelids got heavy and started to close. The ringing of my cell phone pierced the silence of the condo and jerked me awake. I recognized Grant's number.

"Grant? Where are you? Are you alright? Is Dom with you? What the hell were you thinking?" I fired off questions at him.

"Nat, slow down. We're fine." Relief washed over me and tears filled my eyes.

"Where are you?"

"At Crimson. I needed to pick up my car."

"Where's Dom?"

"He is talking to his dad. Apparently Miranda was ready to call in the National Guard. Rico isn't too pleased with his son right now."

"Did you do what I think you were going to do?"

"Yes."

I steadied myself with another gulp of vodka.

"I'm going to go pick up Miranda and we'll be over." Grant hung up the phone. The conversation must have broken through Brittany's slumber because she wandered into the living room.

"Who was that?" she asked through a yawn.

"Grant. He, Dom and Miranda are coming over." I answered.

"What's wrong?"

"Grant and Dominic went to NYC last night to avenge our assaults." Her eyes grew huge with shock and disbelief.

"They did? Wow!" She plopped down on the sofa next to me and grabbed my glass. After she took a generous sip she continued. "I wish I could have seen it. In fact, I would have liked to have killed those pricks myself." From the intense look on her face, I knew she meant it.

"Yeah, they deserved it, but it was a reckless move."

"What do you mean?" she asked.

"Because those deaths are going to be avenged and who do you think the targets are going to be?"

"Will they know who did it? I mean it is the mafia, hits happen all the time."

"I don't think it will take long for them to piece together that these were the same men who came to Philly last weekend."

"Eh, you worry too much Nat. I grew up around this shit and unless Dom and Grant were seen taking them out, or somebody rats on them, they should be fine." She attempted to convince me, but didn't sound too convinced herself. We passed the glass of vodka between us and waited for everyone to arrive.

They took a while and we had moved on to making screwdrivers in the kitchen when they walked in the door. Brittany raised her glass in a toast. "Here's to taking care of business!" I remained silent and my glass stayed on the counter. Miranda didn't look jovial either. Relieved that everyone had returned safely? Yes. Happy? No.

Dominic kept avoiding my gaze and stayed on the other side of the island. He and Grant were both on edge. Miranda and I remained silent. Brittany chattered on like the hostess at a party. She poured screwdrivers for everyone, but the drinks remained untouched. I gulped mine down and moved on to one of the unclaimed glasses. Dominic's cell vibrated on the countertop and he snatched it up and answered with his back to us. He glanced at Grant to get his attention.

"What channel? I'll turn it on." He snapped his phone shut and grabbed the television remote. He scrolled through the channels and ended on CNN Headline News. The screen filled up with the image of a crime scene. Police tape stretched across a sidewalk outside of a brownstone building. Uniformed and plain clothes police officers milled about the scene. I was caught up in the images and not paying attention to the reporter until I heard the name Luigi Genovese. That caught my attention.

"...The murder rate in New York City rose dramatically last night after a brutal slaying that resulted in the death of four victims. One of those victims is Luigi Genovese, alleged boss of the Genovese crime family, rumored to be the most powerful in the country. The names of the other victims haven't been released, but they are believed to be members of NYC's criminal underworld and associates of Genovese. Witnesses reported hearing a series of gunshots and a dark sedan fleeing the scene. Federal authorities have been busy this summer with mob violence escalating in Philadelphia. They are investigating to see if this recent incident is related."

Miranda and I exchanged nervous glances when Philadelphia was mentioned.

"Damn it!" Grant burst. "That made the news quickly."

"Yeah it did," Dominic agreed. "The connection to Philly is a little unnerving."

I went back to refill my glass. Miranda's phone rang and I could hear the angry voice on the other end clear across the room.

"Yes. He's right here. Hold on." She handed the phone to Dominic. "It's my dad. He wants to talk to you."

Dominic took the phone and walked away from the group. I followed his movements with my eyes. I saw him tense up when Marco lit into him.

"But...wait...but..." he couldn't get a word in. "Fine. I understand. Thanks." He hung up and handed the phone back to Miranda.

"What did he say?" Grant asked.

"That we were stupid and impulsive and crossed the line. He said he should probably turn us over to the families. But, he knows why we did it, doesn't understand it, but we're family and he'll back us up. Whatever happens," he ended ominously.

"Do the families suspect us?" Grant pried.

"Uncle Marco didn't know. Apparently there is total chaos in New York right now. The consigliore to Genovese is trying to establish some order. He told us to keep a low profile and he'll let us know if he hears anything."

"He's right you know. That was stupid and impulsive." I never thought I would agree with Uncle Marco.

"Nat, there was no way in hell I was going to let that asshole get away with it." Grant responded, his nostrils flaring.

"What do you think is going to happen when they figure out who's responsible?"

"Yeah, this vendetta isn't going to go away," Miranda chimed in.

"I defended your honor and I'm glad I did it," Dominic said to me. This whole week his face bore a permanent pained expression. That expression was gone and replaced with satisfaction.

Screaming erupted from the couch and we all jumped. We had forgotten that Brittany was even in the room with us. Sometime during the news broadcast she had passed out. Now she tossed in her sleep, kicking and screaming. I had a feeling I knew what her nightmares were about.

Miranda's defensive stance softened as she watched Brittany writhe on the couch.

"Well, what's done is done. They deserved it," spoken like a true Mafia princess. Miranda reached for Grant's hand. Just like that he was forgiven and was the hero again.

Dom looked to me for his forgiveness. That was going to be harder to come by. Not only did he go against my wishes and avenge my assault, but he took a human life. Was the crime I had endured worth a human life? Now, all of our lives could be at risk. I shook my head and looked away from his gaze. I heard him storm off and the sliding glass door to the deck slide open and shut.

"I'll go talk to him," Grant offered. Miranda walked up to me as I drank more of my screwdriver.

"Natalie, I know you're upset, but can you ease up on Dom?"

"Now you're on their side? A minute ago you were just as pissed."

"I was upset, true. They could have been killed…but they weren't. They delivered justice, Grabano style…for what they did to you and Brit."

It was hard to think straight; the vodka was clouding my brain. Maybe Miranda was right. I should have known that Dom and Grant would do this. They were more alike than they knew. I couldn't help but worry that they too would have to pay for their crimes. Secretly, deep down inside, I was glad Mr. Genovese was dead. Now maybe his smell which still clung to my skin would begin to fade.

A month after the hits in NYC, things had started to return to normal. The senior family members had heard nothing linking the crimes to Philly aside from the initial news broadcast. I returned to work and Miranda ran interference with her dad. I had slowly forgiven Dominic and we worked on repairing our physical relationship. The attack had left me uncertain about my body and disconnected with my emotions. We hadn't made love yet and he was patient with me while I healed.

I was working the gun check. It was a Saturday night and the cool crisp of fall hung in the air. Rocco Nucci and his boys rolled in. Rocco winked at me as he walked past the metal detector. He wouldn't be checking his gun tonight. "How ya doin', doll?" he asked me when he stopped in front of the counter. "You're Dom's girl, right?"

"Yeah," I answered hesitantly. Usually they didn't pay any attention to me when they arrived.

"That's right; you're the little spitfire that Mr. Genovese took a liking to the last time he was here." My body went rigid at the mention of that name. "That was about a week before he was whacked, wasn't it?" He stared at me with his dark, beady eyes. I shrugged my shoulders and feigned disinterest. I hoped he didn't see the panic on my face before I looked away. Joey B. stood a few feet away listening to the exchange.

"You know I heard a rumor that your boy had something to do with Genovese's untimely death…know anything about that?" Rocco continued. He was fishing for information and I wasn't going to bite.

"I don't have any idea what you're talking about."

"I'm not the only one who has heard the rumor. It's spreading pretty fast. I'd tell your boy to watch his back," he warned and stepped away from the counter. I managed to hold it together until he was around the corner. The second he was out of sight I fell apart. I was shaking so bad that the teeth rattling in my head was louder than the music in the club. Joey B. radioed for Grant and he was up in seconds. Joey B. filled him in on the exchange and Grant's eyes narrowed. When he turned back to face me I could tell he was in protective brother mode by the way he placed his hands on my shoulders, as if transferring the weight to his.

"Nat, that guy was trying to pry information from you. He doesn't know anything."

"But, he was so dead on. No pun intended."

"The Nuccis are trying to assert themselves again…taking advantage of the change of leadership in New York," he reassured me. "Trust me, there aren't any rumors going around or we would have heard about it. Are you going to be okay?" He studied my face with his eyes.

"I'm fine," I lied. I needed a drink badly. Grant looked at me skeptically before he left. My mind was preoccupied the rest of the night. Rocco's warning kept replaying in my head as if on a loop. Sooner or later the truth was going to surface. It usually did. When the Genovese family found out it was Dom and Grant who executed the boss of the most powerful mafia family in the country, they would retaliate. The ashtray taste returned to my mouth so I chewed a piece of gum. It took the edge off, though not as good as a cocktail. Once the club had emptied and the last gun had been returned, I headed straight to Dom's bar. The urge for a drink was close to uncontrollable by the time the club closed.

At first Dominic didn't want to give me a drink, but after he heard about my run in with Rocco, he figured I needed one. The first drink barely took the edge off.

"You doing okay?"

"No," I answered honestly.

"Well, Uncle Marco has his feelers out. If he hears anything close to what Rocco suggested, we'll be the first to know."

"I hope he doesn't hear anything."

"Me too," Dom agreed.

"So are you meeting with the boys after work?" I asked.

"Nah - I figured we could hang out. I don't want you out of my sight." He winked at me.

"Hmm…what did you have in mind?"

"I figured we could smoke up and hit Chinatown?" This suggestion usually got my appetite going, but that still hadn't returned to normal. Dominic frowned slightly at my lack of enthusiasm. "…or we could go to Blue and have a few drinks – let off some steam," he opted.

"I like that idea better." He looked disappointed that I chose a rowdy club over a quiet dinner. Alcohol was more appealing to me than Dim Sum.

"What if we take tomorrow night off and we run away to Atlantic City for a couple days instead?"

"You mean get out of Philly?" I asked, excited at the prospect of getting away from everything. Dominic must have picked up on my change of attitude and grinned. His dimples flashed and it reminded me that I hadn't seen him smile like that in a while. He must be excited to get out of town too.

"Yeah, it'll be nice. Some ocean breezes, some relaxation. Just you and me."

"Yes - let's do it!" Then I hesitated. "Will we be able to get out of work tomorrow night?" I asked doubtfully.

"That won't be a problem. I'll talk to Miranda." He ducked out from underneath the bar and walked to Miranda's office. He rapped on the door, waited a few seconds and then disappeared inside. I sipped on my drink and felt giddy with excitement. The thought of the salt air and being away from Crimson was an appealing one.

"Hey Nat. How are you?" Grant interrupted my thoughts.

"I'm good."

"All recovered from what Rocco said earlier?"

"Yes. I'm not going to let him get to me." I wasn't about to let those thoughts ruin my ideal getaway either.

"Have you spoken to Brittany lately?" Grant asked.

"No. I haven't actually." Brittany had moved back to her apartment two weeks earlier. She and Dominic had a huge argument over the fact that he refused to bring cocaine back to the condo for her. Dominic had returned home after work and Brittany was waiting for him. She was completely wasted from sucking down a liter of gin. When he showed up empty handed she got belligerent and a shouting match ensued. I tried to intervene but was so drunk I could barely stand up, let alone mediate. Most of the fight is a little fuzzy but I remember the final words that were exchanged.

"If you want coke, get up off of your drunken ass and get it yourself," Dominic shouted.

"I fucking will you inconsiderate fuck!" Brit fired back.

"I'm an inconsiderate fuck? Who has let you stay here no questions asked? You drink all fucking day and eat all the food. No wonder Natalie is wasting away over there." He gestured to me, where I'd helplessly plopped down on the sofa; even standing took a lot of energy these days. "There isn't any food for her to eat."

"Dom, it's not like that…" I attempted to interject, but he ignored me.

"So, Brit, are you going to go out and get your own drugs?" Dominic challenged. Brittany stared at the front door with trepidation, like a dragon was guarding it.

"I...I will." Brittany ran to the guest room and we could hear her throwing stuff around. I went after her to go check on her. She was in a rage and chucked a comb at me. Amazingly, I managed to dodge it.

"Whoa, Brit, calm down. It's just me." I held up my hands in surrender.

Brittany had tears pouring down her puffy face – it was puffy from all of the booze and her eyes were red and swollen. "Nice fucking boyfriend you have there," she sneered.

"I'll admit things got out of hand. But you also have to admit he has a point. We have hidden away up here – we're pretty pathetic," I looked at the collection of empty bottles on the dresser. "We need to get our shit together."

Brittany sighed, defeated. "I know. But I don't think I can." She looked at me and I could see the anguish in her eyes. I felt that in time I would be okay, but Brittany would probably be haunted the rest of her life.

I walked over and hugged her. She wrapped her arms around me and hugged me back. "We'll get through this together." I squeezed her one more time before releasing her. She looked up at me with watery eyes.

"Promise?"

"I promise."

She moved out the next morning and we hadn't spoken since. I called her and left her messages, but she never called back. There were Brittany sightings; she was spotted at various bars completely out of control. Some of the regular dealers that hung out at Crimson also mentioned that Brittany had scored various drugs. It was a relief knowing that she wasn't holed up in her apartment – at least she was getting out.

"Have you talked to Mom lately?" Grant asked next.

"No." I admitted.

"Nat, you can't keep avoiding her. I can't cover for you much longer. You should hear the crazy shit that she's coming up with."

"Like what?"

"Well, first she thought you were pregnant and that's why you've been avoiding her. Now she thinks that Dom is beating you."

"What! She's lost her mind." I had enough to deal with now I had to add my mom's crazy notions into the mix. "Fine, I'll call her," I promised. "But after Dom and I get back."

"Where are you going?"

"Atlantic City for a couple days - Dom is talking to Miranda now about getting tomorrow night off."

"Nice. I think that will do you some good."

"Yeah, me too."

"Alright. I'll hold mom off for a few more days, but you really need to call her. She's worried about you."

"I know." Go figure my mom would start to worry about me once I got in a relationship.

She would probably be the only mother to approve of my previous pattern of getting drunk and hooking up with random strangers – if she only knew.

Dominic came out of Miranda's office with a mischievous grin plastered across his face.

"What are you up to?" I pried.

"You'll see."

"So, we got tomorrow night off?" He nodded. "When do we leave?"

"Let's leave tonight."

"Okay!" I sprung off the bar stool and grabbed my purse.

"You kids have fun," Grant hollered after us, sounding more like a dad than a brother. I rolled my eyes, but he didn't see because my back was to him. Dominic and I quickly left.

Despite the chill in the air, we kept the convertible top down on my car and zipped east on the Atlantic City Expressway. The second we crossed the bridge and left Philly behind, I felt freer. I hadn't realized how oppressive the city had become. The urge to drink seemed to grow less intense the further we drove. At some point, despite my hair whipping around me and occasionally stinging my face, I dozed off.

Dom woke me up as he pulled up in front of the Borgata. The bright lights of the awning shocked me and I had to squint to let my eyes adjust. The valet held the door open for me and I stepped out. Dominic handed the man a twenty with one hand and grabbed mine with the other. A bell hop appeared out of nowhere and retrieved our bags.

We walked up to the front desk to check in. Even though it was almost five in the morning, the lobby buzzed with energy. Everywhere I looked there were well-dressed people; a parade of suits and sequined dresses. I felt a little self conscious in my work clothes. We had stopped long enough at home to each pack a bag, but didn't bother to change.

"Hi, we're here to check in."

"Last name on the reservation please," the concierge asked in a bored drawl.

"Grabano." At the mention of Dominic's last name, the concierge's attitude changed. She stood up straighter and became very attentive.

"Yes, sir. Someone called ahead and made all the arrangements for you. Here's the key to your suite and your massages are scheduled for 2 p.m., after brunch."

I don't know how Dominic did it, but he had arranged a spa getaway in under three hours. That would explain his mischievous grin earlier and I suspected that the person who called ahead was Miranda. He pulled out a roll of hundred dollar bills. "This should cover it," he said and handed the woman a stack.

"Oh, and the GM asked me to give this to you." She handed Dominic an envelope with the Borgata logo.

"Thanks." We stepped away from the counter and made our way to the elevators.

"What's in the envelope?" I pried.

"Gambling receipts."

"What for?" Gambling wasn't one of Dominic's interests.

"Tax audit – it never fails that the IRS audits me and these receipts help document some of my income."

"Oh. That makes sense."

"There's some in here for you too."

"For me? Why?"

"Your income isn't exactly being reported. When was the last time Crimson gave you a paystub?"

"Never. I just get cash."

"Exactly." He shoved the envelope into a side pocket on his suitcase. We were the only ones on the elevator when it reached the top floor. We stepped out onto plush carpet and I followed Dominic down the hall. He slid the key card into the lock and the door swung silently open to reveal an enormous suite. I stopped in the doorway and stared. Never in my life had I stayed in a hotel room this luxurious. The suite was easily the size of our condo. My attention was immediately captured by the floor to ceiling windows. The night sky was beginning to lighten with the new day and I could already envision how magnificent the sunrise would be over the Atlantic Ocean that lapped at the shore, stories below.

All the décor and the furniture were in various shades of rich chocolates and vanillas that blended together to create a lavish, yet cozy atmosphere. A living room area was set-up near the windows, but the focal point was a fire flickering in the gas fireplace. Above the mantel sat a flat screen TV. While Dom tipped the bell hop I inspected the room like a child at Disney World; something would capture my attention and I would run over to it, then something else would catch my eye.

Through open double doors off of the living room and dining room, I spied the bedroom and ran off to check it out. I flopped on the bed and took in my luxurious surroundings. I really was Cinderella in her castle. My Prince walked through the doorway and paused to look at me. I smiled at him and beckoned for him to join me. He didn't hesitate and soon had me in his arms, curled up tight next to him. I was getting used to being touched again and felt safe with him. Feeling more serene in this unfamiliar bed than in our own, I fell asleep. I fell asleep without the need for a million drinks or bong hits to render me unconscious.

Dominic's lips brushed against my cheek and my eyelids fluttered open. The room was bright with sunlight.

"Morning Sunshine," he whispered.

"Unnn," I grumbled. "What time is it?"

"Time for brunch, come on." He clasped my hand and yanked me up into a sitting position. I stretched and rubbed the sleep from my eyes. We had only slept for about six hours, but it was the best night's sleep I'd had in over a month. There was a light rap on the door and Dominic went to answer it. I heard him talking to someone in the other room. I slipped into the bathroom and shut the door.

The bathroom was the one room I didn't inspect and it was like I had unknowingly saved the best for last. I thought the bathroom at our condo was spectacular, but this one put it to shame. Between the marble bath tub and the giant walk in shower, I didn't know which one to choose. I decided on a bubble bath and ducked into the shower at the end to rinse off the suds and wash my hair. The plush towels were warm from the heated shelf they were stacked on and big enough to wrap around my body twice. A soft, oversized cotton robe hung on the back of the door and I reached for it. As I did, I caught a glimpse of my body in the mirror above the marble vanity. My ribs stuck out and the outline of my vertebrae was clearly visible. My skin, usually fair with rosy undertones, had taken on a sallow tone.

My reflection was unsettling. I knew I had lost weight, but hadn't really paid attention to how much. What was most disturbing is I almost didn't recognize the shell I had become. I ran my hand across my ribs and felt the closeness of the bones. My stomach, normally flat, had become concave. My eyes sunk into my head and my cheekbones jutted out like fins from my sunken cheeks.

The encounter with Luigi Genovese had taken its toll. The fact that he had been murdered by Dominic didn't make a difference. The damage was already done. I sighed, feeling the self pity creep in. This time something different happened. Instead of retreating into sadness and fear, I got angry. The anger ruptured forth from some deep reserve. I refused to be the victim anymore. Mr. Genovese was dead, he paid for his crime, but I didn't have or shouldn't have to pay for it any longer. I wanted my life back. Tying the robe tight around my too thin waist, I stood up straight with an assurance I hadn't possessed since before my attack.

Dominic was sitting at the dining room table drinking coffee. I sat down next to him and poured a cup. Although I wasn't hungry, I forced myself to eat. Dominic had ordered an omelet for me that was stuffed with ham, mushrooms and Swiss cheese. I took a bite and discovered that it was quite tasty and I ate another forkful. Dominic stared in shock.

"I don't believe it, you're eating!" He was smiling like he had just won the lottery.

"Um hmm," I acknowledged with my mouth full. I took a sip of fresh squeezed orange juice to help clear my throat. "I need to. It's time."

Dominic didn't say anything; he just continued to stare in disbelief as I managed to eat half of the omelet. That was all I could consume. My stomach had shrunk and it filled up quickly. I set the napkin on the table in surrender. It had taken a lot of effort to eat that small amount, but I could already feel my body thanking me; it had been running on empty these past few weeks, and the fuel was quickly absorbed. I leaned back in the chair and stretched, feeling full and satisfied. The sun pouring in the windows warmed the room. The Atlantic sparkled for as far as my eyes could see and sailboats dotted the horizon.

"How was your breakfast?" Dominic asked.

"Filling," I answered and patted my tummy.

"I'm glad you ate something. I've been worried about you." He reached over and caressed my cheek.

"I know. I just needed some time and still do."

"Take as much time as you need. I won't rush you." I could see the love he felt for me reflected in his eyes. Even as broken as I felt, he still loved me.

There was light knock on the door and Dominic jumped up to answer it. He was talking to someone and the voices grew louder as he walked towards the living room. When he appeared in the doorway he was accompanied by two women, one blonde and one brunette, who were wearing what looked like hospital scrubs.

"You can set up in here, by the windows," Dominic instructed. Both women turned and headed back towards the front door.

"What's going on Dom?" Several options raced through my mind: were we going to get tattoos…maybe a piercing?

"You'll see," was his cryptic answer.

The women returned seconds later and each carried a folding table. They assembled the tables side by side. Once set-up I realized they were massage tables. I forgot the concierge had reminded Dom of our massages when we checked in. They draped cream colored sheets over the tables followed by a deep red chenille throw and set out an assortment of oils.

The blonde woman turned to me. "Hi, I'm Helen and your massage therapist." I shook her hand.

"I'm Natalie."

"Have you ever had a massage before?"

"No, I haven't," I admitted.

"You and your-" she quickly looked at my left hand before continuing, "boyfriend are getting the Live Like A Rock Star massage and you have a choice of Swedish or Deep Tissue."

"What's the difference?"

"Deep tissue is deep, and really works the muscles. It works out any toxins that are trapped in your muscles and tissues. Swedish massage is gentler and helps to increase circulation and release stress. Since you haven't had a massage before, I would recommend the Swedish."

"Okay." I took her word for it. "Dom, which one are you going to do?" I turned to look at him and found he was already facing down on the table and it looked like he was naked, except for a towel draped over his butt. He looked just fine wearing nothing but a towel. His massage therapist answered for him. "Deep Tissue and he's already asleep." She smiled and then continued on massaging Dom's broad shoulders, the oil making his tattoo seem darker.

Helen gestured for me to hop up on the table, like a pediatrician to a child. I started to climb up, when she stopped me.

"You should probably take off your robe first."

I hesitated before I disrobed. My body was probably going to be a shock to this woman. I shyly shrugged the robe off and placed it in Helen's outstretched hand. She looked at my body and didn't have to say anything, her expression said it all. I looked at her apologetically as I climbed up on the table. I was uncomfortable at first having a stranger touch my body, but Helen's hands were gentle and the repetitive motion was soothing. It didn't take long for my muscles to loosen up and for me to doze off.

"Baby, wake up," Dominic whispered in my ear. I jerked awake, my face felt squished from being pressed against the massage table. "The massage is over." I rolled over onto my side and Dom helped me up into a sitting position. I was sleepy, but felt refreshed at the same time. All the tension that I had been holding in my shoulders had been released and the tightness in my neck was gone.

"Wow that was amazing!" I exclaimed. "I feel awesome!"

"You look radiant," Dom commented. "I didn't think you could be more beautiful." I blushed and looked away. "I mean it," Dom added and kissed the top of my head. I eased off of the table and held onto the sides until I knew my relaxed legs would support me. Helen smiled when she saw me upright. She must have seen that she had done her job well. Dom handed me my robe and I quickly slipped into it.

The massage therapists packed up their things and left. I lounged on the sofa with my legs stretched across Dom's lap.

"Is there anything else you have planned?"

"No, this was it. Now we can just do whatever we want." He traced his fingers along my shins. "Is there anything you want to do?"

I looked out the window at the cloudless, sunny sky and realized it was too nice to stay inside. I jumped up of the sofa and reached out for Dominic's hand. "Let's go to the boardwalk!" I hadn't felt this good in over a month and wanted to keep the demons at bay as long as I could. He picked up on my enthusiasm and grabbed onto my hand and heaved himself off the couch. I ran into the bedroom to get changed. He followed right behind. I pulled on a pair of jeans and a long sleeved v-neck black shirt. Since Dominic was watching me get dressed I think he noticed that I didn't put on a bra or any underwear. I turned to watch him dress and he stared at me with hungry eyes. I knew what he wanted, what he had so patiently been waiting for. The thought of being intimate with him made me nervous, but I knew I needed to try.

"Later," I promised.

"Really?" He beamed at me.

"Yes. We'll try," I assured him. Now it was his turn to be radiant and his excitement didn't help to quell my nerves.

Even though it was the weekend, the boardwalk wasn't as crowded as during the summer season. After Labor Day the crowds slowly dwindle. This late in September, the days were still warm and the Boardwalk businesses remained open. Dom and I first visited the Ripley's Believe It or Not! Museum and made our way down to the Central Pier and Arcade Speedway. With each video and skee ball game we regressed. The fried food on the Fairway didn't smell particularly appetizing, but I wound up eating it anyway. At the end of the day, we sat to watch the sunset. First we shared a bench that faced the ocean. The water changed pink and orange to match the hues of the sky. As the sun set further, we crossed the boardwalk to face west. The clouds were as pink as the cotton candy I held in my hand. Once the sun had dipped below the horizon, Dominic and I strolled slowly down the boardwalk, hand in hand. The casino was teeming with activity when we returned and we quickly made our way to the elevators, up to our room.

Dominic led me to the bedroom and I knew what was on his mind. It had been on my mind all afternoon too. Only, it was with more dread than anticipation. I was afraid of not being able to give in and allow myself pleasure. My hands felt cold and clammy and my mouth went dry as Dominic turned towards me. He leaned in to kiss me and I froze.

"Dom, I want to try, just take it slow with me okay?" I pleaded.

He pulled me close to him and ran his hand down my cheek. "I'll go slow, just let me know if you want me to stop and I will." His words helped me relax. I knew I didn't have to worry about him hurting me. He placed his lips on mine and the connection flared. This wasn't an ashtray disguised as a mouth. These were Dominic's soft lips that still held traces of cotton candy. I greedily returned the kiss. All the dread and hesitation dissipated with that first kiss and we fell onto the bed together.

Dominic kept his word and went slow, deliciously slow. The massage had left every nerve ending in my body awake. He trailed soft kisses down my neck to my breasts. His touch was magnified twenty times on my sensitive skin. I begged him to enter me. When he did it was a perfect as our first night together. All the sparks were still there. I hadn't lost them after all. Tears of relief escaped my lashes and Dom kissed them away.

"Are you okay?" he whispered.

"I'm more than okay." I kissed his neck. "That was incredible and I am so glad for that. I really didn't know how I was going to react." I nuzzled up close to him and he hugged me closer.

And despite sleeping in and napping through my massage, I fell asleep again.

Dominic's cell phone pierced the silence. He gently rolled away from me to answer.

"Hello?" His voice was husky with sleep. He sat with his back to me, hunched over. Suddenly his shoulders stiffened and he sat up straight as the person on the other end spoke. I was more awake now and listened in the dark to the one sided conversation.

"When?" Then after a long pause, "Shit!" Another pause. "No, I'll tell her." He hung up the phone and continued to sit there for a few minutes with his back to me. The silence was killing me.

"Dom, what is it?"

"I don't know how to tell you this..."

"Tell me what? Is Grant okay?"

"Yes, Grant's fine. It's Brittany," he turned to face me and grabbed my hand. "She's dead."

"What!" I pulled my hand away from his and sat up. "How...what...when did she die?"

"She hung herself. Grant went by to check on her this afternoon after nobody had seen or heard from her in a few days." I sat in stunned silence. Just hours ago I had made the decision to live; maybe right around the same time Brittany had decided to die.

"Oh my God," I choked out as grief consumed me. Dom moved over to sit behind me and I leaned back against him. He let me cry.

It was a long, quiet ride back to the city. Dom held my hand as he steered with the other and let me be. A million thoughts were competing for attention in my head and I had to sort through them to try to make sense of Brittany's death. *Why didn't she ask me for help? Hadn't I done enough to reach out to her? Didn't she know that things would get better?* I should have never let her move out of the condo when clearly she wasn't ready to live alone. *Did I betray her by beginning to move forward without her?*

As we crossed the Walt Whitman Bridge and the skyline loomed ahead, Dom broke the silence. "Baby, how are you doing over there?" He massaged the side of my hand with his thumb when he asked.

"I'm just trying to make sense of it, you know? Why would she do that? She had options. I should have made more of an effort to be there for her."

"Nat, this is not your fault, please do not blame yourself. Brittany had a lot of issues before…well, you know. Her coping skills weren't there."

"Yeah, but I should have known something was wrong when she didn't return my calls."

"Babe, maybe she needed some distance. You know, to sort things out."

"Yeah, she sorted things out alright." For some inexplicable reason I was angry at Brittany. I had heard people say that suicide is a selfish act, now I understood. What Brittany did was selfish and left me feeling guilty for being able to pick up the pieces of my life. Of course, I wasn't gang raped at gunpoint, so I shouldn't be angry. This shitstorm of emotions sent me into silence again. Dom left me alone as he concentrated on navigating through the inner city traffic.

When we pulled up in front of our building I was surprised to see a familiar sedan sitting in the visitor parking area. The FBI was back. I hadn't seen them tailing me since our initial encounter, so I assumed that I was no longer of interest. Yet, there they sat. *Fabulous.* The dark cloud that had been looming over my head grew darker. Dominic felt me tense up.

"What is it?"

"See that sedan over there?" I tilted my chin in the right direction.

"Yeah."

"My FBI friends are back."

"Hmm. That's interesting."

"More like annoying. I hate being watched." The valet opened the door for me and as I stepped out I waved at the occupants in the sedan and then walked through the lobby doors.

I leaned my head against the elevator wall and closed my eyes. I was exhausted. We had been going non-stop since Dom received the call about Brittany, immediately packing up our belongings and checking out of the hotel. Dominic was busy talking to Grant on his cell phone and getting the latest details about Brittany's death. I tuned him out, unable to hear anymore.

The next few days passed in a daze. I was actually looking forward to going to work, just to be busy. I hadn't been to Crimson since Brittany's death and should have known that work was not going to take my mind off of it. Everyone was sullen and Allegra kept bursting into tears and running for the employee lounge. Not many people knew about what Brittany and I had been through and rumors were flying around about why she did it. Many thought she had just gone off the deep end and the party lifestyle got the best of her. Others speculated that this was a hit disguised as a suicide. Please! Even I knew that a mob hit was made to look like a hit every time – that was part of the message.

I mainly kept to myself. Grant, Dominic and Miranda were quick to shelter me. Miranda had me on the schedule to work the gun check for the next two weeks. Less interaction with my co-workers would be good. There were too many reminders of Brittany in the main part of the club, being sequestered into gun check was a blessing.

The funeral was held on a Tuesday, a week and two days after Brittany was discovered hanging from the ceiling fan in her living room. The coroner said that had Brittany weighed fifteen pounds more, the ceiling fan wouldn't have been able to support her. Despite suicide being considered a sin and the fact that Brittany was raised Roman Catholic, the funeral was still held at the Saint Monica's Church in South Philly. The church was a colossal, stone structure that dominated the corner it was built on. Brittany's mother, a single mom like mine, sat in the front and was consumed with grief. Family and friends filled the first ten pews and even with the hundred or so that had gathered, the church seemed empty.

The priest began the service and his voice echoed off the walls, bouncing around the vaulted ceilings. Several people went up to read and speak about Brittany. They touched on her zest for living and how tragic her death was. How could someone so full of life and energy take such drastic measures to end it so suddenly? I knew the answer.

I wept openly and Dominic kept his arm wrapped around my shoulders through the service. I managed to glance around the audience and was stunned to see Marco sitting in the back. He had some nerve showing his face here.

"...let's hope that this free spirit, who felt trapped here on Earth, has finally found her freedom and most importantly, she has found Peace," the priest spoke his closing sentence.

After the service, the funeral procession drove to Woodlands Cemetery where Brittany was to be laid to rest. Dominic and I followed Grant and Miranda to the cemetery. The early October day was bright and sunny and it seemed odd to be attending a funeral on such a nice day. Wasn't it supposed to be raining and dreary?

"I can't believe Marco was there," I blurted out.

"At the funeral?" Dom asked, trying to make sense of my random statement.

"Yeah, if anyone is responsible for Brit's death, it's him," I spat out bitterly. "He let her get abused and raped; he in no way made any attempt to intervene!"

"You're right, he let it happen. Maybe he was trying to make amends. That whole Catholic guilt thing is hard to shake."

"Don't make excuses for him. It was disrespectful for him to show up today," I snapped.

"He couldn't not show up, Nat, Brit was an employee of Crimson and therefore Marco's employee. He needed to be there." I crossed my arms in front of me and proceeded to sulk the rest of the way. That would explain Marco's presence at the funeral. He was just keeping up appearances – being a concerned former boss. I was still pissed that he had shown up.

To add insult to injury when we arrived at the cemetery and made our way over to the plot, I saw Marco standing off to the side. He didn't have to attend the burial service too. Didn't he know enough was enough? I was incensed; he had gone too far. I broke free of Dom's hand and stormed towards Marco. He saw me coming and pretended to ignore me.

When I reached him I grabbed his arm and yanked him to face me. "You have got some nerve showing up here," I hissed.

"Remember who you're talking to Ms. Ross." His cold, dark eyes seared into mine.

"You're responsible for Brittany's death and I hope that haunts you until you die."

"Brittany was expendable. I'll find another whore to replace her in no time. Are you interested in the position?" He cocked his eyebrow and smirked.

Without thinking I slapped him. All the rage, hurt and fear I had felt since my assault gathered behind my hand and he actually flinched. I reached back to strike again and was stopped. Dominic had caught up to me and held me back. Grant stood beside me and Marco addressed him.

"You better get your sister under control Grant. I'll let it slide this time, but the next time she tries *anything* like this again..." He didn't have to complete the sentence to convey his message. He turned and walked off towards his black Cadillac. Dominic continued to hold me back until his uncle was inside the car. I was trembling with the adrenaline surge - it had felt so good to slap that son of a bitch.

"Natalie, what the hell were you thinking?" Grant demanded.

"He had no business being here. Brittany needs to be left in peace."

"Nat, that was not a smart move," Dom chimed in on Grant's side.

"I'm not sorry. He deserves many more slaps."

"Please Nat; don't push it with my uncle. You know how dangerous he is."

"Fine," I agreed. The rational part of me was returning as the adrenaline surge quieted down and I realized how lucky I was that Marco let me off easy. I turned and spotted Miranda on the edge of the crowd watching us nervously. No one else seemed aware of the exchange. We walked back together to join her. When Brittany was lowered into the ground, except for the sounds of grief, the cemetery was quiet as if nature paused to pay its respects too.

Dominic and I attended the small gathering at Brittany's mother's home. She lived in a small row home on Fitzwater St. The home was too small for all of the casseroles, lasagnas, stuffed shells, cookies and pound cakes let alone the fifty or so people stuffed into the living room and dining room. I made my way through the crowd to pay my condolences to Brittany's mother. She sat on a faded blue loveseat and looked up at me with red, puffy eyes.

"Do I know you, dear?" she asked, trying to recognize my face.

"No - we never met. I worked with Brittany at Crimson. My name's Natalie." I held out my hand.

"Oh, you're Natalie!" she exclaimed and her eyes started to tear up again. I hadn't expected this reaction. "Brit mentioned you in her – in her suicide note," she said the last part softly as if the words themselves inflicted physical pain.

"She did?" I asked my eyebrows lifted with surprise.

"Yes. Here sit down, dear." She gestured for me to sit next to her and took my hand in hers. She was as small as Brittany, but more frail with her graying hair and deep creases framing her mouth. I eased down onto the cushion next to her. "She didn't say much, her note said – 'please tell Natalie that I'm sorry' and that was it. Do you know what she meant by that?"

I lowered my head and tried to compose myself before looking back at the grief-stricken woman. "I think so. I tried to help her through a rough patch recently. But, she shut me out," I responded with a half answer. It was close enough to the truth.

"Oh." Brit's mom looked slightly disappointed as if she was banking on me to tell her why her daughter had ended her own life. I wanted to tell her the truth about her daughter's rape, but it would be cruel to burden this woman further with more turmoil, plus it was too dangerous to reveal.

"I am so sorry for your loss. I only knew Brittany briefly, but long enough to know how special she was." I hugged Brittany's mom and she clung to me, sobbing heavily against my shoulder. I held her until she was ready to pull away, handing her a tissue from a box on the coffee table in front of us.

"Thank you," she sniffed as she dabbed her eyes. "And thank you for your kind words. Brittany may have been a handful at times, but her fearlessness is what I loved the most about her."

"Brit will be missed," I added as I stood up. Someone else was waiting to pay their respects.

Dominic was standing across the room talking to a couple of waitresses from Crimson; his eyes met mine as I crossed the room.

"Ready to go?" I asked when I finally reached him.

"Ready when you are."

I held his hand as he led us through the cramped room and I welcomed the fresh air when we stepped out on to the front stoop. I hadn't realized how claustrophobic the small home was. I needed a drink, badly, but refused to give into the craving. If I was going to get through this, I needed to be sober.

"Take me home," I begged Dominic. I think he sensed the urgency, because several stop signs and red lights were disregarded in his haste to get me back to our condo. I was drained; literally emotionally spent and just wanted to be alone. The second we were home, I drew a hot bath and sunk in up to my chin. The hot water helped relieve the tension that had returned to my shoulders. The quiet solitude of the bathroom was the sanctuary I needed. As my muscles unwound, so did my mind. A little over a week ago I had promised to make an effort and start living again. Sitting there in the sudsy water, I made an addendum to that promise. I was going to live for Brittany too.

The water began to cool down, so I stepped out of the tub. Dominic wasn't in the bedroom, so I wandered out into the living room, with only a towel wrapped around my body. He was in the kitchen cooking something that smelled delicious causing my stomach to growl.

"Feel better?" he asked as he dropped chopped garlic into a sauté pan.

"Tons - I swear baths are therapeutic." He grinned at my answer and tossed some diced tomatoes in with the garlic, the pan sizzled. "What are you making?" I asked, sniffing the air.

"I have chicken parmesan in the oven and I'm going to sauté zucchini in with the garlic and tomatoes."

"I didn't think I was hungry, but that smells so good, I'm actually starving."

"Well, you didn't eat anything today…yet."

"I'm going to go get dressed." I turned to head back to the bedroom.

"You don't have to. You look quite appetizing in the towel." He winked at me.

"Too bad you're busy cooking. I could be your appetizer," I teased. He cursed the sauté pan and I giggled. "I can still be your dessert," I let the towel drop and walked away, feeling aroused as I knew he was watching my nakedness retreat.

I wanted to eat quickly and get right to the 'dessert', but once I bit into the chicken parm I needed to savor it.

"This is delicious! Where did you get the recipe?" I asked.

"Who do you think? Aunt Gloria."

"Ah, yes. " I inhaled another bite of the crispy, cheesy, saucy goodness. Dominic set down his fork to watch me eat. I think I made up for the past month of missed meals in one sitting. Finally, I had to stop. I couldn't shovel another bite into my mouth or I was going to explode. Leaning back in the chair, I patted my taut stomach.

"Did you get enough to eat?" Dom asked as he glanced down at my empty plate.

"Mmmm, that was delicious!"

"So can we move onto dessert?"

I answered his question by straddling him at the table. I was wearing one of his long sleeve button-down shirts, which fit like a dress, and nothing else. He was quick to discover this and his hands eagerly explored my body. This purely human connection grounded me and expelled any negative thought from my mind. Dominic scooped me up and carried me effortlessly to our bedroom. We spent the rest of the night in bed, hungry for each other and making up for lost time, each caress further erasing the invisible scars left by Mr. Genovese.

I woke the next morning feeling more normal than ever. The anxiety that constantly pressed on my heart had lifted. Dominic was sprawled out next to me, the sheet barely covering him. He was deep asleep, so I carefully got out of bed. The condo was still and quiet as I walked to the deck. Once again the sun was shining and filtered through the glass doors. I stepped out into the cool morning air and eased into a deck chair. The sun was warm and the alcove soon toasty. My eyes were closed, but I heard the deck door slide open. Dominic kissed my lips.

"Morning, Sunshine," he murmured. "I need to head out and do some things. You gonna be alright?"

"I'll be fine. I think I might head up to the co-op. It's been awhile."

"Cool. I'll call you later," he bent down and kissed me again. His lips lingered longer this time. "I love you Nat. It's good to have you back."

"I love you too. Thanks for sticking it out with me." He squeezed my shoulder and went back inside.

I sat on the deck for a while after Dom left debating whether to go for a run or go directly to the co-op. Feeling the need to express myself, I opted for the latter. Having made the decision, I was anxious to get going. I hurried inside and showered off the smell of sex, slipped on jeans and a hoodie then headed out the door. As soon as I pulled out onto Columbus Boulevard the familiar dark blue sedan appeared behind me. What could they possibly want this time?

Sure enough the agents followed me to the co-op and parked on the opposite side of the street. I didn't even acknowledge their presence. Brittany weighed heavy on my mind and instead of sculpting, I painted. I focused on the bubbly Brittany, the person I met my first night at Crimson. It was easy to sketch out her face from memory. Then the darker Brittany crept into my mind, pushing the sunny one away. I sketched the other half of her face to include the torment and pain that had haunted her last days. Once this was sketched out on the canvas I worked with acrylic. Using this paint on canvas was so easy to work with, if you made a mistake, you could just paint over it and fix it. I stepped back to look at my progress. It wasn't bad and the difference between the two halves of the face was obvious, if not disturbing. I had done enough for the day and cleaned up the area, leaving the painting to dry on the easel.

I wasn't surprised to see Agent Phillips waiting by my car when I left the co-op.

"Agent Philips," I acknowledged.

"Miss Ross, we need to talk." He was less polite than the last time. I stopped by the driver's side door and waited for him to ask his questions.

"Are you aware that there is a criminal investigation being conducted that involves your boyfriend and your brother?"

My skin turned cold and my stomach suddenly felt full of lead bricks. "What are you talking about?"

"They are persons of interest into the slaying of Luigi Genovese and three others in New York City a little over a month ago."

"You think they did that? Are you crazy? They would have to be crazy to go and do something stupid like that!" I exclaimed, attempting to refute his claim.

"Calm down, Miss Ross. I came here so you can pass a message along," he paused. "The Genovese family has the same suspicions. Your brother and boyfriend need to watch their backs. If they want to talk about available options and get protection, have them contact me." He handed me his business card. I took it with a shaking hand.

"Thank you for your time," he said then walked back to his car. The second he had his back to me I went to open my door, but hadn't unlocked it yet, I fumbled for my keys and managed to unlock the door. As soon as I was safe in the confines of my car, I called Grant.

"Grant, it's Nat. Jesus Christ, we need to talk. Now!" I knew I sounded hysterical and hoped it got his attention.

"What's going on?"

"The FBI just paid me a nice visit and they had some really fucked up news."

"Wait, we can't talk about this over the phone. Where are you?"

"Manayunk. At the co-op."

"You sound upset, are you okay to drive?"

"No." And I wasn't. The way my legs were weak and shaking, I didn't trust myself to accelerate or brake safely.

"Alright. Just stay put. I'll be there soon," he said and hung up. I did what he said and waited inside my car. One of the artists came up and tapped on the window. "Are you alright?" she yelled through the glass. "I'm fine, waiting for someone," I yelled back and gave her a thumbs up. She smiled and continued on her way.

Grant must have broken every traffic law in the book because he pulled up behind my car in less than twenty minutes and during rush hour too. I got out of my car and went to sit in the passenger seat of his Lexus.

"What's going on?" he asked immediately.

I took a deep breath to steady my voice and answered. "Agent Phillips with the FBI wanted me to give you and Dom a message. They're investigating you both in the murders of Mr. Genovese," I winced when I said his name, "and the other three. He also said that the five families suspect you too and to watch your backs." I handed him Agent Phillips business card. "He said that you should call him if you want to talk and want protection."

Grant licked his lips several times so I knew he was upset by my news. He didn't give any other indication that he was affected as he sat there in silent contemplation, chewing on his bottom lip.

"Did he say anything else?" he asked, finally breaking the silence.

"No. That was it. What are you going to do? Are you going to call him?"

"I'm not calling him because he's going to try to get me to testify against everyone in order to save my ass…and I'm not a traitor."

"Oh, so you would rather get killed or go to prison? Great fucking plan, Grant," I responded angrily. "Did you consider me at all? What the hell am I supposed to do if any of those two things happen?"

He was silent again as he mulled this over. "I didn't think of it, because those things won't happen," he reassured me.

I rolled my eyes at this. "What, are you omniscient now? You and Dom did kill those men and it's just a matter of time before the feds lock you up or the five families knock you down. I think that you should talk to Agent Phillips, at least feel him out."

"No. That is not an option," he barked and smacked his hand against the steering wheel hard enough that the horn chirped.

"God, you are so fucking stubborn! I'll talk some sense into Dom."

"Go ahead if you don't want him to trust you ever again. He'll think you're weak and will turn on him and his family just for considering it."

"Yeah right!" I scoffed.

"Fine, find out the hard way," Grant shrugged his shoulders indifferently. His face was stern, making him look older than his 25 years.

"Are you serious? Would Dom really do that?"

"Yes. Family loyalty is first and foremost with the Grabanos. No matter how much you think he loves you, the second he doubts your loyalty, you'll get kicked to the curb and I'll probably be considered a risk then too." We both knew what happened to risks. I felt helpless. Grant uncharacteristically reached over and patted my knee. "Just hang in there and don't worry, everything will work out," His attempt to reassure fell flat because his forced optimism did nothing to break up the knots in my stomach.

"What should I do if the FBI approaches me again?"

"Hear them out, be polite and give them absolutely nothing," he advised. "And let me talk to the boys. I'll let them know about the potential threat with the five families. We'll be on our guard."

I sighed and leaned my head back against the headrest. Life was returning back to normal, the FBI was watching me and lives were in danger. I needed a fucking vacation.

"Hey Grant? Let's go visit Mom for a couple days." He stared at me with his eyebrows raised.

"I thought you were avoiding her."

"I am, well was, but I'm sure she's missing us and you did say she's worried…plus, it would be nice to get away from things for a while," I admitted.

"How about next Sunday and Monday we head up? I can arrange it with Miranda to have Sunday night off."

"One of the perks of sleeping with the manager, huh?" I teased. "That sounds good." I felt better already and was actually looking forward to going home, for once. In the past I dreaded being in the suffocating house trying to live up to my mom's high expectations. I opened the car door and started to get out.

Grant leaned over towards the passenger seat and asked "Are you calm enough to drive? You won't run over any unsuspecting pedestrians will you?" He loved to tease me about my driving. I had one accident in my driving career and will never live it down. Fortunately, it didn't involve any pedestrians as he was alluding to now.

"Ha, ha. You're hilarious," I stuck my tongue out at him and shut the door. He made sure I was safely in my car before driving away from the curb. I pulled out right behind him and attempted to follow him back to the city. He made a game out of weaving in between cars and bouncing from lane to lane that I gave up after the first five miles.

Dominic wasn't home. It was well after seven and I was starving. I spied the leftover chicken parm in the fridge and snatched it up. While my dinner was heating up in the microwave I turned on some music. Believe Me Natalie, by The Killers was on and I danced around the island, my stomach growling louder as the microwave counted down. With my back to the door and the music blaring, I didn't hear Dominic come home and I didn't hear him walk up behind me either. When he wrapped his arms around me I jumped and screamed. I spun around armed with my fork and when I saw it was him, the fork clattered to the tile floor and I hugged him, giggling nervously at my reaction. He laughed too and returned the hug.

"Geez, I saw my life flash before my eyes when you came at me with that fork," he joked.

"I'm the fastest fork in the East." Although the comment about his life flashing before his eyes, even though said jokingly, reminded me of Agent Phillip's warning. Before I could dwell on it, the microwave beeped and distracted me. One thing was for sure, my appetite had returned and with a vengeance.

Steamed poured out of the container when I removed the lid and the chicken smelled just as delicious as it did yesterday. "Do you want some?" I asked Dom.

"Are you going to share?" he teased, feigning shock.

"No, I changed my mind," I crouched over the food, pretending to guard it and hissed. Dom bent over on the counter and lost it. His deep laugh shook his entire body. I realized how silly I must have looked and cracked up too. Soon tears were rolling out of our eyes we were both laughing so hard.

It took a few minutes, but we finally got a grip. "I missed you, baby," Dom said as he joined me at the counter to get his dinner.

"I know I wasn't a barrel of laughs these past few weeks. That felt good. Somehow, I think Brittany would have appreciated it."

"I think you're right," Dom agreed. "She was always full of it." He wacked my butt as he walked behind me to go around the counter and sit at the bar. I followed and sat next to him. We enjoyed a quiet dinner at home. I told him about my plans to go visit my mom. He agreed that it would be good for me to go see her.

"You're not avoiding her because of how she feels about me, are you?" he asked.

"No, that's not it at all. We've never been close, but I know I look like hell and she'll probably blame you. I have been putting off seeing her and delaying it is only arousing suspicions…about you," I paused. "Seeing her will help put those suspicions to rest.

He took my hand in his and kissed the top. "It's definitely time for you to see her. What do you mean, she has suspicions?"

I laughed nervously before answering. "Well, she told Grant how she thinks you're abusing me. Can you believe that?"

He shook his head, his green eyes widening in disbelief. "Wow. She really thinks that?"

"Yes, that's why I need to go see her. Don't take it personally though; she would probably be suspicious of any boyfriend of mine. The fact that you're technically my first serious boyfriend and I'm living with you has probably pushed her closer to the edge." I reassured him and tried to make light of my mom's crazy notions. Dominic looked down at his plate for a few minutes before meeting my eyes. He had a strange expression on his face when he finally did look up.

"What?" I asked.

"Should I come with you? Or maybe she should come here and stay with us for a few days? She'll see that I'm not beating you or anything like that."

"Babe, please don't worry. Grant and I will work things out. If not, we'll consider your ideas as a Plan B, okay?

"I do worry. I want your mom to know me for who I am so she doesn't feel the need to make these assumptions. If this weekend doesn't work, then let's have her down to stay with us." It was so sweet that he really seemed to be bothered my mom's mania. I leaned over and pressed my lips to his.

"Okay, that sounds reasonable," I said, but knew deep down I was going to keep her far away from Philadelphia and the risk of being caught in the middle of a mafia showdown.

Chapter 29

Grant and I drove to York together. The day was overcast and reflective of my mood. The enthusiasm I had once felt of seeing my mom had since waned. I had wanted to see her, but was worried that she would see right through me and know the secrets I've been keeping. She possessed an uncanny intuitiveness and it wouldn't surprise me if she really knew about the antics I had been involved during high school and college. She didn't let on that she knew, but was probably waiting for the day to use that knowledge as leverage.

She wouldn't let my appearance go unnoticed, that I knew for certain. I've always maintained a healthy weight, despite my voracious appetite, but that never satisfied my mother – she always thought I could stand to lose a few pounds.

My appetite had returned to somewhat normal and I had managed to gain back some of the weight I had lost, but not all. I still looked gaunt. As we pulled into the driveway I flipped down the visor to inspect myself in the mirror. My eyes were still a little hollow. I pinched my cheeks to restore a healthy flush. I fluffed my hair and pulled it forwards to disguise my collarbone, which was protruding more than usual. Satisfied, I flipped the visor back up and saw my mom standing in the front doorway waiting for us.

Our childhood home was a small ranch with a patch of grass out front and a somewhat larger patch made up the backyard. The neighborhood was considered working class and nothing to brag about. It was a modest home and the best a single mother of two could provide. Grant's Lexus looked out of place in the driveway. I noticed the paint was beginning to peel and flake off in chunks. One of the shutters around the exterior of the living room window hung askew. I felt a twinge of guilt seeing the house under such disrepair.

"Grant, maybe we should pitch in together and pay for a paint job?" Between the two of us and the money we earned at Crimson, we could easily afford to do that for her.

"Yes, and I'll fix that shutter this weekend." Feeling better, we both got out of the car and grabbed our overnight bags from the trunk. I could already feel my mom's eyes inspecting me from head to toe. Her eyes narrowed and she pursed her lips as she completed her inspection. I inhaled deeply and made my way up the front walkway behind Grant.

"Hi Mom, it's good to see you!" Grant and I said, almost in unison. Grant kissed her cheek and went into the house. I hugged her with my free arm, we were the same height and our cheeks pressed together. When we separated, she looked me over more closely – much like Dominic's Aunt Gloria. For the first time in my life, my mom declared me too thin.

"You need to take better care of yourself."

"I am Mom," I insisted. "I've been through a rough patch lately, but I'm turning things around."

"Trouble in paradise?" she asked with her right eyebrow raised.

"No, nothing like that. One of my friends and co-workers at Crimson committed suicide two weeks ago."

"Oh, I'm sorry Natalie," she gasped, softening her tone. "I didn't know...that's awful! Were you close?"

"Yes we were – especially the past couple of months." I didn't want to tell her about the experience that had bonded us together. Images from that night briefly surfaced before I tucked them away in my sub-conscious again. I winced in pain at the recall. My mom put her arm around me in a comforting gesture and we walked into the house together. Our two frames side by side were small enough to fit through the doorway. The door led directly into the living room, which looked exactly the same as it had since I was in elementary school. The furniture, meticulously maintained, looked maybe five years old, not close to fifteen. My mom went into the kitchen to stir the chili that was simmering on the stove and I walked down the short hallway to my childhood bedroom, which was like stepping back in time to my high school days. The room was unchanged and many of my paintings still hung on the walls. The bulletin board above my desk was covered with concert ticket stubs for my favorite bands and pictures of my friends, mainly of me and Chelsea. A group prom picture showed me with all of my friends, our faces clean and pure – all innocence and excitement for the future – unaware of what the real world had in store for us. I set my bag on my bed, which was covered in the pink bedspread I picked out when I was fourteen, and left the room unable to look at my past anymore. Already the house was having its suffocating effect on me.

Grant was outside fixing the shutter so I hung out with him until he was done. There were no other tasks to attend to so we went back inside.

"Mom how long until dinner is ready?" I asked as I walked into the kitchen. She was making cornbread.

"About 45 minutes," she answered.

"I'm going for a run then," I announced and grabbed a banana out of the fruit bowl that was a constant fixture on the counter. A run would help kill time and get me out of the house.

It felt weird running down the familiar streets of my hometown. My feet took the old route as if on auto pilot and the routine was oddly comforting. Not much had changed since I had last been home for Christmas. A couple cars honked at me as they drove by – probably friend's parents or high school teachers that recognized me.

The last time that I had gone for a run was the day of my assault and after two miles I was winded, so I turned back to head home. A cramp seized up my right side and I slowed to walk it out. As I walked past the grocery store someone started waving at me from the parking lot. It was Chelsea's mom. Not wanting to be rude, I made my way over to where she was loading up groceries into the back of a mini van. The back was already stuffed with bags and this wasn't surprising. The Thompson household still had six mouths to feed, even though Chelsea and her older brother, Jon, had already moved out.

"Hi Mrs. Thompson," I said as I reached the grocery cart.

"Natalie!" Dropping a bag back into the cart, she pulled me into a suffocating hug. Growing up Mrs. Thompson was like my second mom and I was considered another member of the family. "What's one more?" she would always joke – referencing her brood of three sons and three daughters. Chelsea's dad didn't seem to mind one more in the mix either.

It had been a long time since I felt the comforting squeeze of Mrs. Thomson's hug and it felt good. I couldn't prevent the tears that sprang into my eyes. I pulled away and wiped them with the back of my hand, embarrassed at the sudden display of emotion.

Mrs. Thompson looked at me with concern. "Honey, what's wrong?" she asked.

"I forgot how good your hugs are," I admitted. "I didn't realize how badly I needed one." Chelsea's mom looked me over.

"You look terrible honey. Have you been eating?" she asked, reminding me once again of Aunt Gloria.

"I know. I'm working on it. How's Chelsea?" I asked, hoping to distract her. It worked.

"Chelsea is doing just great! She is back from Italy and got a job in L.A. Can you believe it?" she gushed.

"That's great," I said and felt a twinge of jealousy. Chelsea was off pursuing her dreams and I was stuck, unable to move forward.

"You two really need to work out whatever happened between you. You've been friends too long to let a silly boy get in the way," she admonished. If only she knew it was more than a silly little boy, but she was right. We had been friends too long and I missed Chelsea. The more involved I became with Dominic and the mafia lifestyle, I had lost touch with most of my friends. It was like my former life was being swallowed up by my new one.

Chelsea's mom was fishing around in her cavernous purse for something. A few seconds later she pulled out a business card and handed it to me. "This is Chelsea's - all of her contact information is on there. Now I know you both are extremely stubborn, but one of you needs to reach out and make amends. Please don't let your friendship go to waste."

I accepted the card and tucked it underneath the strap of my sports bra as I didn't have any pockets. "I'll try, but I don't know if the damage can be repaired."

"It can, just try," she said as she hugged me again. "And please take care of yourself." I squeezed back as hard as I could. Her hug felt like a mom's hug should feel like – not hard and awkward like the ones I got from my mom.

I continued on my run and waved at the blue mini van as it drove past. Mrs. Thompson honked and waved back.

All the small talk had been exhausted so Mom, Grant and I sat around the dinette table in silence eating chili and cornbread. Grant fidgeted with his spoon and this did not go unnoticed by my mom.

"Grant, can't you sit still?" she snapped. He set the spoon down on the plate underneath his bowl.

"Sorry," he paused. "I need to make an announcement." I dropped my spoon in my bowl of chili and looked up at him, wondering what he was about to say.

"I'm going to ask Miranda to marry me." My stomach dropped and I felt a sudden, overwhelming need to throw up. I excused myself and ran to the bathroom. The chili came up faster than it went down. As I leaned against the bathtub with my head on the toilet seat, I could hear my mom congratulating Grant insincerely and asking him if he was ready to take this next step.

"I am. I want to spend the rest of my life with her," he stated. Another wave of nausea hit and I clung to the toilet bowl as I heaved again.

When there wasn't anything left to throw up, I splashed cold water on my face, washed my hands and opened the bathroom door. Grant was leaning against the wall directly across from the bathroom. I could hear dishes clanging in the kitchen as our mom cleaned up.

"That wasn't exactly the reaction I expected," he said.

"Marriage, Grant? Are you ready to marry a mafia princess? Have you really thought about what you're committing to?" I hissed so our mom wouldn't hear.

Grant grabbed my arm by the elbow, steering me into his bedroom and shut the door. "I have thought about it. First of all, I do love Miranda. Secondly, marrying the boss' daughter not only guarantees me a position in the family, but our safety. If this is the life we are going to live, we might as well be happy."

It wasn't too long ago when I had similar thoughts. Grant was willing to commit to the mafia life one hundred percent and this made me realize that I wanted more out of life. There was finality to his decision - like a nail in his coffin.

"You know it wouldn't surprise me if Dom asks you the same question soon," he said. Fear and panic hit like a wave crashing over me and sent me running back to the bathroom. Grant's laughter followed me down the hall. He probably chalked my reaction up to commitment phobia.

Miranda walked down the aisle on Marco's arm. She was radiant in a cream gown; the veil did little to disguise her glow. Grant beamed as she approached. Dominic was one of the groomsmen and was across the aisle from where I stood among the bridesmaids. All the bridesmaids were dressed in deep red gowns and the white irises that made up our bouquets stood out in stark contrast. Dom smiled foolishly at me and kept winking as if I was in on some kind of inside joke. Annoyed, I looked away from him to watch Marco place Miranda's hand in Grant's.

The priest began a long and seemingly never ending ceremony. Every time I looked over in Marco's direction he was leering at me, his beady eyes watching my every move. Sweat broke out across my forehead and also began to trickle down my back. The church was blazing hot and uncomfortable. My mom sat in the front pew directly behind me and was bawling uncharacteristically.

Finally the ceremony ended. Grant and Miranda were pronounced husband and wife and they pranced down the aisle together, through the wide open church doors, their silhouettes disappearing into the blinding sunlight.

Wedding guests began to filter out behind the newlyweds and I quickly gathered up the skirt of my dress to follow the procession. As I went to pass Marco's pew he grabbed my arm, his fingers were pinching my skin and I stopped to glare at him. Dominic was standing directly behind me, wearing the same goofy grin.

"Come on doll, it's time for the bachelor party."

"Bachelor party? But, Grant just got married. Don't you mean reception?" I squinted at him in confusion. He started laughing a deep, husky laugh that bordered on a cough.

"No, I meant bachelor party," he said, pulling me back towards the altar. I struggled against him and looked to Dom for help, but he followed behind laughing and winking. Marco dragged me around the podium to a door, which was well camouflaged and not visible until we were right in front of it. Dominic knocked and the door swung inwards. Marco stepped across the threshold, bringing me with him. I expected to be in an office, or storage room, but instead we had stepped into the living room of The Speak.

Mr. Genovese sat at one of the small, round tables, He was missing half of his head and brain matter sat on his shoulder like bird poop. His half smile grinned when he saw me looking at him. His remaining eye winked at me as he gestured for me to sit next to him. I cringed and turned away, my stomach rolling. Marco let go of my arm and pushed me in the direction of Mr. Genovese, but I collapsed in a heap on the floor. He laughed and circled around me, a predator sizing up its prey. Once again, I looked to Dominic for help, but he was nowhere to be found. Anxiety enveloped every nerve and I focused on the wood grain of the floor. I counted each line, trying to slow my breathing. Marco stopped circling and stood in front of me, his shoes obstructing my view of the floor, interrupting my count.

"We need a new piñata," he said and a length of rope coiled around his toes. At this strange comment I lifted my head and stared up at him. "Our last piñata is all worn out," he pointed to the ceiling at the end of the room. I followed where he was pointing and a new wave of terror washed over me when my eyes landed on Brittany. Her naked, lifeless body swung slowly back and forth, suspended by a noose. She was beaten and bruised – almost beyond recognition. A puddle of blood pooled on the floor beneath her. Vomit surged up my throat, but was stopped by a noose being tightened around my neck - blocking off oxygen and the ability to scream.

I woke up screaming, but no sound escaped my dry mouth. My hands fought against the rope around my neck that wasn't there. My trembling body was soaked in sweat and I sat up in my childhood bed, the pink comforter grounding me in reality. As my breathing slowed I tried to shake off the nightmare. This was by far the most vivid. I tried to swallow the lump in my throat, but couldn't produce enough saliva. I slid out of bed and padded down the hall to get a glass of water in the kitchen. The house was dark and silent, the only light generated came from the LCD display on the DVD player and cable box.

I grabbed a clean glass out of the dish drain and filled it with tap water, draining it in five gulps then went to refill it.

"Trouble sleeping?" my mom's voice asked from somewhere in the darkness. I yelped and dropped the glass. It clattered into the sink, but didn't break.

"Jesus! You scared me!"

"You were always so reactionary," she commented.

"No. Since when did you hide in the dark? A little warning would have been nice."

She flipped on the light over the dinette table and I squinted, allowing my eyes to adjust. My mom sat at the table with a mug in front of her, a tag from the tea bag draped over the side. She wore an old green and gray plaid flannel nightgown. The one Grant got her for Christmas five years ago. She looked tired and the harsh overhead light created shadows that made her wrinkles look more pronounced. She was once considered a beauty and won the Dogwood Festival beauty pageant in her home town of Phoenixville. After my dad left, her heartbreak had been permanently etched on her face. She used to dye her hair blonde, keeping the gray at bay, but seemed to have stopped as the gray hairs were more prominent than the yellow. I fished my glass out of the sink, refilled it and sat next to her at the table.

"What are you doing up?" I asked.

She shrugged. "I can't sleep."

"Any particular reason?"

"Heartburn; I don't think the chili is agreeing with me."

"Ah."

"What about you? You look like you've seen a ghost."

"Yeah, it was something like that. I had a bad dream, about my friend who died."

"Oh," she replied awkwardly and patted the back of my hand. "I'm sorry."

"I'm also not used to sleeping away from Dom," I admitted. She pulled her hand away from mine as if it had burned her. "Mom, why do you dislike Dom so much?"

She was silent and pursed her thin lips together. Great, this was going be one of the many silent conversations we've had. Surprisingly, she answered.

"I don't dislike him. It's just that you seemed to drop everything: Chelsea, your friends from college, and even your artwork. It's all about him now. What about you?"

"I do stuff for myself."

"I learned the hard way with your father and it was a lesson learned too late – you need to put yourself first." Her words were almost identical to the advice Chelsea had given me when Dom and I first started dating.

"I know that Mom."

"I want to make sure you do. I don't interfere in your life Natalie, I've let you make your own choices, but I see a lot of your father in Dominic and I want to make sure you don't repeat the same mistakes I have made."

"Dominic is not like my father! He is kind, sweet and he takes care of me," I defended him. This was mostly true, but I had forgiven him for not protecting me against Mr. Genovese.

She sighed and regarded me with tired eyes. "So he treats you well, he doesn't hurt you or make you do anything you don't want to do?"

"Not at all, Mom. He is a really great guy." Now his uncle on the other hand, I wanted to add, but didn't. She'd have plenty of time to figure him out if Miranda was going to be her daughter-in-law. "I ran into Chelsea's mom today. She gave me Chelsea's contact info. I'm going to try to make things up with her." This was just the change of subject I needed. Mom lightened up considerably after that and we actually had a civilized, normal conversation and I didn't feel on the defensive. We talked until almost dawn and finally called it a night when we were both yawning more than speaking.

Grant and I left the next afternoon and I was actually sad to say goodbye to mom. We each hugged her and promised to call when we arrived back in the city.

"So you and mom seemed to be getting along," Grant mentioned.

"Yeah, we had a good talk last night."

"Wow, that's amazing," he joked.

"I know, right? I'm glad we came to visit though; guess I needed it too."

"We're family; it's always good to go home." I nodded in agreement and stared out the window at the passing farmland. The leaves were beginning to change color, shades of reds and yellows blazed the tree line. Farmers were readying the fields for winter, pulling in their last harvest of pumpkins and gourds.

"Speaking of family…when are you going to pop the question to Miranda?" I asked.

"I'm going over to her parents' house for dinner tonight. I will speak to Marco in private there and ask for her hand." This was typical for Grant, a very traditional approach.

"Well, break a leg. I still don't understand why you would want Marco as a father-in-law."

"I'm marrying Miranda, not her father," he pointed out.

"Yeah, but Marco has a way of making his presence known," I replied.

"He's not so bad."

"What? Not so bad?" I yelled at him. "Did you forget about what he did to me?" I couldn't believe he didn't see Marco as a monster, like I did. Love must really have clouded his vision.

"You just have to get to know him. He's in a very powerful position and has to do certain things to maintain that position."

"Oh, I know him, I still feel his hands around my throat every once in a while," I yelled back at him. Grant winced, but didn't say anything else. We rode the rest of the way in silence. I couldn't believe Grant was defending Marco. He had already crossed over to the dark side and I was now beginning to see it.

Grant dropped me off in front of the lobby and I got out without saying another word; I figured the slammed door said enough for me. Dominic wasn't home and it was nice to have the condo to myself. I grabbed a diet coke out of the fridge and plopped on the sofa. Turning the television on, I watched without paying attention. The news came on and the top story was about another mob related slaying that had occurred on Passyunk Avenue. I changed the channel. It was comforting to know that Grant was out of town when that occurred and didn't pull the trigger. Dominic, on the other hand, could have. I shuddered at the picture of him holding a gun and blowing somebody's brains out without any remorse. Lack of sleep caught up to me and I dozed off as the sun set and the apartment grew dark.

The deadbolt sliding in the door woke me up. The sound reminded me of the safety being released on a gun; something working the gun check familiarized me with. The kitchen light came on and Dominic peered around the entertainment center. He smiled when he saw me lying on the sofa.

"I'm sorry if I woke you," he said.

"It's okay." I yawned and stretched. "What time is it anyway?"

"A little after nine," he answered and sat down next to me. I propped my legs up on his lap. "So, did you talk to Grant? Did you hear the news?" I was still disoriented and shook my head. Then it dawned on me what Grant was doing tonight. Secretly, I hoped that Marco would refuse Grant. "Grant and Miranda are engaged," Dom announced.

"Oh," was all I could say, feeling more disappointed than happy. "Marco was okay with it then?"

"Oh my God, Uncle Marco is thrilled. He was already making wedding plans like he was the mother of the bride!" Dominic chuckled.

"Were you there?"

"Yeah, my mom and dad were too. It was a family dinner." For some reason this comment bothered me and made me feel excluded. Dominic must have picked up on my distance and put his arm around me. "I tried calling to invite you, but your cell went right to voicemail," he explained. My phone sat on the coffee table in front of us and I reached for it. Sure enough, the battery had died and the phone shut off. I tossed it back on the table and snuggled closer to Dom.

"I'm sorry; I'm just feeling a little cranky right now."

He moved my hair aside and started softly kissing my neck. I couldn't help but giggle as his stubble tickled. He continued to leave a trail of kisses up my neck, sending goose bumps down my body. He paused at my ear. "I know how to put you in a good mood," he whispered suggestively. I was already feeling better as the familiar tingling sensation spread out from my core. I reached for his face and pressed my lips to his. We kissed and ripped each other's shirts off. I pushed him back on the sofa and climbed on top. He was right, he knew exactly how to improve my mood.

Chapter 30

Word spread fast at Crimson about Grant and Miranda's engagement. Grant strutted around the club like a prize thoroughbred. Just like in my nightmare, Miranda was radiant, her pale skin luminescent, like a pearl. I couldn't remember ever seeing Grant so happy. His face was always heavy with seriousness and that seemed to have lifted. He actually looked his age and not older. Although I wouldn't have made the same choice, I couldn't begrudge his happiness.

Miranda's ring finger was barely visible underneath the giant rock that Grant had given her. The disco ball above the dance floor didn't sparkle nearly as much as the princess cut diamond. It was the envy of most of the Crimson girls. Every time I ducked into the employee lounge to freshen up, the engagement, the ring and the upcoming nuptials were the main topics of discussion.

Dominic's description of his uncle was dead on. Marco was behaving like a mother of the bride. I had settled into a routine whenever I worked the VIP section and Marco was present. I ignored him. He had stopped giving me any attention after I had slapped him at Brittany's funeral, and that made ignoring him so much easier. Tonight he was sitting at his usual booth surrounded by his boys. His brothers, Al and Rico, were among them. Even though the wedding was a year away, Marco was busy discussing the wedding and how many people to invite. By the sounds of things, they were going to have to rent one of the stadiums to accommodate the guest list. Knowing the Grabanos, they probably owned one of the stadiums anyway. The conversation steered towards the inclusion of the Five Families in New York and that's when the tone became more serious.

"I don't want to give them an opportunity to do anything at Miranda's wedding," Marco stated.

"Yeah, but if we don't invite them, it will be received as a slight and will only make matters worse," Al reasoned.

"Do you really think they would mar a sacred event like a wedding?" Rico, Dominic's father, asked.

"Of course they would take advantage of an opportunity like that. I'm surprised they haven't settled the score yet; killing Luigi is all the reason they need, not to mention the others," Marco added. Everyone around the table grew quiet. Marco caught me eavesdropping and his eyes got dark. I looked away, feeling my face flush. So Grant had warned them about the New York families' plans for retaliation. I wondered if Dominic knew. If he did he was really good at appearing calm. One thing that was becoming increasingly clear to me was that it didn't matter how high the body count got. There was always going to be one family trying to establish power and control. Reading about it in the paper or hearing about it on the news is one thing, but actually knowing the people that are being killed, and the ones that are doing the killing, is entirely different – and extremely disturbing.

I hurried over to another table to take drink orders. Even though my back was facing Marco, I could still feel his penetrating gaze. I wondered if he saw the fear in my eyes before I turned away from him. Grant and Dominic were moving targets, the conversation I overheard just confirmed that, and my stomach was twisted so tight, it hurt to breath.

Dominic sensed the tension the second I sat down at his bar and ordered a drink. I hadn't drunk anything alcoholic the past couple of weeks, but I surrendered to the craving tonight. The vodka and tonic went down way too smoothly and didn't quench my thirst. I ordered another one. This too disappeared quickly and left me wanting more. When I ordered a third, Dominic raised his eyebrow and hesitated. "Nat, what's up? Why are you drinking like you're on a mission?"

"No reason," I lied.

"Uh hunh," he said as he set another drink down in front of me. From the first sip I could tell this drink wasn't as strong as the first two.

"Let's run away together," I blurted out. He laughed and set a clean glass on the shelf. He picked up a dripping wet martini glass and started drying it.

"Where did you have in mind?" he asked.

"I don't know," I slurred. "Anywhere." He set the martini glass down, flung the dish towel over his shoulder and looked at me.

"When?"

"Now, tomorrow, I don't care, just soon."

"We can ask for some vacation time. Let's plan something."

"Not a vacation, I mean let's move, let's leave Philly behind and go somewhere new," I corrected him. His smile disappeared when I said this and his eyes got dark, reminding me of a green version of Marco's.

"Why do you want to move? Aren't you happy here with me?"

I took another long sip before I answered. "I am happy with you, but I think I need a change of scenery," I looked up at the VIP section where Marco and his crew still sat. "And I think it would be safer for you to get out of Philly too."

Dominic reached across the bar and took my hand in his. "Is that what you're worried about? That something's going to happen to me?"

"Yes," I said quietly. "I know that the Genovese family knows you and Grant took out Luigi." He caressed my hand as I spoke. "Grant is set on marrying Miranda and staying here; I thought I could convince you to leave." He reached over with his other hand and lifted my chin so he could look in my eyes.

"I'll be safe, Grant will be safe. This stuff happens all the time, please don't worry." He kissed the tip of my nose.

"I don't know if I can do that. How can you be so calm knowing that someone wants you dead?"

"It's what I grew up around; I'm used to it."

"You may be used to it, but I don't think I ever can be. I still feel like I'm on a Sopranos episode." Dom laughed again and his face was all smiles and dimples again. Any seriousness was gone. He kissed me quickly on the lips and went back to cleaning up his bar. I drained the rest of my drink, but didn't ask for another. My body was already comfortably numb.

Dom and I walked across the dimly lit parking lot to his Mustang from Miranda's Mercedes. We were both pretty stoned and the pot had helped to mellow me out even more. I was relieved to see that the FBI hadn't shown back up, although I still looked around for the familiar sedan. After the last interaction with Agent Phillips, he hadn't maintained his surveillance or attempted to contact me again. He had conveyed his message.

Dom pulled out onto Columbus Blvd. and I stared out the window at the deserted neighborhoods. Several of the surrounding warehouses were boarded up and crumbling into dust.

"You're awfully quiet," Dom interrupted my silence.

"Hmm, just thinking."

"About what?"

"Would you ever leave Philly? I mean, have you ever wanted to see what else the world has to offer?"

He didn't hesitate to answer. "No. I would never leave my family. Besides, there aren't any reasons to leave. I have everything I could possibly want." He set his hand on my thigh and gently squeezed. "Why do you ask?"

"I was just wondering. I never planned on staying here after graduation...thought it would be nice to live somewhere else for a while." Dominic was quiet and he stared straight ahead. I saw his jaw tense up. The tops of his knuckles were white from gripping the steering wheel too tightly.

He pulled in front of our building and handed the keys to the valet. The elevator ride to our floor was silent. Dominic flipped the lights on in the entryway to the condo and took my jacket. He still hadn't said anything. I was getting nervous.

Finally he broke the silence. "Are you thinking about leaving?" he demanded. His voice was sharp and his eyes angry. I took a step back.

"No! It's just," I paused. "I love you and I'm happy with you. It's the craziness around us I want to leave. The death and the violence..."

"You can't leave, remember? Uncle Marco will have your head – and Grant's – if you leave," he reminded me. His eyes flashed in anger as added emphasis.

"That's why I thought if we left together, he wouldn't mind so much."

"That's not going to happen," he glared at me.

"So, I'm stuck here, there aren't any other options?"

"Stuck here? Is that how you feel? I thought you were doing okay, I thought we were okay," he said with a pained expression on his face. I rushed to him and wrapped my arms around his waist. I looked up at him.

"We are and I love you. If I am stuck here I couldn't think of a better person to be stuck with," I leaned my head against his chest to hide my face. "I'm just freaking out, feeling trapped and helpless, you know? I'm sorry." I wasn't going to push the issue anymore tonight. Right now there didn't appear to be an alternative, but I would find one.

He kissed the top of my head, wrapping his muscular arms around me and hugging me close to him. "I'm sorry too. You deserve to be able to go and do what you want, wherever you want. I'm sorry that if you did, you would be hunted down. Uncle Marco meant what he said." This sounded more like a threat than an apology.

"I understand," I said. I pulled away and faked a yawn. "I'm going to bed." I wasn't tired but went to bed anyway. Dom came in about an hour later and I pretended to be asleep. He curled up next to me and fell asleep almost instantly. His soft snores whispered in my ear.

The condo was still and gave me plenty of time to think. Most of my friends from high school and college were off pursuing their dreams. Becoming a permanent resident of Philadelphia was never part of my game plan. Yes, I loved Dominic, but I didn't love his family. Yes, Dominic would let me pursue my artistic goals, but within the confines of the city. Ultimately, I would always be tethered to the criminal underworld, where violence governed. Brittany had grown up around the mob and she couldn't hack it. Was I strong enough to handle this lifestyle?

Dom was never going to leave and neither would Grant. I resigned myself to stick it out and try to make it work. What other choice did I have? I sighed and turned to face Dominic. He slept so peacefully. His full lips were parted slightly and the traces of stubble shadowed his face. His thick black hair was tousled and hung over his dark eyebrows. I traced the lines of his tattoo, of the word "famiglia" branded on his arm and he slept on, unaware of my light caress.

The room started to lighten with the onset of daybreak and sleep still hadn't come. With another sigh, I rolled over and got out of bed. I quietly slipped on track pants and a hooded sweatshirt from my alma mater. I grabbed my iPod, put on sneakers and left the condo. The concierge looked up briefly when I walked by and waved. The doorman held the door open for me and I was off running towards Penn's Landing. Whenever I had too many thoughts weighing heavily on my mind, going for a run usually helped. Rush hour traffic was beginning to build as the city woke up. The sidewalks were still clear and I ran uninterrupted past Penn's Landing and up to South St. I crossed over and went down 7th street. As I approached the Italian Market the streets and sidewalks were too congested to keep a consistent pace, so I turned around and headed back to the condo. By the time I approached our building, my legs were quivering like Jell-O.

The endorphins had worked their magic and cleared my head. I caught my breath in the elevator and reveled at the stillness, the million different thoughts pinging around had ceased. A steamy hot shower was sounding really good and I couldn't wait to get inside to strip off the sweaty clothes. I opened the door and was surprised to see Dominic up. He turned as soon as he heard the door swing open.

"Where have you been?" he snapped. I was taken aback by his intensity.

"I went for a run," I answered defensively and set the iPod down on the kitchen counter.

"Oh," he replied and visibly relaxed. "Sorry, I didn't mean to bark at you."

"What's that all about anyway?" I asked, not ready to accept his apology. He never cared where I went and had never questioned me before.

"I thought you might have left me," he admitted. "I tried your cell phone, but you left it here. You know you should really take that with you."

"Thanks for the advice, Dad," I mocked. "Maybe I'll go running next time with my purse too, you never know when I'll need to reapply lipstick or get a piece of gum. Did you really think I had left?"

"I didn't know what to think. I woke up and you weren't here and after last night's conversation..." he looked at me with sad eyes. "I'm sorry, I overreacted. Forgive me?" I stood with my arms crossed over my chest and debated. I was going to forgive him, but wanted to make him sweat a little bit.

"I can't leave, remember? Besides, would I really leave my purse, my car and you behind?" I smiled at this last part to let him know his apology was accepted. He smiled a huge smile and I couldn't help but walk up and kiss him, even though I felt gross and didn't want any close contact. His dimples were impossible to resist. "Now please stop all the crazy stuff," I said sternly as we separated.

I shook my head at Dominic's silliness as I walked down the hall to our bedroom. My ponytail swung back and forth like a pendulum. The sweatshirt was yanked off before I even walked into the bedroom. The shower was calling my name.

Hot water coursed over my body and rinsed the sweat off. The heat relaxed my muscles and the exhaustion from missing a night of sleep set in. Dominic came into the bathroom and leaned against the vanity.

"Hey baby?" he asked.

"Yeah?" I answered as I rinsed the conditioner out of my hair.

"Wanna go to the haunted house thing at Eastern State Penitentiary tomorrow night?"

"Sure, that sounds awesome! I hear it's really scary." Dominic and I both like horror movies and anything paranormal. We were looking forward to the costume party at Crimson. Apparently everyone went all out for it. We were going to dress up as Frankenstein and the Bride of Frankenstein. In the past my Halloween costumes were lame because I was always broke, but that wasn't going to be the case this year.

"Cool, I'll make the arrangements," he stood up to leave the room, but not before peeking in the shower first. I splashed water at his bare chest and he laughed as he attempted to dodge the droplets. He was still laughing when he left the room.

A line wrapped around the corner of Eastern State Penitentiary. The old prison was modeled after ancient European castles and looked out of place on Fairmount Avenue. The neighborhood had grown around it and the fortress loomed over the row homes and businesses that surrounded it. Parking was hard to find, but Dominic expertly navigated his Mustang into a space on a narrow, one way street, that looked like it might have been an alley at one point. We had to walk several blocks to the Penitentiary. Even though it was almost ten at night, and a Tuesday, the line was long. I walked up to stand in line, but Dominic grabbed my hand and we continued walking past the crowd to the front.

"What are you doing?" I asked and tried tugging him back. You didn't want to cut in lines in Philadelphia because the residents were quick to turn on you and not afraid to express their opinion on the matter.

"My dad knows the accountant…we don't have to wait," he informed me.

"Figures. That is so typical." I said and rolled my eyes. Laughing, Dom walked up to the ticket taker at the entrance and handed him a card. The guy waved us through. I could hear the people waiting in line start to grumble so I hurried through.

"This is one of the reasons I could never leave Philly; the connections make everything so easy," Dominic gloated. Ever since our little argument, Dominic had picked up the annoying habit of pointing out everything that was fabulous about living in Philadelphia. He could have worked for the Chamber of Commerce.

We proceeded down a corridor that seemed endless. I could barely see in front of me and creatures, ghouls and psychopaths lurked in every corner and shadow. I clung to Dom and screamed at every sudden movement. The thrills left me feeling queasy and nervous – I loved it. By the end of the tour, we were laughing at our ridiculousness. Even Dom jumped and got spooked. I continued to hang on his arm as we walked to a corner bar for a quick drink. A cool wind had picked up and Dom's warmth felt nice.

The bar was packed too. Many of the patrons had been to the Penitentiary and were sharing stories. Dom found us a table in the back where it was quiet. "I know the owner," he explained. Of course he did. He held my hand across the table and only took his eyes off of me to order our drinks.

"That was fun, wasn't it?" he asked.

"Oh my God, that was so realistic. They really know how to do it up. I thought that place was creepy enough during the daytime."

"Philly has so many cool places," he started in on the marketing pitch again.

"Dom, I'm not going anywhere, you don't have to try to convince me to stay. You sound like a damn tourism commercial for the city."

He smiled, his green eyes twinkling. "Was it that obvious?"

"Uh, yeah!" I couldn't help but laugh at him. Where he got these notions was beyond me.

We took our time sipping our drinks. I enjoyed not being at a bar surrounded by Crimson people. The change of scenery was refreshing. When we got up to leave, Dom left a generous tip on the table for the waitress before we squeezed our way through the crowded bar.

Outside, the neighborhood was quiet. We huddled close against the wind as we walked the few blocks to the car. The narrow street was dimly lit and most of the houses were dark, indicative of the late hour. Dom held the door open for me and shut it as soon as I was settled in the passenger seat. I busied myself with the seatbelt and getting comfortable. Dom slid in and turned the key in the ignition. The engine roared to life. Headlights were coming down the road and he sat, waiting for the car to pass before he pulled out. I bent down to scratch my ankle when I heard a car backfire. I thought it was the car coming down the street because it was close. The car backfired again and the driver's side window imploded. Shards of glass flew through the air in slow motion. I stared at the sparkling fragments, confused. A series of bangs erupted around me. Dominic made an odd gasping sound and slumped against the steering wheel. Something wet splattered against my face.

I screamed and sunk down in the seat. A bullet whizzed by my ear. Had I not moved, it would have hit me. My window shattered and I was showered in glass. Dominic groaned and clutching his neck, leaned over to the glove compartment. He made another grunting sound and he fell forward against me. That's when I saw a dark green sedan stopped alongside the Mustang. Both the driver and passenger were firing rounds into the car. I could hear the bullets punching into the steel chassis. We were vulnerable and exposed. I popped open the glove compartment and pulled out Dominic's handgun. My experience working the gun check taught me how to release the safety and prepared me for the surprisingly dense weight of the piece.

Without hesitation I started firing back. The sound was deafening. Amazingly, I hit the guy in the passenger seat. He yelped, dropping his piece onto the street. The driver fired a few more rounds and I felt a searing pain in my right shoulder, causing me to almost drop the gun. Lights appeared in the second story windows of several homes, but no one ventured out. This was good, my aim was terrible and I would hate to hit someone with a stray bullet. I fired off one last time and it was a direct hit. The passenger's face looked surprised and his lips formed an "O" before his eyes went vacant and blood started to ooze from a tiny hole in his forehead. He crumpled against the driver who shoved him over, put the car in drive and sped off.

The neighborhood was eerily quiet, but more lights were coming on. Adrenaline rushed through my veins as I contemplated my next move before hysteria and shock took over. I needed to get us out of here.

"Dom, baby? Can you hear me?" He moaned and tried to sit up. Instead he rolled over so his head was in my lap. He was struggling to breath and making a horrible sucking sound every time he inhaled. He was still holding his neck and staring up at me. "We need to go," he wheezed. I nodded and cradled his head while

I slid out from beneath. My fingers were sticky with blood when I removed them from his head.

My shoulder burned, but I ignored the pain. I only had a few seconds to act before someone came out of their house or the cops showed up. I jumped out of the car and ran round to the driver's side. After throwing my back into it, I succeeded in shoving Dom over enough for me to get behind the wheel. Thank God the car was already running because my shaking hands would never have been able to get the keys in the ignition. I threw the car into drive and pulled out onto the street. As soon as I was clear of the parked cars, I floored it. One bad thing about Dom's car was that it was a classic and very identifiable. I needed to get off the roads fast and get Dom to a hospital even faster.

Dom curled up on the seat and I kept one hand on him with the other on the steering wheel, paying more attention to the sounds of his breathing than the road. I don't know how many red lights I ran. At least the side streets weren't policed as often as the main roads, like Broad St. I fished Dominic's cell out of his jacket pocket. It took me three tries to dial Grant's number.

He answered on the fourth ring. "Yo, Dom, what's up?"

"Grant!" I screamed. Just hearing his voice was causing me to fall apart and I couldn't afford to lose it yet. "Dom's been shot! He needs to go to the hospital." I cursed the tears that were pouring down my face and blurring my vision.

Grant was all business. "Where are you?"

I could barely make out the street signs as I passed through an intersection. I just went past Sansom, I'm heading south on 12th St. I'm taking him to Pennsylvania Hospital."

"No you can't do that!" He yelled. "The cops will be all over him."

"But I think he's dying!" I yelled back at him.

"Come to our house. I'll be out front."

"Stay on the phone with me. I don't know if I can make it." Grant stayed on the phone and spoke in a calm, rational voice, which helped me to focus on the road. A hell of a lot of good it would do if I wrecked the car.

The Mustang screeched to a halt in front of Grant and Miranda's townhouse, Grant was already running into the street, Miranda right behind him, her face pinched and pale with worry.

"Get in the back," he ordered. I complied and clumsily climbed over the seat as Grant took over behind the wheel. Miranda opened the back door and sat down next to me. I was covered in blood. It was hard to tell which belonged to me or to Dom.

Miranda gasped. "Natalie, you've been shot too!" She leaned over to inspect the damage. Grant whipped his head around to look.

"What! Holy shit, are you okay?"

"I'm fine," I snapped. "Just pay attention to the road." Grant was speeding through South Philly, the neighborhoods whizzed by in a blur. My shoulder ached and I felt sick to my stomach.

"I need to lie down," I whispered, feeling faint. Miranda helped me and guided my head onto her lap. She ran her hands through my hair, picking out bits of glass, the repetitive motion was comforting. My pulse beat loudly in my head and everything shifted in and out of focus.

"I killed someone," I murmured.

"What Nat? What did you say?" Miranda was leaning down over me.

"I killed someone," my voice sounded very far away. The adrenaline was wearing off, being replaced by shock and making my eyelids heavy. Then everything went black.

Chapter 31

I woke when the Mustang slammed to a stop and Miranda got out. A chorus of panicked voices filled the car and I felt it rock. I managed to open my eyes enough to see Dominic being lifted out by his father and Dr. Russo. Then the door by me opened and Grant was peering in at me.

"Can you walk?"

"Yeah, I think so."

He held his hand out and I latched on. He half pulled me out of the car and my legs shook when I stood. Dizziness swirled around my head and I felt myself getting sucked under again. I remembered Grant swearing before he scooped me into his arms.

Voices faded in and out. Two men were arguing and then a woman was crying. Just as I was making sense of the words, unconsciousness wrapped its arms around me again. Time passed and I hovered just underneath the surface. My shoulder was on fire, a slow burn that steadily built until it felt like millions of hot needles were jabbing repeatedly, deep through the muscle and tissue. Eventually the pain forced my eyelids open.

The room was brightly lit and hurt my eyes. I quickly closed them and slowly eased my eyelids open again, allowing time to adjust. I looked around the room and realized I had been here before. I was lying on the examination table in Dr. Russo's office. The door was open and I could hear hushed voices drifting down the hall. I attempted to sit up, but between the searing pain in my shoulder and the pounding in my head, I was immobilized.

"Hello?" I called out. The voices stopped and I could hear someone running down the hall. Grant appeared in the doorway. His long sleeved, blue shirt was stained with patches of dried blood. He looked anxious and exhausted.

"Hey," I said, smiling weakly.

"Natalie, you're awake!" Grant came and stood by my side. "How do you feel?" he asked while studying my face.

"I feel like I've been hit by a train...how's Dominic?"

"It was touch and go there for a while, but Dr. Russo worked his magic. Dom was shot in the neck and it nicked his carotid artery. He was close to bleeding out. He also took a bullet in the chest and it collapsed his lung. Fortunately, he's stable now." Relief washed over me.

"How long have I been out?"

"Almost a day. Dr. Russo kept you sedated so you wouldn't move around too much. You're lucky, the bullet passed clean through your shoulder."

"If I was lucky I wouldn't have been shot in the first place." He smirked like I had just made a funny. I hadn't.

"Natalie, what the hell happened? Did you see who shot at you?" His questions triggered too many bloody memories and I started to tremble. I closed my eyes, hoping to block the images, but they were in my head and closing my eyes didn't make a difference. "You don't have to tell me now, but I will need to know eventually," he said when I didn't respond to his questions. I nodded my head in acknowledgement. Just this slight movement made the pounding worse.

Grant must have seen the pain register on my face. "Dr. Russo will be in soon. He's checking on Dominic right now."

I opened my eyes and looked at my brother. "Dominic is here?"

"Yeah. We couldn't take him to the hospital. Fortunately Dr. Russo is a great doctor. He's in the next room."

I reached my hand out towards Grant. "Help me up."

"What?" he asked sounding surprised.

"Help me up," I demanded. "I need to go see him." I winced as I tried to sit up and inhaled sharply. It wouldn't surprise me if my arm just fell off.

"I don't think you should be moving." He warned as he grabbed me around the waist and helped me off the exam table. I thought the floor was going to rush up and meet me, but Grant kept a firm grip on my good arm. "You are so stubborn," he grumbled.

"And you're not?" He grinned at the return of our brother sister banter and helped me to the door.

Dr. Russo wasn't the only person checking on Dominic. His mom and dad sat in chairs by his bedside. Dom's mom, Angela, held his hand and leaned forward towards him. She didn't look up when we entered the room, but Rico did.

"Natalie!" He gave me a light hug, careful not to bump the sling. "How are you feeling?" He whispered, careful not to disturb Dominic.

"I'm good considering...I'm more worried about Dom. How's he doing?"

"Alright. He hasn't regained consciousness yet, but Dr. Russo has him pretty well sedated." We all turned to look at the patient of interest. Unlike my exam table, Dominic lay on a hospital bed and was hooked up to a heart monitor and an IV. Both saline and blood dripped down tubes that led to his arm. Rico turned back to face me. "Thank you, Natalie, for saving him. I don't think he'd be here right now if it wasn't for you." Rico's green eyes, so much like his son's, misted up with tears.

"What happened?" Angela asked from Dominic's bedside.

It took me a minute to answer. I felt the blood drain from my face and felt dizzy when I thought about the man I had killed. Grant must have seen me waver and reached out to steady me. "I'm okay," I reassured him. Dominic's parents deserved an explanation. After all, if he hadn't defended my honor, he wouldn't have had a hit out on him and he wouldn't be lying there unconscious. I took a deep breath and began. By the time I finished I was shaking uncontrollably and Grant guided me to a chair. Reliving that night was awful and had drained what little energy I had.

Angela regarded me with her eyes, dark like molasses. "You're very brave, braver than I could have been in that situation." I nodded my head. Brave or not I had still killed a man. "Thank you for saving my son."

"I think he would have done the same for me."

Angela's eyes flickered slightly and she glanced sideways at Rico. "Of course he would," she agreed, but it didn't sound sincere.

The pounding in my head increased so I leaned back and closed my eyes.

"Natalie, let me take a look at you." I looked up to find Dr. Russo was standing over me. "On a scale of 1 to 10 how would you describe your pain level? Ten being the worst."

"My shoulder is about a seven and my head a four. Did I bump my head and not remember?"

"No the sedative can give you a headache when it wears off. Did you want some more pain medicine?"

"No. I'll be fine." I didn't like how cloudy the pain meds made me feel. It was hard to stay focused on anything. The pain gave my thoughts clarity. I thought about how different my reaction was to this traumatic event. When I was assaulted all I wanted to do was mask the pain with alcohol or drugs. This time I needed to keep my head on straight.

Dr. Russo escorted me back to my room for a more thorough exam. He removed the bandages from my shoulder and I hissed as the tape tugged against the raw skin. He cleaned the wound, which was an agonizing process and I clenched my jaw tight to keep from screaming.

"How's your friend? The one that I treated the last time you were in here?" Dr. Russo asked as he examined my wound.

"She's…she's dead," I stammered, the last part coming out in a hoarse whisper.

Dr. Russo set down the gauze and iodine bottle and looked at me. Small, silver glasses framed his eyes.

"I'm sorry to hear that. Do you mind if I ask how she died?"

"Suicide."

"Ah, such a shame. She couldn't get past that night could she?"

"No."

"And now you're in here with a gunshot wound," he turned away to remove the surgical gloves and wash his hands in the small sink. "That's how the mob works. Once you're in their grasp, it's hard to escape."

He said this with such conviction; I suspected he too was trapped. Curious, I waited for him to face me again before I asked, "Are you speaking from personal experience?"

Dr. Russo glanced at the closed door. "Yes, you could say that," he answered in a hushed voice. "I used to have a thriving private practice up on the Mainline." I'd only been up to the Mainline once. The affluent suburb was beautiful and reeked of wealth.

"What happened to it?"

"I have a gambling problem and racked up quite a bill with Marco. I lost everything: my wife and kids, the house. I managed to convince Marco I would be an asset to his organization. He agreed and I walked away with my life and medical license."

"Surely you've paid off your debt?"

"Probably, but I've seen and heard too much. The Hippocratic Oath doesn't mean anything to Marco."

"So you have this South Philly practice instead?"

"Yes and I see my kids every other weekend. Although they're both in high school now and don't come as often." Dr. Russo sighed. "You seem like a nice girl, Miss Ross. I'm sorry for this trauma you've endured." Dr. Russo patted my good shoulder. It was more of a fatherly gesture than a clinical one.

"Thanks, but none of this is your doing."

"I think you're well enough to go home. I don't see any signs of infection and your bed at home is probably more comfortable than this." He lightly slapped the side of the examination table I was perched on. I couldn't imagine anyone taller than me being able to sleep on it. Their feet would hang off the edge. "I want you to come by on Monday so I can take another look." He handed me written instructions on how to care for my wound and a white paper bag, like what you would pack a school lunch in, that was full of gauze, antibacterial ointment and a lot of pain reliever.

"How long until Dominic is able to come home?" I asked.

"Well, it's hard to say. He lost a lot of blood and was in shock. Once he regains consciousness I'll know more."

"Shouldn't he be in a hospital?" I asked, hoping I didn't offend the kind man.

"Yes, he should. Nobody wanted to hear it. I argued with them for close to an hour, but Marco refused. His parents listened to Marco. End of story." It didn't surprise me that Marco had something to do with it. Dr. Russo helped me down off of the exam table. "Your brother will take you home. Please take it easy and don't exert yourself. We really need to stop meeting like this," he said with a smile.

He left the room so I could get changed. Someone had brought me clean clothes; a soft, cotton button down shirt and sweat pants. I didn't recognize them and assumed they were Miranda's since we wore the same size. I was relieved to get out of the hospital gown and into the comfortable outfit. I winced a few times as I slipped my injured arm into the shirt sleeve, but managed to put it on and the fabric was soft enough, it didn't irritate my injury. Thank God I didn't have to put on a bra, that would have been near to impossible and torture.

Clutching the paper bag and my purse in one hand, I walked down the hall to the waiting room. Grant was dozing in one of the plastic chairs. I hadn't noticed until now just how ragged and run down he looked. He must not have slept since I pulled up in front of his house like a NASCAR driver pulls into the pit. I nudged his foot with mine and he jerked awake. His eyes were bloodshot, usually how he looked after smoking a joint, but I knew he wasn't high.

"Hey, the doc released me, ready to take me home?"

"Yes, sure." He stood up and took the bags from my hand.

"Thank you Dr. Russo," I said as we were almost out the door. "Oh, wait! How much do I owe you?"

"It's already been taken care of, you just focus on healing," he answered from behind the small reception desk.

"Oh. Okay, thanks." I waved with my good arm and followed Grant out into the street. The sun burned my eyes and I had to squint and catch my bearings. Grant went ahead and pulled his Lexus up to the curb. He hopped out and helped me into the car. I felt like a helpless child as he fastened the seatbelt for me.

Grant spoke to me as soon as he was driving down the street. "Natalie, I am so sorry you were shot. I should never have gotten you a job at Crimson."

"Grant, please don't blame yourself. You warned me and I didn't listen," I placated him.

"I thought I could keep you out of the major stuff and you would have a job until the end of summer...you know save up some money? It all went wrong so fast and spun out of my control. You getting shot is my fault; if Dom and I hadn't killed Luigi and his boys, this would never have happened." I could see the torment on his face. Grant was always going to be my protective big brother; I just didn't realize how much he was shouldering the blame.

"Grant, you can't control everything, especially me." I paused, dreading the next question I had to ask. "I need to know something...now that I killed one of the Genovese soldiers, are they going to come after me?"

He didn't say anything, but I could read the answer on his face, especially when the fine line of sweat formed on his upper lip. The answer was clear. While I had successfully defended us, a target had been placed on my back as well. Now Grant, Dominic and I were wanted. How could they protect me now?

Grant must have felt the stress and panic radiating off of me in waves. "Don't worry Natalie, the Grabanos are on the offensive now and won't let anything happen to you, or to Dom and I."

"You can't guarantee that. If that was the case, Dom and I wouldn't have been attacked in the first place!" I stopped to calm down, my breathing was accelerating with my heartbeat and it made my headache worse.

"You might have to lay low for a few days, which you need to do anyway…doctor's orders." I groaned, once again I was going to be cloistered away in the condo, afraid to go outside. I didn't know which was worse, the idea that people wanted me dead or the guilt that I had taken a human life. Being alone in the condo without any distractions was going to magnify these two concerns and that was a daunting thought. "Marco and the boys are figuring out their next move. Everyone is on full alert and waiting to hear any news from New York and what plans are being made there," Grant informed me.

This alarmed me. "What do you mean next move? Marco's not planning on retaliating, is he?"

"Hell yeah he is! The Genovese's tried to kill his nephew; they might as well have attempted to take out Marco. You don't mess with his family."

"But, you guys started it!" I yelled.

"No, the second they messed with you and Brittany is when it started." Grant replied, his voice flat.

"But Marco let them get away with it…he fed us to the wolves!" I choked, the tears were building up. This was ridiculous. Reasoning with mafia logic was like trying to reason with a room full of preschoolers.

"That's the way it's done and has been for decades. Just stop worrying, everything will be worked out," he said with more annoyance in his tone than reassurance. I wanted to believe him, but the bullet hole in my shoulder contradicted his statement. I didn't say anything to that effect, it would be a low blow and I could tell Grant was already stressed to the max.

We were silent the rest of the way. The doorman opened my door and looked alarmed when he saw my arm in a sling. Like the last time I stepped out the car looking battle worn, he kept his mouth shut. Experience must have taught him that the less he knew the better. I wished I knew less; I would definitely be better off.

Grant got the door to the condo and held it open for me. The garbage had turned rancid in our absence and the odor permeated the apartment. Grant immediately snatched the bag out of the can.

"Where does this go?"

"Down at the end of the hall there is a garbage chute," I instructed. Grant left and I dumped the contents of the white paper bag onto the counter. The short ride had left me drained and in pain. My shoulder ached, a deep, throbbing burn that couldn't be ignored. Reluctantly, I swallowed a pain pill.

Grant returned moments later and surveyed the condo. "Is there anything else you would like me to do? Are you hungry at all?"

"No, I'm not hungry, but I feel nasty. Could you, um, help me take a bath?" I was mortified that I would have to ask my brother to do this and my cheeks grew hot. He seemed just as embarrassed and froze at my request.

"Err, sure," he answered, lacking his usual confidence.

"I would ask Mom, but since she doesn't know I was shot, I don't have anyone else."

"What about one of your girlfriends? Wouldn't it be better if one of them…or Miranda?"

"None of them know about this…besides I've kind of lost touch with them and Miranda's well, I'm more comfortable with you."

"Oh. I guess so."

"I wouldn't ask you if there was anyone else. I'm not thrilled about having to be naked in front of you because that's just weird and wrong on so many levels. You won't have to like, wash me or anything. I just need help getting in and out of the tub."

I saw relief wash over his face at this, "Okay, I can do it and you're right, it is going to be weird," he said with a laugh, running his hands through his hair and looking nervously in the direction of the bathroom.

I filled the tub with steaming hot water and extra bubbles. Grant waited until I was ready to step into the tub to assist me. He averted his eyes as much as he could while I concentrated on not slipping. To say it was an awkward moment for both of us would be an understatement. By the time I had finished cleaning up, the pain medicine had kicked in and I was drowsy. Grant helped me out and I managed to dry off with one arm. Grant pulled one of Dominic's button-down shirts out of the walk-in closet and helped me to put it on. Then he helped me with the sling.

"I need to head to the club and get ready for tonight. Will you be okay here on your own?" he asked.

I yawned. "Yes, I'm ready to crash." I slid into bed. Dr. Russo was right; it did feel good to be home.

"Well, call me if you need anything. I'll stop by later to check on you."

"Okay," I yawned again and was asleep before he even left the bedroom.

I walked up the stairs at The Speak. Even though I didn't want to go, some invisible force propelled me forward. I knew Mr. Genovese would be waiting for me behind the door on the left. Instead of heading there, my body turned to the door on the right. I expected to see Brittany on the floor and braced myself.

The scene was different and it took me a few moments to make sense of it. Brittany was on the floor, her naked body propped against the far left end of the sofa. Her head hung forward, limp against her chest. Her legs, mottled with bruises and smeared with blood, splayed out in front of her. She reminded me of the way Raggedy Ann dolls would sit. Just one glimpse convinced me that life no longer existed in her body. The three men that Grant shot months ago sat next to each other on the sofa, their bloodied bodies leaned against one another like drunks trying to support one another. This was silly though because they were all dead and missing part of, if not all of their heads. On one of the club chairs, across from the sofa, sat the man I had shot. A dried stream of blood ran from the hole in his forehead, down the side of his nose and down the rest of his face, by his mouth. The rusty stream had dripped off of his chin and pooled into a giant brown stain on his gray sweatshirt. His cloudy eyes stared out ahead and he still had the same surprised look on his face. I wanted to run from the room, but the invisible force kept me glued in place.

What was going on behind the macabre audience of corpses had my attention. Instead of Brittany being brutally raped, with the gun forced into her mouth, it was me. I watched myself get violated time and time again. First by the driver of the car that had parked alongside us and shot up the Mustang, then by Marco, then some other rough looking thug types I didn't recognize. One after the other, they had their way with me and had the audacity to high five one another when they finished. I couldn't look away. I wanted to yell at myself to do something, but my other self's eyes were empty- indicating that I had mentally retreated to some far off place and couldn't hear myself.

Marco walked up in front of me again and gestured to the man holding the gun in my mouth. The man nodded in understanding and pulled the trigger.

I woke up screaming.

My heart was racing and my whole body shook violently. With every tremor, stabbing pains bit at my gunshot wound. It took a while for my screams to taper off to a whimper. Thankfully the walls were thick in this place, or the neighbors probably would have come running.

There I lay on the bed, curled up in a fetal position on my good side. Trembling, sweating, whimpering in pain, and alone. There was no better time than the present for a pity party. Tears rolled down my face and I sobbed, for what seemed like hours, before I pulled myself together. It seemed like every other month I was facing a crisis and the cumulative impact was having a devastating effect on my overall well being. Instead of dwelling on the fact that I was alone like it was a bad thing, I decided to take advantage of it for some serious, uninterrupted soul searching. I didn't know how much more stress my body could handle. Now that I'd taken a life, I could feel my moral fiber beginning to fray and I needed to fix that before the damage became irreparable. I was a murderer. Instead of inspiring people through art, I was contributing to the violence I so despised. I could go to prison or get gunned down in a dark alley and become another statistic – just a blip on the headline news.

I got out of bed to get a glass of water and didn't bother turning on the light; the darkness provided a veil of anonymity that was comforting. I moved through the condo like a ghost. The pain medication bottle was barely visible in the faint light provided by the kitchen appliances. Even though the bottle called to me, I ignored it. Soul searching shouldn't be done in an altered state.

I moved away from the counter and from the temptation. As I did this, my arm bumped my purse and it went flying off the counter. Its contents spilled across the tile floor. Sighing, I flicked on the lights to clean up. I kneeled down and began picking up the miscellaneous items; my cell phone, wallet, keys, gum, lipstick, lighter and random pieces of paper. Two pieces caught my eye; Agent Phillips business card and Chelsea's business card. I paused and contemplated putting them back in my purse. Instead, I set them on the counter. An idea was forming, just on the outside of my brain, I could feel it.

I finished picking everything up and hung my purse on the back of one of the barstools, grabbed the two business cards and went to the bedroom. I flicked on the bedside lamp and sat cross legged on the bed with the two cards laid out in front of me.

I needed out. If I didn't escape I was going to be consumed and would probably wind up hanging from a noose like Brittany. Like many others before me, I could turn myself in to the FBI and ask for witness protection in exchange for evidence. The only problem there was that I was now a murderer and the only evidence that I had implicated people I loved. I couldn't clearly tie Marco to any of the crimes; he conveniently orchestrated things, but was never directly involved.

My eyes shifted to Chelsea's card. She lived on the other side of the country and had no connection to the Grabanos. Dominic, Grant, my mom, even Chelsea's mom all knew that we had a falling out. If I showed up on Chelsea's doorstep, would she turn me away? I didn't think so, we had been friends since the first grade; I had faith that she would be there for me, especially considering how dangerous my situation had become. Was this feasible? I had plenty of money saved up, thanks to my mom, who taught me not to live beyond my means. Plus, the fact that Dominic paid for everything helped.

A plan began to form. Dominic wasn't going to be home for a few days and Grant was going to be working for the next couple of nights. Sneaking away would be easy, but staying undetected would be tricky. How would I keep the mob from looking for me, from hunting me down? This was a question I didn't know how to answer. And the question kept me awake until Grant came to check on me. I heard the front door unlock and quickly set the business cards in the night stand drawer. I grabbed the latest issue of Cosmo and was pretending to read when he came into the bedroom.

"You're awake."

"You're observant," I cracked at him.

"And feeling better as your sarcasm is returning," he replied with a grin. I was feeling better. I was mapping out a different future for me and felt somewhat in control again.

"Can I get you anything?"

"No. I'm good. Any word on Dom?

"He's doing better and regained consciousness about an hour ago. His dad told Miranda that the doctor thinks he'll make a full recovery."

My sigh came out as a big whoosh. "That is excellent news!" It also meant that I needed to speed up my plan. I might not have the courage to leave once Dom came home and seeing him again would just make it harder.

"Natalie, you okay?"

"Huh, what? Yeah, I'm fine."

"You kinda zoned out there for a bit."

"Did I? Must be the meds," I said.

"So you don't need anything?"

"Nope. You don't have to hang out, I'm fine."

"Okay, call me if you do need something," Grant said before leaving. I listened for the front door to close before I pulled Chelsea's business card out. She was an assistant costume designer for Warner Brother's studios.

I grabbed a notebook out of the drawer and started jotting down my escape plan:

1) Close out bank account

2) Get oil change and tune-up on car

3) Buy a GPS

4) Get a new cell phone number

5) Set up PO Box and have mail forwarded

6) Pack

7) Write mom and Grant letters so they won't worry about me

8) Ensure that bridges aren't burned and Marco won't kill Grant for my departure and won't put a hit out on me.

9) Write a letter for Dominic, explaining why I had to leave.

10) Do all of the above and leave.

Items one through six were easy, but the last three were a hell of a lot more complicated and my window of opportunity was closing. By now I was completely exhausted. My shoulder screamed at me and I knew I needed to rest. I set the notebook on the table and tried to sleep, but the pain kept me awake. Finally, I gave up and went to take another pill. Before drifting off to sleep, I tried to think happy thoughts, hoping to keep the nightmares at bay.

I woke up refreshed. By some miracle I slept a deep, dreamless sleep. Besides feeling stiff and experiencing a little twinge of pain every now and again, my shoulder felt pretty good.

It was close to noon and I didn't have much time to get things in order. I called down to the concierge and asked them to call me a cab. I quickly brushed my teeth, brushed the tangles out of my hair and freshened up. I didn't look fantastic, but I wasn't looking to impress anyone. I called Grant and told him I was going to nap and that he didn't need to stop by until he was on his way to work. Fortunately, he sounded relieved and I didn't have to worry about him discovering my absence.

My first stop was the nearest branch of the Philadelphia Credit Union. I closed out my checking and savings account. After I left, I wished I had made it my last stop because walking around with close to twelve grand in cash on me was stressful. I went and picked out a new cell phone and number. I would cancel my old contract once I left the city. Radio Shack also sold Garmins, so three items on my list were eliminated in one afternoon. Once I was able to drive my car, I could cross item number two off. With the easy stuff taken care of, I would be able to focus on the more challenging tasks.

I made it back to the apartment in time to change back into my lounging clothes and hide my new purchases before Grant stopped in. I was tired from the exertion of shopping and didn't have to put on an act for him.

He helped to clean my wound which had scabbed over on both sides of my shoulder. Another day and still no infection - that was a good sign. I was more tolerant of the cleaning process this time around and only hissed a few times.

"Ouch!" I blurted out.

"Sorry, I'm almost done. Hold still." He had a firm grasp on my elbow to prevent me from moving. "This isn't right Nat. I shouldn't be cleaning your bullet wound. You shouldn't even have to know what it's like to be shot," he shook his head in disapproval.

"I shouldn't know what it's like to kill a man and neither should you, yet here we are." I shuddered at the memory and this caused my shoulder to bump harder against Grant's hand. I winced at the contact.

"Hold still," he reminded me, tightening his grip. He finished taping the gauze to my skin and sat back to look at me. "Did you eat anything today?"

I had to think about it. "No, I didn't," I admitted. I didn't have the energy to lie to him. He frowned at my response.

"You need to eat Nat. You need all of your strength in order to heal." He went into the kitchen to survey the options. He pulled out a can of soup and I scrunched up my nose. He sighed and put the can back in the cabinet. He pulled out a jar of peanut butter and grabbed the loaf of bread off of the counter. The first slices he pulled out were fuzzy with green mold. He grimaced and tossed the whole bag into the garbage. Still determined, he opened the freezer and spotted one of my favorite treats. Triumphant, he spun around and dropped a bag of pot stickers on the counter.

My stomach growled when I eyed them. "Cook 'em up. You know I could house that whole bag in one sitting." He started me out with six and then prepared six more. It was like having a personal chef. I was going to miss Grant. Despite all the craziness of the past few months, our bond did grow stronger.

When I was full, and Grant was satisfied that I had eaten something, he got ready to leave. "Tell everyone at work I said hi," I told him as he stepped out the door. It was extremely difficult acting normal. I was just going through the motions. As soon as I had my follow up appointment with Dr. Russo on Monday, I was leaving. I just hoped that Dominic didn't come home in the next four days. There was still a lot I had to accomplish in that short period of time.

The deadline had me antsy and once again I couldn't sleep. Instead, I stayed up to write the letters to Grant and to my mom.

Mom,

Sometime I will be able to explain to you why I had to leave. There are a myriad of reasons and many I can't tell you right now. There is one reason I can tell you now, and I know you will understand – I am putting myself first. Life has spun out of control for me these past nine months and I need to go get my head together.

I know we haven't always had the best relationship, a lot of that has to do with me. When we do see each other again, I want to wipe the slate clean and start from scratch. I'm all about new beginnings these days...

Please don't try to find me. I will contact you when I'm ready. This hasn't been an easy decision to make, but I need to do it. I started to lose myself, just when I was beginning to figure out who I am.

Love,

Natalie

This was a lot harder than I thought it was going to be. By the end I had a lump in my throat from tears I refused to spill. I moved on to Grant's.

Grant,

First of all, I know I promised to stay and I hope that my leaving doesn't put you in harm's way. As I told Mom in her letter, I was starting to lose myself. Not just physically shrinking, but my mind, my life, my goals...everything. You seem destined for this lifestyle, but it's not for me. The more I tried to conform to it, the more lost I became. I have nightmares full of death and violence. Now I'm responsible for destroying a life and I am at my breaking point.

Please let Marco know that I am not going to the feds. The only information I have implicates you, Dominic and now me. I would never turn against my own family and I think Marco will understand, and I hope appreciate that.

Please don't try to find me. I'll be okay. You have protected me thus far, now it's time for me to protect myself. I wish I could be there for your wedding. You and Miranda are perfect for each other and I wish you a lifetime of happiness. You really are the best big brother. Thank you for all you've done. I will be in touch, when I feel it's safe.

Love,

Nat

That was the solution to Marco and I hadn't thought of it until I started writing Grant's letter. It made sense that I didn't pose a threat to exposing the Grabanos since I was just as dirty now. Grant would soon officially be part of the family and that should count for something too. I hoped it was enough. I debated writing Dominic's letter since I was on a roll, but these two letters had already left me drained. His letter would have to be written another day.

Chapter 32

I was still in bed when Grant came over the next day with a fresh bag of bagels. "Based on the food situation in your kitchen, I thought you could use these for breakfast." On our nocturnal schedule it was common to eat breakfast at one or two in the afternoon. Using the bagels as bait, Grant drew me out of bed and I followed him into the kitchen. I chattered on about random things just to fill the silence. Grant set down the bread knife and eyed me suspiciously.

"What?" I asked.

"Aren't you going to ask me about Dom?" Shit, I wasn't keeping up the façade very well.

"How is he doing? Still improving I hope?" I asked, recovering quickly.

"He's doing great, better than expected. Dr. Russo is letting him go home to his parent's house this weekend. He'll probably be home here by Monday," Grant was still eyeballing me as if gauging my reaction. "He's been asking for you. I think you should go see him this weekend. He would like that."

"Yeah, I can do that. Definitely." My deadline had just been moved up by a day. I might not be able to see Dr. Russo before skipping town. If Dominic was coming back Monday, I needed to be gone by then. My mind went into overdrive reconfiguring my schedule.

"Nat? Natalie?" Grant snapped his fingers in front of my face to get my attention.

"What?"

"You were zoning out again." He set a toasted sun dried tomato bagel (my favorite) in front of me and snatched up the bottle of pain pills. He opened the bottle and inspected the number of pills inside.

"What are you doing?" I asked him.

"You're not yourself and I just wanted to make sure you weren't overdoing it with these things," he shook the bottle like a rattle.

I rolled my eyes at him. "I'm not taking any. I took a couple the first night, but that's it," I paused. "You're right though, I'm not myself. You're probably used to lodging bullets in people's heads, but I'm not."

"Oh, right." Grant quickly set the bottle of pills back on the counter. "How are you doing with that?"

"Can I ask you something? Do you ever stop seeing them…the people you've killed? Every time I close my eyes, his face is there. I've had terrible nightmares, not just the guy I shot, but of those three men you shot at the after-hours place."

Grant shrugged his shoulders. "I don't know. It's never really bothered me. If I stop to think about it, I feel remorse. So, I don't think about it and it doesn't affect me." I shook my head in amazement. I didn't know how he could just switch it off. His ability to do that is probably what made him a successful soldier for the mob. We may look alike, but that is where the similarities ended.

We stopped talking to eat our bagels. It wasn't an uncomfortable silence, just another breakfast with my brother. I felt a twinge of sadness when I realized this was probably going to be our last breakfast together for a while.

Grant set his bagel down and cleared his throat. I looked up at him. "Nat, I don't know if you'll ever stop seeing dead people," his eyes twinkled when he said this. "But I will do everything in my power to keep you from having to shoot anyone again." I always used to think Grant's overprotectiveness was annoying, now I was beginning to realize that it was just his way of displaying his affection.

"Thank you."

After we ate, Grant checked on my injury and cleaned it. Each day it hurt less and less and I was pleased with my progress. Grant left shortly after that. Once he was gone, I surveyed the condo. I didn't have much to pack. All of the furniture belonged to Dominic. I had sold all my Ikea furniture from the apartment I shared with Chelsea to another student. My winter clothes could be donated since I wouldn't need them in LA. I really hadn't left much of an imprint here and that was comforting. It would be easier to extricate myself.

Only having the use of one arm slowed me down, but I managed to pack a bag of clothes and stashed it in the walk-in closet so Grant wouldn't see it. I called the concierge and arranged for laundry to be sent out. The clothes would be returned folded and easier to pack. Plus, I hated doing laundry, so much so I was willing to pay someone to do it.

The afternoon was slipping away quickly and I still needed to set up a post office box to forward my mail. I called the concierge desk again and had them call me another cab. It took longer than I planned and I was running late getting back to the condo. Grant was going to stop by before heading to work. The cab sat in downtown traffic and I started to get anxious. What if Grant got there early and came across anything, like the notebook, or the suitcase. Finally, the congestion freed up and the cab found an opening to turn down a side street. The sun had already set by the time we pulled up in front of my building.

"Good evening Miss Ross," the doorman said as he held the door open for me.

"Good evening. Has my brother been by here at all?"

"Yes Miss. He is already upstairs. He arrived here a few minutes ago." Shit.

Grant was pacing when I opened the door. "Where were you?" he barked the second I entered the condo.

"I needed to get out, I went downtown."

"You were supposed to be lying low. It's not safe for you to be wandering around out there."

"I was feeling a little stir crazy, besides I'm fine. Nothing happened."

"You should have called me; I would have taken you out."

"You do enough for me already – you should be spending time with your fiancé."

"Next time call me," he ordered.

"Fine," I said through my teeth. So far he was acting like this was the only issue, which was a good sign. If he had uncovered any of my plans, I would be probably be hauled away to some mafia style intervention. "Sorry. I'll call you next time."

"Good." We both stood as if we were facing off. In a way we were, our stubborn streak had caused us to bump heads many times before. I continued to glare at him, just to give him a hard time. He clenched his jaw and then burst out laughing. "You are hilarious when you try to act tough," he teased.

"I am tough. I'm a killer," I attempted to joke back, but didn't find it amusing. I could tell by the stern look on Grant's face that he didn't find it funny either.

"Are you hungry?" he asked, changing the subject.

"I could eat." He smiled at my signature answer.

"Miranda is on her way. She's bringing pizza."

At the mention of pizza, my stomach growled. I wondered if LA had pizza as good as Philly. In fact, I wondered a lot about LA. I had never been there and hadn't really done any research. It was like that game I played in elementary school, where you spun the globe and wherever it stopped under your fingertip, was where you were going to live. It was an impulse decision, but one I was going to stand by.

As if on cue there was light knock on the door. Grant opened it and Miranda walked in carrying a pizza box. She was dressed for work and looked stunning. I glanced down at my track pants and flannel shirt. I looked like a bum in comparison. Miranda set the box down on the counter and the light glinted off of her engagement ring.

"You're going to blind somebody with that thing," I teased.

"Your brother knows his jewelry," she beamed at Grant and stepped up on her toes to kiss his cheek. Grant blushed, for probably the second time in his entire life. Yeah, he had fallen for Miranda hard. It was reassuring to know that I wasn't leaving him alone. He was going to be alright, even though Marco was going to be his father-in-law.

"Dominic misses you," Miranda stated. She must have misinterpreted my wistfulness.

"How is he?" I asked and took a bite out of a slice of pizza. Grease dripped down my chin and I had to set the slice down to reach for the napkin. Only having one arm to use had its inconveniences.

"He's good. He's going to be moved to Aunt Angela's and Uncle Rico's tomorrow. He wants you there," she stared at me, her green eyes so much like Dominic's. I knew I needed to go see him. They would think it odd if I didn't.

"I'll be there," I promised. My nerves started to flitter and I lost my appetite. The half eaten slice remained on the paper plate, the grease beginning to congeal.

Sleep was elusive and I tossed and turned, although my movements were limited - whenever I went to toss or turn onto my injured shoulder I would wake up. I was awake when the sun peeked above the horizon. The sky lightened and went from dark gray, to gray and eventually to a clear blue. I watched nature's canvas from the deck. A blanket formed a cocoon around my body to keep out the morning chill. The ferry boat, which looked like a yellow dot on the river, had made several trips back and forth from Camden to Philly before I stood up to get ready. Miranda would arrive soon to take me to see Dominic.

Leaving Dom was going to be the most difficult. I had surrendered my heart, my soul, my whole being to him. Not having him around this week had helped. I was already able to imagine life without him. Now, I was going to visit him and was terrified he would be able to see right through me and know what I was up to. The feelings he brought out in me, even with just the touch of his hand, were going to be painful reminders of what I was leaving behind.

As I got dressed, I mentally prepared myself for our reunion. I needed to stick to my plan and not let my heart interfere. I forced myself to focus on the images of the man I shot and of Brittany after she had been all but destroyed by those men. This helped to fortify my resolve. I could do this, I told myself. Miranda arrived and I went downstairs to get in her Mercedes.

"You look tired," she commented. "Trouble sleeping?"

"Yeah, my shoulder makes it hard to get comfortable."

"I bet. I've never been shot before, I bet it hurts…what did it feel like?" She asked with morbid curiosity. I thought about the best way to describe it so she could relate.

"Remember when you got your ears pierced and you had the incredible pressure at first and then as the blood rushed to the ear your lobe got hot?" she nodded her head, her eyes focused on the road, but listening to every word I said. "Then the pain starts. Like a stinging, burning, throbbing pain?" she nodded again. "Well it's like that magnified by a thousand times." She slowed down for a red light and turned to stare at me. Her mouth hung open slightly.

"That sounds horrible!"

"It is." The light had turned green and she turned her attention back to the road. I could see her glance at me out of the corner of my eye.

"What?" I asked.

"What was," she hesitated. "What was it like to shoot someone?" She seemed intrigued to know and kind of excited, like she was living vicariously through my big mafia moment.

"I think I prefer getting shot."

"Oh," she said, sounding disappointed, "That bad, huh?"

"Indescribable. It was like I could see the moment life left him and he just toppled over." I shuddered and looked out the window. She didn't ask any more questions the rest of the way.

Miranda couldn't find parking anywhere near Dominic's parents house. She parked two blocks over and we walked through the South Philly neighborhood. While Dom lived in a brand new, contemporary condo, his parents were old school. Their brick row home was sandwiched in between other brick row homes. The white aluminum awnings over the windows were identical to their neighbors. It was hard to tell the homes apart. We could hear the people inside the house before we saw them.

"Geez, everyone seems to be here," Miranda muttered as she opened the door. Voices tumbled out onto the small porch and Miranda wedged her way into the crowd, I followed close behind. The Grabanos had turned out in full force for Dom's homecoming. I recognized about half of the people pressed into the two front rooms. Careful not to jostle my shoulder, I used my good arm to elbow through. Aunt Gloria spotted me first.

"Natalie!" she cried and bulldozed through to reach me. She pulled me into a hug and I winced as my shoulder connected with hers. She heard me hiss and pulled away quickly. "I am so sorry! Did I hurt you?"

"I'm fine," I assured her.

"Natalie, dear, I am so glad you and Dominic are safe! What an ordeal. And you, quite the heroine I hear!" She beamed. "Are you hungry? Franco and I brought plenty of food." She ushered me into the dining room. The large table was laden down with every imaginable pasta dish, fresh baked rolls, antipasto and my favorite, eggplant parmesan. Aunt Gloria grabbed a plate and started piling on heaping spoonfuls of food. She shoved the plate into my hand.

"I'll be right back hon!" She spun around and disappeared into the kitchen. I stood there holding the plate in my only free hand. There wasn't anywhere to set it down, so I just stood there awkwardly. Angela, Dominic's mom, spotted me and came over next. Angela moved in a very controlled manner, almost subdued, the exact opposite of Gloria who buzzed around in fast forward. Angela took the plate from my hand.

"My sister…she's been on a mission to feed the world since I can remember," she chuckled quietly. "It's a good thing she married a chef." Angela regarded me with her deep brown eyes. "Are you ready to go see my son?" she asked. I'd only met Angela a few times and she always referred to Dom as 'her son' around me, almost possessive in a way. She hadn't warmed up to me the way her husband had. I nodded.

"Follow me." I followed her into the kitchen, where she set the plate of food on the counter. She went through a separate doorway and up the stairs. We walked into Dominic's childhood bedroom and I instantly looked to the bed. I was surprised to find it empty. Confused, I surveyed the rest of the room and found Dominic sitting in a chair by the only window.

The sun filtered in through the window and accentuated the shadows under his eyes. Like me, he had lost weight. His usual olive toned skin was pale. Dominic's face lit up when he saw me and I hoped my face mirrored his emotions. Truth was I was feeling nervous and shy. What if he sensed I was pulling away? I forced the uncertainty to the back of my mind as I crossed the room. He reached out for my hand. I looked down into his eyes and saw that the same spark was there. He may look pale and weak on the outside, but internally he was healing. Angela silently left the room and shut the door behind her. We were alone.

"Hey you."

"Hey." I squeezed his hand.

"God, I missed you. How are you doing?" he asked, glancing at my sling.

"I've missed you too and I'm getting better each day. It still hurts, but I wasn't hurt nearly as badly as you," my voice started to crack. "I thought you were going to die!" Tears spilled down my cheeks. Damn it, why did I have to care so much? Leaving would be so much easier if my heart wasn't invested.

"Hey I'm fine. I didn't die. Don't worry." He pulled me onto his lap. I protested at first, afraid of hurting him, but he hushed me. "Babe, my neck and chest got shot, my lap is fine."

"Are you sure?" I held his gaze.

"Positive. In fact, having you on my lap might do me some good." He winked at me. Yeah, he was feeling better. I shot him a look and gently rested my head against his chest, comforted by the sound of his strong heartbeat.

"So, what were you up to while I was unconscious?"

"Nothing really, Grant's been checking on me. He actually helped give me a bath – it was horrible!" Dominic started to laugh but cut it short. His face pinched up in pain. "Are you okay?"

"Yeah, it just pulls when I laugh." He touched the giant gauze pad that was taped to his neck. "I'm sorry you had to be there – had to experience a shooting. I should have been more careful."

I looked down at my lap, not quite sure what to say. Then Marco came barging into the room and our moment together was disrupted.

"How's my favorite nephew?" he boomed. Then he saw me. "Natalie, thank you for saving my boy," he said before clamping his hand down on Dom's shoulder making him flinch. Marco regarded my injuries briefly before turning back to his nephew. I was forgotten as Marco dominated his attention and the entire atmosphere. Dom looked past Marco's shoulder and mouthed "sorry."

"It's okay," I mouthed back.

"Love you," he said.

"Love you too." I turned and left the room. The sadness formed a lump in my throat and gallon sized tears started to pour down my face. I ran to the bathroom. Was it wrong for me to leave him like this? I knew that had he been given the chance to say goodbye, he would have used it to convince me to stay. I knew I wouldn't be strong enough to deny him. I was glad Marco arrived at the end. Seeing him was a reminder of why I needed to leave.

I managed to get myself under control. With a heavy heart and puffy eyelids, I made my way back downstairs. The volume of so many conversations being held in one area was deafening compared to the quiet of Dom's room. Miranda saw me coming down the stairs and met me at the bottom.

"Ready to go?" she asked. I nodded. More family had arrived and we squeezed our way through the boisterous crowd. I followed her out the door and to her car, too numb to pay any attention to where we were going. I probably would have wandered around for hours trying to find the car, had I been left alone. "Why do you look so devastated? Did you guys have a fight or something?" Miranda asked as she pulled the car out into the street.

I flipped the visor down and looked in the mirror. Yikes, I thought to myself, and attempted to wipe away the rivers of mascara, but only succeeded in smearing them across my cheeks. "No, we didn't have a fight. It was very emotional seeing him again." My tone was harsher than I had intended and I felt bad, but Miranda kept to herself for the rest of the car ride and I appreciated the silence.

My laundry was ready at the concierge desk and one of the staff helped me up to the front door. Perfect timing, I could pack the rest of my clothes. It was Saturday and I planned to leave Monday, right after my morning follow up appointment with Dr. Russo. I would be gone by the time Dominic arrived.

Something rubbed my head. I groaned and moved away. Next something was tickling my ear, I tried to swat it away, but my arm was in a sling. The little bit of movement sent a shooting pain down my arm. I woke with a jerk. Grant leaned over the back of the sofa looking down at me and laughed.

"You're such a shithead!" I growled at him.

"I called your name. Man, you were out cold." I glared at him. I didn't remember falling asleep. I remembered sitting on the sofa to watch a movie and that was it.

"What time is it?"

"After six, I'm on my way to work and thought I'd check on you. You didn't answer your phone."

"Wow, I really was out." I stretched my legs out and yawned.

"Do you need anything while I'm here?" Sleep still clung to my brain like a fog and I had to think about it.

"I think I'm all set. Thanks bro!" I gave him a goofy grin and he smiled back.

"You're such a dork," he said and bipped me upside the head.

"Hey, that's not fair. I'm defenseless," I gestured to my sling. He rolled his eyes at me.

"I'm going to head to work then."

"Have fun. Don't worry about checking on me later. I'll be fine and will probably be asleep."

He left and I went to fix something to eat. The morning with Dominic weighed heavily on my mind and he stayed in my thoughts while I gathered up more things to pack. My new cell phone was charging on the dresser and the instructions to the Garmin were strewn across the bed. I crawled into bed to read them, but wound up thinking about everyone I was leaving behind. Sneaking around behind their backs and not saying goodbye to their faces haunted me. I imagined my mother would feel abandoned and betrayed. Grant would be angry and then extremely worried. Miranda would probably react the same as Grant. And Dominic...I didn't know how he would react. Hurt? Betrayed? Sad? Or would he be angry for a little while and then move on? It hurt to think about and I started to cry, which turned into big, heaving sobs.

Once again I slept. Violent images flitted across my REM cycle, disturbing and graphic, but not lasting long enough for me to wake up screaming. My cell phone ringing woke me up instead.

"Hello?" I answered my voice rough with sleep.

"Hey baby, it's me,"

"Hey," I yawned. My eyes burned from the tears and slumber. I looked at the clock, it wasn't even midnight yet. My schedule had been completely thrown off since the shooting.

"Sorry about earlier. I wish Uncle Marco hadn't interrupted." His voice was soft and soothing. I didn't realize until I heard it, how much I had missed the sound of his voice.

"I'm sorry too."

"Can you come by again tomorrow?"

"I don't know. I'll try."

"What do you mean you don't know? Do you have other plans?"

"Grant or Miranda has to drive me around and I don't know if they're available," I explained.

"So take a cab, I'll pay for it...or I can come home early!" He sounded more excited at that idea. I had to stall him.

"No, I'll come see you. I think your mom would like you home a little bit longer. She was really worried about you." This seemed to appease him and he lightened up.

"What are you wearing?" he asked. So this was going to be one of *those* calls. That would explain his impatience.

"Unbelievable, Dom. Just two days ago you were practically in a coma and now you're horny?"

"I've had time to rest up. Ya know, recharge the old battery." His voice was husky now. I couldn't help but laugh at him. "What are you laughing at? Although I can picture the way your skin flushes when you laugh and your breasts jiggle just the slightest bit, making your nipples harden..." He started to breathe heavy. I gave in. He was too irresistible and this was going to be our last intimate time together. I could at least leave him satisfied.

I woke up Sunday morning with the deadline looming. I was basically ready, except the letter to Dominic had yet to be written. Dr. Russo said I could take the sling off periodically and for longer periods each time. If I was going to drive to his office, I needed to get my arm used to motion. Sunday mornings were a good time to drive in Philadelphia. Traffic jams didn't exist, unless the Phillies were in the World Series. My car was waiting for me when I got downstairs. I put one of my suitcases in the trunk then slid in behind the steering wheel.

It had only been about a week since I had driven, but it felt like a year. The gear shift seemed foreign to me when my weakened arm shifted it into drive. I drove around the block then three blocks and on until driving was comfortable again. It might take more breaks than usual, but I would make it California.

I pulled into Jiffy Lube and got the oil changed. The last item on my list was the letter to Dominic and I knew that had to be done tonight. I promised Dom I'd visit and dreaded having to look him in the face again. Still feeling confident behind the wheel, I drove to Dom's parents. I found a parking spot right out front.

Angela answered the door.

"Hi. Dom asked me to visit today." She stepped aside to let me in. The house was so quiet compared to the day before – and spotless.

"He's upstairs," she said. Angela and her sister Gloria were exact opposites. Gloria never hesitated to give a hug and Angela remained distant, more reserved. She wasn't mean to me, but she didn't get too close. I had a feeling that she and my mom would get along great. Sometimes I would catch her looking at me, regarding me with what looked like sympathy on her face. She looked that way at me now. "Do you remember where his room is or would like me to take you up?"

"I remember. Thank you." I walked up the stairs and past the family portraits that lined the staircase wall. His door was closed so I knocked lightly before turning the knob. Dom was sleeping. His heavy breathing could be heard across the room. I crept over to the bed and curled up alongside him. He woke up then and smiled when he saw it was me.

"You made it," he said and I nuzzled closer, enjoying the smell of him. He had been gone so long that his scent had faded from our sheets.

"I'm here." He squeezed me and kissed my forehead. We lay there in the silence for a while, enjoying each other's company.

"Hey Dom, can I ask you something?"

"Sure."

"Your mom...I can't figure her out. She looks at me weird – it's hard to explain – but, it's like she's sad for me or something."

"She probably is. My mom has never liked the mafia life, but it's what she grew up around and she loves her family," he paused and looked down at me. "She probably sees you struggling with this too." He caressed my injured shoulder.

"You haven't thought about leaving again; have you, especially with the shooting and all?" My body tensed up. Why was he so damn perceptive?

"No."

"Good. I'm glad I got my first bullet wounds out of the way. Now I know what to expect."

"Your first?"

"Yeah, these won't be the only ones. My dad, he was shot four times and Uncle Al's been shot a couple times, but Uncle Marco has the luck. He's been shot at seven times and only hit once. He's a legend..." Dom dozed off, midsentence, like a drunk. I lay there watching him sleep. My arm draped up over his head and I played with his thick hair. I knew that my decision to leave was the right one. I couldn't deal if he got shot again, especially if the next time was fatal. I slipped out from under Dom's arm and managed to get off the bed without disturbing him. Just as quietly as I had entered the room, I left. Before walking out the door, I turned and blew a kiss.

I found Angela in the kitchen making lasagna. "I'm leaving now," I announced.

"Good." Wow, that was rude!

"Excuse me?"

"Leave. Get out while you still can," Angela set the serving spoon down and looked at me. "If you stay, you will grow roots that will be imbedded here and you will never leave." Her eyes looked haunted and I'm glad Dom had explained her history to me, otherwise I would probably think she was nuts.

"I've been planning to leave," I admitted. She looked relieved when I said this.

"When?" I hesitated and she sensed it. "Let's sit." She gestured to the dining room table. We sat down and I still didn't know if I should tell her. "Natalie, I wish I could turn back time and make a different choice. I don't regret the love and I wouldn't trade my children for anything, but if I could go back to when I was eighteen, knowing what I know now, I would have run. I see myself in you."

"I've made my choice and I am leaving. After the shooting…I just can't do it anymore."

She nodded, understanding. "When I got the call that my son had been shot, well, that was my worst fear coming to reality. Thank God he survived. A parent shouldn't outlive their child. And Rico too, I'm always on edge waiting for the next call." Her eyes glistened with tears and she smiled faintly at me. "When do you plan on leaving?"

"Tomorrow, after my appointment with Dr. Russo. I need to do it before Dom gets home otherwise, I'm afraid I won't be able to." Once again she nodded in understanding.

"Where will you go?"

"I have a plan and hopefully it works out."

"Do you have enough money?"

"I think so." Angela stood up and walked over to the hutch. She grabbed a small ceramic jar and fished out a wad of bills. She handed the money to me.

"I don't know how much is there, but every little bit helps."

Stunned, I took the money. "You don't have to…"

"I want to help, Natalie," she said, cutting me off mid-sentence. "Go, start over." She smiled a conspiratorial grin. "I'll stall Dom as long as possible so you can get a good head start. Don't worry about him, he'll be fine. He's a Grabano," she added, as if that explained everything. "Go and don't look back."

I stood up and she walked me to the door. "Thank you," I whispered, the tears in my throat were constricting my vocal chords.

"I wish someone had done the same for me," she said, a wistful look in her eyes. She hugged me then and this time it reminded me of her sister, Aunt Gloria's hugs. Maybe they were more alike after all. "Be safe."

I walked, well floated to my car. Being able to tell someone my decision, and have it reinforced, lifted the tremendous weight I had been carrying. Now, I felt almost buoyant. I was going to be okay, Dom was going to be okay. It had felt like my world had been imploding around me, but I could see that reconstruction was possible.

Chapter 33

After packing the last of my belongings and taking a long, hot bath I was ready to write Dom's letter:

Dearest Dominic,

You're probably wondering where I am and why I am not here to welcome you home. I am so sorry, but I knew that if I waited for you, I would never leave. I haven't been able to adjust to this life, your life, and when I shot that man, that was the proverbial straw that broke the camel's back. I love with you all of my being, but I need to love myself more. Between being attacked, your uncle's craziness and the murder...I can't take another day. Please let your Uncle Marco know that I am not going to rat him out. I would only be implicating you, Grant, and now myself. Your life is here, your family is here and this life is for you - it's all you've ever known. I really tried to make it work. If I stay my life would be full of regret and I would probably resent you one day.

I am going away to start over. As I told Grant in his letter, please don't try to find me. Just let me go.

All my love,

Natalie

Tears were oozing out of my eyes and it was hard to see the words I had written. I had to move away so the ink wouldn't smear. Several drops were already wrinkling the paper. I crawled onto the bed and curled up into a ball. The tears fell until my body wasn't capable of producing anymore. Never had I felt more drained, completely and utterly drained.

***

The alarm went off and my eyes sprung open. The day had arrived. I quickly showered, pleased to see that the massive bruise around my healing wound had faded to a mottled greenish yellow. It only took two trips to pack up my car. I did a final sweep of the condo and placed the letters for Grant and Dominic on the kitchen counter. I would mail my mom's letter on the way out of town. I bid a silent farewell to the home Dominic and I shared then walked out the door.

The End

Read on for a preview of Clean Slate, Book Two of The New Mafia Trilogy – available now!

CLEAN SLATE

Chapter 1

LOS ANGELES

I sat in my car just outside the entrance to the Warner Brothers studio lot. The security guard had his back to me as he attempted to page my former best friend. He hung up the phone and glared at me through the small window of his "office", which was smaller than a toll booth. He had been working on a crossword puzzle when I pulled up and seemed annoyed that he actually had to do his job. The phone trilled and he answered mid-ring.

"Security," he paused. "Yes, there's a Natalie Ross here to see you?" He pivoted in his chair so his back was to me again. "That's right, Natalie Ross. I checked her ID – it's a Pennsylvania license." There was another pause and I waited, holding my breath until he said, "I'll send her in."

Well at least she was willing to see me. My heart rate kicked up a notch as I pulled through the gate. With the convertible top down and sunglasses on, I already felt like I fit into Southern California. I just needed to work on my tan. My skin was so white it created a glare. The guard had handed me a visitors badge and a map of the studio grounds. He'd circled where Chelsea's office was and drew a line indicating the best route; it looked like a maze.

I had just arrived in Los Angeles after driving cross country in record time. The long drive from Philadelphia had been an interesting one. For the first half of the trip I had developed a nervous habit of looking in the rearview mirror every two minutes. I kept expecting to see my brother Grant, my ex-boyfriend

Dominic or other members of the Philly mob behind me in hot pursuit.

A string of violent events precipitated my journey west. First, I had discovered Grant was a hit man for the mob after unwittingly being at the scene of one of his hits, which happened to be a triple murder. That same night I learned my boyfriend, Dominic, was also a Mafioso. Then, I was sexually assaulted by the Don of the most powerful mob families in the country, a member of the Five Families out of New York City, who Grant and Dominic murdered. I knew I needed to get out after I was shot in a drive by, which almost killed Dominic and resulted in me lodging a bullet in the forehead of a member of the New York mafia. Despite threats that my brother and I would be killed if I left, I ran away. To avoid losing myself completely, I left the love of my life and my family behind.

I spent many sleepless nights in hotel rooms. Every time a car door shut outside my window I'd jump. Whenever someone paused outside my door, I'd hold my breath and clutch at the knife I kept beneath my pillow. By the time I hit Montana, I relaxed a little bit, cut three inches off of my hair and got bangs, which really made the shape of my face look different. Hopeful that I wasn't being followed, I stopped checking the rearview mirror and concentrated on the journey ahead.

Now I was about ready to beg my best friend for forgiveness and I prayed that she would throw me a much needed lifeline. She hadn't been expecting me and we hadn't spoken to each other in over nine months. Not since the night we had a huge argument over Dominic and I moved out of the apartment we had shared. She claimed I was forgetting who I was and who my friends were. I couldn't tell her the truth - that I had already sworn myself to the mafia in order to save my brother's life, and my own. But, she deserved the truth now.

I parked in a spot marked with a visitors sign and turned the car off. I grabbed the map off of the dash and looked around. A giant warehouse the size of an airplane hangar loomed in front of me.

Doors lined the exterior wall every ten feet or so. I chewed on my bottom lip as I tried to figure out which door to enter. Turns out I didn't have to figure it out as Chelsea emerged from one. She squinted and raised her hand above her eyes to shield them from the sun. I stuck my arm up and waved, noticing a brief hesitation before she started walking towards me.

My stomach was in knots as I stepped out of the car to meet her. She was thinner than I remembered. Her round, rosy cheeks more defined. Her hair was longer too and hung in blonde waves past her shoulders.

Chelsea stopped a few feet away and I felt her eyes surveying me. She would be quick to notice the dark circles under my eyes, more pronounced by the swollen bags that sleepless nights and crying jags had created. She wouldn't miss that I too had lost weight. Although where Chelsea's weight loss left her looking leaner and healthy, I was gaunt.

"Jesus. You look like hell!"

"Yeah…well, I feel like I've just come from there," I responded.

"What are you doing here?" Her stance hadn't softened. This was going to be harder than I thought. My hopes of her running out and pulling me into one of her bone crushing hugs quickly dissipated.

"I'm sorry to bother you at work, but this was the only address I had. Your mom gave me one of your business cards."

"Are you moving here?" Chelsea looked behind me at the numerous bags in the backseat. "Did you and Dominic break up?"

"Can we talk after you get out of work? I'll tell you everything…and it will explain a lot."

"Um, sure, I guess so."

We made arrangements to meet at six o'clock and I would follow her back to her apartment. I turned to get in my car.

"Nat?"

I turned back to face her.

"Are you okay?" Chelsea's expression had softened.

"I don't know." Unconsciously I shrugged my shoulders and winced as the reawakening nerve endings screamed. Chelsea's eyes moved to my right shoulder. I was wearing a white tank top and the strap wasn't wide enough to conceal the healing wound.

"What is that?" she asked at the same time sliding the strap over. The bruising had faded to a faint jaundice yellow, but the scar tissue surrounding my injury was still red and raw.

"I was shot."

She jerked her hand back with a gasp, "What?"

"This is part of what I want to talk you about later and please don't tell anyone you saw me. Not even your mom."

"Does this have something to do with why Grant called me a couple of days ago?"

I wasn't surprised Grant had already called Chelsea and I was glad that she didn't know I was coming.

"Yes and I promise to tell you everything. There's a really good reason for the secrecy. Okay?"

Chelsea didn't say anything, just nodded her head in agreement. I think my statement stunned her into silence. She stared after my car as I backed out and pulled away.

Chapter 2

I followed Chelsea's rusted out, hand-me-down Volvo wagon down a palm tree lined street. She pulled into the drive of a huge apartment complex. We wove through visitor parking, past the leasing office and up to a gate. She punched in a code and the gate rumbled open on its track. She gestured for me to follow close behind.

Chelsea and I walked up to her apartment building, which had a beige stucco exterior. A water fountain filled up the center of a small courtyard.

"My apartment is tiny, but it's affordable," Chelsea commented as she unlocked the door.

Her one bedroom was decorated like the apartment we had shared in Philadelphia. The same futon, coffee table and entertainment center furnished the living room. A recliner appeared to be the only new piece of furniture. I was surprised to see that Chelsea had held onto a couple of my paintings and these hung on the walls. Maybe she didn't despise me after all, I thought to myself and took my flip flops off before stepping onto the white carpet to sit down on the futon.

"Your place is really cute."

"Thanks. The best part about this complex is that it has a pool and a gym. A pool, isn't that awesome?"

"That is cool." I didn't remind her that the condo where Dominic and I lived had those too, but that was an exception since most places didn't. L.A. was definitely a different world from Philly. I just hoped it was far enough away.

"Do you want something to drink?" Chelsea asked from the kitchen. I looked over my shoulder to see Chelsea framed by the breakfast bar. She didn't seem as defensive as she was earlier this afternoon. Her curiosity must be killing her right now. I chuckled remembering how she would interrogate me after every date with Dominic.

"I'll just have some water." Since arriving in the more arid climate I was constantly thirsty.

Chelsea sauntered in to the living room and set the glasses on the coffee table. She sat down cross legged on the futon, looked directly at me and said, "Okay, spill."

Her gaze was unwavering, so I took a deep breath and began.

"Dominic and Grant are part of the Philly mob."

"What?" she shrieked. "Are you fucking with me?"

"I wish I was," I paused. "You know that after hours place I told you about?"

"The Speak, right?"

"Yes. Dominic took me there one night after work and that same night, Grant was there and he killed three men."

Chelsea's blue eyes widened and her mouth hung slack.

"It was awful! There was blood everywhere and…" I broke off with a shudder. "That night I was sworn to secrecy in order to protect Grant and myself."

"You haven't told anyone this?"

"No. But it gets worse." I took a sip of water, wishing it was something stronger. "Dominic's Uncle Marco is the boss of the mob and he's an awful man."

Chelsea watched me place the glass back on the coffee table, my hand shaking so bad, water spilled over the sides.

I told her how Marco forced me into the room with Mr. Genovese, the head of the Five Families and how he had assaulted me.

"I got off easy though," I continued. Chelsea reached for my hand and held it tight as I told her about my coworker, Brittany, who was brutally raped by Genovese's men. I told her about the pressure and the fear, but also how powerful it felt to be part of the mafia.

"Two weeks ago someone tried to take Dominic out. We were both shot." Chelsea's eyes shifted to my shoulder. "I shot one of the men, who was firing rounds into Dominic's Mustang, and killed him."

"You killed someone?" She stared at me in disbelief. Ashamed, I lowered my head and nodded in confirmation.

"I had to. Otherwise I'd probably be dead right now."

"Whoa!" Chelsea sat back and analyzed me in silence. I plucked at a loose thread on the dark green futon cover. "So you ran away to my place, just like you did when you were nine."

I laughed, having forgotten that time when my mom and I had a horrible fight. I packed my dolls, my piggy bank and some candy into my backpack then ran away to Chelsea's house. Of course her mom called my mom and I spent the night before going home the next morning. "I guess so. I hated losing you. I hated not being able to tell you what was going on. You have no idea how surreal it's been."

"What are you going to do now? Are you going to get arrested?"

"I honestly don't know. I'm more worried about the mafia than the police. They could still come after me so I need to keep a low profile for a while. Nobody knows where I am."

"And that's why Grant called me."

"Yeah, but obviously you didn't know where I was either. I still don't know where I'm going to go. Unless..." I looked up at Chelsea and she knew me well enough that I didn't have to finish asking.

"Yes, you can stay here. You're much too interesting to not have around," she teased.

I smiled and breathed a deep sigh of relief. "Thanks."

"I'm glad you're here. I missed you." Chelsea pulled me into a hug that made my shoulder ache, but I didn't pull away. Even though I was in California and in this apartment for the first time, I felt like I was home.

About the Author

E.J. Fechenda has lived in Philadelphia, Phoenix and now calls Portland, Maine home where she is a wife, stepmom, and pet parent all while working full time.

She has a degree in Journalism from Temple University and her short stories have been published in *Suspense Magazine*, the 2010 and 2011 Aspiring Writers Anthologies, and in the *Indies Unlimited 2012 Flash Fiction Anthology*. In addition to writing The New Mafia Trilogy, she is working on The Ghosts Stories Trilogy. E.J. is a member of the Maine Writers and Publishers Alliance and co-founder of the fiction reading series, "Lit: Readings & Libations", which is held quarterly in Portland.

E.J. can be found on the internet here:

Facebook: https://www.facebook.com/EJFechendaAuthor

Twitter @ebusjaneus (https://twitter.com/ebusjaneus)

Tumblr: http://ejfechenda.tumblr.com/

Made in the USA
Middletown, DE
13 July 2024